"O'Neill's lively style is so filled with vivid descriptions and complex characters that the reader's experience is virtually cinematic. . . . In the hands of this brilliant author, even the ugliest events are depicted with the most musical cadences, soaring arias and symphonic resolutions. Filled with inspired twists and turns, the tale is utterly compelling, creating a world where desperation and love coexist." —*The Washington Post*

"A larger-than-life, gritty love story that reads like a fable. . . . The greatest strength of O'Neill's work, however, is her wholly unique narrative voice, which is at once cool and panoramic, yet shockingly intimate and wisely philosophical. The novel brims with shimmering one-liners." —*The Boston Globe*

"Art, love, imagination—these values are held aloft in O'Neill's novel, with Pierrot and Rose floating through life as 'collector[s] of beautiful moments.' . . . The nature of the theatrical spectacle Rose and Pierrot and company have created speaks to the mesmerizing effects of the novel itself." —*San Francisco Chronicle*

"It is stunningly, stunningly good. . . . O'Neill, always an original and enchanting storyteller, is at the height of her powers. *The Lonely Hearts Hotel* is a feat of imagination, accomplished through the tiny, marvelous details she scatters across the page." —*LitHub/The Toronto Star*

"O'Neill is an extraordinary writer, and her new novel is exquisite. She has taken on sadness itself as a subject, but it would be terribly reductive to say that this book is sad; it's also joyful, funny, and vividly alive." —Emily St. John Mandel, author of *Station Eleven*

"Heather O'Neill's style is laced with so much sublime possibility and merciless reality that it makes me think of comets and live wires and William Blake's 'The Tyger.' Between prose like that and a story like this, you have a book that raises goose bumps and the giddiest of grins." —Helen Oyeyemi, author of *What Is Not Yours Is Not Yours*

"Because this book is so filled with delightful things, it would be easy to overlook how finely it is made. *The Lonely Hearts Hotel* sucked me right in and only got better and better, ultimately becoming much tougher, wiser than I was prepared for. I began underlining truths I had hungered for but never before read. By the end I was a gasping, tearful mess." —Miranda July, author of *The First Bad Man*

"A fairy tale laced with gunpowder and romance and icing sugar, all wrapped round with a lit fuse. Each of Heather O'Neill's sentences pricks or delights. If you haven't read her other books, start with this one and then read all of the rest."   —Kelly Link, author of the Pulitzer Prize finalist *Get in Trouble*

"[Walks] the hypnotic line between tragedy and fairy tale . . . O'Neill's prose is crisp and strange, arresting in its frankness; much like the novel itself, her writing is both gleefully playful and devastatingly sad. Big and lush and extremely satisfying; a rare treat."   —*Kirkus Reviews* (starred review)

"In a love story of epic proportions, O'Neill's excellent historical novel plumbs the depths of happiness and despair. . . . At the very end of the tunnel are floodlights to the stage, sad clowns, gigantic moon props, chorus girls, and the one thing that time and distance cannot diminish—true love grander than any circus act. This novel will cast a spell on readers from page one."
—*Publishers Weekly* (starred, boxed review)

"O'Neill is a mistress of metaphor and imagery ('her sobs were flung on the deck'). This is brilliant tragicomedy . . . in a melancholy love story that brings to life the bygone days of theatrical revues. It's a little weird and a lot of fun."
—*Booklist* (starred review)

"This simultaneously heartbreaking and life-affirming novel depicts the range of the human experience through the eyes of its almost preternaturally charismatic hero and heroine. . . . O'Neill's prose is gorgeous, with arresting imagery."   —*Library Journal* (starred review)

"All at once, *The Lonely Hearts Hotel* is whimsical, melancholy, tragic and delightful—a wonderful feat that re-creates the ambivalence of life. Throughout the novel, the bleakest of realities are colored by magic, and the most joyful moments are cloaked in subtle gloom. . . . [A] highly original work of fiction."
—*BookPage*

"O'Neill's fairy tale spins a bittersweet spell. . . . Brazen, offbeat and thoroughly bewitching, *The Lonely Hearts Hotel* mixes the sacred and profane into an effervescent love potion."   —*Shelf Awareness*

"Magical and charming and sexy and raunchy and enchanting."   —*BookRiot*

"O'Neill fuels her prose with a frothy charm that's almost self-deprecatingly simple, letting its depth sneak up on you. . . . It's the kind of book that both bookworms and casual readers would discuss with friends over coffee, appreciating its humor and quotability."   —*Open Letters Monthly*

THE LONELY HEARTS HOTEL

HEATHER O'NEILL

RIVERHEAD BOOKS
New York

RIVERHEAD BOOKS
An imprint of Penguin Random House LLC
375 Hudson Street
New York, New York 10014

The Library of congress has catalogued the Riverhead hardcover edition as follows:

Names: O'Neill, Heather, author.
Title: The Lonely Hearts Hotel : a novel / Heather O'Neill.
Description: New York : Riverhead Books, 2017.
Identifiers: LCCN 2016036295 | ISBN 9780735213739 (hardcover)
Subjects: LCSH: First loves—Fiction. | BISAC: FICTION / Historical. |
FICTION / Literary. | GSAFD: Love stories.
Classification: LCC PR9199.4.O64 L66 2017 | DDC 813/.6—dc23
LC record available at https://lccn.loc.gov/2016036295
p.   cm.

First Riverhead hardcover edition: February 2017
First Riverhead trade paperback edition: January 2018
Riverhead trade paperback ISBN: 9780735213746

Printed in the United States of America
1   3   5   7   9   10   8   6   4   2

Book design by Meighan Cavanaugh

THE
LONELY
HEARTS
HOTEL

THE BIRTH OF A BOY
NAMED PIERROT

On that day in 1914, a young girl banged on the door of the Hôpital de la Miséricorde in Montreal. She was pudgy and had round apple cheeks and blond ringlets. She was only twelve years old.

Her older cousin, Thomas, had gone overseas to France to fight. She had been crazy about him since she was a tiny thing. He was wild and did handstands and took her to see bands in the park on Sundays. He was brave and always told her that he would like to be a soldier someday. He had come over to her home one afternoon the previous winter and had said that he would give her a medical exam to see if she was fit for active duty, the way that boys had to do. She had really wanted to know whether she could have been a soldier too if she were a boy. He'd said he had to stick his penis inside her to test her internal temperature. When he was done, satisfied with her perfect health, he had handed her a little red ribbon that had come off a cake box. Then he pinned it to her jacket as a badge of honor for the consummation of her grand service to her country. When the Archduke Ferdinand was assassinated, Thomas prayed for months that Canada would declare war, to get away from his pregnant cousin.

Her parents sent her to the Hôpital de la Miséricorde. Every day there were young pregnant girls lining up outside the hospital, with their big bellies that they could no longer hide from their families. They had been thrown out of their houses. Some had had time to pack their suitcases first. Others had just been pulled by their hair and tossed out the door. The girls showed up with handprints from their fathers on their faces, bruises they tried to hide beneath their pretty blond curls or straight dark hair. They looked like porcelain dolls that had fallen out of favor with their children.

These girls had thrown their whole lives away just to have five lovely minutes on a back staircase. Now, with strangers living in their bellies, they had been sent into hiding by their parents, while the young fathers went about their business, riding bicycles and whistling in the bathtub. That's what this building had been established for. Out of a great kindness for these miserable wenches.

The nuns gave the girls aliases when they came in through the big doors of the Hôpital de la Miséricorde. They said that the names were for the girls' own protection, but they obviously had the added role of humiliating the girls and reminding them of their new scorned and sinful status. There were girls named Chastity and Salome and Dismal.

The apple-cheeked girl was christened Ignorance by the nuns. She became known as Iggy. She had no regard for the fact that she had a potbelly with the most precious package in the world inside it. She wrestled a cat one day. Another day she leaped from one bed to the other as though they were ice floes. She did cartwheels down the hall. The nuns tried their very best to stop her. They had occasion to wonder whether she could be so remarkably naive or if she was trying to have a miscarriage, thinking somewhat irrationally that she would get out of there early.

When her baby boy was born blue, it didn't surprise anyone. He looked like a stillborn baby. The doctor checked the pulse. There was not a sound coming from the boy's heart. The doctor put his hand in front of the mouth to check for breath, but there was nothing.

They left the baby on the table, its arms at its sides. Its bow legs fell open. The priest didn't know what happened to these babies in limbo. He waved his rosary over him—did his funeral rites. He turned away from him. He would take the baby away in his large handbag that he kept especially for such occasions. He would have him buried behind the church in a bread box. You didn't have to have fancy coffins for this kind of death.

Then strangely and surreally, the boy's penis began to rise straight up. And then the baby coughed out a cry, color began to appear in his skin and his limbs twitched. The erection had brought him back from the dead. The priest wasn't sure whether he was witnessing a miracle. Was this the work of God, or was it the work of the devil?

When the nun from the Hôpital de la Miséricorde brought Iggy's baby to the orphanage to spend the rest of his childhood, she told the nuns there to watch out for him. His mother had been trouble, and even though he was nothing but a baby, they were sure there was something not quite right about the boy. A black cat was at the nun's feet and followed them in. All the male babies at the orphanage were named Joseph. It was thus also an imperative to come up with nicknames for them. The nuns at the orphanage called this baby Pierrot because he was so pale and he always had a rather stupid grin on his face.

THE MELANCHOLIC BEGINNINGS
OF A GIRL NAMED ROSE

Rose was born to an eighteen-year-old girl who didn't know she was pregnant until she was six months along. Rose's mother hadn't particularly liked Rose's father. The boy waited for her on the corner of her street every day. He would always beg her to come into the alley with him and let him have a peek at her breasts. She decided to give in one afternoon. Somehow she thought that if she made love to him, he would go away and leave her alone. Which, actually, proved to be the case.

When she realized she was pregnant, the girl hid it under baggy clothes the whole time. She gave birth to a tiny baby girl at home in the bathtub. It had purple lids over its eyes. It looked like it might be thinking about a poem. The girl's sisters all stared at the little baby in shock, not knowing what to do. They forgot to put their hands over the baby's mouth and it let out a cry that summoned everyone in the house.

With tears streaming out of two black eyes that she'd gotten from her father, the girl wrapped the baby up in a little blanket. She put on her black coat and boots. She was supposed to go straight to the church. Babies were abandoned on the church steps all the time. The baby's fists opened and closed like a pensive sea anemone. But before the girl left, she got on her hands and knees and secretly begged her mother for fifty dollars. Her mother, with a mixture of disgust and compassion, handed her daughter the bills. The girl whispered "Thank you" and hurried out the door.

She passed the church and walked another mile and knocked on a door at the end of a lane. There was a woman who lived there who would take your baby off you for fifty dollars. For the fee, the woman promised, the baby would not be put in an orphanage.

A woman with gray hair the color of gunpowder and wearing a coat opened the door for Rose's mother. In the kitchen, she said she would make sure that the girl was given to a rich family in Westmount. She would be dressed in beautiful white outfits with elaborate little collars, which would make her look like a flower. She would have a governess and an Irish wolfhound. She would be read to all the time from great fat books. For a small fee. For a small fee. For a small fee she could secure a home and good fortune for her daughter.

What a foolish imagination Rose's mother had to have had to buy what this woman was selling. It was no good to have an imagination if you were a girl and living in Montreal at the beginning of the twentieth century. Intelligence was what she needed. But she never listened to anyone.

A MAN, taking a shortcut home from the factory, found Rose wrapped in her blanket in the snow beneath a tree in Mount Royal Park. She was frozen and had two little round spots like blue roses on her cheeks. The man put his ear up to the girl's face and felt that her cheeks were as cold as stones, but he heard a tiny, tiny exhale. He tucked her deep into the folds of his coat and ran with her to the hospital. At the hospital, they put her in a bucket of warm water. When her eyes flittered open, it was a miracle of sorts.

The police went to the park and found other babies in the snow, each having turned into a stone angel. The terrible merchant's identity was uncovered and she was arrested. As she was being dragged into court, all the people threw snowballs with rocks embedded in them at her. The woman was sentenced to be hanged. Although everyone was indignant and outraged about the fate of Rose, nobody came forward to adopt her. All anyone could afford was indignation.

When the policemen brought the baby to the orphanage, they said, "Watch out for this one. Nothing good was ever meant to happen to her." All the girls at the orphanage were named Marie, and so was this baby girl. But her nickname, which she would always be known by, was Rose, because the two bright spots on her cheeks had turned from blue to red, then took two more weeks to disappear.

···⟨ 3 ⟩···

A HISTORY OF INNOCENCE

The orphanage was on the northern boundary of the city. If you went to where the city ended and then walked two thousand paces, you would come upon the orphanage, although it isn't there now. It was an enormous place. It was not the type of building that you would want to bother making a pen-and-ink sketch of because you would surely get incredibly bored drawing all those identical square windows. It would require no artistry on your part and, therefore, you might find your time more creatively spent illustrating a running horse.

Before the orphanage had been built, orphans were housed in the nuns' motherhouse downtown. And that had been too much temptation for the orphans. They did not sufficiently understand their otherness. They believed that they too were a part of city life. They were meant to be servile. It was better here in isolation.

The building was teeming with abandoned and orphaned children. Although many actually had parents, they were taught to consider themselves, for all intents and purposes, orphans as well. There were two separate dormitories, one on either side of the building, one for boys and one for girls. There were identical beds in the dormitories. The children lay tucked up in their blankets like rows of dumplings on a plate. There was a small wooden trunk at the foot of each bed in which each orphan was to keep their personal effects. These trunks usually contained a nightgown or pajamas and a toothbrush and a comb. There was sometimes a special rock hidden inside too. There was a pillbox with a broken butterfly in one.

There was an extensive garden behind the orphanage that the children tended. There was a chicken coop where little round eggs appeared as if by magic every morning. Tiny fragile moons that were necessary for survival. The children reached into the nests ever so carefully to retrieve the eggs without breaking their shells. With the sleeves of their sweaters pulled over their hands, their arms were like the trunks of elephants swallowing up peanuts.

There were two cows that had to be milked every morning. The task of milking a cow always required two orphans. One to whisper sweet words of calm into its ear and the other to do the milking.

THE CHILDREN were all quite pale. They never had enough to eat. Sometimes they would find themselves just fantasizing about eating. While they were sitting in class, sometimes they would look down and tell their bellies to hush—as though there were a dog underneath the table begging for scraps.

They never had enough clothes in the winter either and were cold for months. The tips of their fingers went numb when they shoveled the path to the chicken coop. They would hold their hands up to their faces and breathe against them to generate just a handful of heat. They would tap-dance about to keep their toes warm. They would never completely thaw out under the thin blankets at night. They would pull the blankets over their head and wrap their arms around their legs, trying to hug themselves, trying to make themselves into little warm bundles.

They were never quite certain when a blow might fall, but they were struck by the nuns for virtually anything. It was the nature of such a system of beatings that a child could never really determine when he was going to be hit—they could not predict or control it completely. In the wisdom of the nuns, the children were wicked just by virtue of existing. So it followed, really, that all their actions were wicked. And they could be punished for actions that, if committed by other children, would be considered benign.

Herein is recorded a brief summary of certain infractions that were the cause of corporal punishments, meted out to children from January to July 1914.

From *The Book of Minor Infractions*:

A boy raised his legs up in the air and made a bicycle motion with them.

A small girl looked at a chipmunk and made clucking noises in an attempt to communicate with it.

A boy was standing on one foot while holding his refectory tray.

A little boy was staring too quizzically at his reflection in a spoon.

A little girl was humming "La Marseillaise."

A boy was stomping the snow off his boots in an overly aggressive fashion.

A girl had a hole in the knee of her stocking that she hadn't darned.

A girl drew a smiling face on a zero in one of her math equations.

Seven children wiped their noses on their sleeves.

A girl could not resist the temptation of snow and grabbed a handful of it and shoved it in her mouth.

A boy managed to come to breakfast with every article of the clothing he was wearing inside out.

A girl claimed that she woke up in the middle of the night and saw a man with goat feet tiptoeing around all the beds.

Three children could not remember the name of the ocean between Canada and Europe.

A girl spelled out words in the air with the tip of her finger.

A little girl looked into the sun at an angle to make herself sneeze.

A boy pretended to pull his thumb off his hand.

A girl was treating a peeled potato as though it were a baby and hid it in her pocket to protect it from being boiled.

For reasons unknown to him, a boy decided to deliver his Confession in the voice of a duck.

IT WAS SAD for all the children. They were so in need of love. The beatings affected their self-esteem. Because they were beaten every time they found themselves lost in thought, they began to find that their minds were afraid to wander. Their little brains were not allowed to amuse themselves or to dally happily in the magical Elysium of the mind that was childhood. But Pierrot's and Rose's personalities both survived this cruel regime.

THE MOTHER SUPERIOR always took particular notice of the boys and girls in the younger group, the two-to-six-year-olds, who were lodged on the second floor. The first thing Pierrot and Rose had in common was the black cat. The Mother Superior was always trying to get rid of the black cat, which seemed to haunt the orphanage. It had spiky hair and looked as though it had just climbed out of a vat of tar and was miserable about its fate. There were days it could never be found. It would seem to just disappear into the walls. But one time she found it in Pierrot's bed. They were asleep, wrapped up in each other's arms like lovers. She chased it right out the window. She was sure that was the last time she would ever lay eyes on it.

And then she saw it again, talking to Rose. The little girl was crouched down and was speaking to the cat as though they were going over some very important business together. But Rose was so young she couldn't even speak proper words yet. She was just uttering garbled, burbling noises. They sounded like water in a tiny pot bubbling over. The cat was listening carefully to what Rose said and then hastened out the door, as if to deliver the message to the insurgents.

When Pierrot and Rose were both four years old, the Mother Superior saw the two of them pretending that the black cat was their child. They kept kissing the cat on the head and handing it back and forth.

"You've been a naughty kit-kat. Silly bad thing. Dirty raggedy scamp. You'll go straight to hell," said Rose.

"Yes. You've been bad and whiny. You don't get milk. No milk at all. No milk one bit. No milk for you," insisted Pierrot.

"If you cry, I'm going to poke you in the nose."

"Owww! Owww! Owww! I don't want to hear it."

"You smell bad. You have to scrub your paws. Bath time. Stinky creep."

"Naughty sinner, naughty, naughty, naughty. With mud for paws."

"Soooo shameful. Look at me. Mister Shameful."

They had never been taught words of affection. Although the two had only known harsh terms and words of discipline, they had managed to transform them into words of love. The Mother Superior immediately made a note to keep the two children apart. Boys and girls were kept in separate dormitories and classrooms, but they played in the common room, ate in the same large cafeteria and did their chores outside in the field together. It was necessary to thwart all love affairs in the orphanage. If there was one thing responsible for ruining lives, it was love. They were in their pathetic circumstances because of that most unreliable of feelings. These affairs sometimes began years and years before the children themselves were aware of their affections, and by the time they became evident, they were impossible to uproot. So the nuns were all instructed to keep Rose and Pierrot away from each other.

Not these two delinquents, she thought. Not these two unlucky found-lings. They had already escaped death. And still they were expecting more.

~∙≋[4]≋∙~

THE EARLY YEARS OF A BRILLIANT IDIOT

Pierrot was a late bloomer. When he was a baby, he didn't do much of anything at all. He wouldn't even sit up but just lay on his back, staring at the ceiling. And then when he finally learned to sit up, he couldn't be bothered to talk for months and months and months. He let the other children do all the talking. He was too delighted listening to the others to say anything himself. He would burst out laughing at odd times when you weren't sure what he could possibly have found funny.

The Mother Superior was quite sure that before he was six years old, she would have to pack his stuff into a suitcase, draw him a little map with the directions to the insane asylum and send him on his way.

The nuns almost separated him from the other boys, but he seemed to play well with them. The other boys didn't cast him aside like they usu-ally did with oddly maturing children. This seemed to imply that they thought he was somehow at their level. And children were the best at knowing such things. Once he did open his mouth, at age three, he seemed bright enough.

But perhaps what really saved him from being in a straitjacket for the majority of his life was the unusual skill set he was developing. He was able to do handstands and cartwheels. He could do a backflip as if it were a natural thing for a child to do. He also had a flair for theatrics. Pierrot would pretend to sit on a chair, even though there wasn't anything underneath him—a subtle act of absurdity that amused the other children to no end. Pierrot also often acted as though he had just been struck by lightning, sizzling in one spot and then dropping dead to the floor. He would sometimes be found in the backyard in the winter, picking imaginary flowers and sniffing them.

Pierrot's blond hair made him look serious and angelic when he wasn't doing something absurd. He was so slender. He just got taller as he got older, but never broader. It was hard to imagine that he would ever hit puberty. Pierrot was capable of great wondrous thoughts by the time he was eleven. Everywhere he went, he seemed to leave a trail of them behind, like the tail of a kite flipping around in the breeze. Usually one formulates an idea or desire and then subsequently says it out loud. But with Pierrot, the thoughts were so on the tip of his tongue that he sometimes had the impression he was saying them first and thinking about them later. He seemed to be as much in love with the gymnastic feats of language as he was with its meaning. And therefore he was known to say things that were much wiser than he himself could understand.

Pierrot was to be a paradox to all those who met him. On the one hand, he was utterly brilliant, and on the other hand, there was no way he could be interpreted as anything except a fool. But because he was so entertaining, Pierrot was always presented when the archbishop was visiting.

Although it was not the type of question an archbishop usually bothered volatile orphans with, he asked Pierrot—purely out of curiosity as to what his answer might be—who he imagined that his parents were.

"Oh," said Pierrot, "I imagine some woeful skinny teenage thing who got seduced by a thug. These things happen, and there is nothing that anybody in the whole world can do to stop them. Let's be honest—I was born in the most unfashionable of gutters."

The archbishop, along with others, realized that if you put a blazer on him, Pierrot could fit in anywhere. He could have passed for the prime minister's son. You could imagine him giving a little speech on the radio when his father passed away—on how he felt about losing such a grandiose papa.

PIERROT'S MOST REMARKABLE SKILL, however, was that he was able to pick out certain tunes on the piano after only a few lessons. He was a natural. He couldn't be bothered to learn to read music but just played by ear, composing his own tunes or improvising them. Reading a musical score was too much like classwork for Pierrot. And he was terrible at math and science and geography and history and spelling. Very soon Pierrot was able to play much better than the Mother Superior herself. He played so quickly. The notes were like mice scurrying across the floor.

If he had been born anywhere else, he would have been a musical prodigy. But he was raised in an orphanage and so he played the piano in the cafeteria at dinnertime. He would play a religious tune that the Mother Superior requested, but every now and then he couldn't help himself and would start inventing his own numbers. He would turn the little hymn into a jazz number. Everyone would start laughing and clapping their hands. They wagged their heads violently, looking like piggy banks being shaken.

When he went off script like that, the Mother Superior would come up and close the piano lid and sometimes whack him on the palms with a ruler. She always let him play again, though. There was nothing else she could do. There was no way the children could listen to the instructors or other children playing when they knew Pierrot was in the room.

It was Rose, of course, who crossed the line one evening and got up off her chair and began to dance to the tune Pierrot was playing. Rose did a sweet cartwheel, her legs straight in the air and her dress down over her head. When Pierrot saw, his mouth dropped open in amazement. Then he bent forward, as though he had just the tune to accompany her wild display. He tapped out another pretty bar of enthusiastic melody in order to encourage the girl. Rose danced, wagging her hands over her head as if she were waving to a soldier departing on a train. A nun, wasting no time, leaped to her feet, headed toward Rose and smacked her on the back of the head, causing her to tumble to the floor, while another took care of Pierrot. The Mother Superior didn't like that these particular children were being punished at the same time, as it might breed in them a sense of solidarity. But what choice did she have?

Even the often rigid and ornery Mother Superior was fond of Pierrot. He did a rather endearing impersonation of her that always made her laugh. Nonetheless, she smacked him like she did all the other children, until the arrival of Sister Eloïse.

SISTER ELOÏSE WAS YOUNG when she arrived at the orphanage—only twenty-two, in fact. She had a high forehead, yellow eyebrows, cheeks that were covered with freckles, a pretty nose and pink lips. She had a curvy, healthy figure that needed to be seen naked to be appreciated. Any man would have found her attractive. The first time Pierrot saw Eloïse, she reminded him of a glass of milk. She reminded him of clean sheets blowing in the wind at the exact moment when the water evaporated from them and they became dry and light and easy again.

All the children believed that when a new young nun entered the orphanage, she would remain kind, she would remain tender, she would act just a little bit like a mother. Their hopes were always dashed, of course. The Sisters always became wicked, slapping and yelling at the children after a few months. The older children never even got their hopes up because they knew a transformation was in the works.

But Pierrot had high hopes for Sister Eloïse because of the way she treated him. She came by his desk and looked over his shoulder in class. His handwriting was always so terrible. His hand was always trying to write some other word than the one he wanted it to. She did not smack him on the back of the neck the way the other Sisters invariably did when they looked at his disastrous handwriting. She took the chalk out of his hand and wrote *love and cherish* with perfect skill and ease on his blackboard. Like a bird that flies without any fear of falling.

When he passed by Sister Eloïse, she smiled at him and he blushed and shuddered.

Sister Eloïse, although young, was put in charge of the children on the third floor, who were between the ages of seven and eleven. She noticed things about the children before the children themselves did, a skill the Mother Superior saw in very few nuns. Eloïse was able to punish some children preemptively. Although some of the other nuns disputed the morality of this, they could not deny that it was effective.

PIERROT WAS LOST IN THOUGHT one day when Sister Eloïse took his arm and led him to a corner.

"Look under my dress. I have a treat for you."

He peeked under her habit like a photographer peering under the black cloth of a camera, intent on capturing the elusive mysteries of the world. When he stuck his head out again, confused, she had a small cookie with raspberry jam in the palm of her hand. The children were never given any sweets. He felt ashamed afterward that none of the others were able to eat this cookie with him and that he couldn't tell them about it. The cookie was delicious, but it tasted of death.

When he was smacked for trying to scrub the floor by attaching the rags to his feet and skating on the surface, Sister Eloïse intervened. After that he found that he was not hit or beaten for anything. He would have been delighted by this phenomenon if it extended to the other children, but he discovered, to his consternation, that none of the other children were spared. He was the only one not being brutally punished. It made him feel singled out and guilty. And he noticed that Rose especially seemed to be hit more than ever. He saw Rose with a black eye feeding the chickens. It made him suddenly want to be beaten. He wanted to have the same fate as Rose. He didn't know why.

⋅⋅≺⟦ 5 ⟧≻⋅⋅

NOTES ON A YOUNG PROVOCATRICE

Rose was an ordinary-looking little girl. She was definitely not unattractive. But she wasn't one of those children so absolutely lovely that you can't take your eyes off them. She had black hair, with eyes to match. She looked a bit like the snooty expressionless doll that was popular in the high-end stores back then. Perhaps her only remarkable feature was how pink her cheeks would get when she was out in the cold. It was the only time people would remark that she was beautiful. When she was inside, it was as though that attractiveness just melted away.

Like Pierrot, Rose also, from a very young age, had a fondness for dissimulation. Rose pretended to be a kitten at the foot of the bed. She mewed in the cutest way. She was able to make a steam-whistle noise. She was able to make her cheeks go really round, just like those of a trumpet player. Rose would plop herself down on a chair and make a farting noise. All the other children loved that.

Perhaps it had to do with her first deep, deep nap in the snow, but

Rose was a remarkably introspective child. She wondered about the difference between what was happening right in front of you and all the strange stuff that goes on in your head. She sometimes thought that there wasn't a distance between the two. Sometimes she thought it was just plain silly that we were paying all this attention to the real world when there was this wonderful one in our minds that we could just as well be engaging in. So she would suddenly act as though the real world had no import.

All the other girls laughed in delight when they realized that tonight was going to be one where Rose completely lost her mind. She bent forward and draped a coat over her body and head. She stretched her arm up in the air to look like an ostrich's neck. She climbed onto the edge of her bed frame like it was the rigging of a ship. As if it were a ship cable, she walked delicately across it. She called out, "Land ho!" A crowd of children scrambled up onto the mattress. They wanted to get aboard this lifeboat. They wanted to arrive in this new land—and explore whatever it was that Rose was going to explore. To see everything Rose was going to see.

She hopped from one bed to the other as though trying to escape a wicked pirate who had breached the deck and was out to kill her—out to stab her in the heart for refusing to love him. Such was the quality of her performance that the little girls could see the evil man pursuing her. They would hold their small hands to their mouths to stifle their terrified cries.

One of the girls got so worked up one night at the performance that she fainted. The other girls gathered around her, blowing in her face and waving pillows back and forth above her. They were trying to revive her. If the Sisters came in, they would put an end to all of these marvelous games forever.

Their favorite of Rose's performances by far were those when her imaginary friend, a bear, came to visit. And he would always be demanding Rose's hand in marriage. All the girls scooted down one chair at the dining table because they wanted to leave a space for her imaginary friend to sit. In the dormitory at night, Rose would sit on the edge of her bed, looking straight ahead, spurning the affections of the beast.

"You must be completely out of your mind. Why would I marry a bear?" She paused to listen to what the bear was saying. "Well, for one thing, how in the world could I trust you around any of my friends? I'm quite sure that I would turn my head for just a minute and when I turned it back I'd find that you had swallowed them whole."

The little girls exploded with mirth. Their laughter was like a pheasant that burst startled from a thicket.

"And you are always eating all the honey. That just isn't right! You know that I like to have a spoonful of it in my tea, and every time I go to pick up the jar, I see that it is completely empty."

They laughed again at this big bear that didn't have the sense to know when enough was enough.

"Also, you are a bum. You sleep for the whole winter. I know it's cold out, but that doesn't mean you can just sleep right through it. How will the bills get paid? Do you think I want to spend the whole winter listening to you snore?

"No, I will not kiss you. No, no, no. Get your huge paws off me."

The little girls clapped their hands and screamed in delight. They forgot themselves, pulling their dresses up to their chins and shoving their fists in their mouths. One girl laughed so hard that she peed in her underpants a little.

While Pierrot was in the boys' dormitory entertaining the boys, Rose was putting on a show for all the girls. Because of the separation of the boys' and girls' wings, they were never really a part of each other's imaginative worlds.

Not yet.

THE NUNS WERE AWARE that Rose stuck out, and perhaps it was for this reason that she was punished more than all the other children. In fact, the frequency with which her name appears in *The Book of Minor Infractions* at the time is rather alarming. Sister Eloïse didn't like how other girls paid attention to her. She was adored for being creative and witty, which was not right, in the nun's estimation—she strongly believed that girls should be admired only for being good.

She hated that Rose was trying to better herself intellectually, something that a girl had no business doing. She caught Rose taking the newspaper pages that the fish had been wrapped up in out of the garbage can and reading them. She saw an old janitor pass something to Rose, which she tucked under her sweater. Upon investigation, the Sister found it to be a history of France, with the first chapter missing. Sister Eloïse knew that this couldn't be the first time this clandestine exchange had taken place. In one of the bathroom stalls, she noticed that a panel on the floor seemed loose. She pulled it up and spotted a stashed pile of books there: Victor Hugo, Cervantes and Jules Verne!

As Rose's punishment, nobody was allowed to talk to her that day. Rose wore a sign around her neck that read *Ignore me*. If any girl was caught talking to her, she would find herself wearing a sign just like it around her neck too.

Another time, Rose was made to stand on a chair for fraternizing indecently with her imaginary bear. She had to hold a great atlas on her head. The atlas was filled with maps of all the countries in the world.

Rose carried a white mouse around in her pocket, a gift from the gardener. At night when she slept, she kept the mouse in a jar at the bottom of her trunk. Upon discovery of the glass residence one morning, the Mother Superior filled the bottle with water in front of everybody and screwed the lid back on. The mouse floated about with its arms spread, as if it were truly amazed by life.

The cook always gave Rose cigarettes. The cook liked to have company when he smoked. She would smoke while perched on the counter with her legs crossed, listening to the cook rattle on about his brother-in-law.

When Sister Eloïse caught her, she made Rose stand in front of everyone and smoke an entire pack of cigarettes. All the children watched her smoking. She did it so elegantly. Rose blew a smoke ring and the children applauded. They had no idea how she was able to playact at being an adult so well.

"It's very hard being a dragon," Rose said, "no matter what they tell you. Every time I turn around, it just so happens that there is a knight standing there, poking me in the behind. Excuse me, but do I show up at your house and poke you in the behind? No, I do not."

As always, laughter erupted around her, the way water leaps up around a statue in a fountain. Pierrot laughed the hardest. He thought Rose was marvelous. He thought she was a rebel. He was intimidated by her.

Rose felt as if she could smoke every cigarette in the whole damn city. Later that day, Rose found herself over a bucket, puking.

When she caught Rose with her arms around the bear again one evening, Eloïse decided she had had enough.

Ordinarily, Eloïse's thoughts were like pieces of well-crafted china delicately placed on the shelf of a locked glass display case. When Rose came into the room, each of her words was like a mortar shell, and the shelves began to shake and the ideas began to fall off and smash to the ground. Eloïse's anger was irrational, and it was also impossible to stand.

"What are you doing?"

"I don't want the little ones to be afraid of the dark. I want them to know that the creatures of night are sweet."

"There's nothing in the darkness. They just have to trust in God and everything will be all right. God is all around them in the dark."

"But sometimes we like to imagine talking bears. I am inviting them to come out and to sit with us and have a cup of tea."

"You're summoning the devil."

"No I'm not. It's only a game."

"How dare you talk back to me?"

Rose found herself sitting in the cupboard for the better part of three days. When she was finally released, Pierrot noticed her in the corridor, squinting because the light was blinding, her arms stretched out in front of her.

At the orphanage, those caught masturbating had their hands whipped with a ruler fifty times. And then they would stand on a chair in the common room wearing red gloves so everyone would know what they had done. There was a different little boy standing up on the chair every few weeks. And then one day there was the lovely Rose. Nobody could believe it. But perhaps most shocking was the look on her face. She stood with her chin up in the air, a look close to pride on her face.

Pierrot sometimes told people that was the moment he fell in love with Rose.

⊰ 6 ⊱

PORTRAIT OF BOY
WITH UMBRELLA

Pierrot had his eyes scrunched up as he masturbated one night when he was eleven. His lips were screwed over to the left, and his toes poked out from under the blanket and were stretched out wide. He opened his eyes and was startled to see Sister Eloïse standing at the foot of his bed. He was horrified. His penis was making the blanket stand up like a tent.

He was certain he was going to be severely punished. Instead she gently took his hand while putting her finger up to her puckered mouth, indicating that he should be quiet. Making it seem as though she were somehow complicit in his crime. She tiptoed prettily in front of him and he followed. She took him into the bathroom with her. He thought that she was perhaps taking him away so that she might beat him without waking up the other children. She was probably going to make him climb into a bathtub filled with cold water, a not uncommon punishment at the orphanage.

At the sight of the bathtub filled with water, Pierrot began to tremble and shake. Children in Montreal had an absolute terror of the cold. You might assume they had built up a resistance to it, given the long winters, but the opposite was true. The cold had persecuted and tormented them to such an extent that they were more wary and frightened of it than children anywhere else. In the same way that children who are bitten by dogs are horrified by the creatures their whole lives.

"Take off your clothes and get into the bath," she said.

Pierrot's teeth chattered as he pulled his nightgown up over his head. His whole body trembled as though a train were passing by the window. Sister Eloïse looked down at his penis. Although it had lost its erection, it was still larger than the penises of other boys his age. When he noticed her looking, he put his hands over it, embarrassed once again. He stepped into the bath, forgetting the cold for a moment, as if it could hide him.

The minute his foot plunged into the water, he was shocked by its warmth. It was startling and felt so good. It was as if he had been expecting a smack but had received a wondrous, delicious kiss. He hurried into the bathtub and sank into its great warmth. He had never taken such a warm bath before. The baths the children took once a month were always tepid and filthy.

He didn't bother with why or how he was allowed to have such a treat. There was no time for logic right now. He just loved the feeling. He was at one with the warm water. The faucet looked like an elephant with its ears flared out. Eloïse screwed its ears and more warm water spurted out of its nose and Pierrot closed his eyes.

When he opened them again, he saw that Sister Eloïse had taken off her habit. She was wearing a thin slip. It was odd to see her hair. Even though it had been cut short, he could still see that it was soft and fair. It was like something one might discover in a milkweed pod. She shook her head, as though she had long luxurious locks.

"I'll wash you," she said.

Pierrot stood up and Eloïse began to vigorously move a bar of soap this way and that all over his skinny body. Her slip got splashed with water as she scrubbed and rubbed him. He could make out the shapes of her large round breasts under it as it became soaked. He couldn't say why but he felt frightened.

The bottom of the tub was slippery under his feet and felt as insubstantial as a thin layer of ice. As though he might crash through it any minute and descend a hundred feet down into the cold waters that lurked just beneath him.

"Do you want to feel something strange but also really nice?" Eloïse asked.

Pierrot shrugged. Like any child, he was always up for experiencing new and possibly delightful things. Now, however, he hesitated. Although something prevented him from saying yes, he did not say no. In the future, he would always remember that he didn't tell her no.

Putting the soap and washcloth on the side of the bathtub, she straightened up on her knees. She took his penis in her hands and leaned forward and put her mouth around it. She had just the tip of it in her mouth and was licking and sucking on it. His penis grew so quickly. He thought it would keep growing and growing. As if it were some magical beanstalk. He felt terrible, but so good.

He had the sudden urge to grab her head and ram his penis to the back of her throat. He tried to stop himself but his hands and fingers reached against his will. They just wanted to touch her silky hair with their fingertips. The moment he felt the hair, he couldn't help himself. He took two fistfuls of it and pushed his penis deep into her mouth and it exploded. The feeling was so enormous that he didn't know whether it was a good feeling or a bad feeling. It was more frightening than anything else. He also knew that it was something that he could easily spend the rest of his life doing.

His penis throbbed in her mouth. A tremor went through his whole body, as though he were a flag moving in the wind. She gagged and coughed. She pushed him back gently. She spit into the bath.

"You can go back to bed," she said.

Pierrot climbed out of the bathtub. He dried himself off hastily and put his nightgown back over his head. He hurried back to bed, shivering now and on tippytoe. Freezing rain began to fall outside and it sounded like there were a hundred children running behind him. He had a chill and had to get under the covers so that he could go back to sleep and wake up out of this strange dream. He didn't even know what they had done exactly. He hadn't known what being sucked off was before then. But he knew it had to do with sex.

He was too young to be married to the nun. She was married to God! What would God say if He knew about this? And God knew absolutely everything, so He certainly would know about this. How could he have been so stupid, to go and upset God? He had been considering himself lucky of late, as he was no longer beaten like the other children.

He wept into his pillow. He didn't know why he was weeping. The next day he began crying when he looked at his porridge. His big teardrops made the porridge tasty.

Sister Eloïse continued to wake Pierrot up in the middle of the night. It happened too many times for Pierrot to count. It continued to happen as the winter melted away outside. Once, he was concentrating so hard while Eloïse sucked him that it caused small buds to burst through the branches of the trees, and then the leaves unfurled when he came. The next day, he pulled his black turtleneck on to go outside. He had trouble getting it over his head and he sat on his bed and imagined he looked like a pawn in a game of chess. When he went outside, the spring wind had come back. It was telling the children about how it had gone in a ship to Paris, how it had taken a train to Italy. The children danced with the barefooted, carefree wind.

Pierrot didn't tell any of the other children what was happening. It was as if the things that occurred between him and Eloïse were just dreams. It was rare that any of the children spoke of their dreams. What use was it to bring up a two-headed horse that had poked its head into the dormitory? At night the monsters under the beds begged him to come make love to them.

Sister Eloïse made Pierrot swear that he wouldn't confess to the priest about what they had done. She said that what they had done was a secret, but it wasn't a sin. And that being able to keep a secret was a sign of being in love. But the feeling of wrongness was there. Was that feeling proof of something? That there is a distinction between good and evil? But Pierrot didn't dare tell the priest. And so, on top of everything else, Pierrot felt that he was going to hell.

OTHERS NOTICED a certain change in Pierrot. Whereas before he had always seemed to be an almost unfailingly happy child, he now was taken by great bouts of sadness. He would tell the others to leave him be, that he was afraid of death and needed to weep. He seemed to perform sadness.

He curled up into a little ball as though he were literally a ball of despair. And he rocked back and forth, until finally he rolled right around into a somersault. He would always act shocked when he rolled over, then he would stick out his limbs in all directions, startled. All the other children laughed.

He ran, threw himself up against the wall, smacked against it like a bird against glass and then slid right down again.

He was standing outside in the garden. He had taken the Mother Superior's umbrella and was holding it over his head. The children asked what he was doing and he said he was waiting for it to rain.

The children ran up to Pierrot when he got into one of these moods. For some reason, his sadness made their own go away. Their unhappiness was something that could be very easily mastered. It made their bad moods seem like something silly. Sadness was nothing to be afraid of. You could laugh at it. It was as absurd as a sneeze. It lasted as long as the pain from the sting of a bee.

Pierrot just stood there, all alone under his umbrella. A hen walked by with its chest way forward, like a toddler learning to walk. All the children got tired of watching Pierrot and went off to have fun. Except for Rose. She was left staring at him. She tiptoed over, bowed her head and went under the umbrella with him. She held his hand and Pierrot felt better almost immediately, as though Rose were a solution to all great philosophical conundrums.

"I'm a terrible person," Pierrot said to her.

"I'm quite wicked too," Rose said, and she smiled at him.

Pierrot knew that Rose was punished every time she spoke to him. All her words were contraband, treasured items from the black market. A sentence from her was like a pot of jam during wartime.

"Does it bother you?" Pierrot asked her.

"No. We won't be here forever. When we go, we can do as we please."

What an idea! There was the possibility for escape? Pierrot had never considered that. He had been a child for his whole life, so it seemed reasonable to expect that he would continue to be one for the rest of it. But there was the possibility of being free.

Rose pointed across the field in front of the orphanage. You could see the city being built every day. There was a different cityscape every time you looked. There would be new turrets and garrets and roofs and windows and crosses. They were approaching the orphanage, a fleet of warships getting closer and closer to the shore.

Three nuns came out with sticks above their heads to separate the boy and girl. Rose dropped Pierrot's hand and ran across the yard.

LATER THAT NIGHT Pierrot whispered the words "I'm quite wicked too" under his breath. He liked that. He liked to have her words in his mouth. He wanted to open his mouth and hear her laugh. He had a strange longing that he couldn't put into words or logically understand: he wanted to be one with her.

ROSE WAS LET OUT of the cupboard and went back to her dormitory later that night. She was glad it was nighttime because the bright lights would give her a headache. She supposed she was lucky. She had been inside for only five hours this time, not days.

She had spent the whole time in the cupboard wiggling her back molar. It had come loose when she was struck on the side of the face for talking to Pierrot. She had it now, in her pocket.

Sister Eloïse had told her that she was a slut and that she had been trying to tempt him. Maybe the sister was right. She did have an urge to be near Pierrot. It always got her in trouble. She risked everything for him.

The other girls had already gone to sleep. There was a full moon outside and it lit up the dormitory with an eerie light. She sat on the edge of her mattress, unlaced her shoes and tucked them under her bed. She reached beneath her dress and peeled off her stockings. She stretched out her naked legs in front of her and admired them. The nail on her right big toe was completely black and about to fall off, because it had been stomped on by a cane. Her left knee was dark blue from landing on it when she was knocked over.

She pulled her white dress over her head. She hadn't unbuttoned enough buttons and she got tangled up in it, looking like a butterfly trying to get out of a cocoon. She wrestled it off, folded it and put it in her trunk. There was a violet ring around one arm where she had been yanked.

She took off her onesie underwear. It was thin, like a bit of smoke escaping from a cigar. There were marks across her back where she had been beaten with the cane. And her side was still light brown from where a rib had been cracked in a previous beating. There were three drops of blood at the bottom of her onesie because she had gotten her period. They looked like rose petals.

A young girl's body is the most dangerous place in the world, as it is the spot where violence is most likely to be enacted.

Rose pulled her nightgown over her body and leaped into the bed. She wiggled under the blankets. She thought about Pierrot. She didn't know what it meant to always want to be close to someone. She wanted to have the same experiences as him. She wanted to hit him and have a bruise appear on her body.

"I'm a terrible person," Rose whispered at the ceiling.

"I'm quite wicked too," Pierrot whispered back.

IN WHICH THE SNOW IS
CUED FROM BELOW

Christmastime was magical in Montreal. The snowflakes were enormous that time of year. They were so white that sometimes it hurt the children's eyes just to look at them. There was such whiteness everywhere. There was such a cleanness to it.

At Christmastime there was much work to be done at the orphanage. They were always putting on plays at the town hall for the public. In 1926, for instance, they put on a play about Daniel and the lions. The children all had manes made of skullcaps and yellow yarn fitted on their heads. They had to be very careful not to let the yarn fall into their soup before the show. Rose was in that performance, and the audience had laughed loudly at her distinctive roar and the way she shook her head.

The following year, the one in which Pierrot and Rose both turned thirteen years old, the orphanage's creative committee, consisting of nuns around a dinner table, decided to put on a production about winter. The night before the performance, all the children dressed up like snow angels. They had wings made out of white feathers that had straps to wear on their shoulders and little wire halos that were attached to the back of their out-fits in order to float over their heads. They held their white gowns up over their knees so that the hems didn't get completely covered in mud and dirty snow as they hurried into the horse-drawn cart. The clip-clopping of the horses' hooves sounded like a roomful of children with hiccups.

The children walked out onto the stage. They put their hands together in prayer. They looked downward at the floor, with their lips tucked in. They were afraid to look at the crowd because it might cause them to laugh. They all tried to hurry out in a straight line. One of the children turned her head and looked at the audience. She froze for a couple of seconds and all the children coming up behind crashed into her.

There was a song about the winter. The children all sang *whoooo whoooo whoooo* to mimic the sound of the wind. They put their arms up in the air with their fingers spread and waved them back and forth as though they were tree branches. Some very small children came out on the stage and began to beat the surfaces of metal drums to create the sound of a storm. And then the racket stopped and all the children looked up. Then, to the audience's delight, paper snowflakes began to fall from the sky above the children's heads.

The children sang "Silent Night" as they fell.

Rose was walking off the stage when Pierrot was heading out onto it. He caught her hard by the wrist. "Stand here. I want to play this tune for you."

The snowflakes had not yet stopped descending when Pierrot appeared from behind the curtains. He strolled toward a large brown piano that had been rolled out into the center of the stage. Pierrot had never met the piano before. He settled in on the bench and hunched his head over the keyboard and wagged and wiggled his hands over the keys before even touching them, as though to warm up. When he pressed the keys, his fingers jumped back in surprise. The keys were so much lighter than those of the piano at the orphanage. They were so much more willing to be his accomplice. This was a piano that liked to be played, unlike the other, stubborn one. He ran his fingers over the keys, enchanting both himself and the audience. His playing sounded like laughter in a school yard. The tune sounded nonsensical at first, but then the audience picked up the tiny, delicate, sweet melody that he was improvising right before their eyes. It sounded like the world's most magical jewelry box had just been opened.

It was the bar of music that he had played the first time Rose began dancing. Pierrot had been working on it every day since. Remembering how she couldn't resist it, he had wanted to seduce Rose again. Rose closed her eyes, listening and enjoying the tune, ignoring the rest of the world. She began to dance from one foot to the other, swaying to the music backstage. There was suddenly the sound of laughter right behind her. She thought that she was safe behind the black curtains, thick as the night in a moonless forest. But when Rose opened her eyes, she was standing onstage, facing the back curtain. She very slowly turned around; the audience was looking right at her.

Everyone in the audience became completely quiet the minute they saw Rose's pale, shocked face. They couldn't take their eyes off her. She looked so surprised that she was alive. They couldn't figure out why exactly they found her so beautiful. What was it that was making them stare? Was it the giant eyes, which seemed to be preternaturally black? Was it the dark hair? Was it the rosebud mouth? Her rosy cheeks?

Pierrot kept playing. He played hesitantly, as if the tune were also trepidatious and surprised to find the audience there. Rose smiled at the audience. She flapped her arms in the air as though she were trying to ascend to the heavens, to escape the situation she was in. But she hopped upward and landed on her butt.

They all laughed at her adorable expression and antics as she continued to find ways to fly off the stage. Rose felt the admiration from the audience. It was like standing in front of a fire that was emanating heat. And every time she made any movement, it was as if she had tossed a log into the fire.

At that moment, Sister Eloïse ran out from the back. She had to stop what was happening on the stage. But she didn't watch where she was going. She tripped over the rope attached to one of the buckets filled with fake snow that had mysteriously not tipped over. Of course, now it seemed to have no trouble reversing. A heap of paper snow spilled out over the stage. Rose scrunched her head into her shoulders and put her hands out on either side as though she were caught in a snowstorm.

She spun as she shook the paper snowflakes out of her hair. Then she wrapped her arms around herself, the way people do when they are freezing at a bus stop. She started to hop from foot to foot as though she were trying to keep warm. Then she began dancing a dance of a snow angel. She acted as if the ground were cold to her toes and the wind kept making her swirl around. She stood on the tip of one toe and raised her other leg high above her head. She quickly brought it down before the dress slipped down completely. She was wearing white darned stockings underneath and black lace-up boots.

And Pierrot played along. They were so synchronized that it was hard for anyone in the audience to discern whether Pierrot was playing along to her dancing or whether she was dancing to his music. It seemed to everyone watching that they had rehearsed this number carefully for years.

Pierrot began to play so wildly that there was nothing for Rose to do but make a little flip in the air with her hands behind her back. She flung her body forward as if in a front dive. For a moment it did seem that she was about to obtain flight. And then she tucked up into a roll, wings and all, and ended up right at Pierrot's feet.

Pierrot played the last notes of his song. She put her hand out. He took it. He helped her to stand and they walked to the center of the stage and took a bow.

A very wealthy woman was seated next to the Mother Superior. She was the cousin of the former prime minister. She had a hat made out of distressed velvet. It looked almost like she had just come off the battlefield and had a bandage wrapped around her head. It went so far down over her face that you could only judge her expression by her thin lips, which were usually constricted into a tight frown. She had a mink stole that seemed not to want to behave, as it kept slipping off her neck and getting into fights with another audience member's Pekingese. She leaned in to the Mother Superior.

"*Ces deux-là sont extraordinaires.* I must have those children perform in my parlor," she said. "I'll make a sizable donation."

And her words changed the orphans' lives.

On the way home, Rose put a snowball against her cheek where Sister Eloïse had punched her the minute she got offstage. She was sitting in the back of the cart with the other girls. The Mother Superior was seated up front, Sister Eloïse at her side.

"I think the minute we get back Rose should be put in the cupboard for a week," Sister Eloïse suggested.

"She's been punished enough."

Sister Eloïse was stunned. The Mother Superior turned and looked at her harshly. "I don't want you hitting her in the face again. She'll be black-and-blue for two weeks now."

"I think it's time to send Rose out to work. Before she really gets us into trouble."

"Not just yet, Sister Eloïse. Not just yet."

THE MORNING AFTER THE PLAY, Pierrot swiped a pair of wings from the costume closet. He wore them as he tiptoed along the corridor. He had no intention of ever taking them off. It had been a triumphant night for him, as he had gotten Rose to dance for him.

Sister Eloïse let him wear the wings. She couldn't bring herself to tell him to take them off because they suited him so. It came to seem natural to everyone in the orphanage to see him in those wings. The whiteness of the wings was so bright, it seemed that Pierrot himself was radiating light. He wanted Rose to notice his wings, though. She was afraid of even looking at Pierrot because her jaw was still blue.

When he passed her in the hallway, Rose put her mop against the wall and couldn't restrain herself from running her fingers over the feathers. "What kind of bird do you think these feathers come from?" she asked.

"I don't know. A swan?"

"You had better stop wearing those wings, then. A swan might fall in love with you. And as you probably know, swans mate for life."

"You are a funny one, Rose."

Sister Eloïse caught him chasing Rose around. Rose expected to be attacked, but the beating did not come. Instead Eloïse took away Pierrot's wings out of spite. She put them back in the box where they would be kept until next Christmas and then could be used to worship the one who was truly God's favorite: Jesus.

But they were called on to perform again sooner than that. The Ladies Charity Society was so impressed by Pierrot and Rose's spectacle at the town hall that it recommended the act to other charity organizations. The two children were asked to perform all over the city.

Sister Eloïse was furious when the Mother Superior told her. Her face became pale, as though she had just received the news that she had a terrible illness.

"Mark my words," Sister Eloïse told the Mother Superior, "this will be disastrous. You have to humble these children. They are going to have to get used to working in factories and being maids when they get older. If they get used to all this fancy living, they'll be done for. They won't want to accept their lot in life and they'll turn to crime."

The Mother Superior shrugged. "We need the funds, Sister Eloïse."

"But you always told me we should keep those two apart."

"Sometimes these things are impossible to stop."

Eloïse stormed out of the room. She kicked a black cat that got in her way. Rose and Pierrot were going to fall in love. She knew it sure as day. Everybody knew it. But nobody cared now. Money was an abstract idea, like God, and so it trumped all earthly considerations. She shook Pierrot awake violently that night. After she made him come in her mouth, she felt more secure, but not much.

When Pierrot and Rose began traveling around town together, they were surprised to discover that they were able to do similar tricks. He pulled a paper flower out of her head. She pulled a striped ball out of his. They looked at each other in amazement. They were both able to do handstands. All the rocks fell out of his pocket. Her dress fell up over her head. They laughed at each other upside down.

They would visit rich people's parlors. They needed only a couple of things to perform, and almost all the rich people were in possession of these: a piano and a nearby carpet. They would sometimes move a small coffee table off the carpet to give Rose her proper theatrical venue.

Pierrot would sit on the piano bench and begin to play his odd, miraculous tunes. He would sway his head in ecstasy as if he were a genius performing Rachmaninoff for a thousand spectators in Prague and not a tinkling ditty he had composed himself.

And Rose would do a strange pantomime. She had one in which she pretended she was being blown about by the wind. At one point she would be blown over backward and do a little backflip and then stand up again. When Pierrot finally finished his windy tune, she would wobble slightly as though she were dizzy and discombobulated. And then she would take the world's loveliest bow.

She did quite risky acts at times too. Like once, she brought out her bear character. She sat eating an imaginary pot of honey. She told the bear that she didn't want to share, as the bear would just be a glutton and pig out. Finally she said okay, and the bear devoured every drop of honey as she watched, shaking her head and tsking, telling him that he would certainly have a bellyache now.

When she was done, the woman of the house had tears in her eyes. The woman said she had no idea why. Rose's performance was the saddest thing the woman had ever seen.

. . .

UNLIKE SOME CHILDREN when falling in love, Pierrot and Rose never fought. Their temperaments were suited to each other's. When they were onstage, there was something of this sympathy that people were able to sense. It was like watching a tiny little married couple when they performed. They were able to intuit each other's movements.

Indeed, wherever they were, they were always able to act in an oddly harmonious way. It was almost as if they were a monster with four child hands. The Mother Superior watched them setting the tables while conversing with each other. They did it quickly and at no point did either of them reach for the same utensil or the same dish. And they set the tables without once bumping into each other, a feat that had not been accomplished in many years.

THE PATRONS would ask Pierrot and Rose questions. They would try anything to get them to talk. Because wasn't it amazing that even though they were orphans, they sometimes had things to say, and clever things at that.

Sometimes the patrons would even ask them really sad things. It wasn't, of course, particularly kind to ask them such sad questions—and they wouldn't ever ask an ordinary child about something that would no doubt upset them. But Rose and Pierrot were orphans. There was something magical about hearing them talk about their tragic circumstances in such high-pitched voices. They were metaphors for sadness. It was like someone playing a requiem on a xylophone. It wasn't something you heard every day. They especially liked to ask about the children's origins.

"My mother was very sick," Pierrot said. "She coughed all the time. I would put my hand on her back, hoping that it made her feel better, but I'm afraid that it didn't make her feel better at all. *Une nuit, elle toussait à mort.*"

"My parents both worked in a hotel, and it caught on fire," Rose explained. "They panicked and shoved me down the garbage chute. I ended up outside in the trash. They would have got into the garbage chute too, but they were too big."

"My papa went to war and he died," Pierrot sadly admitted. "A grenade landed near him and it blew him into a million bits. And my mother was so upset that she jumped out the window."

They made their beginnings up. They had no intention of wearing their hearts on their sleeves. They kept their hearts neatly tucked away in their chests.

"My father was hanged for murdering my mother."

Everyone in the room gasped. Rose looked over at Pierrot to indicate that he had gone too far.

"I wanted to kill them both off in one sentence," Pierrot said when they were outside.

BECAUSE THEY TRAVELED TOGETHER, they developed intimacy. This was something other orphans didn't have. Intimacy makes you feel unique. Intimacy makes you feel as though you have been singled out, that someone in the world believes you have special qualities that nobody else has.

"I bet there are all these people just like us on other planets," Rose said whimsically one evening. "I bet people are alive up on the moon."

They both looked up at the moon. It was like a child's face that needed to be wiped clean with a rag.

"What do you think it's like up there?" Pierrot asked.

"It's probably just like this planet except everything is lit up. Like if you have a glass of milk, it lights up. And when you drink it, you look down at your belly and you can see it shining through."

"And the apples look like they're made out of silver, but you can bite into them."

"And the white cats glow so much, you can use them as lamps for your room."

"And everybody has white hair just like old people—even the babies."

They found out just how funny they were by hanging out with each other. They began to develop a new language. They had a different dictionary and every word had a slightly different meaning for them than it had for anyone else. No one else could understand what they were saying to each other. Every word they spoke was a metaphor.

SINCE THEY WERE BOTH very good with sleights of hand and magic tricks, it was easy for them to steal. One day Rose slipped a load of sugar cubes into her sleeves and then shook them out into her pocket. When she got back to the orphanage, she held out her palm, which now gripped a stack of sugar cubes, shaped like an igloo. The children opened their mouths like baby birds and she dropped a sugar cube into each one. This way the other children were not jealous of her and Pierrot's escapades. They began performing as a duo for the children as well.

They performed their more experimental numbers for the other orphans, different from the ones they put on in the living rooms of the elite. They were both able to pretend to weep. They wept so hard that it began to appear ludicrous. The children all began to laugh. Rose held up a rag to her face to absorb her tears. Then she held it out in front of her and wrung it, to hear water splash all over the floor.

One afternoon in the common room, Rose and Pierrot placed their chairs next to each other's. They shook up and down as though they were trembling on some train tracks. It was such a simple pantomime and yet it was so delightful that all the children found themselves laughing and laughing. They were surprised that something so simple could be so humorous. They kept rumbling on their little train seats for about half an hour.

Rose imagined that she saw, out the window of the train, places she had seen in books. She imagined that she was in Paris. She had seen a drawing of it in a children's book. The hero of the book, a goose that carried a suitcase in his hand, declared that it was the most beautiful city in the world. She passed crowds of people, all wearing berets and striped shirts, with baguettes under their arms and cigarettes between their lips.

Pierrot wasn't even imagining what was going on outside the train. He was imagining the suitcases all stacked on top of their heads and the stewards coming and going with little trays of sandwiches. He was imagining that he and Rose were rich and they were able to afford the sandwiches.

Finally a nun came in and swore she would beat the two of them if they didn't knock it off. What would she have to do in life to be on one of those trains and to see those amazing things? Rose wondered as she marched off to bed.

DURING THIS TIME, Pierrot began to feel more conflicted than ever about Sister Eloïse. What perhaps disturbed Pierrot the most was that he couldn't stop thinking about their sexual acts. He would relive what they had done together the night before. The image in his head was bestowed with such a mixture of shame and pleasure that it made his penis grow hard. He began to think about dirty things all the time. He was horrified by his thoughts. They were completely mad. They were like the people at the foot of Mount Sinai engaged in an orgy.

He imagined all the girls lined up on their knees as though they were waiting for Communion, waiting to give him blow jobs. He was somehow absolutely horrified by the knowledge that he wanted to fuck all the girls at the orphanage. He thought that Sister Eloïse must have seen it in him and that was why she had brought him to the bathtub.

He tried not to think dirty thoughts about Rose. Because he spent so much time with her, he thought she would find out. But he thought about her more and more. Rose hardly had to do anything in the fantasy to bring him to a climax. He imagined her chewing on a lock of her hair. He pictured her dropping a book and then bending over to pick it up. And once he had a fantasy where she took the tip of her finger and spelled out the word *prick* in the air.

Perhaps sensing that Rose was beginning to dominate his inner life, Eloïse wanted more and more from Pierrot. She didn't want to be a virgin anymore. She wanted to have sex with Pierrot. Then they would be husband and wife, in her mind. Then they would have something that he and Rose did not have. Then she would be his first love and he could never abandon her. Everything would be as it should in the universe. The problem was not that Eloïse did not have a sense of right and wrong— she most certainly did. Perhaps the most dangerous people in the world are the ones who believe in right and wrong but what they ascribe to as "right" and "wrong" is completely insane. They are bad with the conviction that they are good. That idea is the impetus behind evil.

So one night Eloïse brought Pierrot into a small coatroom beside the chapel. There was a pile of hymnals on top of a radiator that was covered in a pattern of roses. It was where plumbers and doctors hung their coats when they visited. There was an old couch for them to sit on and tie up their boots. Although it had been destroyed by a cat, you could still see the pattern of a medieval princess frowning and pointing at a dragon like it was a naughty dog. Eloïse lay down on the couch and told Pierrot to go inside her. Pierrot at first couldn't figure out how to do it. They fumbled with his penis together. Once he was inside her, a strange feeling of guilt seized hold of him. The sordid reality of what was happening struck him. Eloïse's big tits had rolled off to either side of her body. He could see the blue veins in them, as though she were made of marble. Her blond pubic hair seemed to cover half her torso. He wanted to get out of her but couldn't figure out how other than to come. He was afraid that he would lose his erection.

Pierrot closed his eyes and imagined Rose. And he only pictured her lying beneath him as he held her nipple gently between his teeth. He ejaculated like a white wild mustang bursting forth from its enclosure. He lay there on the couch, sweaty and stinky and depleted, but he felt like the first time had been with Rose. And he would be faithful to her from now on. Pierrot decided right then and there that he would rather die than touch Sister Eloïse again.

"I think we should wait until we are married to do all this again," Pierrot said. "It's disrespectful to you. I want to be with you once everyone else and especially God can witness it."

This is what Pierrot told Sister Eloïse in order to escape her embraces. Sister Eloïse had never felt so happy.

❖ 8 ❖

THE SNOWFLAKE ICICLE
EXTRAVAGANZA

One afternoon when Rose and Pierrot were performing at a patron's house, a huge snowfall began to tumble down from the sky. The snowflakes fell in big clumps, as though they were children with their arms wrapped around one another and toppling downhill. As Rose and Pierrot performed their little routine, unbeknownst to them, the city was being covered with snow. As soon as they were done with their show someone parted the curtains and noticed that all the trees had turned white.

Pierrot and Rose were underdressed, both having arrived in only their black threadbare coats. And although they both had thin scarves tied in knots around their necks, neither of them had a hat on their dear head. When the lady of the house saw them ready to leave in those outfits, she rummaged through her things to find them some headwear she didn't want. She found Rose a white fur hat. It was too large and extravagant for a girl so young, but it would certainly keep her warm. She gave Pierrot a man-size overcoat and a pair of galoshes that were two sizes too big.

She gave them a fruitcake to take back to the orphanage and a suitcase filled with old teddy bears. And off they marched down the street like an old couple who had been turned into children by a witch's magic spell. The snowflakes settled on their hats and shoulders as they headed home.

"She was really nice, wasn't she?" said Pierrot as they walked down the street. "Or was she too nice?"

"I think she's sad because she never fell in love. Except she needn't worry, because love doesn't exist."

"How do you know that?"

Rose wiped a large snowflake from her eyelash and raised her head to try to catch one with her tongue. Pierrot put his hands out to catch some.

"I read it in a Russian novel," she said, looking at Pierrot again. "The Russians have figured everything out because their winters are so long. It makes them very thoughtful."

"How do you know all these wonderful things?" Pierrot asked.

One of the things that Rose really enjoyed about Pierrot was how quick he was at understanding what she said. She couldn't count on her hand the times when she had told an especially clever thought to one of the nuns at the orphanage and their response was to consider having her lobotomized.

They passed a billboard with a group of posters plastered to it, advertising a show that was going to be performed downtown in the near future.

There were the Parisian cancan dancers. There was a group of tap dancers from Poland. There were aerialists from Bulgaria. There was a contortionist who claimed she had mailed herself in a box from Germany. There was the White Bat Orchestra from Russia. There was a group of Ukrainians who shot themselves out of cannons. There was a Russian flea circus. A man with a big mustache and a fur hat yelled at the wee little fleas. He brought them across the sea in a suitcase with a fancy lining. They each got their very own matchbox to sleep in. Pierrot and Rose agreed that if they had any money, this was the show they would go to.

"I think I would like to make a show of my own," Rose said. "I am going to find all the clowns in the world and take them out of whatever circus they are in and make them perform in mine. I am going to find really, really sad ones too. I need some who can ride on bicycles."

"Oh yes. You should have a clown who always falls off buildings and then cries."

On the trolley, Rose took a piece of paper out of her pocket and a stub of a pencil. She put the paper on the seat between her and Pierrot. She began to write down everything she had just told Pierrot.

"We can travel from town to town and be world renowned. There will be stories about us in the newspaper."

Pierrot looked impressed. As he always lived entirely in the moment, it never occurred to him to look into the future. But Rose was always looking so far ahead.

"Let's leave our act to the very end," Rose declared. "Let's make a giant moon, and we'll dance underneath it together."

"What if the moon falls on our heads and kills us?"

"We'll hang it from really strong ropes."

"What will the revue be called?"

Rose looked at him intently for a brief moment. And then she looked back down at the paper and scribbled on it. She held it up afterward, and at the top of the page, in bold letters, was written: *The Snowflake Icicle Extravaganza.*

"What do you think?"

"Lots of clowns, right?"

"All the clowns we can find."

They knew they worked well together. The melted snow dripped down from Rose's hat and fell on her nose, warm like holy water.

"If you have a good show, then you get to travel the whole world. Can you imagine that?" Rose said. "Packing all our gear into trains and boats and heading out to the world's most wonderful places."

"I never did. That's a marvelous thought."

Pierrot sat there for a moment, letting his head grow and expand so he could fill it with all this new information. He considered her dreams to be downright miraculous.

"It'll be a lot of work, though," Pierrot said. "I personally consider myself a very lazy person."

"Well, my darling, you can be lazy when you're lying in your coffin."

The trolley came to their stop and they descended the steps onto the sidewalk and back onto the road. The snow fell all around them. They began to cross the field to the orphanage. The top layer of snow had hardened and now cracked under their feet like the surface of crème brûlée, something they'd never had the privilege of tasting.

"I like it when you call me darling," Pierrot said.

"You do?"

"Yes. It's surprising just how much I like it."

"Why don't you try saying something like that back to me?"

"Okay . . . well . . . how are you today . . . sweetheart?"

They both started to giggle.

"Well, and so, how did that make you feel?"

"Really, really good."

"Really?"

"Yes."

"Sweetheart."

"Darling."

"Sweetheart."

"Darling."

They paused, just staring at each other. The snowflakes fell down, landing on their noses, landing on their lips, melting and turning them redder.

"Sweetheart."

"Darling."

And their lips shone and grew darker and became more and more enticing to each other. This was how they made a marriage vow at thirteen years old.

THEY CONTINUED TO TOUR AROUND the city into the spring. Colors began appearing everywhere on what had previously been a white page. The blossoms were like underwear blown off the laundry lines. The orchids hung over the cast-iron gates like girls in just their petticoats yelling at the postman for a letter. And they continued to tour into the fall, when all the leaves were like colorful candy wrappers, leftover from the very sweet days of summer.

Rose and Pierrot performed in all the big houses in Montreal. They were perfectly bilingual so they were able to perform in both French and English households. The city was the most magnificent in the world. It wanted to tell the two orphans its stories. What city doesn't like to brag about itself? The gargoyle fauns leaned off the front of the buildings, whispering about their sex lives. The fat catfish in the greenhouse swore they had stock market tips. The horses on the carousel reared their heads, ready for a battle against the mermaid statues in the pond. An electric train rode around and around a tiny mountain in the toy-shop window, while its Lilliputian passengers dreamed in tiny berths. Rose and Pierrot's feelings for each other during this time grew deeper and deeper.

Two years passed in this way. In 1929 they were both fifteen years old, and so what happened next was probably inevitable.

When they were inside the orphanage, they were often separated, as all the girls and boys were. Rose was coming out of Confession when she saw Pierrot. He was sitting on a bench by the wall outside the visitors' coatroom, with a big, stupid smile on his face.

"What are you thinking about?" Rose asked him.

"I don't want to tell you because I think I might upset you and make you really rather angry."

"Oh, just tell me what you were thinking about and stop playing this ridiculous game."

"Can I tell it to you in your ear? I don't want anybody who is passing by to hear what I am saying."

"Nobody can hear us."

"I would be mortified if anyone else knew what I was thinking."

Rose turned her head forward so he could get up close. She could feel his lips against her ear. His breath entered into her ear before his words did. Her impulse was to both pull away to stop this unpleasant thing from happening and to pull his head closer to her. The duality of this sensation made it so intense.

"I want to take off your stockings, and I want to look at each and every one of your toes. I want to put each of your toes in my mouth."

The words were just shocking. The reason they were shocking was because she did not quite believe them. She had heard rumors of such words, naturally. But she hadn't quite accepted them as being absolutely true. It was as though he were holding up a jar with a mermaid in it. Or walking down the street holding a unicorn attached to a leash.

She opened her mouth to respond, but she found that her mouth was dry and her throat seemed to be empty, with no words at all. It was like opening an icebox and expecting to find bottles of milk but finding nothing.

"And then I want you to touch my penis. Just take it in your fist and squeeze it really hard."

She looked down and she could see his penis pushing up his pants.

"It grows and gets hard anytime I think about doing these types of things to you."

SISTER ELOÏSE NOTICED that they were whispering. She hurried into the chapel and went into the coatroom through its back door. She sat on the couch in the room and listened through the transom to what Pierrot and Rose were saying on the other side of the wall. There was an opening of some sort in every wall for this purpose: no one could have any privacy.

Pierrot wasn't actually whispering when he put his mouth up to Rose's ear. All he had done was lower the register of his voice to make it huskier. It was almost like his words had taken their clothes off. And so Sister Eloïse heard each of them.

She was so angry. It was so vulgar. He didn't want to have anything to do with her physically yet pretended that he was a pure child wanting an innocent and holy union. And now here was Pierrot with the vocabulary of the Marquis de Sade, as sophisticated and well versed as Casanova.

She was filled with a terrible and uncontrollable rage. But, as always, her rage was not directed toward Pierrot. She was filled with loathing toward Rose, who was really only the passive listener. Rose hadn't even been able to respond. It was as if Rose were being offered a box of chocolate-covered cherries to eat. It was as if Rose were going to receive everything Sister Eloïse had ever talked herself out of wanting.

ON THE OTHER SIDE of the wall Rose stood up quickly, frightened by Pierrot's words. Or it wasn't exactly that she was afraid of them, but they made her feel like doing odd things. It was as though her body had a mind of its own. She wanted to strip naked. She wanted him to call her Mrs. Pierrot.

Rose needed to reflect upon these strange knee-jerk reactions before acting on them. The new sensations and desires she was feeling were delightful and confusing all at once. So she jumped up and darted off. She had just entered the dormitory and was leaning against the wall when Sister Eloïse came for her.

SISTER ELOÏSE hated Rose's face too. It was so calm and blank, open to everything. It was a face that all sorts of people fell madly in love with. She always wanted to take that face like it was a piece of wet clay and mold it into a different expression, one that was bitter and filled with rage and discontent. But no matter what she did to Rose, Rose always looked up at her afterward with that same unscathed face.

Eloïse stopped herself from doing anything to Rose at that moment. She thought she would kill the girl if she didn't walk away. She hurried off down the stairs.

Rose looked after Eloïse. She had never understood the Sister.

ROSE WAS MOPPING THE FLOOR in the vestibule by the front entrance of the orphanage. The tiles at the bottom of the flight of stairs were brown and white. There was a yellow stained-glass window with an image of a lamb that the light shone through. It shone on Rose as she assiduously mopped up the area, for it was where the most footprints seemed to gather, like they were fish in a net.

Sister Eloïse was waiting and waiting for Rose to make some sort of mistake, to perpetrate an infraction. It usually didn't take very long. You only had to observe a child for several minutes before they made some sort of ridiculous mistake. What on earth was as flawed and imperfect as a child? She needed Rose to make a mistake not only to justify to the other children the punishment she was going to rain down upon Rose, but to justify it to herself.

Rose found the sunlight intoxicating. It made her sleepy. It made her dreamy. It blinded her to the physical world around her. The mop in the bucket made the sound of a pig rooting for truffles. She flopped it onto the floor. Rose began thinking of the words Pierrot had said to her. She couldn't help it. She then, for a short moment, took the mop in her hands and began to dance with it while washing the floor. She began to fantasize about dancing with Pierrot, his arms around her waist and his fingers secretly reaching down to her behind.

Sister Eloïse saw it instantly. She quickly grabbed Rose by the scruff of the neck, her arm like a cane yanking a performer offstage. Sister Eloïse felt like Samson. Her beautiful hair had been cropped off, but she was filled with supernatural strength. She could have lifted anybody up over her head. She could put her hands on either column at the entrance of the building, push hard in either direction and watch the whole building come crashing down.

Instead she directed all her fury and strength at Rose. She pushed her down so she fell to the ground. She thrashed her over and over and over again. She hit her on the back with the broom handle. She hit her until it broke. Eloïse had forgotten how much she liked hitting another human being. She just wanted to hit her again, but harder. She felt that she could just stand there whipping the girl again and again until she was dead. Every time she hit her she hated her even more. It took over her entire body. Every inch of her was furious.

Rose lay on her side, curled up like a dog. All the bruises blooming like violets. All the bruises like storm clouds. The little beads of sweat like raindrops on her nose. All her bruises spreading out like the tip of a pen touching a wet cloth.

Still Sister Eloïse continued to hit the girl, until Rose was unconscious and the Mother Superior cried out, "That's enough!"

THE MOTHER SUPERIOR KNEW THAT Eloïse would end up murdering Rose. And an uproar would no doubt ensue. She had been looking for a reason to stop Rose and Pierrot from going around town. True, she had made a pretty penny off them. A new solarium in the nuns' sleeping quarters had been built, and the indoor plumbing had been upgraded. But there had been more patrons requesting visits, which would entail repairs beyond the income that Rose and Pierrot were bringing in. And in any case, isolation was necessary for an orphanage to keep running. You couldn't discipline the children if there were interminable people checking in and participating in the children's lives. And an orphanage could not be a happy place.

The Mother Superior was of the opinion that happiness always led to tragedy. She had no idea why people valued the emotion and pursued it. It was nothing more than a temporary state of inebriation that led a person to make the worst decisions. There wasn't a person who had experienced life on this planet who wouldn't admit that sin and happiness were bedmates, were inextricably linked. Were there ever any two states of being that were so attracted to each other, were always seeking out each other's company? They were a match made not in heaven but in hell.

The Mother Superior looked at Rose's body lying on the raised bed in the infirmary. She was half-conscious, covered in terrible bruises and attached to an intravenous drip. The Mother Superior thought this was what came of allowing children to think of themselves as unique. Or particularly, this was what happened when you allowed an orphan to think of herself as unique.

SISTER ELOÏSE WAS ASHAMED to tell anyone why Rose was in the infirmary with a curtain drawn around her. So no one knew at first. They assumed she was in trouble and locked in the cupboard. Pierrot was sure that Rose was angry with him. Once his erection had gone down, he began to feel the little bit of shame that always came. He felt that he had gone too far. My God, how insensitive he had been! The more he thought about it, the more he was shocked and appalled by his behavior.

Just the day before, Rose had been telling him about her amazing plan that was surely going to make her world famous, and would probably include him. And how had he responded? By telling her that he wanted to introduce her to his penis!

Pierrot whispered at the door of the cupboard, but she didn't answer back.

Every time he thought about it, he thudded the heel of his hand on his forehead. He kept knocking his head against the wall as though it were a boiled egg whose shell he wanted to crack open. He just couldn't even think about it! He was a perverted lowlife. To revive his spirits, he imagined the Snowflake Icicle Extravaganza that he and Rose would collaborate on once she forgave him.

The first day of spring came and Rose was still in the infirmary. A small crucifix with a blue ceramic Jesus nailed to it hung above her head. A butterfly passed by the window. It had made its wings out of the pressed petals of flowers.

⋅≈∦ 9 ∦≈⋅

IN WHICH PIERROT IS
MISTAKEN FOR A GENIUS

Legend had it that Albert Irving—a very elderly citizen of Montreal—adopted Pierrot after hearing through a window of an orphanage the sound of a child playing the piano. He was a thin man who walked with a slight stoop and he was, that day, wearing a black suit and a top hat and an imported white silk scarf. Unlike his neighbors, he knew nothing of the talented pair who resided in the orphanage. He would occasionally contribute money to the orphanage, among other public institutions, in order that he might be called a philanthropist, but he rarely ventured inside it. It made him far too depressed to think of the terrible little unfortunate children who lived there. He quite liked to honk his horn and have a Sister come out; he'd hand over a sizable check and be on his way. The driver of his great black car had already opened the back passenger's door for him to climb in when the tune began to play slowly, each note like a bird alighting on the window ledge.

The playing so charmed him that he went right up all the stairs, despite his arthritis, and banged on the door. He was escorted to the Mother Superior's office. The Mother Superior was seated at her large desk, piles of books and papers on it. Behind her was a shelf covered in statuettes of different saints, who all looked up toward the ceiling. The lovely playing filled the corridors, bewitching the old man. He felt things that he hadn't in years. He almost felt like dropping his cane and skipping down the hallway. It was a great medicine. He was so wealthy that he was able to acquire whatever he wanted. He immediately set his sights on having the pianist for himself.

He asked to be introduced to whoever had been playing the piano, and a pale and slender blond-haired boy was brought to him. Pierrot stood in the doorway and smiled brightly.

"Were you playing the piano, my boy?"

"You could say that, or perhaps you could say that the piano was playing me. Or at least that we were having a conversation."

"Do you mean to tell me that the piano keys were making conversation with you? What a delightful idea, my boy. Now, I don't suppose you could give me an example of something the piano has said to you?"

"The piano was just now telling me how it feels so odd when it rains. The rain can cause you to suddenly feel guilty for all the tiny crimes you have committed, like not telling your friend that you love her."

"I do know that feeling. I've felt it quite a few times. And up until this moment, I really thought I was the only person who did. Well done and bravo, my boy. Because you have made me feel less alone in the world and less like a madman."

"You're exceedingly welcome, oh distinguished guest. And thank you for letting me know that I have been able to bring delight to someone as obviously esteemed as yourself."

The Mother Superior rolled her eyes, but Mr. Irving could not stop smiling.

THE MOTHER SUPERIOR SHRUGGED when Mr. Irving returned to inquire about Pierrot a week later. She leaned back in her green leather chair and put both hands up as though she didn't have anything to hide from the old man. "It's always been a debate among us Sisters whether that boy is bright or completely idiotic," she said.

"Do you know that is quite often a feature of an artistic mind?" asked Mr. Irving, who was seated on a smaller chair in front of the desk, leaning forward.

"If you want to see it in a positive light. But I'm going to tell you something that is true about all these orphans. They are wicked. They are thieves. They aren't quite human. A child needs a mother and a father in his life for him to have any sense of morality. Pierrot is the laziest boy I ever saw. He's distracted as easy as you please. If a bird flies by, he drops what he is doing and just stares straight up at it."

"Perhaps he is so affected by beauty that he will risk a beating just to gaze upon it."

"Do you really want a boy this old? They can be quite set in some terrible ways."

"Yes, I think he is the right age for me. I am much, much too old to look after a young child. And my other children never spoke to me when they were that age. I find young men very interesting. They are right at the beginning of their ideas. Their personalities can be so ferocious or so weak. I think that boy has an extraordinary character. And to think that he was able to develop it while living in an orphanage. Do you know anything about his mother?"

The Mother Superior shrugged again. She was just overwhelmed with disgust at all the stupid girls who had been such fools to get themselves pregnant. She vaguely remembered some story about a particularly naughty girl who went by the name of Ignorance at the Hôpital de la Miséricorde. But it hardly seemed worth scouring her memory for such a girl.

"They all seem to be the same girl to me."

The Mother Superior seemed rather concerned that Pierrot wasn't going to be forced to work all day long. Mr. Irving promised that he intended to use Pierrot as a servant—as his personal valet. Actually, he changed his mind about what he was going to use Pierrot for right in midsentence. But it was some sort of job.

"I will make a sizable donation to the orphanage."

PIERROT WAS GIVEN a cardboard suitcase to put his things in. It had belonged to a mother who had died in childbirth. The lining was printed with dark purple plums. Pierrot sat on the edge of his bed and put the suitcase on his lap, using it as a desk. He had a piece of paper and a pencil he'd borrowed from another boy. He quickly wrote Rose a letter.

Dear Sweetheart,

I don't know what in the world came over me. I'm a clown! You know that. I am going to stay with a peculiar gentleman so that I can play him piano to soothe a certain pain that seems to be plaguing him. Please write to me at this address to say that you have forgiven me. And I will write you piles of love letters. And, of course, we will be reunited soon.

"I'd hurry up if I were you. Before the man changes his mind," the Mother Superior said.

As he was leaving with his coat, his enormous scarf and his empty suitcase, Pierrot passed in front of Sister Eloïse. She thought he was going to tell her how painful it was to part from her. Instead he walked right by. She took his hand, and he pulled it from her with a small shudder, indiscernible to anyone but Sister Eloïse. Knowing that he was leaving made him feel bold. He stopped in front of the Mother Superior, who was standing at the door a few feet away from Eloïse, and handed her the letter, not caring that she was witnessing the interaction.

"Will you tell Rose that I love her and that I will be coming back for her?" Pierrot asked the Mother Superior. "And that I will most definitely marry her once I have found my fortune."

Soon after Pierrot left the building, Sister Eloïse stole the letter off the Mother's Superior's desk and ripped it up into a hundred pieces and threw it in the trash. It lay at the bottom of the basket like butterflies that had died during a sudden frost.

As HE EXITED THE GREAT DOOR of the orphanage, Pierrot felt guilty about leaving, especially since he hadn't seen Rose for weeks. He knew that it was all his own fault. He could have done something to make the old man hate him. He could have explained to the man that he was a degenerate, and then he surely would have left Pierrot behind! But the truth was he wanted to go. Living with Sister Eloïse had become intolerable for him. Here was a chance to exist without her breathing into his ear ever again. Yet he was betraying Rose, wasn't he? If he stayed, he would eventually convince her that he wasn't a lout. Even if she continued to despise him, wasn't it his duty as a lover to remain and accept that acrimony? But the truth was he saw an opportunity and he was taking it and he was leaving her behind. As he walked down the street next to the chauffeur, who was collecting him, he noticed that the black cat was following him. The cat was making him feel so awful.

"Don't leave me in this terrible building. Who will put out a little bit of milk if you don't? I'll starve! I'll starve!

"Who will snap my fleas? I will itch to death. They will eat me alive. One morning I will wake up and I'll be nothing but a bone.

"Who will say one nice word to me? Everyone will be accusing me of bringing them bad luck. It will just be so untrue. They will throw rocks at me. They'll pour boiling water on me. They'll swing me by my tail. My life isn't worth living without you. You owe me something. You owe me something!"

Maybe that was what the ones you loved did to you: they made you feel lousy. Pierrot tossed his suitcase in the trunk and hurried into the back of the car. It wasn't only Rose he was abandoning, was it? It was all the children. He used to entertain them and make them laugh. They depended on him for this. But he was going anyway!

·◦⟨ 10 ⟩◦·

IN WHICH ROSE IS INSTRUCTED OF HER NEW FATE

Two weeks later, Rose was better and ready to go back to the dormitory. She took off her hospital gown and pulled her black tights up under her dress. She walked down the corridor, whose walls were painted blue. There were stone flowers carved above the arched windows. She walked through the wide-open doors of the common room. It was raining outside and all the children, chatting and playing with dolls, turned to look at Rose. They looked apprehensive: Rose wasn't aware that Pierrot had left.

Sister Eloïse marched over quickly to tell her that Pierrot was gone and there would be no more touring for her. She wasn't really much of an act on her own, was she? This struck Rose like a small bolt of lightning. She might as well have been Rip Van Winkle. She had been in the infirmary bed for a hundred years, only to find that everything about the world that was familiar and dear to her had irretrievably disappeared. But Rose stared at Eloïse, refusing to let her know that this upset her. She nodded and walked off, hoping her legs weren't making her body shake.

Rose didn't understand why Pierrot would have left without saying good-bye. It didn't even seem possible. Especially since he was so effusive with his emotions. Over the next couple of weeks, she waited for some message from him. Why were there no letters, at least? There was a boy in the orphanage who had received letters from an older brother who had stayed in Europe after the war. They were the most wonderful missives. The boy read them out loud over and over again. The children crammed around him when he read them, as though he were a famous person and they wanted an autograph.

The children wanted to know what in the world had happened to Pierrot, and what adventures he was having. They fully expected reports to arrive that Rose would certainly share with them, the way she shared everything else. But letters never came. It made her feel insecure. It showed her that a person's personality could change radically, that you could never really know someone. In fact, you could probably never know yourself. You could think of yourself as the most fun-loving, generous person but actually be cutthroat and indecent.

The Mother Superior came in one afternoon in the fall to tell Rose that she was being sent off to work as a governess. The Mother Superior was eager to get Rose away from Eloïse. But there were other reasons to send her off as well. Of late, the nuns were feeling pressure to send out all the older children to work. They had to make room for all the new children who were being dropped off.

The Great Depression had come to Montreal.

THE NEW ARRIVALS CAME in the backs of cars with priests. The doorbell seemed to ring every day that month. That morning, the Mother Superior had opened the door to see a priest holding the hands of two children, a girl in a white sweater and blue leather boots, and a boy with a crooked bow tie and no shoes at all.

Earlier that week a handsome boy had arrived with a large duffel bag containing his Sunday clothes and a teddy bear with a missing eye. He was followed shortly by a girl with blond ringlets whose parents had both died of consumption. She had a small oval tin with blue roses on it, filled with pastilles. That was her inheritance.

There was another boy who was pigeon-chested and went around shaking the other children's hands saying, "How do you do?" He turned out to be very frank. He said his father had shot himself after losing money in the stock market. And his mother's new husband thought he was too ugly to keep.

There was a solemn-looking boy whose lips were so full that it looked as if he were kissing the window of a train.

Once the doorbell rang and there was a girl in a small black coat and lace-up boots holding a baby in her arms. "*Bonjour,*" she said. "This is my brother. My mother said I should bring him. She didn't give him a name. But if you please, I would like him to be named Emmanuel. I am not to leave the blanket."

Women gave birth at hospitals. And the second the doctor cut the umbilical cord, they were pulling their moth-eaten stretched sweaters over their heads and running to the front door to get away from feeding an extra mouth.

One boy was brought to the orphanage by his mother. She was wearing a navy blue coat, torn at the shoulder, and men's shoes tied with pink ribbons. She got down on her knees in front of the boy. "I will come back for you, my darling. I will think about you every single second of the day. As soon as I get work and a new apartment, I'll come back for you."

The nuns had little patience for these women. They would leave a bizarre list of instructions. About how their child liked to be sung to before going to bed and how they liked their milk to be warmed. And how there was a poem that they liked to have recited to them while each of their toes was wiggled.

The more effusive a mother's instructions were, the more likely the child was never to lay eyes on her again. Or so the Mother Superior believed. It wasn't love that was making those proclamations. Love was a paltry, meek thing; it was guilt that spoke in such operatic statements. Their instructions went into the fire, along with the letters Pierrot kept sending to Rose.

There was a small boy who spoke a language nobody could understand. He seemed to be saying that he was missing his pet goose, though they weren't sure. He came with a suitcase filled with bone china that looked a hundred years old. The nuns took all the dishes out of the boy's suitcase. They gave the suitcase to Rose to pack her things in.

The suitcase was blue and had green and yellow stripes on the inside. It had a funny smell to it. Rose stuck her head in the suitcase and inhaled. It smelled of another country. It smelled of a large family.

Rose liked the idea of traveling, though she knew that she wasn't going very far. Still, she wanted to leave the orphanage. She felt humiliated because Pierrot had abandoned her without a word. She thought all the other children in the orphanage were looking down on her. And *that* she couldn't tolerate. She didn't care what sort of environment she was in, so long as she wasn't seen as someone who had been jilted by her lover.

She put on her coat and packed her fur hat and gloves. The other children gathered around her to say good-bye. She kissed them on their cheeks and hands. She did a final little backflip before leaving. The children applauded sadly, knowing that the circus had folded up its tents and left the orphanage.

Rose climbed into the car waiting for her outside. The car bounced like a raft going over rapids. She was driven around and around a circular road to the top of a hill. The houses became more and more magnificent as she got closer to the peak. They were high enough above the ground that they didn't know anything about the rising tide of poverty. They were by and large unaffected by the Great Depression. The driver got out of the car to open a gate in front of a house, then drove through. It was a large redbrick house that took up a whole block. It was very pretty. It had a small blue flag waving from the top of one of the turrets, its own little kingdom.

The driver honked the horn and a maid in a uniform came out through the front door to meet them. A small pug was standing at her feet, looking up at Rose.

"Hello, my dear," said the maid. "Let me show you to your room and you can get settled in."

The maid shooed the pug through the door and closed it behind the dog. She and Rose then went into the house through the back entrance. They walked up a narrow, white staircase that led up from the kitchen. Her room was on the top floor of the house, where the children's rooms were.

"You will be looking after the children for most of the time. I hear you're quite good with the younger children."

"Yes, I guess. I mean, I like to make people laugh. Children laugh very easily. But I also quite like the idea of making adults laugh."

The maid looked her over. Rose looked at the maid with a blank expression that she knew made her impossible to read.

"They also told me that you were a rather peculiar girl."

The maid opened the door onto the bedroom that was to be Rose's own. It was sort of amazing to her, as she had always slept in a row of children. The girls woke up in the morning and climbed out of their identical beds, wearing their identical nightgowns. They resembled paper dolls that had all been cut out at the same time. And it was a question of mathematics as to whether they were one person or one hundred and thirty-five identical people.

The room was tiny and the walls were white, as if to remind the girl that she was to remain chaste. There was a little bed and a little white desk in the corner. There was really only enough space in the room to kneel down at the side of the bed, to pray at night. The only ornament was a mirror with a charming steel frame soldered into the shape of flowers. She leaned in to look at it but immediately felt vain, as though she were checking in on her own appearance.

ROSE WAS GIVEN a light blue dress with a bib that she was to wear every day while she worked in the house. She was also given a white starched hat that made her look like a nurse. After she dressed, she went down to the kitchen to meet the maid, who had promised to give her a tour of the house.

She followed closely behind the maid, who looked to be about thirty. The house was so big that if she got lost, she would never find her way back to her room, not without a map. She was introduced to each room as if it were itself a charismatic resident of the house, with its own particular needs.

There was the smoking room, where great cigars were smoked by important people. The walls were a khaki green, but were you to remove the paintings, you would see squares of emerald green, the color the room was initially painted.

There was a library filled with valuable information and statistics about the world in leather-bound volumes.

"Will I be allowed to borrow some of these books?"

"Oh, don't be an idiot. These are just for show. No one actually reads them."

There was a room that was especially for drinking tea after one o'clock. There were blue flowers on the walls, and there was a grandfather clock. Its loud ticking sounded like a suicidal man cocking his rifle over and over again.

There was an art room with an easel in the middle. There was a little table with a vase of dried flowers on it. There were all sorts of containers with every shape of paintbrush, to re-create virtually any object in the world.

Furthermore, there was a business room, a billiard room and a greenhouse. There was a room with a little swimming pool in it. There was a lone pair of boy's trunks floating on the water like some sort of sea turtle. There was one room that was filled with artifacts from someone's travels. There was a shrunken head in a glass case. Rose asked if she might have a peek through the telescope that pointed out a window, as the sun had just gone down.

"Oh, very well," said the maid. "But please don't make a habit of it."

When Rose peeked through the telescope, her eye was the first to gaze into it in the past five years. The household had given up entirely on looking at the heavens. Rose jolted back and stumbled a couple of steps. She had not expected to see the moon so close up. It was terrifying. It no longer looked like the surface of a scuffed, white figure skate. It was gray and busted up and angry. It looked like it was made of gunpowder. It was as though she had just opened the door to find someone standing there naked. It was difficult to look at the moon. She thought that she had seen a face in it.

. . .

THE MAID INFORMED ROSE that Mr. McMahon was often away on business or slept in his apartment downtown. When he did come home, it was always late at night after they'd all gone to bed. On the other hand, his wife barely left the house.

They stopped at the master bedroom to say hello to Mrs. McMahon. She was lying in bed on top of the covers, fully dressed. She had on a beautiful blue velvet dress with buttons on the front, and a pair of black boots. She also had a wet rag lying on her forehead. McMahon's wife had a fantastic and voluptuous figure. She herself knew that it was her body that had won Mr. McMahon over when he was young. He would do anything to see her gigantic breasts. Even with the rag over half of Mrs. McMahon's face, Rose could tell that she was a great beauty.

"Well, go and meet the children. Hazel and Ernest. They are truly possessed. And I'm not just saying that because I'm their mother."

There was little evidence of any children living in the house, outside of the nursery, which she hadn't seen yet. Still, she did see their tiny SOS signals as she went from room to room. In the art room, there was a pencil drawing of a boy whose head had fallen off. There was blood spurting out of his neck and head. On the glass of the window in the room with the pool someone had written *HELP* with the tip of their finger.

They turned down the corridor toward the nursery. A little blond boy who looked to be about six years old, wearing a zebra mask and holding a whip in his hand, was standing at the end of the hall. The maid practically jumped out of her skin when she turned and saw him there.

"I've been putting up with bullshit from lions for too long," he said.

A girl came out of the room with a hobbyhorse in her hand, which she planted firmly on the ground as though it were a spear. She had dirty-blond hair and brown eyes, and looked to be about seven. She was naked except for her underwear and socks.

Rose had the feeling that the children were wild. That when she stepped into the bedroom, it would be an overgrown jungle with lush tropical vegetation and wild boars and butterflies with wings as large as tennis rackets.

THE MAID CLAPPED HER HANDS loudly in the direction of the children. They both jumped like small animals and hurried, shouting, into the nursery. She led Rose into the nursery and left her with the children to get acquainted. The nursery was a large room, painted light blue, and had small cumulus clouds painted along the top edges of the walls. There were splendid toys on all the shelves and an exquisite dollhouse modeled on a Victorian manor. Hazel and Ernest just stared at Rose.

"Did you see the wolf come in through the back door?"

"What—what—what—what the hell are you talking about?" they demanded.

"I met him in the backyard just before I put the washing on the line. He was trying to steal some of your father's clothes."

They both ran to the window to look out to the backyard to see whether they could spot the wolf.

"He's not there anymore. I confronted him about taking your father's clothes and he said he'd ask your mother if he could have some of them."

"Are you crazy?" screamed Hazel. "You can't send a wolf up to see Mama! He might eat her."

"Well, I'll see what's going on up there."

"Mama doesn't like to be disturbed," Ernest said.

"Well, if she's being eaten by a wolf, I'm sure she won't mind me interrupting."

"Hurry, please!" cried Hazel.

Rose went down the stairs. The children looked at each other, at once terrified for their mother and impressed by Rose's bravery. When Rose walked back up to the nursery, she was wearing one of McMahon's suits and a top hat she'd discovered in a hall closet.

"I hear there were some children looking for me. I am Mr. Wolf."

Hazel stood up from her chair so abruptly that it toppled over behind her. She began applauding, so happy that she was getting a story without asking for one.

"Look at me. I'm not a monster. I just want some clothes so that I can get a regular job. Oh, perhaps I'll eat a child once in a while. That's my nature. But only the very naughty ones. Only the ones who skip school and who I catch going down the street in the middle of the day. Or I wait outside the candy store to see which child has been a glutton and then I gobble them up. Or I toss little pebbles up at windows—and see which children are up late at night. If they are up late at night, of course, it is because they want to be eaten by me."

They didn't know quite how to take her story. The rush that it gave them was unlike anything else. It was better than drinking *chocolat chaud* all in one gulp. It was better than hanging upside down from the jungle gym at the park. And then, to their utter amazement, Rose took the top hat off, handed it to the little girl, did a backflip and deliberately landed awkwardly on her behind.

The children applauded, not quite believing their luck. The pug, looking like a little old man wearing a bathrobe, stood by unimpressed.

·≈{ 11 }≈·

PIERROT'S REVERSAL
OF FORTUNE

Despite the Mother Superior's adamant advice, Pierrot never did a day's work. Unless you counted keeping Irving company. Pierrot was given a huge bedroom in the mansion. All the rooms seemed too big. Pierrot felt he should carry around a megaphone so that he could talk to Irving when they were at opposite sides of a room.

You could ride a bicycle quite comfortably through the house. Pierrot knew this because he had tried it. He would hear the little bell in his room ringing, indicating that Irving wanted his company. To save time, he would get on his bicycle, propped up against the wall in the hallway, and he would head down the corridor to Irving's room as though it were a luxurious country road. He would call out "Hello" to the servants he met along the way.

He cycled over a half dozen carpets en route to Irving's bedroom. Each of the carpets illustrated a distinct natural environment. He crossed a field of red poppies. He crossed through a field with sheep and dragons. He crossed through a dense green jungle.

There were incredible chandeliers all throughout the house. They looked like trees after an ice storm. At one point in his life, Irving had been an aficionado of chandeliers, collecting them in all the great cities of Europe. He had since relinquished this passion, but it wasn't like chandeliers would just go away. They still hung in every room. It was as if

Pierrot were passing underneath various galaxies before arriving in the dining room.

What would Rose think, Pierrot wondered, when she saw how he was living? Would she think that he had come up in the world, that he was classy now? Would she forgive him for suggesting all those improper things?

He arrived at the dining room just as the meal was being served. He sat across the table from Irving every night. He was served the same magnificent plates as Irving. He exclaimed loudly for the first three months when the dish was set in front of him. And for six months he would stop the conversation to remark on how marvelous the food was. After that he became used to the extravagant dinners and became more attuned to the philosophical nature of the conversation, as opposed to the food on the table.

He was Irving's constant companion and they discussed all sorts of things. Irving would ask Pierrot his thoughts on the paintings he had collected through the years, which hung on the walls. There was a still life of bloated carnations. There was one of clouds lit up from lightning. One was of a peregrine falcon wearing its typical striped pants. Hawks all dressed in an Elizabethan manner, never changing their style. There was a little girl with a blindfold around her head, wandering all alone with her arms stuck out. It was as though all the other children had been called inside but she hadn't heard. He told Irving how he had played this game with Rose and the other orphans. Pierrot explained that this painting was the most magnificent, as it illustrated the universal and terrifying condition called childhood.

"Well put," said Irving. "It is indeed one of the most valuable in my collection. Your experience has made you a connoisseur of fine art. Come see my portraits of dogs."

Pierrot never brought up Sister Eloïse. He never told Irving that for the first time in his life he could go to sleep feeling safe. For the first few weeks, he had dreams where Sister Eloïse would be sucking him off. He would have called them nightmares were it not for the fact that he ejaculated in his sleep. The shame he felt afterward sometimes made him cry out in the darkness. But soon he learned to sleep the deepest sleep he had ever slept. He went into the Land of Nod without scattering any bread crumbs to find his way back. The freedom that he had was exquisite and was so joyful that it almost drove him a little mad.

Pierrot thanked Irving every day for the great gift he had given him. Everyone else in Irving's life had turned against him. It was in part because he had so much money. And when you have that amount of money, then as now, everybody near and dear to you believes that the money should be theirs. His children thought he was greedy for not giving them greater trust funds. His money had made all his children dull and dependent. They lay in bed with their spouses, cursing him. All his children's spouses hated him passionately. They were convinced that the money was theirs even more, as they had married his children for his money.

Pierrot truly loved Mr. Irving. But then again, Pierrot truly loved just about everyone he came into contact with. When Irving's children found out about his relationship with Pierrot, they hated that Irving was happy. Their greatest hope was that Irving would grow old alone, miserable and regretful of his stingy actions. But they went over to see Pierrot in a pair of roller skates, pushing Irving in his wheelchair in circles in the middle of the street.

THE DOCTOR CAME BY to check on Pierrot at the daughter-in-law's suggestion. She said the boy was stark raving mad and might kill her father in his sleep, having mistaken him for a dragon.

She came to visit once and Pierrot had been on the roof. The gray clouds lined up behind him like the aristocrats from Versailles filing up for the guillotine. He had a great big gardenia behind one of his ears. He was brandishing a poker from the fireplace in his hand. He screamed out,

"Come hither, all dragons. I do not fear you. I will slay you all in one afternoon. Because I am a knight."

The neighbors all quite agreed with her diagnosis of insanity. He was spotted doing handstands in the yard every morning. He cycled down the street, his long scarf trailing behind him. He called out "Good day" to everyone. When Pierrot turned sixteen, Irving fired the chauffeur and gave him the keys to the car. Pierrot drove the car recklessly, right up onto the lawn. He honked his horn instead of ringing the doorbell.

But Irving did not choose to scold Pierrot or chastise him. The child had a madness to him, but it was indeed such an incredibly lovely madness. These were the marks of a genius. The boy was eccentric. He reminded Irving of all his own absurd antics. If he were a young man, he too would be brandishing a poker on the rooftop, demanding that the dragons show their ugly faces.

And what was more, Irving adored Pierrot's piano playing.

When he heard the tunes, he would remember how it felt to be absolutely guilt-free. What it felt like to be a good person. He felt young again. There was no such thing as time when Pierrot played the piano. Irving would close his eyes and he was nine years old, in a striped bathing suit with just the tips of his toes in the freezing water. He had his eyes closed to make a wish on a birthday cake. He was about to wish that he would become prime minister.

No, he would not listen to any doctor condemning his dear friend. He didn't like that Pierrot wasn't treated with the respect the doctor would accord to Irving's other children. So they went to the tailor to get Pierrot new clothes.

"I can't stand to look at second-rate clothes," Irving declared from the passenger seat. "I'm purchasing it for me and not for you."

On the way to the tailor downtown, Pierrot managed to almost run over a line of schoolgirls, a couple of distinguished young ladies and seven cats. At the shop, Pierrot insisted on a roll of checkered multicolored material. The tailor was assigned to making a suit of the highest fashion out of the ridiculous material. He wore a yarmulke on his head and had pins sticking out of his mouth as he scurried about, furtively measuring Pierrot's skinny dimensions with a piece of chalk. And a week later the suit was delivered to their door.

Irving was sitting in the garden drinking tea. Pierrot came out in his new suit with his arms spread. A swallow passed overhead, its tail feathers as thin as a seamstress's scissors.

"It makes me very happy to see you walking around in that dapper suit. Who were your parents? I wonder. Surely it was some pretty girl from a very wealthy family, tempted at the Valentine's Ball. You are obviously an aristocrat. You are my own young prince. You and I are in the same predicament. Nobody knows us for who we truly are. But we won't be lonely anymore because we have each other. We will enjoy life together. Free from the preposterous names that people have attached to us. What does the past have to do with us? What does the past have to do with any of us?"

WHENEVER ANYONE ASKED QUESTIONS about the orphanage, Pierrot would tell them about the wonderful Rose. He told them nothing about the cold and Sister Eloïse and all the lonely children he had left behind in her care. That just filled him with a guilt impossible for the hardiest heart to withstand. Pierrot continued to send letters to Rose. He sent them every few days, but she never returned them. She must be furious with him for leaving. Perhaps it might be best to let her go. But thinking and obsessing about her allowed him to block out any other memory of the orphanage. It was as though she were the only thing that had ever happened in his childhood. The thought of her climbed and twisted around each of his thoughts like a rosebush.

MR. BEAUTY AND MISS BEAST

D espite her entertainment value, Rose wasn't an especially good governess. She didn't care that the children were wild, and she seemed to have no intention of disciplining them or training them to be civilized. She was more of a kindred spirit to them than anything. She just played with them and took care of their general needs.

They set fireworks off the back balcony. They were supposed to wait until Christmas, but they couldn't. They regularly ate dessert three meals a day. Once they ran into the kitchen with their faces covered in green face paint. Hazel stopped for a second and looked at the cook.

"Greetings, Earthling," she said.

Rose never cleaned up after the children either, only pulling out her small lemon-patterned rag when the lady of the house passed by. One of the maids started screaming when she discovered the bathtub was filled with frogs. Hazel came in and informed her that she and Rose had kissed them but were waiting to give them the opportunity to turn into princes. Maybe it wasn't something they could do at the drop of a hat.

"Maybe there are naked princes wandering the earth, looking for the damn girls who kissed them and then just took off."

One night she was up late eating a bowl of whipped cream with the children. The whipped cream suddenly reared into a white stallion on its hind legs. Ernest was so hyperactive when he was finished eating all that cream that he ran down the street in his underwear and threw a baseball through a friend's window.

On another afternoon, a snowman appeared outside the house with a knife in its chest and red food dye spreading down from its wound. And a large flat stone for a mouth that made him look as though he were screaming at the top of his lungs.

Although Hazel and Ernest were becoming even wilder under Rose's tutelage, there was no way anyone would fire Rose because the children had clearly decided that she was going to stay. There would be a terrifying uproar if she left, the likes of which the house had never seen.

There were days when Rose decided to be absolutely quiet, as if life itself were a silent film. She would gesture her needs and desires. She rubbed her belly to ask the children whether they were hungry. She scolded them by making an extremely dour expression, stomping her feet and wagging her finger viciously. It was the only time the maid witnessed Rose chastising the young savages. And it was in jest.

She was teaching the children how to do cartwheels and backflips in the nursery one afternoon. Their knees were all bloody from doing front flips and falling. They were bleeding happily at the kitchen table, eating chocolate cake for lunch. The maid thought she might need to have a word with Mrs. McMahon about Rose to save her own neck.

"She keeps them out of my hair, so what do I care if they're off murdering small animals?"

"I don't mind myself, Mrs. McMahon. We all quite like the girl. I'm just telling you so that if you see your children running around the backyard buck naked, you don't get alarmed and blame me."

"Fine. Fine. I grant you immunity."

Despite the telescope being off-limits, Rose often found herself looking through it.

She placed her little rag down beside her so that she could pick it up and begin dusting the telescope at a moment's notice, if need be. She focused the telescope so that she could look at the moon up close. It always startled her, as though she had turned around and there was the moon, following her down the street. Or she opened her bedroom door and there was the moon, lying in her bed, under the sheet.

She tried to see whether there was an alternate reality up on the moon. She looked at it closely, expecting to see herself and Pierrot standing up to their ankles in silver sand with their arms stretched out toward the earth.

When she looked through the telescope, she always asked herself the big questions. Who made us? And why did that being put us in the middle of all this great emptiness? What did anything matter? Why did they put all those stars so far away? Why did they put strange creatures at the bottom of the ocean? Why did they give us the minds to find them, if they didn't want us to find them? She wondered whether if she went to university and studied astronomy and mathematics she would be able to answer these questions.

One day Hazel came to peep through the telescope too. Rose put a chair beneath it so that she would be at eye level. They took turns looking deep, deep into the universe: Saturn like a knee that had been dipped in iodine, Neptune like a peach covered in mold, Jupiter like a half-sucked jawbreaker, Mercury like a large shooter marble, galaxies like crushed candy, galaxies like the suds from a bubble bath blown off the palm of your hand.

"You are so lucky," she said to Hazel. "You get to be educated! How wonderful is that? I would love to go to school and learn to read giant books of mathematical problems like they were novels. Don't you always find that math problems are quite beautiful to look at? I do. They remind me of funny little insects pinned to a corkboard. And you wonder so much about their origins."

"I never pay attention when the tutor comes over."

"Well, I think you should. Try to be good when he comes over."

"I find that I can't help being bad. I promise and promise and promise myself that I won't be a bad person. But then I just do something bad."

"That's because we're girls. We're supposed to only have emotions. We aren't even allowed to have thoughts. And it's fine to feel sad and happy and mad and in love—but those are just moods. Emotions can't get anything done. An emotion is just a reaction. You don't only want to be having reactions in this lifetime. You need to be having actions too, thoughtful actions."

THE OTHER SERVANTS became quite fond of Rose. She was in the kitchen juggling eggs. The maids and the cook were screaming with laughter, yelling that she was for sure going to break all of them.

She walked across the banister in her stocking feet. She was carrying in all the plates from the dining room and pretended to trip. Everybody shrieked. They all thought she was quite mad. They loved when she tried to get through an open door but was pushed back in an imaginary wind tunnel. It was quite extraordinary.

They had never met a girl who made jokes about farting. When she bent over to pick something up, she would make a loud farting noise. It always made them guffaw noisily. She had such a good sense of humor.

They had never seen the children so happy. Rose was able to control them just by virtue of being crazier than them. They were all three of them sitting in the backyard wearing Napoleon hats made out of newspaper. The servants were very surprised that she had grown up in an orphanage and that she hadn't been lobotomized.

ONE NIGHT Rose was sitting by herself in her room. It had been raining all evening. The soft sound of the rain on the rooftop sounded like young girls sneaking off in stockings to elope. She felt lonesome for Pierrot.

Rose pulled her suitcase from beneath her bed. She kept her most precious belonging in there. She took out the plan she had drawn on a piece of paper on the trolley when she and Pierrot were little kids. It seemed like the most absurd plan in the world. It had come to her in a fit of inspiration. Who really knew where these fits came from? Perhaps it had been an angel whispering in her ear. There were doodles on the margins of the paper, a vine creeping up a white wall.

It seemed so fantastical and silly. It was a make-believe story that she would tell the children. She had a future as a domestic house cleaner. She wasn't qualified for anything else. But she kept the piece of paper near to her. It was the closest thing she had to a photograph from her childhood. It made her nostalgic for all the good times at the orphanage, without remembering the bad.

But she also had to learn her place.

·⟨ 13 ⟩·

PORTRAIT OF PIERROT
AS A YOUNG ARISTOCRAT

Although Pierrot was elegant by nature, Irving decided that he could further enhance the young man's sophistication. He made Pierrot walk around while balancing an encyclopedia on his head. Pierrot became quite good at balancing things in this manner. One afternoon Irving, hearing a commotion in the kitchen, entered to discover all the servants crowded around Pierrot as he balanced a small stool with three books and an apple on top of his head.

"Never let anybody tell you that you can't pass as an aristocrat. Remember, it's all superficial. It has to do with mannerisms. You can learn how to be an aristocrat by following a few rules in a very short book. There is nothing to it."

He gave the boy a small copy of a book called *Manners for the Perfect Gentry*.

He taught Pierrot to hold his chin up higher and to cry out that he didn't know why on earth he wasn't in Italy. The absurdity of it all did not faze Irving in the least. He was at an age where even being alive was absurd and so he had retired from the realm of common sense.

IRVING ENROLLED PIERROT in a private school. He thought Pierrot would be good at school, given his artistic temperament, but he was wrong. The boy was brilliant on the debate team. No one on the opposite team understood what he was saying, and so they had great difficulty responding to or challenging his points. However, he failed in every other subject. Pierrot couldn't handle any kind of structure, or hard work, or discipline. He refused to learn even basic algebraic equations. And he refused to learn the birth date of a single war. He wasn't even accomplished in music class, as he couldn't learn to read music. Pierrot ended up missing most days at school and staying home with Irving.

IRVING DRANK EVERY NIGHT. One day, when Pierrot was seventeen, a bottle of very expensive wine was sent over by the mayor as a gift for Irving's endowment to Montreal's art museum. Irving was loath to drink it alone and so he told the servant to fill the boy's tumbler to the brim with wine as well.

"Have a drink, my boy. I need to make a toast and I need someone to raise their glass and drink to it. A toast must be seconded." He held up his wineglass and Pierrot held up his tumbler. "Let us toast that we were born intelligent men. There are more and more stupid people born in the world every day. We are lighthouses for brilliant ideas lost in the dark, searching for an audience."

They clinked their glasses together. Pierrot knocked back his wine. He loved the warm feeling at the back of his throat and its strange burgundy sweetness. He put the glass back on the table when he was done. The alcohol entered his heart and was sent out in a gush through all the veins in his skinny body.

For a moment Pierrot felt as though a trapdoor had opened beneath him and he was plunging downward. He felt as though he had slipped off a diving board and was now doing somersaults under the water. He felt numb. He picked up a fork and pressed it against his skin. He was surprised to find that he hardly felt anything, no matter how hard he pressed.

A similar thing was happening to his mind. When he thought about things that had previously caused him pain, they only tickled him. He was always afraid to think of the other children he had left behind at the orphanage because it would break his heart. But now he thought about them and their memories had no power over him. Not only did the thought of them no longer cause him any pain, they no longer caused him to have any reaction at all.

After the seventh toast, Pierrot had finished four tumblers of wine. His lips were dark red, as if he had kissed a Parisian whore. His teeth were purple, as if he had bitten into an animal. He was feeling hot. So he unbuttoned his shirt and flung it onto the floor. He sat there like a mad Roman emperor.

He started laughing. He picked up his chair and he carried it to the other side of the table and he sat next to Irving. He put his arm around Irving and announced that he was swell. He jumped up when the maid came in and gave her a big kiss on the lips.

"Sit down! Let this be a lesson to you. No matter how wild you get, the one rule you have to follow is don't impregnate the servants. A pretty servant girl is like a cupcake—you can have some pleasure in it, but only in a momentary way. You don't want to commit to her. There has to be a division between high and low. Looking down on people is an important motivator.

"I became the man that I am in order to look down on people. That's why a doctor found a vaccine for smallpox, you know, not because he was interested in helping out all those sick people, but because he wanted to make all his doctor friends jealous."

Pierrot stood up on the table and stuck his arms in the air. "Look at me way up here!"

"Well, you don't have to be so literal, my boy. Think in terms of the big picture, will you?"

"Let me get my notebook!" Pierrot exclaimed. "I have to record these instructions for my edification. I have so much to catch up on."

Sometimes when Irving was particularly loquacious, Pierrot would take out a notebook and write down things he was saying. Pierrot had a way of looking so intently: his eyes would open up so wide. He would wear the most compassionate expression and his dazzling blue eyes certainly never hurt. It inspired Irving to share his most improbable pensées.

"Appearance is the most important thing. People are rarely curious about anything else. They don't go the extra mile. Just get yourself a well-tailored suit and never mind personality, et cetera . . . Did you get that?"

"Yes, marvelous. The words are dancing about the page, but continue."

"Love. Such an absurd idea. It's worse than God."

The truth was that the very last thing in the world Pierrot needed was to spend time with a half-mad, old millionaire. He was the only orphan being raised like a member of the very wealthy elite. Naturally this was problematic, given that he didn't have a penny to his name. He really needed the constitution to work in a factory, or perhaps as a salesman.

Pierrot needed some order. He needed some sort of discipline. He needed to find a way to toughen up. This was ruining him. He would never be able to hold any sort of job after this. The Mother Superior had been right. Now, thanks to Irving, he had a life philosophy that he could not afford to have. This was a common denominator of most addicts, which Pierrot would become.

As it grew late into the night, the flowers dropped forward on their stems, like girls who had fallen asleep on a church pew.

PIERROT LEARNED to mimic Irving's ways. After living in a rich household for two years, he was able to act in a hoity-toity manner. As he walked down the street in Westmount, if you did not know who he was, you would think he was a rich boy for sure. You would assume he had grown up on that street. That he had a mother who had adored him and tied absurd white bonnets onto his head. You would have assumed that he had had a governess, who would have counted his little fingers for him. She would have shown him a globe and traced her finger from Montreal all the way across the ocean, as if "across" were a place that a person could go.

Pierrot would read to Irving in the evening. Irving wanted the classics he had read as a boy recited back to him. Pierrot was such a good reader. Whatever new words he saw on the page one day would the very next day become second nature to him. They would be natural on his tongue. Because he could remember words intuitively without understanding them. He would glance over the newspaper and now all the words were in his pocket. His verbal dexterity increased over the years.

"Do you ever wonder about all the stars in the sky? Science is always saying the most peculiar things about the heavens. But I don't think they are at all true. I think if you got yourself a tall enough ladder, you could get up to those stars and then just pluck them down and put them in buckets. And all you would need is just one single star to stick inside a stove, and it would heat up your whole house for the winter. All you need is two brave men. One man brave enough to build the ladder that goes all the way up to the heavens. And another man brave enough to climb it."

"Well said, my wonderful child. Well said."

Is there any difference between acting like a really intelligent person and being a really intelligent person? Who in the world, just by looking at him, would know that he had been raped? The further away he got from those events, the harder they were for him to deal with. He realized how abhorrent and weird they were, and he had no idea how a person was supposed to behave after surviving such a thing. He had no other choice but to act as though it had never happened. And if no one could tell, perhaps it *hadn't* ever happened? Pierrot hoped this were true.

But deep down he knew, no matter how clever he seemed, that he was a creep.

·⊰ 14 ⊱·

PORTRAIT OF LADY AT ODDS WITH THE WORLD

Some of the women in the neighborhood were quite satisfied with their roles as housewives. They would wave at Rose and the children. They would join garden clubs, drink iced tea and read books. Their hair would be mounted in an enormous bundle on their heads and sprayed until it stayed there. Mrs. McMahon could never bring herself to be one of those happy women. She seemed to be frustrated almost every day for the two years that Rose had lived there.

. . .

MR. MCMAHON'S WIFE WAS ALWAYS accusing her husband of cheating on her. She was miserable because of it. She took out her frustrations on everyone in the house. Her misery filled up all the rooms. If there were a teacup left on the table, it would be filled with unhappiness.

She stormed around the living room, throwing things onto the floor and against the wall. Her face could display every kind of different expression imaginable. It ran the gamut. Each of her expressions was like an opera of sorts. She had been raised to know that women were supposed to look blank and that it was inappropriate for them to show emotions in public. That to openly have emotions would be like being a prostitute hanging out a window with her breasts exposed for all to see. But she didn't care.

She threw a vase at the wall and put a hole in it. Then she went over and tore the wallpaper off in great sheets.

She held up a cushion as though she were considering devouring it or something. And when she seemed to realize that there was really no damage she could do with a pillow, that a pillow could never be a cannonball, she looked defeated by the awareness of her impotence.

She sat down on the sofa, buried her face in the same pillow and wept. She sobbed—they were huge sobs that came from deep in her lungs, like someone bringing up a net of fish from the bottom of the sea. Her sobs were flung onto the deck, with all the contents of the deep flipping about, desperate and exposed.

The family lived in terror of these rages. They made Mr. McMahon miserable. The children would sit quietly and look pale, incapable of doing anything until the woman was done with her fit. But Rose wasn't a part of the family and so she felt herself to be free of their misery. She sat reading a novel.

. . .

SHE JUST WANTED HIM to admit that he was cheating. She needed some sort of absolute proof. He always denied it. She smelled it on his clothes. Rose stood next to her as she smelled all his clothes. And then the lady of the house collapsed to the ground.

Rose took all the clothes and smelled them herself. They were wonderful, those smells that had upset McMahon's wife so much. They were the smells of beautiful women on the other side of town. That was the side of town away from all this domestic life. Where all the theaters were. All the cabarets. All the traveling performers.

Rose inhaled deeply. She imagined she was on a train with a brass band arriving from New York City. One of the singers, a beautiful black woman, laughed so hard she spilled her drink on her fur collar. Rose could smell the gin.

She smelled cigars. That was one of her favorite smells. Maybe because it was a generous one. She imagined all these businessmen sitting around a table, smoking cigars and talking about work and making money.

She would find herself fantasizing about being at that table. Which was a peculiar fantasy for a young girl to have.

Rose thought McMahon's wife was a psychic genius. She was able to tell what he had been up to on any given night. You could tell by his expression that she was right. She had no business being a housewife, really. She probably had a mind built for being the world's leading criminal investigator. She could be out in the world tracking down society's most heinous criminals or cracking enemy codes. Instead she was stuck in the house, focusing all her intellectual acumen and perspicuity on piecing together exactly what her husband had been up to that evening.

TO COMPENSATE HERSELF for the horrific treatment she had to endure at the hands of her husband, she bought herself the most expensive outfits. She was always shopping to remind herself that she had acquired some sort of power by being married to a rich man. All the fantastic couches covered in flowers. The paintings on the walls, the display cases filled with delicate china tea sets, the rich carpets that swallowed sound like quicksand, the closet filled with clothes—they were all beautiful evidence of her betrayal.

And she would boss around the staff to feel as if she had servants. So that she wouldn't have to feel like a servant herself.

ALTHOUGH ROSE WAS NOW SEVENTEEN, Mrs. McMahon wasn't afraid of the girl stealing his affections. McMahon, she knew, wasn't attracted to girls without large breasts. He had never been attracted to odd birds like Rose. She couldn't understand how any man would be attracted to Rose. She didn't act delicate or attractive. Rose kind of disgusted her. She had no feminine qualities, and yet the child went around acting as though she were a girl.

MRS. McMAHON HAD ROSE COME and scrub a burgundy stain on the wallpaper, caused by having thrown a wineglass at it. Mrs. McMahon was sitting in an armchair covered in patterns of ships and anchors and mermaids as if she were in the fat arms of a tattooed sailor.

"Does it bother you?"

Rose just looked back at her, confused.

"Being ugly, I mean."

"No, not at all."

"I mean, maybe you don't realize you are ugly. Because if you look in a mirror you can't really see yourself. It's what men think about you physically that counts."

"I know, ma'am. But I've come to terms with it."

"I can never decide whether or not you talk too much."

"Oh, it depends on the forecast. My conversation is probably something like the rain. On some days it pours, and then on other days there's just a clear sky—not a word in sight."

"I'm surprised they let you talk like that at the orphanage."

"I was sometimes punished for it."

"Sometimes I wonder if you're safe around the children."

"That's up for you to decide, ma'am."

Mrs. McMahon sighed, for a moment relenting. Rose kept knocking back the insults as though she were playing tennis.

"Oh, hush. You know those two monsters will go into hysterics if I send you away. You've cast a spell on the two of them. Tell me, have you ever known a woman cursed with two such contrary brats? They're spoiled rotten. There's no redemption for either of them. It's not as though I don't love them, but I just don't have a lot of hope for them. It's because their father has made me so miserable. That's why they are the way they are."

She reached over and grasped Rose's wrist, her grip like a handcuff. It was as if she had no intention of letting go until Rose agreed with her.

"I should have married somebody else. I'm in the wrong marriage. I have the wrong children."

Instinctively Rose stepped back from Mrs. McMahon, as if her employer were a deep hole she might fall into. She was alarmed and confused by the older woman's grief. She could sense the enormity of what had been taken away from her but could barely comprehend it.

15

PIERROT'S SAD CAREER
AS CASANOVA

After three years of sending unanswered letters, at eighteen years of age, Pierrot could only conclude that Rose was eternally annoyed with him. He wished she would just write one letter back that confirmed his suspicions. But it seemed absurd to continue to write to her, and so in that third year he stopped. The lack of closure bothered him a little bit more every day, until it somehow became a part of the fabric of his being.

He felt like something was missing from his life, almost as if something was supposed to happen by the end of each day but never came about. It was like reading a book and finding out at the end that the last two pages had been torn out. He often checked his pockets, not knowing what it was that he felt he had misplaced.

He could never really get to know anybody in the way he had known Rose. He wanted to visit her, but he was afraid of seeing Sister Eloïse. He thought that somehow he would be a little boy again and that she would be able to hurt him. Finally he decided he would take matters into his own hands and go visit Rose. He would simply tell Sister Eloïse to get out of his way. He was pretending to be a rich man now, and he wanted to tell Rose that he loved her and that he was not the degenerate she believed him to be.

He drove the car quickly down to the orphanage. He spun the steering wheel as though it were a lock whose combination he was solving. He honked his horn the whole way. He honked it in part so that everyone would stand back and he would get there faster. But he also honked it out of joy. He imagined Rose hearing the honking and looking up from scrubbing the floors, knowing it was him. He was like a flock of geese announcing their return from the south, and that all the false rulers should get right the fuck out of their thrones. The pigeons sitting on top of statues should move over.

Sister Eloïse, having heard the ruckus of his car, came to the orphanage gates to investigate. She was surprised to see Pierrot, and to see the outfit he was wearing. Perhaps if he had been wearing anything else, she wouldn't have been so cruel to him. But although she had braced herself for his presence one day, she wasn't quite ready for the figure he cut as he stepped out of the car. If anyone were to see him, they would never have known that he was an orphan. He wore a tailored suit and polished shoes. He had a wonderful haircut. He reached into the backseat and pulled out a bouquet of flowers wrapped in brown paper. The flowers looked all tousled, like children who had been awakened by a fire alarm in the middle of the night.

His manner too made him seem rich. He was light on his feet, the way rich young men without a care in the world are.

For a second Sister Eloïse thought the flowers were for her. Then she realized she had been an utter fool. As Pierrot leaned against the gate, the bouquet was tilted toward her; there were roses inside, and she knew who they were for. She felt so deeply humiliated by her assumption that her face went red. How many times would she be surprised that he had forgotten his promise to love her?

Pierrot hoped Sister Eloïse would just pretend that what had happened between them hadn't occurred at all. It was criminal, after all. He began by playing that game, hoping she would go along with it.

"I'd like to see Rose, please."

"She isn't here anymore. She hasn't been here for years."

"Ahhhh! Of course she left years ago! Because I sent her a lot of letters and not one of them was answered, which led me to believe she was not receiving them. Because, as I'm sure you will concede, Rose always had a particular fondness for me. And an affection like that doesn't dissipate every day."

"You'd be surprised. Romantic love is a mirage. It was created by the devil—and like most of his creations, it is very short-lived."

"I understand. You know I'm always grateful when you share your life philosophy with me. And it is an interesting theory. Nonetheless, I would like to have Rose's address. We're both eighteen years old, and there's no harm in giving me her address. Even if she doesn't want to see me again, at least she can tell me that, and I'll be fine with it. It's just that we never got to say good-bye to one another. It gives me a feeling of loose ends."

"Do you think I would give you her address so you can disturb her? You idiot. Don't you realize how many years it's been? She's married. She has three sons. I don't know very much about her husband, but I understand that he's very brutal."

"I never came to visit her because I was so frightened that she was angry with me."

"How stupid. How weak. You should have been much more courageous, don't you think?"

"Yes."

"Why would she like you? You're a pervert. You seduced me. You ruined my life. You were the one who started all that filth between us. You're going to hell. I'll never forgive you. I told her about us."

"You did? Why? You said we were never going to tell anyone. What did she say?"

"She wept like a baby and then said she never wanted to see your stinking face again. She was very thankful not to have been led into temptation."

And then Sister Eloïse walked away, satisfied that she had thrown water on that squalid little passion once and for all. Pierrot hurled the flowers on the ground. He yelled out once, facing the city, his back to the orphanage. He stood there for a moment, waiting to see whether his shout would have any effect at all, whether it would cause the city to topple down. It did not. He got in his car and quietly drove off, convinced only of his own cowardice.

IT WAS TRUE what Sister Eloïse had said. He was a pervert. He was grotesque. He was only good for dirty thoughts. He hated himself.

As he drove home, he spotted a group of girls, each wearing a beige beret, which made them look like a cluster of mushrooms. He stopped in front of them and invited them to climb into the car with him. He thought that he might make love to every single one of them. They all giggled and yakked at the top of their lungs. They were having a swell and dangerous time, until they heard a honking behind them.

A police officer pulled them over. He couldn't quite believe there were so many girls in the car. He had no idea how they could have fit in there.

The police officer watched the girls as they scrambled out. They all seemed to be in a state of disarray. As though they had been crammed in at funny angles. As if they were clothes that had been packed in a trunk and now they were straightening themselves back out. The officer couldn't make out their entire bodies. It was like they were a box of doll parts that had gotten all mixed up. There was a shoe with a buckle. There was a bum in pink underwear, flashed for a brief second. There was a knee like a peeled apple waiting to be bitten into. There was a skinny arm, with fingers that were all stretched out toward heaven. There were a bunch of bouncing yellow curls.

Pierrot thought they looked like a beautiful, exquisite beast with a hundred limbs that could take you into its myriad arms and make love to you. Pierrot sighed. What in the world would it take to make him happy now?

16

ROSE SMOKES CIGARS

Before she turned eighteen, Rose rarely saw McMahon. He was always at work. He had some sort of massive club downtown that did really well. He never let his wife or his kids come to the restaurant because he kept those parts of his life separate.

Everything she knew about him she learned from the other governesses at the park. She shooed the children away to hear more. "Leave me alone, children. I just want to talk to people my age. I will tell you a story about a seagull that swallowed an umbrella and then spent the rest of its life as a swan."

"Oh, oh, oh, oh! Tell it to us now!" the children cried.

"No, I need half an hour alone."

But the children remained within earshot, so the governesses really couldn't go into any sort of scandalous detail.

"*C'est un propriétaire de boîte de nuit.* He runs the Roxy downtown."

"That big nightclub! I would just love to see the acts they put on there. I can't wait to be old enough to go down and see all the shows. I think that I could be onstage."

"*Pour vrai!* Do you have any talent?"

"Lots. I was a famous performer when I was a little girl. I went from living room to living room."

"Can you sing?"

"No, I can't carry a tune. I mean, I know how to make a tune sound funny."

"Can you tap-dance?"

"No, not really. I've never taken a lesson. Do you think it's possible to tap-dance without ever having had a lesson?"

"Noooo!" they all said at once.

"I'll show you something that I *can* do, though."

She jumped up off the bench and leaped a few feet from them. She found a spot on the grass. She then did a handstand. Hazel, acting as her intrepid assistant, put a large ball on her feet, which she began to spin.

Some people looked at the ball spinning at quite an extraordinary speed. But many others chose to look at her underwear, or her skirt, which was now up over her head.

She stood back upright. Her face was beet red.

"I know a lot of other tricks that I can show you. Maybe not today, because we have to go, but next time."

They did not know what on earth to make of this girl. They knew that what she was doing was truly magical, and they felt they could watch her do it for hours and hours and hours. But they also felt she would never make a single penny off it.

She certainly seemed crazy. But she simultaneously made them think that there was nothing in the world wrong with being a crazy girl. And that maybe the world needed a couple more crazy girls.

The other children in the park also loved when Rose showed up. She always made them all laugh. They would gather around if she was talking to her friend the bear, who after all these years was still after her, still seeking her affections.

The peacocks in the park were all white, and they walked with their wedding dresses trailing behind them.

SOMETIMES AFTER HER PERFORMANCES with the imaginary bear, she would find herself feeling quite blue. Because the bear was the only one she kept in touch with from the orphanage. She sometimes thought she would run into Pierrot, but she never did. The other governesses all understood that Rose was the type of girl to easily fall into temptation. They knew this from overhearing her strange conversations with the bear. The invisible bear seemed to be getting more and more aggressive.

Rose brought the children home. They shared a bowl of chocolate-chip ice cream. The chunks of chocolate looked like flotsam from a ship that had just sunk.

SHE BUMPED INTO MCMAHON one night after she had put the children to bed and she was walking down the hall with an atlas on her head. It had been one of her punishments at the orphanage, which she had managed to transform into a fully fledged trick.

"You're still the governess."

"Yes."

"Congratulations. But why the fuck do you have a book on your head?"

"What are you talking about? What book?"

"For the love of God, are you one of those lobotomized kids from the orphanage?"

McMahon was like this great ship that went back and forth to the different worlds. He had in his brain all those marvelous theatrics.

"Tell me about what you saw tonight."

"There was a Parisian troupe. It was a disaster. The whole troupe had clearly lost its mind somewhere on the road. You would actually be surprised how often that happens. After seven years on the road, they should all be committed."

"Oh, how lovely! Tell me more, please don't stop."

"They were all dressed up as white mice. They had cloth ears stuck up on their heads and long tails stuck to the asses of their leotards. It was called the Opera of the Souris en Pantoufles. So I really don't know why I was still shocked when they tiptoed out dressed like rodents. But there you go.

"But one girl on pointe didn't have a shirt on. They all looked so stoned that it's hard to say whether that was an artistic choice or whether she forgot to put her clothes on before coming out onstage. I really thought she was a boy because she was so flat-chested, but plenty of other people in the audience figured out pretty quickly that she was a girl, given the general amount of hooting and hollering. In any case, the police busted the show because she was only fourteen."

"What's it like to be able to watch the most stupendous acts from all over the world every night?"

"You can get used to anything, I suppose."

"Will you take me one night?"

"Are you out of your mind? This conversation is over. Scurry back to your nursery. I'm putting ideas into your head, I can see that."

"But I need to see this wonderful world. I used to be a performer too, when I was little. Perhaps you saw one of our famous Christmas performances. At City Hall? The *Journey of the Star of David*, perhaps?"

"No. I run the Roxy downtown. All the spectacles that are worth seeing are up on that stage. Did you perform at the Roxy? No? I didn't think so."

"Everyone used to fall in love with me."

"Trust me, I'm not in love with you."

"You're not my type either."

"You probably need new chores or something. Go away now. And this will be the last time I speak to you. Do you understand?"

"Yes. I will never speak to you again. I will communicate only in ways that transcend words."

He wanted to protest again, but he knew that it was useless, so he let her leave. It was best to get her away from him as soon as possible. Before she walked away, she moved the tip of her toe on the floor, like a piece of chalk writing words. He wondered what she spelled.

. . .

ROSE HEARD FROM the other governesses that McMahon was a heroin dealer. It was actually quite amazing what the other governesses knew. The girls were so positive about McMahon's other profession. Their employers talked about it. And they had seen the police come to McMahon's door in the past to question him. He also ran brothels.

"I heard that whenever a new girl comes to the city, Mr. McMahon is always the first to sleep with her. He makes sure that she is addicted to heroin. Then she is too crazy to ever leave. You should see all the girls who work in his whorehouses downtown. They are all addicted to drugs."

"My cousin wanted to do something else, but Mr. McMahon wouldn't let her. All the money she made sleeping with men she had to pay to Mr. McMahon for her room and board. She doesn't have a penny to her name. She wants to jump out a window."

"They are like slaves. They don't even know they are alive anymore. There was this girl and she spent the whole day with her eyes closed."

"Why? Why would she do such a thing?"

"Well, in the first place, she was really stoned, and when you are stoned, it can be really difficult to open your eyes. And I think that she was a really good person. She liked to see only goodness in everybody and everything. And then she knew that there was nothing but ugliness in the world she found herself in, so she just kept her eyes closed the whole day. She didn't even take a peek to see what the men she was having sex with looked like."

Rose was fascinated by these tales about McMahon, but even more she preferred the dirty sexual stories. Those ones made her think of Pierrot. They were her favorite types of fairy tales. She loved that women shared these types of things. Whenever one of the governesses had a story to tell, all the other governesses quieted down to listen to her. The pinecones lay on the grass around them, like cigar butts the gods had discarded.

93

She liked knowing she wasn't the only woman in the world fascinated by these things. She closed her eyes and pictured the scenarios as though they were short little movies in which the man pursued the woman all around the room.

Sister Eloïse had taken all the girls aside when they were little. She had warned them that they were all the children of women who had not been able to resist temptation. It was in their blood. They had inherited this weak trait from their mothers. They should understand it as a weakness. Like people who had inherited weak lungs from their parents had to be wary about climbing stairs. Had to be wary about going out on wet, cold days.

When they experienced those feelings, when they felt lust, they should understand immediately that this was a disease.

ROSE TIED A BLINDFOLD over her eyes. She spent the whole day like that. McMahon saw her in the yard with the blindfold on. She was taking the garbage out to the curb. For a moment he watched her with alarm, as it looked as if she might walk into the street and get run over by a car. He began to open the window, to call out to her.

She started moving around the garden with her arms out in front of her. This was disturbing because there were no landmarks near her. In her head, she might be wandering on the North Pole. She might be in the middle of the desert. She might be about to walk the plank of a pirate ship. Wherever it was, it was miles and miles away from him. And then, maybe more disturbingly, his children appeared. They were wandering from the porch of the house into the yard with their hands out in front of them. They had black blindfolds tied around their eyes too. They had all departed from him. They were all in the land of make-believe.

It occurred to him that nobody in his family really loved him anymore and that they had all found a way to escape to freedom.

17

PIERROT AND THE APPLE

After seeing Eloïse again and learning that he had lost Rose, Pierrot began to be revolted and shocked by pleasure. There was a dumpy blond woman in a green velvet jacket getting ready to play the accordion on a street corner as he walked past. She pulled on the instrument and it let out a long exhale, like a woman in labor trying to breathe. Then she began to play "The Accordion Waltz." He adored that tune, but now it made him feel sick to his stomach. He sprinted off down the street to get away from it.

PIERROT WAS WALKING HOME with a tiny debate trophy in his hand. He stood on the edge of the pond in the center of the park. He hurled his trophy into the water and it made a terrific splash. It was as though a champagne bottle had been shaken and then uncorked. He felt a little bit better.

"You're not supposed to throw things in there, you know."

Pierrot turned and saw a teenage girl in a tartan jumper and black bow tie standing there. "Will you kindly refer to me as Dr. Pierrot?" he said. "And I'm sorry to tell you this, but you are exhibiting all the classical symptoms of a fatal illness. I'll have to do a nude examination, if you don't mind. Is there a private place we can find at your house?"

The girl's face went red and her eyes went wide when he said this. But then she smiled.

Maybe if he made love to this girl, he would go around feeling guilty about sleeping with her and not Eloïse.

THE GIRLS WHO WORKED as servants at the house or in the neighborhood knew that Pierrot was a fool. They knew that if they hooked up with him, they would be miserable and looking after their children on their own and living off charity for the rest of their lives. They would find themselves living in a tiny apartment with cockroaches underneath the wallpaper and eating oatmeal for dinner. He promised you good times. But poor people knew that all good times had to be paid for. You'd be scrubbing laundry for extra pennies late at night. No thank you. If they wanted to hear a Shakespearean sonnet, they would take a collection out of the library and read it themselves. Pierrot didn't impress them. They didn't think he had the sophisticated language of an intellectual. They thought he had the mellifluous tongue of a hustler.

In their minds, Pierrot was a man who would deliver a pithy aphorism to a newspaperman upon his arrest and then never be heard from again.

His looks were fundamentally appealing to girls, however, and the rich ones could not resist him. Rich girls didn't know the bite of poverty. Their parents could buy them a husband like Pierrot. And when they met Pierrot, they wanted their parents to make such a purchase. He was like a pony. He snuck into their windows at their request. They would kiss his neck. He would do whatever they told him to do. But Pierrot always felt lost afterward. Once he climbed out of a girl's window and up onto her roof after she heard her father come home. He sat up on the roof not knowing how to get home, since he had left his shoes behind.

There was a black cat up there too that was yawning, having come to terms with its bad luck.

ONE AFTERNOON, after making love to a girl named Juliette who lived in a giant house on top of the hill, he found himself particularly blue. As he was walking down the corridor to the front door he passed a large display case with glass doors. He couldn't help but notice, on one of the shelves, a glittering red apple. When he put his face up to the case, he saw that it was covered in tiny red jewels. He wanted the fruit. It was an urge he couldn't resist. He stopped for a moment, looking up and down the hall to see if anyone was there, and listening for footsteps. When he was sure that he was alone, he opened the cabinet door slowly and gently. He reached in for the apple.

The apple itself was just begging, begging to be plucked. It always considered itself somewhat of a fake because it could not be consumed. There is no pleasure whatsoever in immortality. But while it was in Pierrot's pocket, it felt a sense of adventure. And when Pierrot balanced the apple on his head outside, the hard fruit beamed with reflected sunlight.

Pierrot knew that everything in the world was alive. Everything was composed of molecules that shook and vibrated and hummed. There was no such thing as permanence. Even the most stalwart object—such as a statue in the park—was struggling to keep itself together.

AS HE WAS WALKING HOME he began to feel like a thief. Wonderful! he thought. I am not only a pervert but also a thief! Life is a path that you go along, discovering worse and worse things about yourself. He was not quite sure how he could return the apple. He thought of sneaking over in the middle of the night and putting it back. He thought about mailing it, but then he worried it would be traceable. They would know it had been him.

He climbed into the large maple tree in the middle of the park. He was, as you would imagine, an excellent climber. There was a hole in it that he had often seen squirrels dart in and out of. Pierrot reached his hand into the hole and then let the apple fall. From the sudden *thud* of the falling fruit, one could assume the hole wasn't particularly deep.

Pierrot scrambled back down the tree trunk. He felt relieved. He wasn't entirely sure whether he was free of the apple. But he did feel that at least he could forget about it for a moment. During the next weeks, he stopped thinking about it altogether because Mr. Irving began to get sick.

That night five squirrels sat staring at the glowing red apple. They had no idea how in the world it had gotten there. It wasn't edible. One of the smaller squirrels just kept looking at it. It was the closest that an animal had ever come to believing in God.

·◦❙ 18 ❙◦·

ROSE AND THE APPLE

Rose found a strange book in Mrs. McMahon's room, behind the bed. She hadn't really meant to go snooping. But she was cleaning up the shards of a teacup Mrs. McMahon had flung angrily against the armoire by her bed. She had to move all the items to get at the shards, and then she noticed a small, dark red book. She was always magically, magnetically drawn to books. Even if she didn't read them, she would want to smell them or to run her fingers over the pages or just flip through them. It had never occurred to her either that a book could be a secret. They were written for other people to read, after all. They weren't personal. Another one just like it could be found in a shop.

She sat cross-legged on the floor and opened the book. It was filled with illustrated panels. They had onion paper that you peeled away as you would a curtain on a window to get a view of what was going on outside. Or that you pulled down like a sheet from a bed to see what body was lying underneath.

At first she thought she was imagining what she was seeing, that her eyes were playing tricks. But she continued to stare at the drawing and it did not change at all. The figures were obstinately naked. They were in an amorous position. They didn't shout in alarm and scurry around the room, grabbing at their clothes, throwing them on and shouting out excuses about what they had just been doing. The woman's legs were still spread. Her dress was still hiked up over her hips. Her head was still flung back in ecstasy. Her mouth was still open, and her eyes languorously shut. The man still had his tongue out. His head was still between her legs. He still had his pants off. He was still holding his penis.

Why hadn't she just given Pierrot what he wanted? If it happened now, she wouldn't be able to resist. She would have wanted him to touch her so badly that she would have made whatever promise he had wanted her to make. She always found herself going back to that moment in her mind and reliving it. Each time she would say, "Yes, I don't care about anything in the whole world other than you." And then she would have a different sexual fantasy in her head. Of what Pierrot would do to her.

SHE HAD URGES. Instead of trying to fight them, Rose let them play out in her mind. She let them unwind slowly.

They were like water seeping underneath a door and filling up a room. Desire flooded in. And all the cups and plates floated on top of it. And the chairs were knocked over. And the books began to open up as they spun around, wanting each of their pages to be read at once. And then finally her bed began to rise up off the floor, and there was nowhere for it to go but out the window and toward the moon.

She would look at different men, on the sidewalks, in the park, at the markets. If she was able to make eye contact and hold it for more than three seconds, she would know exactly what they wanted to do to her. Somehow knowing that she had gotten this information from them made them blush and look away. Every man thought he was dirtier than every other man. If we all knew that we were all perverts, we might all be a lot happier.

SHE DID THIS INSTEAD of having sex. She went around reading men's minds.

She went inside them as though they were bureaus and she was opening their drawers. She looked underneath the folded articles of clothing. She found their dirty postcards. She pulled them out and had a look at them. And what lovely things she did find there.

She was on a trolley and she began to imagine what sexual fantasies were in the men's heads. A man with an enormous mustache got down on his knees and lifted her skirt and began to lick her pussy. He wouldn't wash his face for the rest of the day. He would go to sleep with the smell of pussy all around him like a cloud.

There was one who would have her lick whipped cream off his penis. She almost laughed at this. The poor fellow—it was what he wanted more than anything in the world and yet he was afraid to ask for it.

There was one who just wanted her to tell him that he was a filthy animal the whole time they were fucking.

She stared at one man, reading his mind, while her own desire was like a balloon, growing and growing and growing inside her. She just needed him to take a pin and pop it, so that it would explode, so that she would cry out.

Rose rang the bell on the trolley. She descended at her stop and walked off.

She imagined making the man feel understood. As though he had just made love in exactly the strange manner that he had always wanted. He had just met the woman who had fulfilled all his desires, and he wouldn't need anything ever in the world again. And there she was walking off down the street, not even looking back at him. As if he were clothes in a changing room that she had tried on for size and then discarded.

. . .

McMahon came home early one night. When people come in from the cold, you can feel it all around them like a shawl of some sort. And when people return from doing something wicked, it also surrounds them. You get a shiver in their presence. Rose felt it one day when McMahon walked in, and she knew that the girls weren't wrong about him. He had done something nefarious very recently. He had a cigar between his teeth, and the smoke coming out of it looked like a skinny girl pulling her undershirt down to her knees.

McMahon was always looking at her. He was wary of her. It was as if he had a premonition that she would destroy him. It was actually a kind of animal instinct. It was the way a cat felt when a dog walked by. Rose was a predator and he was prey. He was a man. He shouldn't be afraid of a girl like that. She was so skinny. None of this seemed right. Shouldn't he be the one to destroy her? It was a new feeling for him, and he needed to understand it. It was attractive.

She was making shadow puppets of a bird on the wall. It was a black crow. And somehow the black crow managed to fly from the bedroom wall and down the hall and into his bedroom. It was waiting to pick on his corpse.

McMahon was enormous. She had fallen into his gravitational pull. He was the center of everyone's universe in the home. That happened in any home. You either fell into someone's orbit or you had to force everyone to be in yours.

That night in her bed, Rose imagined that she told McMahon to get down on his hands and knees and to kiss her gently, one hundred times, between her legs. She imagined fastening both his wrists to the bedposts with ties and then riding him wildly.

If you can imagine something, then it is possible within the physical laws of this universe. So says some Greek philosopher.

She lay on the tiny bed, spent and happy, knowing that certain things were possible to her that she had not thought possible before. The fantasy had proved revelatory. She fell asleep with the satisfaction of an explorer who had just spotted land through his binoculars. While seagulls circulated over her head crying loudly, "Land ho! Land ho!"

THE CHILDREN'S MATH TEACHER was quite interested in Rose. He tried to make conversation with her when he came by. He loaned her a book by Victor Hugo. When she opened the pages, she found a pressed flower between them. She held up the tiny flower, whose aging process had been stopped.

They sat together in the backyard. There were white flowers wilting in the yard as if a child had had a tea party and left the pieces all over the carpet. He told her about his little house and how much money he made. "I would like to start a family. And I think that with you I would have very pretty and very happy children."

She found herself yawning during the conversation. She yawned and yawned and yawned and yawned. She found the idea of life with him so boring.

All the other servants thought it was a good idea to marry him. He was so handsome and so polite, and he wouldn't beat her. And although Rose was young, they thought it a good idea that she get married before she ended up ruined. She had no desire for him, though. Her desire was a strange calling that she couldn't ignore.

McMAHON LOOKED LIKE A BEAR. He was always lumbering around in the house late at night. He would turn the lights on and knock things over and rattle dishes, unconcerned about whom he might be disturbing.

He ate leftover turkey by himself in the dark. She could hear his great snoring from all the way down the hall.

She liked the idea of being ruined. She was curious to see what would happen to her if no man would marry her. It seemed like the most likely way to have an adventure. Even though she was able to make people laugh all day, she sometimes wanted to be tragic.

And then one night Rose ran into McMahon on the way from getting Ernest back to sleep. Their eyes met. There was something new in the darkness of their eyes. They looked and looked, trying to find out what the new thing might be. What it was that they recognized in each other. Then they both realized it all at once. They'd had sexual fantasies about each other the night before. The insight was so shocking to Rose. It was as though there were a noose around her neck, and she heard the floor drop. It was wonderful.

"Don't touch me or I'll scream."

"What are you talking about? Are you crazy? Why would I want to touch you? How dare you talk to me like that!"

"I would never let you touch me just like that, just for nothing. I don't have any desire for you, so you will have to pay me whatever I ask for, when I ask for it."

McMahon stared at her. "I don't want you. How can you speak to me like this? Aren't you worried that I'll fire you? Aren't you worried that I'll throw you out onto the street?"

"No."

"You're not?"

"You won't throw me out."

"So you want to be a whore?"

"If you are going to put it that way, then yes."

Of course, Rose was worried he was going to have her kicked out of the house. She was terrified that things wouldn't work out; this was incredibly risky. She was well aware. It reminded her of a trick she used to perform when she was in the dormitory—she would pile eight or nine Bibles on her head. She would walk around like there were nothing at all unusual about what she was doing. This was so risky, because if the Bibles fell, they would make such a huge thud on the floor that the Sisters would arrive to punish Rose mercilessly.

She put her index finger up to her lips and whispered a *shhhh*, then she hurried out of the room.

This was a new act for her. And like all new acts, it made her really nervous.

The acts that made her the most nervous were always her best. That's what you always felt when genius was in the room: humbled that it had visited you, and terrified that you might blow it.

She sat on the edge of her little single bed, trembling. But McMahon did not fire her. Instead he observed her every day.

His wife was so beautiful. His wife looked like sunshine bursting through the window. There wasn't a single person in the world who wouldn't think his wife was incredibly beautiful. When McMahon first met her, they went out all the time. When she walked into casinos, everyone started winning. When she walked into a room, everyone felt better about themselves. They found themselves to be funnier or wittier and more charming. So everybody always wanted her around.

But she would never have set eyes on him or given him the time of day if he hadn't become filthy rich. His money had indeed bought him love. Given what he had seen of the world, the exchange of love for money seemed to be one of the commodities that never wavered—it was as dependable an investment as electricity. But she always reminded him implicitly that he was a criminal.

The girl had looked at him with such desire.

SHE TOLD HIM THAT for a dollar she would act like a kitten. He gave it to her. She put a little bowl of milk on the floor, and she got down on her hands and knees and lapped it up. Then she stood up and walked away. He didn't know what to make of what he had just seen. He was frightened. It made him feel guilty, as though his life had been a crime and he was suddenly feeling remorse for it.

THERE WERE MEN WHO LIKED all sorts of odd and depraved perversions. He owned brothels, after all. The things they liked were so ridiculous, it made him think of them as children. He would never engage in that nonsense.

ROSE WALKED UP TO HIM and held up her wrists for McMahon to see. There was a black ribbon tying them together. "How in the world did this happen?" she asked.

He had no idea how he was supposed to answer that.

ROSE STARTED SINGING "HAPPY BIRTHDAY" as she walked by with an imaginary birthday cake. Each time she blew out an imaginary candle, McMahon felt as though his heart were a flame she had blown out. He was dead. He died nineteen times. That was how many imaginary candles there were on the imaginary cake.

HE COULDN'T FIGURE OUT whether she had genuine designs on his destruction or whether she was just a pervert.

SHE WAS STANDING WITH A BANANA. She slowly lowered the banana so that she was holding it at her hips. As though it were a penis.

SHE PUT DOWN the laundry basket. She leaned up against the wall and began kissing it. She kissed it tenderly and a little bit hesitantly, as if she and the wall were touching each other for the first time. As if they were experimenting with kissing before getting into something deeper.

. . .

SHE WAS LEANING AGAINST the back door, outside the house. She had a jacket on. Her hair was all messed up from the wind. She had the mop standing upside down next to her.

"Oh, I don't know if he's that handsome. I think there are better-looking men at the nightclub. You find every man good-looking."

The mop was leaning a little in toward her, her confidante.

"Really? You would. Oh, I don't know myself. I don't know if I'd let him touch me."

For a second it seemed to him as though the mop were shaking, holding in its laughter too. Were they laughing at him because they thought that he was a fool or because they actually liked him? When any woman agreed to reciprocate your affections, weren't they all thinking a mixture of both things?

HE HAD NO IDEA WHAT it would be like to make love to such a girl. He wondered about making love to her the same way he had wondered about lovemaking when he was a virgin. How could she be more experienced than he was? Maybe the priests had lined up to make love to her. He had heard that this was quite common. But how would that make her so brash?

He wanted to make love in her peculiar way. He wanted her to whisper the rules to this strange new type of lovemaking into his ear. He would follow the rules. He would abide by every one of them. He would get down on his knees and worship her if it was one of the rules. He really hoped that it was.

MCMAHON'S LONGING TO BE with Rose made no sense to him. He wanted it to go away, as if it were the flu or some oddly unbearable pain. The only way to get rid of it would be to make love to her.

She was standing in the hallway with an apple on her head like William Tell—desperate. Inviting anyone to have their way with her. He couldn't resist her. He took the apple and stuck it in her mouth so that she wouldn't be able to cry out when he entered her.

MCMAHON TOOK HER in the nursery. The pile of bricks toppled over. There was a giant dollhouse. All the little dolls seemed to be staring out the windows at Rose. They were gathered in the rooms, watching Rose the same way the orphans used to look out at the snow falling, the strange wonders of the outside world that did not belong to them. There was a row of tin soldiers on the windowsill. They weren't on her side. Even though they were only three inches tall, they were men. There was a hobbyhorse standing in the corner. It was handmade out of orange yarn and had purple buttons for eyes.

Rose was so slender compared to McMahon. It wasn't just a matter of size. It had to do with years. The older you got, the thicker you became. She had only been alive for nineteen years.

She liked that he was enormous. She felt as though she were scaling him like he was a mountain. He picked her up and carried her around the room as if she only weighed ten pounds. The Sisters would never pick her up and carry her just for fun. Just because they couldn't resist. Just because they wanted to get her head up close to theirs. They never picked her up at all.

When he went down on her, she couldn't believe how amazing it felt. It was like she had been thrown into a lake. She wanted it desperately. And she cried out in a pretty cry of joy when she came. And she hated herself for having sex with someone other than Pierrot. But then again, hating herself was part of what made it feel so good. The self-loathing that arrived right before you came was at the very extremes of feeling.

If this was how good sex felt with somebody you hated, what might it actually feel like with somebody you loved? she wondered. She'd always had an inkling that she was the type of girl who would love sex. But she had not realized she would enjoy it so much.

MᴄMᴀʜᴏɴ ᴡᴀs ᴛʜᴀᴛ ʙᴏʏ in the story who had to keep his finger in a hole in the wall of a dam. And he suddenly couldn't stand the responsibility anymore. He just wanted to pull his finger out of the hole and go on to other activities in life. He was a prisoner to the hole. So finally he yanked at the finger and the flood came on. And it destroyed everyone around him and all of civilization, and everyone perished in the *swoosh* of the great waters.

And he was drowned for a moment and he experienced the euphoria that the drowned are supposed to feel just before life lets go of them, like a child letting go of the string of a balloon.

Rᴏsᴇ ᴡᴀs sᴛɪʟʟ ᴛʜʀᴏʙʙɪɴɢ as she hurried down the hallway. She loved the feeling of McMahon oozing out from between her legs.

Aɴᴅ ᴡʜᴇɴ MᴄMᴀʜᴏɴ got out of bed the next morning, he felt as though he were made out of ashes.

Tʜᴇ ɴᴇxᴛ ᴅᴀʏ the maid was in the nursery and she saw the apple sitting there. How funny to find an apple just sitting there without an owner, without a history. She picked it up and bit into it. It was the most wonderful apple she had ever tasted.

·⟨ 19 ⟩·

A SPOONFUL OF DREAMS

Pierrot had a dream that he was sitting in a room that had a thousand lightbulbs suspended from the ceiling. The electric light was so great that it was as if it were shining from God. Irving believed it was a sign. He invested heavily in GE. Irving had begun to make investments based on Pierrot's dreams. His returns were paying off wonderfully. He rarely listened to his adviser but to Pierrot instead. He told Pierrot he would leave him some money because he had rightfully earned it.

Pierrot yelled, "Don't talk about such things!"

But Irving was frail, and the years were hard on his health. Pierrot helped Irving into the bathtub one night, as was his custom. Irving sat with a little tumbler of brandy in his hand as Pierrot shampooed his hair. He poured a bucket of soapy water over his head to rinse it and Irving noted that his brandy now had a soapy taste.

Later Pierrot sat next to him in the large bed, underneath the purposeless enormous canopy, and spoon-fed him soup. He held a napkin close by, and he dabbed any spill from Irving's chin.

Irving stopped going outside because he didn't want anyone to see him this aged and this incapacitated. He could only bear for Pierrot to see him this way. Pierrot didn't judge people. Their walks were now confined to the mansion.

Because it was wintertime, Irving was fretting that he would never live to see another summer and see his roses. Pierrot hired a landscape painter to come into the bedroom and paint roses all over the walls. Irving wept when he saw the beautiful mural, thinking that he had died and had found himself, to his surprise, in heaven.

ONE MORNING Pierrot had taken off his fancy suit, and it was hanging from a coat hanger. He was wearing a green undershirt and a pair of the old man's pajama bottoms that tied at the waist with a string. He walked into the bedroom, carrying a tray with a plate covered in cheese and bread and some peaches that had been left by the grocer outside the front door. When he saw that the old man was frozen in time and looking at the ceiling, Pierrot dropped the tray and cried out.

There was a chandelier above his head, made out of eight thousand glass beads, like pieces of ice from a hailstorm had all been frozen mid-fall.

Pierrot called for the undertakers to come. He sat next to Irving's body, holding his hand, occasionally whispering, "There, there." The undertakers came and took the old man away on a stretcher, stepping over sweaters and plates in the hallway. The house was so quiet and empty once the large front door thudded to a close. He wasn't sure what he was supposed to do, but before he knew it, Irving's son arrived.

Pierrot put his clothes on hastily, intimidated by the severe, middle-aged man. He pushed his wild, unwashed hair from one side to another, attempting to look normal. He shuffled through the papers on the night table. He was looking for an item of great importance for his future. He found it underneath a cup of coffee that was resting on a top hat that was on a pile of records that was balanced on an empty cake box that was on top of a copy of Jules Verne's *Twenty Thousand Leagues Under the Sea*. Pierrot had read the book three times to Irving. He showed Irving's son the piece of paper, which was the amendment to Irving's will.

The son threw the will immediately into the stove. Pierrot was left with not a cent at nineteen years of age.

· · ·

BUT EVEN WORSE, though he had been Irving's closest companion over the past four years, Pierrot had to stand at the back of the crowd at the cemetery. The fat, middle-aged women were all dressed in black at the funeral, like a group of cello cases abandoned backstage during a performance. The fedoras on the men were like a cluster of snails. Irving's children's lives were to be enhanced by their father's death because of their inheritance. Pierrot was the only one left out in the cold.

Pierrot was also the only one who actually missed the old man.

HE WANTED TO CRAWL INTO Irving's grave and shoot himself in the head. Then he could be buried with Irving. They would meet again in heaven, lying on an enormous bed in the sky.

Pierrot was wandering and stumbling toward the grave so haphazardly that he bumped into a large statue standing between him and the grave. He stepped back to take a look at it. It was an enormous gray stone angel, whose hair was whipped up in a frenzy. He couldn't say whether it was female or male. Just one of its stone toes could crush him.

But the angel with its enormous sword was blocking his entrance into Paradise. The angel seemed to be clearly informing him that he needed to back away. So he turned around and went the other way.

PIERROT TOOK THE TROLLEY DOWNTOWN. It was a neighborhood where you could loiter properly. A horse clip-clopped by like a little girl wearing wooden clogs. Who could Pierrot turn to now? He thought of all the people at the orphanage he had left behind, but he would never be able to find them now. Too much time had passed. Time was not like physical distance. There was no road map you could acquire to travel over it.

He spotted a piano in the window of a department store. He couldn't resist. He needed to play it to calm down. He walked through the door, climbed into the window display and began to play. The instrument had a loud and bright sound. He had played a rambunctious piano like this as a child, when touring with Rose. The taut assertive notes had almost seemed to make her mad. She had stomped around to the music like a soldier dancing on the enemy's grave. She had held out her finger under her nose as though it were a mustache. Remembering that made Pierrot smile.

As he played a young woman with blue eyes and a cloche over red curls stopped on the sidewalk and stared at him. Then she disappeared. The next thing Pierrot knew, she was sitting next to him on the bench. Her eyes were preternaturally big, as if she were looking through magnifying glasses.

"And who are you?" Pierrot asked.

"I'm Poppy. What's your name?"

When the girl spoke, he could see that one of her front teeth was missing.

"Well, Joseph, actually. But you can call me Pierrot."

"You have a terrific outfit."

"Thank you. My father had it tailor-made for me. He passed away today, and I don't have a cent in the world."

"You play the piano very well."

"I was hoping to find work playing it."

"You're outta luck. All the piano players used to play for silent movies, and now they're all laid off. I know a movie theater that needs someone to mop up the sticky floors. Want the address?"

"Yes, absolutely. That would be a dream come true for a newly made pauper like myself."

"All right—1340 Saint Catherine Street West. Tell them Poppy sent you. Actually, tell the manager the Redhead from Heaven sent you. That's how he knows me."

"Thanks. You are an angel."

"That's what they say. Hey, I was wondering if you wanted to accompany me to Chinatown. I don't like to walk alone, and you look like you need some cheering up."

"Okay."

They walked together to Chinatown. There were buildings covered in red glazed bricks. The edges of the roofs were curled at the tips like slippers. They sold parts of chicken different from what Pierrot usually ate, like the feet. There was a grocery store that sold different types of delicacies, like pickled eggs. The mannequins in the window displays were wearing silk kimonos decorated with gold dragons and multicolored butterflies. There was a small house of worship with a gold plaque and Asian letters on it. There were chop suey restaurants on every corner.

The girl hopped daintily over the puddles filled with chicken grease and other horrors. There was a room where you could get heroin at the back of the store, where they sold dragon's beard candy. Everybody came home with a cloudy look on their faces and a pink cardboard box filled with white, stringy candy.

They ducked into an alley and went into a door at the end of it. There was a young Chinese girl sitting on a stool behind a table. She was wearing a gray dress and silver stockings and blue leather high heels that were scuffed at the toes. Her black hair was tucked behind her ears, and she was reading an Agatha Christie novel. There was a bowl on the desk holding a black fancy goldfish that swirled around like a paintbrush dipped in black ink. When they entered the shop, she rang the bell on the desk without even looking up. An older Chinese man dressed in a traditional silk outfit came to lead them to the back.

There were framed prints on the wall. There were couches and daybeds all over the room. For a moment Pierrot was shocked by all the people lying on the thin mattresses on the floor. They still had their coats on. They looked like they had been shot on their way to work. Their foreheads were sweaty. They had their arms around strangers. It wasn't a sexual thing at all. They were still a little bit conscious. They were trying to peep out of one eye. They were like little kids in their beds, forcing themselves to stay awake so that they could hear more of a fairy tale their mother was reading.

Poppy found a stack of three thin mattresses stacked one on top of the other like a layered sponge cake. She purchased a pipe, lit it up and inhaled from it. Then she handed it to Pierrot to do the same.

HE FELT AN ITCHING on his back right below his shoulder blades. The itch bothered him. He felt that he had to get to it. If he could just touch the tip of his finger to where the itch was, he would be able to stop it. He tried to reach back over his shoulder in order to scratch it, but his fingers couldn't reach. And then he tried to get at the itch from underneath, but that also proved impossible.

Then the itch started to burn and to be painful. There were two pressure points. They were pressing and pressing and pressing. It was as if there were something alive under his skin trying to burrow its way out. And then he felt the skin break. And two wings burst out. And as soon as they did, he felt a wondrous calm.

He moved the wings around. Wasn't it just so wonderful to have these extra limbs, ones that reached out into space in such amazing ways? For his whole life he had been confined in a box, and now he was finally allowed to extend himself in all directions.

Pierrot felt as though he were flying. Everything around him had become immaterial. There was no such thing as matter, only energy. He floated up off the bed. He was up by the ceiling. There were flowers on the tin ceiling. The lightbulb singed his tie. There was no limit to how far up he could go.

He closed his eyes and floated. Pierrot drifted away. He knew that he ought to take a peek at his whereabouts in the universe so that he could find his way back. His eyelids were great, heavy velvet curtains, very difficult to draw. Perhaps he had floated out a window, into the Milky Way.

As the effects of the heroin wore off, the wings folded up and retracted into his shoulder blades. He was surprised the wings were able to fit back in once they had been outside of him. But they were gone.

·⋇[20]⋇·

IN WHICH MRS. McMAHON
HAS AN IDEA

What were you talking to the governess about?" McMahon asked his wife later.

"Oh, Marie. Or actually, Rose. That's what she likes to be called, you know."

"Is that what the children call her?"

"Of course. They'll do anything she says."

"Then why doesn't she get them to behave? Why does everyone else have ordinary children but we somehow brought wild animals into this world?"

"Maybe she just doesn't care. Or maybe she doesn't know they're misbehaving."

"You give her too much freedom. She can't handle it. She's like a little dog let out of a cage."

"She's a romantic. Can you believe it? Her mother gave birth to her and then kicked her out the door, and she still believes in love."

"Who is she in love with? Did she tell you his name?"

"She doesn't use his real name when she talks about him. He has some stupid nickname. But his real name is Joseph. She says she's going to find him. When she does, she doesn't want to marry him, she just wants to be his lover. She says he can do handstands and twirl a ball on his feet. She has a dream that she's going to find him and go on the road with him."

"Why do you listen to that?"

"Because it's like a fairy tale."

"Does she have any contact with him? Does she have any idea where he is?"

"I'm going to the orphanage tomorrow. It's so simple. I'll ask where the little idiot was sent to live, and then we'll go visit him. If he even remembers who Rose is, I'll give her a dollar."

"I'd love to see this fabled creature too."

"I'll tell you all about it. I'll be taking the car, by the way."

McMahon intercepted Rose on her way home. She was carrying a basket of bread and fish that she'd purchased down at the market.

"Don't come close to me. Don't touch me," Rose said as soon as she saw him.

"Don't go in the house."

"Why not?"

"My wife found out about us."

Rose fell down on her knees. She began tearing at the grass. She pulled huge clumps of it, as though it weren't listening to her and she needed a reaction.

"I've made a mess of everything! What in the world will I do now? What will come of me? I've ruined your family. I was finally getting along with your wife. Oh why, oh why, oh why am I such a pervert? It's the ruin of me, of course. I have such demented thoughts in my head, you have no idea."

She rolled over onto her back and flopped both arms out to the side, martyring herself.

"And the children," Rose said. "They are crazy already. Please don't tell me that they knew anything about this. They'll go completely out of

their minds. They'll end up killing small animals. They'll end up murderers. I'll probably be like this my whole life. It's my great character
flaw. I'll probably have hundreds of strange degenerates for lovers. Someone will write a terrible novel about me."

McMahon looked down at Rose in her supine position. She was so
lovely, he thought. She was so absurd. How could he not adore that absurdity? Until then his feelings for Rose had consisted mostly of perverted desire and the subsequent reactions of fear and revulsion: the
typical emotions that played themselves out when he had an affair with
any woman. None of them had surprised him in the least. Those emotions couldn't tame or threaten a man like him. But he was surprised by
the emotion that he was having right then, looking at Rose. Actually, it
would be safe to say that he was shocked by it. He was feeling that very
rare thing: love.

He could have dropped her off at the door of any of his brothels.
There were so many girls with similar backgrounds to Rose's. They all
used bad judgment. We all make mistakes. And isn't that what money is
for, so you don't have to pay for them?

"Sister Eloïse was right about me." Rose spoke to the sky. "I thought
that it was nothing at all to go around waltzing and cavorting with a
make-believe bear every night. But she knew what I should have known,
which is that there is no such thing as make-believe. I probably was invok-
ing the devil. It wasn't a bear I was dancing with but the devil. I'm cursed."

But she was so lovely! She was plagued with remorse. And racked with
guilt. She believed she was a sinner. He remembered the wonderful days
when he was able to feel all those things. Rose would make him feel them
again. He would be a brute for her. He would never let another man have
her, especially not an orphan. He reached his hand out and gently took
hers. She got up off the ground.

She trudged along beside McMahon. The ribbon in her hair was beating
around wildly in the wind, like a black stallion not wanting to be broken.

SKETCH OF MAN WITH MONKEY

After the heroin had lost its effect, Pierrot felt how close to the ground the thin mattress actually was. He opened his eyes and the world seemed more mundane and miserable than it ever had. He looked at Poppy, sleeping with her mouth wide open and her skirt up over her panties, and found her too sad to bear. He got up and quickly stepped between the mattresses, then out onto the street alone. As he walked his legs felt inadequate. They got him places so slowly. As though he were walking through water. How awkward this ordinary life was. Everything he took for granted was incrementally harder.

He got himself a room at the very cheap Cupid Hotel, whose bricks were painted pink.

Pierrot went to see the owner of the Savoy movie theater, as Poppy had suggested. The Savoy was one of the less popular theaters in town. There were always lightbulbs that had blown out on the marquee. It wasn't even where a theater should be. Theaters usually existed in a row with others that were just like it. This one was squeezed between a dental clinic and a ceramic-tile store.

The prices of movies and popcorn were written in white letters on a black frame on one side of the door. The other side had the poster of the movie being shown. The plot involved an incredibly handsome man who tries to rape a woman on a train for two hours, and to both her and the audience's delight, finally succeeds.

The inside wasn't as garish as the other theaters downtown either. The lobby had white walls with molding at the ceiling but little else. In the theater, there was a black curtain with sparse gold tassels at the bottom that pulled open smoothly to the sides and always seemed to get stuck at exactly the same spot. But the seats were black and soft, and there was an orchestra pit that still had a lonely, beat-up piano in it.

The owner was sitting in a tiny office at the back. He was a very short man with white hair who breathed through his mouth. The man laughed and laughed when Pierrot told him the Redhead from Heaven had sent him. He said he did need an extra usher and cleaner, since his last one had contracted tuberculosis. Pierrot could play the piano during intermission while the audience got snacks. He said his dearly departed wife used to play the piano during the silent-film era and that's why he couldn't bring himself to scrap it. But Pierrot wouldn't be paid more than the other ushers.

Pierrot changed into a red uniform and porkpie hat. He hurried up and down the aisles during the newsreels. A Betty Boop cartoon came on—the adorable buxom Betty was having herself a funeral. Pierrot stopped for a second to look up at it and laugh but quickly got back down on his hands and knees with his small broom to sweep up spilled pink popcorn. During intermission, Pierrot plopped down on the piano bench. He desperately needed to play a tune. He hadn't since Irving's death, and he had to find some way to articulate his grief.

The moment Pierrot put his fingers down, notes leaped out. What a happy piano! It looked beaten up, but it had a young soul. It loved to be played. It laughed easily under Pierrot's fingertips. It begged him for more. Like a girl who encourages you during sex with pretty gurgles and gasps. He forgot his predicament for that instant and lost himself in the tune. He played his tune for Rose, the one that had made her dance in the cafeteria. Perhaps she would be in the theater one day with her husband and children and the tune would remind her how she had loved him once, and why.

When he was done and it was time for the movie to come back on, surprisingly the audience clapped. The owner was leaning over the balcony railing with a cigar in his mouth and tears in his eyes. The ticket girl, wearing a golden sailor hat, had come out of the booth.

As he began to play a tune during the next intermission, he felt the wings move. They wanted to break free of his skin once again. They were frustrated now. Especially since they had already felt unfettered freedom—so they were so anxious to be in that state once again. They were so aware, and indignant about their restrictions.

Pierrot tried to ignore them but they would not leave him be. They kept trying to spread themselves out. They never stopped pushing. They were pushing against each other like two children in a school yard or in the backseat of a car, ever frustrated at the other for infringing on their space.

HE SPENT HIS ENTIRE PAY on heroin. His body immediately relaxed, as though he were naked and lying in a bathtub.

BECAUSE HE SPENT HIS PAY on heroin, he was always short on rent. The landlady was on his back for rent every night when he left. He would often try elaborate ruses to get into his hotel room without the landlady catching sight of him. They had changed the lock on the front door. He would crawl up the back fire escape and into his back window.

He lost weight. All his clothes seemed a little bit baggy. If he didn't put on suspenders, his pants would probably fall right down to his ankles. As if he were standing in a puddle.

He once spent three minutes attempting to climb into his jacket, which kept trying to run away from him. The minute he put one arm in, the other one seemed to slip out. He seemed suddenly aware of the mathematics and geometry of mundane actions, and once aware, he could no longer take them for granted. But he found it wonderful. Putting on a jacket was as perplexing as folding an origami swan.

Then one night he crawled up the back fire escape to find that they had also bolted the window.

Pierrot was tormented by his addiction. The wings were wrapped around him like a straitjacket. He spent the money on heroin and kissed his room at the Cupid Hotel good-bye. Not a month after leaving Irving's house, he lay down on a piece of cardboard in the park to sleep.

The leaves fell down on top of him. He kept his eyes closed, but the ground grew up around him. The roots of the trees reached up like the great arms of wrestlers, and they rolled around his limbs like boa constrictors. The beetles and other insects crawled into his nose and ears. They devoured his brain. And then it was hollow, like an Easter egg that children had already blown the yolk out of.

If anyone was to come along and tap him, his shell would shatter.

HE LEARNED HOW TO SHOOT UP, so he could get more for his money. The heroin would probably kill him within five years. Knowing that somehow took the pressure off everything. What did anything matter if you weren't going to get old? He could live the rest of his life as a child. What a blessing.

A child's main job was to be happy. If Pierrot was happy, he was doing his job. He sat on the trolley with his eyes closed, as big a grin as was anatomically possible spread across his face.

He walked down the aisle of the trolley. He was holding out a flower. He held it out for everybody to smell. They all backed away from it as if it were going to squirt water in their faces.

HE STOPPED AT A PLAYGROUND one day when he was high. He didn't feel that he was in any way superior to the children playing there. They were his people! The children looked so hungry that their eyes stuck out like oversize stones on silver rings.

Children were always amused by Pierrot. They could see right away that he was a lot of fun, that he always got in trouble, that he knew how to clown around, that he didn't fit in with the other adults.

He hated being stuck in a body so much bigger than theirs. He couldn't fit his ass into the swings. The slide was much too narrow for him to whiz down it comfortably. Pierrot sat on one slide and discovered that his feet were already at the ground. What did that mean? If he were an intelligent type of scientist, like Newton or Galileo, he would be able to deduce some fantastic rule of physics from it.

A father chased him out of the park. He thought it was inappropriate for Pierrot to be talking to children in the playground, for him to be there at all. He was now twenty years old, after all.

When the evening came, a black bat flew by, like the charred remains of a burned will.

·◦[22]◦·

THE TEN PLAGUES

McMahon got Rose a room in the Darling Hotel at Sherbrooke and Mountain Streets. It was a fancy neighborhood. The buildings were all stately. There were iron awnings at the front of the buildings, with lights underneath. The very rich inhabited their own universes, lived under their own skies. Limousines would drive up under the awnings. The drivers would hurry out and go around the side to allow extraordinary men and their wives to step out.

There were doormen with gold-buttoned uniforms in the lobby. A woman strutted by with a great yellow stole wrapped around her fat shoulders, like caramel poured on top of ice cream.

"Clean up my room, please," she said, mistaking Rose for a maid.

Rose had never lived in such a room. It had its own bathroom and a kitchenette. She supposed that she ought to get down on her knees and kiss McMahon's feet. But she didn't feel she owed him anything for this. She closed her eyes. She wondered why she had not been allowed to take her suitcase this time. Every young woman should travel around with her own suitcase. She imagined her body cut into pieces and piled into her suitcase with rocks and tossed into the Saint Lawrence River.

All she had was the plan she'd made with Pierrot, which she kept in her pocket. Her toes sank into the beige carpet as if into sand at the edge of the beach.

SHE LAY IN BED so long that day, she felt like a strange illustration on a children's quilt. A small pirate on a ship with a patch over her eye and anchors revolving like stars around her head. She didn't see the point of doing anything at all.

She felt guilty about everything. She even felt guilty about lying in bed all day long. McMahon had brought her a bottle of golden whiskey. There was a little round glass shaped like a planet on the bedside table next to her. She sat up, her legs dangling off the edge as if she were sitting on a doctor's examination table. She poured the liquor into the glass. It lapped up on both sides of the glass, like waves crashing against a rocky shore.

She drank it. Her body was set on fire. It was as though there were a little thermostat knob under her spine. It was cranked higher and higher. She was warm like a cast-iron radiator covered in a pattern of roses. All she wanted in the world was to be warm. If someone tried to grab her toes right then, they would get burned.

She didn't want to make love to McMahon at first. She spurned his affections. She was so regretful of having made love to him in the first place that she supposed she wanted to reject him entirely now.

She had begged McMahon—if he was going to leave her in that hotel room to rot, the least he could do was to please get her some books. He asked her what kind she wanted and she said, "New stuff. Something adventurous."

When McMahon told the bookseller he was looking for "adventurous stuff," he interpreted it as meaning "dirty books." He handed McMahon a little pile of books, including ones by the Marquis de Sade and Colette.

Poor Rose went wild as she read them. On every page there were loads of schoolgirls in enormous piles rubbing and rubbing against one another until they achieved orgasm. She was so wet that she trembled and banged her knees, trying to get through the story without tossing the book aside and touching herself. When McMahon walked in, Rose jumped into his arms. Her underwear was soggy up against him.

Rose smelled of roses. If she touched you, you would also smell like roses for days. The furniture in her room smelled like roses. The mattress in her room smelled of roses. Maybe it was because she was twenty and had just bloomed into a woman. They made love every afternoon after that.

ONE MORNING ROSE WOKE UP to discover that she had been crying in her sleep. She touched her cheeks and was surprised to find that they were damp with tears. McMahon played her a record. When a woman began to sing, Rose wept some more. McMahon said she should knock it off because it wasn't a particularly sad song.

"I think there's something odd happening to me. But it's not like I'm sick or anything. I've just been feeling so odd. And I don't think I can ignore it anymore."

McMahon insisted she go see a Dr. Bernstein he knew. Bernstein was known to administer all sorts of drugs to himself. He was ahead of his time. He was treating himself for all sorts of diseases of the mind. He knew that these were the same as physical ones. He did not believe that anything was spiritual. All ailments were physical. He wanted to find a cure for melancholia.

He could only practice out of an apartment, and only covertly. It was not really clear how he had lost his license. He'd had a good practice. He had lived in a grand sort of house on the Golden Square Mile. Some people said that he had been on the front. He was shell-shocked, just like the patients he was supposed to be treating.

He was writing his own book, called *An Interpretation of Sadness*. He thought sadness was contagious. If you sat next to someone on the bus and they were sad, even though you didn't speak to them, you would find yourself overcome by sadness later that night. It is a disease that parades as a mood.

"He treats irrational illnesses. He believes in diseases that nobody else believes in. He hasn't found them in laboratories. He found them inside books. This new invention of sadness for sadness's sake is going to have more damaging effects on the human psyche than modern warfare will."

Rose put on her clothes to see this doctor. She was actually rather smelly. She was wearing the same underwear and undershirt as when she had run away from the McMahon house, and she certainly hadn't made an effort to change them. She hadn't had time to pack anything. She was stuck with only her maid's outfit. When she put it on, it seemed as though it had shrunk. The maid's outfit didn't have very much strength left in it. The little stitches at the side snapped. The dress had just plain given up. It wasn't as if she had gained any weight, because she really hadn't eaten very much at all. Mostly her diet consisted of whiskey for breakfast, whiskey for lunch and whiskey for dinner. She put on her coat. The buttons seemed to have grown in her absence and didn't want to squeeze into the holes.

. . .

SHE HAD THOUGHT that seeing other people would cheer her up, but the effects of the Great Depression were everywhere. Someone had jumped out a window the night before. The landlady was pouring a bucket of water over the dried bloodstain. The water turned red and rolled out onto the street. Rose leaped backward as the bloodied water spread out on the sidewalk and almost touched her shoes.

As she walked farther down the street a little girl ran by her with a jar with frogs. She released them into the sewers. "We're being evicted," the little girl told Rose. "And we can't keep any of the pets."

Rose wondered if the frogs would find a way to survive in the sewers. Perhaps they would multiply and be everywhere in the city in a year. You would go to your bathtub and find it filled with frogs that had climbed out of the drainpipe. Rose shuddered.

A group of boys passed her. They were wearing dirty clothes, and shoes that looked too big. One boy was barefoot. Their heads were shaved, surely because of lice. They must have slept in the same filthy bed, and the mites were contagious. Who knew what other vermin were in the houses. There were the remains of a burned mattress in the trash. The bedbugs had gotten to be too much. It seemed like everyone in the city was itchy.

A stray dog hurried by. It had once had a job protecting a family, no doubt. But now no one could feed it. It looked in the window of the butcher shop. They were selling all sorts of ghastly pieces of meat.

She passed the line for the soup kitchen. There were so many men, all in clothes that had become too big, making them look like circus clowns. A man in the line removed his hat, as though in deference to a pretty lady. His face was covered with boils.

A man came out of the soup kitchen, clanging a large pot with a big spoon. It made the sound of great thunder. He was announcing to the men that they could go inside now.

Rose saw a boy holding a newspaper. On the front page it described a horror story about the prairies. There were grasshoppers everywhere. They were eating all the crops. They were insatiable. They came in huge swarms.

She thought she would keep her eyes closed until she passed the street. As she cut through the park, she saw men sleeping under the trees and on the benches. She had wondered why there were so many men sleeping in the park. They wanted to nap through this part of history. If everyone just closed their eyes, did that make the world go dark?

Montrealers had spent the entire 1920s out partying, making money off the Americans who came up looking for legal liquor, and maybe the Great Depression was a punishment for that. All the women with short skirts had really enraged God.

Rose arrived at the doctor's apartment building. The small lobby had red tiles. She rang his doorbell and then began the long climb up the spiraling stairs to the seventh floor. Rose knocked on the door. Dr. Bernstein answered. He was a middle-aged, sophisticated gentleman. He was wearing a suit, and his white pompadour looked like a wave about to crest. He gestured for Rose to enter. It was a small apartment, but it was quite amazing how much stuff was in there. Rose couldn't help but gaze around the room as she stepped in.

There were framed ferns and flowers on the walls, and tiny butterflies pinned to corkboards. In addition, the shelves of his room were covered with all sorts of strange things. There were geraniums on all the windowsills. He had a shelf full of seashells that he had collected when he was young and full of adventure. What beautiful days those were when he had piled these things into a tiny blue tin bucket. He had thought he would figure out the world.

"You'll notice I'm a bit of a naturalist."

He had a tiny aquarium with a cocoon in it, as he liked to raise butterflies. They would flit and fly around the room. He would get stoned and watch them. The butterflies from warm places were truly magnificent. They had such beautiful wings.

"Ooooh my, you do have some exquisite bugs."

"Thank you. I discovered my interest in insects at school while I was studying biology. I wrote a paper on the sex life of slugs that was widely read by students in universities."

He sighed as he led Rose to his examination table.

"But my father encouraged me to enter medicine. He told me it was much nobler to worry about humans than about bugs. But you know, he was wrong. Because people are wicked. They are cheaters and liars and degenerates and drunks, and the science of medicine just keeps them alive so they can murder and commit even more sins. But I have yet to find anything about the workings of insects that has disappointed me."

Rose sat down on the examination table. He pulled up a wooden chair that had once been painted pink and had once been painted blue and had once been painted white. The nature of its deterioration caused all the colors to show.

He handed her a pretty teacup. It was filled with hot water and a few seeds from when he had squeezed the dregs of a lemon into it.

"So I see you've been stricken by my old pal, Melancholia! Why is it that we never give sadness its due? Why do we insist on keeping so many things secret? Tell me about your relationship with sadness, please."

"Even when I was a little girl I wanted to make everybody happy."

When she spoke, phlegm cracked her voice. Since she hadn't spoken in a while her words seemed to be covered in rust. She was glad to talk to the doctor. She always liked to have meaningful conversations. Sometimes you tried to talk to people and nothing worked. The words were all stiff and slow.

"I always had this gift. Even though we were in this big orphanage where we weren't supposed to experience anything like happiness or joy, I was still able to see beauty every day. As a child, I existed in a strange, prolonged state of glorious rapture."

"Nostalgia and Melancholia are thick as thieves. Old pals from grammar school, one could say."

"There was only one other child in the orphanage who was able to do this. He was known by everyone as Pierrot. He could feel it too. That wonder. He was also a collector of beautiful moments.

"The times did not encourage such children to survive. The rest of them are all lying in tiny wooden boxes in the cemetery. Like packaged dolls to be opened on the final miraculous Christmas.

"I decided it would be wonderful to invite a great bear as a visitor to the orphanage. And he had a great big heart. He had a heart the size of ten of the mothers. He had such a big heart that he couldn't help but be a pervert. Could he? He couldn't help but be a little inappropriate. But wasn't it better to have someone who was always gushing annoyingly about love than someone who was reserved with it? They had never had someone pinching their cheeks and squeezing them so hard that they could barely breathe. The big dirty philandering bear was a dream come true."

"When we accept our perversion, we accept ourselves."

"I wouldn't have been able to express any of that then, of course. But I was a very complicated little girl. I think I was so interested in navigating these strange emotional seas that I became a pervert. Or I lack moral fiber. Either/or. But I would like you to know that I am trying to combat this . . . well . . . complicated aspect of myself. And can you deduce, doctor, what is wrong with me?"

"You'll have to take off your underwear and lie on the couch with your legs back up in the air."

"Why in the world would that be necessary?"

"So that I can check my prognosis."

"And what is said prognosis?"

"There's a certain sort of melancholy that is a symptom of pregnancy."

In the aquarium a butterfly began to emerge from the cocoon. It looked at first like an umbrella that someone was having trouble opening, and then each wing fluttered out. Dr. Bernstein held a little box of chocolates for her to choose from. Each one looked like the face of a crying baby. But they were actually shaped like roses.

ROSE WALKED AWAY from the building, frightened. She didn't have any of the symptoms of pregnancy usually considered typical. She wasn't sick in the morning. She hadn't even missed a period. She did, however, know strange things. She was able to guess people's middle names. She knew how old cats were. She always knew what numbers were going to come up on the die at the barbotte tables. She was surprised to be accumulating so much money. She was making a tidy profit just through betting on them.

Things that were unhappy called out to her. She lifted up a rock to discover a beetle underneath it, squashed. She opened the back door of a restaurant and a bird that had accidentally been trapped inside flew out. Perhaps it was all coincidence.

SHE DID NOT TELL MCMAHON for fear it would make it more real.

SHE BEGAN throwing up in a bucket. What happened if an unwanted child gave birth to an unwanted child? It was as though she were in a hall of mirrors, except that instead of getting smaller in each one, she got younger and younger.

BUT IT DIDN'T HAPPEN that way. Instead she had a cramp one morning. She went to sit on the toilet. And when she was done, there was the world's tiniest baby floating in the toilet. She put her hands up to her face. She pulled the chain and her firstborn was flushed.

23

OF MICE AND WOMEN

The bulk of McMahon's money had always come from dealing drugs and running brothels. McMahon had made a small fortune in the heroin trade, using the old Prohibition routes to bring the drug into the United States. He had about twenty-five brothels operated by madams. He was more hands-off about those. The madams sometimes just paid him to have a building in their names, as they weren't allowed to legally own anything themselves. And, of course, he gave his brothels a heads-up when the police were going to raid them.

All that was underground, but he was openly the owner of the Roxy and several other clubs. If he hadn't been a greedy man, he could have lived well just off his clubs, because they generally did very well. Montreal had never had Prohibition, so it had become a party town for Americans. There were cars full of people looking to drink at piano bars. Since it was also a port town, it was filled with sailors. They wore white hats at the backs of their heads, and they howled away at the moon. The sailors took Montreal clap all over the world.

Because it was a sin city, there was money in entertainment, and McMahon could afford to make his clubs lavish places. He hired out-of-town acts. He even had burlesque stars. They had big asses, with ostrich feathers on them. And eyelashes so long there was nothing much they could do other than blink wistfully. They breathed fire. They spun hoops around their hips.

Rose started going to see McMahon at work. She would read a book in the corner of his office because she didn't want to spend the day alone. A girl named Poppy showed up once when Rose was over. She had curly red hair and a missing front tooth. She was a prostitute at one of the lower-end brothels that McMahon owned. She had no chest at all and was wearing a transparent shirt with no bra, as though having only two raised nipples were a selling point. She had a thin brown mustache above her lip that made it look like she'd just been drinking chocolate milk. Maybe God hadn't quite decided what sex she was going to be. She was swinging her arms around and spinning the globe in the office. When McMahon asked what the hell she wanted, she said she needed a lawyer because she'd been arrested four times in the past six months.

"It's not fair. Madame makes me go to prison for everyone."

McMahon told her that the brothels were run entirely by their mad-ams and not him. But he'd see what he could do, if she got lost right away. She nodded at him, did a quick about-face and hurried back out the door. McMahon didn't mention Poppy again—he pretended no one had walked into his office. But she had made an impression on Rose. She went to find the curly-haired whore for advice on how to not get pregnant again.

When Rose went out, she would button up her coat over her maid's outfit. It was still the only dress she had. When McMahon told her that he would buy her a dress, she got on her knees and grabbed his collar and begged him not to. She still felt much too guilty. If he bought her a dress, she would be indebted to him; she would have to do something in return and would be trapped in that life forever. Although she couldn't really put all that in words.

THE BIG CLUBS WERE ON Saint Laurent Boulevard, which had an alley running behind it, where gentlemen could leave quietly out the back door in search of a brothel. Rose went down to the side streets that shared the alley.

All the dwellings looked more or less the same. They were two-storied squat duplexes made of red bricks. They had different-colored doors. Every now and then there would be a prettier house with a balcony or a tin molding with maple leaves along the roof. Some had concrete squares next to their door, the Virgin Mary leaning forward out of them with supplicating hands.

A young mother wearing a red kerchief on her head and carrying a baby on one hip and a big cloth bag with groceries in it on the other passed Rose. There was a look of women who breast-fed while they themselves were hungry. Their skin was gray and their teeth were rotten and wiggly. A little girl trailing behind her wore a gray cotton dress with pink flowers. She wore only one sock as, presumably, there just hadn't been time to put on her second one. The child was carrying a bag of onions like it was a war buddy she was going to have to leave behind eventually. The family smelled like urine, probably because of the baby's diaper.

The women in the brothel were the only ones without children. But Rose realized, looking at their slow mannerisms, that they all seemed to be addicted to heroin. Being a woman was a trap. Something would bring you down before you turned twenty-three. The only time the world shows you any favor, or cuts you any slack, is during that very brief period of courtship where the world is trying to fuck you for the first time.

THE DUPLEXES FOR THE WHORES were usually nicer. They could afford pretty curtains and a doormat. The whores in the windows were like chocolates in an Advent calendar. The madam let Rose in. She pointed the way to Poppy's room. Rose walked down the hall and knocked on a door. It swung open and there was Poppy, wearing an undershirt and nothing else. She had a great big strawberry-blond bush and scabs on both of her knees. Rose wondered what odd sexual practice caused her to skin both her knees. Poppy looked at her visitor, trying to place her.

"Oh yeah, you're with Mac."

"My name's Rose."

Poppy gestured for Rose to come in. She slammed the door and sat down on the lumpy double bed that seemed to be made of old oatmeal, in the center of the room. There were magazines lying all over the quilt.

"You're named after a flower too."

"It's not my real name."

"Jesus, I'm not really Poppy either. Everyone goes by the name of a flower here, in case they get arrested. I've changed my name about seven times, but everyone always calls me Poppy. I guess it suits me. My real name is Sarah. I'm Jewish, if you can believe that. I make less money than all the other girls, so when the madam gets a tip that there's going to be a raid, she always hides the better-looking girls in the ceiling and lets me get arrested. I think that it has more to do with my personality than my appearance. I mean, I have naturally curly hair. Not that anybody knows that it's naturally curly because you can fake it. Maybe people aren't as impressed by curly hair as they should be."

"I think you're very pretty."

"Not that I really think that much about it at all, in the end."

"What are you reading?" Rose asked, pointing to the *Better Homes and Gardens* and *The Chatelaine* magazines on Poppy's bed.

She looked at Rose with enormous eyes, which made her look like a little kid.

"Oh, I can't read very well. I like them for the recipes. There's one for jam that I'm interested to try. I make the city's most amazing jam. Look at this."

She knelt on the bed and leaned over to pull open the door of the armoire at the foot of it. Sure enough, there was a shelf with ten jars on it.

"My jam is so good, I'd be a millionaire if I were a man. You know, there are sometimes articles in the magazines about how it's all right to be a woman. I don't know if I believe it, though. My crotch is always itchy. I get sore every time I have sex."

"What do you do for it?"

"Sit in a pot of water and pray to God."

They laughed together. They heard the girl in the next room moaning wildly.

"Be careful, sweetie, don't hurt me. I'm new to this. Ooooh, that feels so strange."

"Listen to that!" Poppy said. "Isn't she good? The men all love her. She's so pretty. She's done by four o'clock, then she goes to the penny arcade."

"Oh daddy," said the voice through the wall. "Teach me how to do it so I can show your friends when they come over."

Poppy put her hands over her mouth and exclaimed, "How does she think of that?"

"Do you get along with the other girls?" Rose asked.

"Yes. I'm good to them. I go to prison for them, and I read all the girls' fortunes. Give them advice and such. I can do yours!"

Poppy rolled across the bed as though she were rolling down a hill, fell off the other side, then jumped up and went to get the pack of cards on the bureau. Rose found Poppy so fascinating to look at, even if men didn't find her attractive. She loved how openhearted Poppy was.

"Where did you learn how to read cards?" Rose asked.

"There was an old French-Canadian woman who lived upstairs and had no legs. She showed me. She also taught me how to make jam and maple butter, and also how to swear in French. Those are, like, the only things that I know how to do well."

She shuffled the cards like a madwoman. Then she held out the deck for Rose to cut them. Rose took off the top half of the deck. Poppy flipped the card that was on top of the second half.

"The death card! You're going to wreak havoc in this world, miss."

"I didn't need cards to tell me that."

"What do you need to know?"

"Where to get condoms."

"Ha-ha-ha! That's hysterical. Let's go to the pharmacist. I only have five left, and I need them for myself."

Poppy threw on a light blue sweater and a red pleated skirt. There was a crashing sound from downstairs, undeniably the sound of a door being smashed in. Poppy looked out the window. Police officers were already hauling out two girls from the parlor downstairs.

"It's the police again! I'm not going to jail. Forget about it! Let one of the pretty girls go. Come on."

They ran out of the room and into the hallway. They ran into the bathroom. There were already two girls pulling up a ladder behind them into the crawl space.

"Come on! Let us up!"

"*Cachez-vous ailleurs.* There's no more room up here," one of the girls called down.

"Damn you."

The cops were coming up the stairs now. Poppy hurried Rose into a bedroom and pulled her into the closet. Poppy shut the door behind them, and Rose looked around to discover that they were in a tiny closet with striped green wallpaper. There was a piece of plywood at the back that Poppy pushed aside, revealing a large hole, which they promptly squeezed through. Rose put the plywood back and then turned to find that they were in another closet. This one had blue wallpaper with tiny berries on it.

They could hear the police open the door to the first closet and swish all the clothes along the clothes rail from one end to the other to make sure that nobody was in there. The coat hangers made the noise of knives being sharpened. When the police slammed shut the closet door, Rose and Poppy quietly opened the door of the closet they were in and stepped out into the room.

They were in a bedroom that looked geometrically identical to the one they had just left. Its decor was the opposite, however. It was dingy and the wallpaper on one wall was different from that on the other. There was a frame with a painting of an old woman with a long neck and no chin, like an ostrich. The linoleum didn't have any flowers on it.

There was a child's bed with a swan painted on the frame. They climbed out the window. They went down the fire escape and into the backyard.

"Well, what do we do now?"

"We go on about our business like nothing happened. Let's get those condoms. One second, though."

Poppy opened the door to a shed made of corrugated iron at the end of the yard. There was a small wire chicken coop with a hen sitting in it.

"I have my money hidden here. And I've also got my trusty getaway roller skates! There's an extra pair for you. Try them on."

Poppy came out holding a pair of roller skates in either hand. They strapped the roller skates to their shoes. They were still so young, after all. They were only twenty years old. They laughed, even though it was the so-called Depression. Poppy was much more adept at roller skating than Rose was. She had to grab Poppy's arm several times. They rolled out of the alley and careered onto the street.

Poppy was swirling around the people. A lot of them were annoyed, as though Poppy were the world's most irritating bee. Rose flung herself around a lamppost to catch herself from falling, but she was getting the knack of it quickly. In their roller skates they felt fearless. They felt like they were moving at the speed of light. By the time anybody could figure out the girls, they would already be gone.

They passed a fat woman in a green velvet jacket sitting on a chair, playing accordion, a hat in front of her. She was playing "The Accordion Waltz." She was just playing the last bars of the tune. They began to dance with each other. Poppy executed an elaborate move. She put her arms akimbo and kicked her legs up in the air, doing a cancan of sorts. Rose tried to imitate her and fell on her ass. They laughed and laughed.

They tried to spin around while holding hands and they both fell forward, landing hard on their knees. Now Rose understood why Poppy had scratches and scabs on her legs. It wasn't from making love but from horsing around on roller skates. Poppy breathed on Rose's skinned knee. Her breath on the cut felt so cold. It was as though Poppy had suddenly blown all the clothes off her body.

Her body was made out of sugar. If she stood in the rain, she would dissolve.

Poppy told her to wait outside the tiny drugstore and ran in to get the condoms. She hopped up the step and glided right in. She had the paper bag tucked in her pocket as she exited the store.

"Do you want to go to the movies? If you ever want to see a movie, you should go to the Savoy Theater," Poppy said. "They have the best pianist in the city there. He's really good-looking—he gives me the chills. Although maybe you don't like the chills?"

They took another route home for fun. They passed a long row of people in line for a soup kitchen. They passed in front of the brothel and the door was boarded up. Poppy didn't want to go in. If the madam was still there, she would be infuriated with Poppy.

"I'm going to get in so much trouble for this. I should have just got arrested. I've done that so many times before. I'd be released in a couple of hours. Who cares?"

Poppy pulled her curls straight up with both hands out of frustration.

"Why don't you come with me?" Rose asked.

"Are you crazy? Do you think that McMahon would let a girl like me come anywhere near his personal life? Then you don't know the man you're having sex with. Oh, never mind. It isn't your problem."

"Well, where do you want to go?"

"Why don't you come down to Chinatown?" Poppy asked. "We can get high together. It'll be my treat. It's quite lovely. That always makes me forget about my problems."

"No, I don't want to get mixed up in that."

"I've been doing heroin since I was fourteen. I never get hooked on it. You can do it once in a while if you want to."

Poppy lifted up her skirt to show Rose that she had track marks on her thighs.

"Are most of the girls on drugs?"

Poppy screwed up one eye, pretending she was giving it some considered thought.

"Yes. Tulip overdosed last month. She was really pretty. She was only working at the brothel for three months. She started to get so stoned. She went out on the street corner naked and started blowing kisses! She woke up blue one day. It's a better way to go than Magnolia. She cried all the time. She jumped off the roof. You think it's easier than working at a laundry because you can go out on Sunday nights and read magazines, but it's not. You never make any money. You can't save up because you have to spend all your money on rent and their crummy food. It's all a big swindle. Gets some of the girls too down."

This was how McMahon made all that money, Rose thought. This was what paid for his mansion and his big meals and his cars and his clubs. This was what his flashy universe looked like backstage.

"Do you want to get out of there?" Rose asked.

"They're going to kick me out, and I don't know what I'll do. I met McMahon when I was fifteen. I was cuter then. Just because I make less money than the other girls doesn't mean I'm worth nothing, you know?"

They were both working for McMahon. That was why Rose had gone to her. Not only for birth control but to see who she actually was, who she would be when her currency on the dating market plummeted. Rose unbuckled her roller skates and handed them back to Poppy.

"Will you come back and have your fortune read?" Poppy asked.

"Yes, I promise."

Rose walked for a few steps, then spun around, came back and squeezed her mouth up against Poppy's in a kiss. Then she ran off.

"The condoms! The condoms! The condoms!" the curly-haired girl called out after Rose.

24

POPPY SINGS A LOVE SONG

Poppy had been kicked out of the brothel for that day with Rose. She had been robbed and raped a few days later while turning a trick on the street corner. She had two black eyes and a little bandage on the bridge of her nose when she ran into Pierrot again. He had been sleeping in the park and had a couple of twigs in his hair but seemed to be doing better than her. She was like an injured deer. She knew that violent men were watching her every move. She knew they only acted the way they did in secret, with only women and children witnessing their actions. She wanted to walk down the street and not be murdered. When she saw Pierrot, she remembered he owed her a favor.

"I want you to pretend to be my pimp," Poppy told Pierrot. "I always feel I'm in danger because I don't have a husband or a boyfriend. You don't have to do anything. You just have to exist."

"Thank you. I will try to live up to your expectations."

"Oh, I haven't set them very high at all. You've got that fancy suit. People will think that you're a pimp. They'll leave you alone. They'll assume you're crazy and that you have a gun."

She found a small room in a cheap hotel. It had blue wallpaper. She had cut some photographs of movie stars out of the newspaper and stuck them on the wall above her bed frame. She said they didn't have to touch each other. She said he could stay in the same bed as her because it was convenient. She had a black ribbon tied around her neck.

"Your ribbon is pretty but odd. I keep thinking that if I untied it your head would roll right off."

After he said this, Pierrot looked rather terrified.

The mattress was lumpy. She left on her undershirt and tights at his request. Her tights were white with brown stripes, like the wallpaper in a basement that had been flooded often. She couldn't sleep all night because she was so excited. Pierrot fell asleep right away.

In the alley below, a raccoon dragged his tail behind him like a kid pulling along its favorite blanket.

PIERROT ASKED HER ONCE how many men she had slept with. She stuck out her arms in front of her, her fists closed. She then opened and closed her hands in rapid succession, the fingers spread out wide, like a child's drawing of a sun that has a bunch of lines for rays.

He had trouble counting how many times she did this. He wasn't sure whether it was five or six. And then she ended with three fingers stuck in front of her.

He knew she was exact about the figure because she believed that if you kept track of how many people you slept with, then you weren't a prostitute. You were some sort of Casanova. It was a philosophical stance. Or perhaps it was a scientific stance.

WHILE PIERROT SWEPT UP POPCORN and played the piano at the movie theater, Poppy would go out and pick up men on the street corner. She tried not to make conversation, because they might see her teeth and try to find another girl. She just smiled demurely. She would do a little swirl and hold up her coat at the back, as she had been told that her ass was her best feature. She had a little bottle of Lysol. She would mix it with water and then douche with it in the evening to kill what the men had left inside her. She still had her high heels on. They were boots that laced up to her knees. The heroin made her so lazy that she couldn't take them off for days. She used more when she was with Pierrot. She was able to quit when she wanted to, or go for days without it, unlike Pierrot. He needed it every single day, which was very expensive.

Poppy had a million other ways of making money too. She had become quite well known in the neighborhood for reading tarot cards. She made baked beans with black-market brown sugar over a hot plate in their room and sold them in the neighborhood. If you ate a bowl, all your problems in the world seemed so insignificant. You might have a belly-ache the next morning, of course. Poppy was the type of girl who provided temporary solutions. Perhaps that was why the teeth had rotted out of her head. She was the personification of dessert, wasn't she?

She pushed a baby carriage all around the city. Every time she got back to the hotel and pulled it clinking up the stairs, the carriage would be filled with all sorts of amazing things. But never a baby, of course. She had some perfume bottles that she got from the dumpster of a beauty parlor that was going out of business. She filled them with gin she'd made in the bathtub. She gave people a one-cent discount when they brought back the old bottle for her to refill.

She went door to door selling old clothes. She once got into a fist-fight with another Jewish peddler who was also going door to door selling clothes in the same neighborhood. She was so mad at him that she stayed up all night cursing him, until Pierrot suggested she stop. She showed Pierrot some of the baby clothes she was trying to sell. There was even a tiny black suit for a little boy to wear to a funeral. This was the closest they had ever got to romance. They slept in the same bed but didn't have sex.

. . .

THEY LOOKED LIKE A COUPLE. They both had the harried look of people who had come of age during the Depression. Their youth was the only thing that was keeping them from being total bums. Their youth was like the last dollar in their pockets. They were fairly attractive. Or, they would have been attractive if they had more to eat.

POPPY HAD some very appealing qualities. For instance, she could bend forward at the waist at a ninety-degree angle while saying silly pleasantries to you.

"I'm not going out tonight," she said one evening.

She sat on the side of the bed. She had on a bustier to prop up her small breasts. She had on some garter belts. She had on a pair of old underwear. She spread her legs. She tilted her head. She was trying to pose in a suggestive way.

She had washed all her underclothes by hand with soap so they would smell nice. And she had put some effort into her hair as well. A lot of people said she had an unusual color of hair. She washed it and fixed the curls around her face.

She wasn't going to be paid for this. What was she doing it for, then? She was taking the very dangerous and risky move: exchanging her time for love. She wanted Pierrot to love her.

She and Pierrot had a good thing going on because they were surviving. She was worried that he would leave because the relationship wasn't consummated. She thought he would owe her something if she let him sleep with her.

Pierrot stared at Poppy's provocative outfit, which didn't excite him in the least. There were so many holes in her stockings that they looked like oil paint on water. And her blue bustier was missing buttons up the front.

She winked at him saucily, like a doll with an eye that didn't close properly. He sort of felt he should act more like a man. He asked her to bend down and show him her ass.

He kept a little postcard tucked away behind the cupboard in the bathroom. It was of a pair of naked ladies and a man locked in a ménage à trois. It always gave him a hard-on. He looked at it and then wandered into the other room with his eyes shut, looking in the darkness for those two women.

He closed his eyes tight and pushed his penis into Poppy. She yelled out in surprise and delight that it was finally happening.

Pierrot was thinking of flying foxes. He was imagining peeking into peepholes at girls changing out of wet bathing suits. He imagined they were the Dionne quintuplets and he was making love to all of them. They would fight for their chance to go first. They would yell at Pierrot that he had already made love to that particular quint and that she was actually coming back for seconds.

Poppy thought about all the gin in the bathtub. She had been thinking about what they would eat for dinner. She was thinking about who owed her money. She was thinking about a little gosling she had chased around the backyard in her rubber boots when she was little, for just a moment, and then she went back to thinking stressful thoughts. It's sort of impossible to be absentminded and vacant and daydreamy during sex. You are either enjoying it intensely or you are in a state of high stress.

Pierrot had a fantasy about making love to a housewife up against the meat counter. She held her little number in her hand. He was trying to come before the butcher got to that number and called it. Because she would be distracted and tell him to get the hell out of there. He wasn't even sure what that fantasy meant. It had something to do with the Great Depression, though. For whatever reason, it made him burst inside Poppy before he could withdraw.

When he was done and lying next to her, he did take a long look at her face. There was something so affable about it that he gave her a big kiss on the cheek.

When he was making love to a girl, in his mind he made love to about thirty-three girls on average. He felt guilty that he had to do this with Poppy. She didn't cross his mind once while he was having sex with her. Although he hadn't been with any woman since they had met, he felt as though he were cheating on her now. He felt terrible.

But when he was done, he shot up and stopped caring. He closed his eyes and fell asleep in the chair with a cigarette in his hand. The ash of the cigarette grew and resembled the trunk of an elephant.

POPPY FOUND A RING in one of the coat pockets she was rummaging through. She was happy. She put it on her left hand. It had a blue glass stone the color of blue eyes that had been crying. She figured people would assume that she and Pierrot were married.

At one point Poppy was bragging to the neighbors about how Pierrot was so possessive of her—he would never let her talk to any other man. He felt that Poppy was tricking him into becoming some horrible version of a man that he had no interest in being. He knew this was what she believed love was and that she was just trying to be normal, but he didn't like it at all. It seemed sordid to him. He felt bad about himself all the time.

He did like to make her laugh nonetheless. She would toss back her head and open her mouth and reveal the terrible brown mess in there. They had a jar of money. They kept saving up money so they could buy some new teeth for Poppy. But then every time the money got to the top of the jar, they would spend it on heroin. She would hold up a warm rag to her face the next morning and really regret her actions.

What could be more darling in a woman than regret?

HE FELT THEY WERE never quite meant to be together. Pierrot's old infatuation with Rose started popping up. He used his love for Rose as an excuse never to commit to anybody, and now he used it to find fault with Poppy. She was kind of crass, wasn't she? When she was thinking up a solution, she would sometimes stick her hand down the front of her pants. She would burp while she was eating. She always stuck her tongue way out at the side of her mouth when she was doing a chore. She was obsessive. Poppy had all these piles of rags in the living room. She was going through them and sorting them. The bottoms of her feet were black. She was holding her breasts in two hands. "Tits for sale!" she yelled out.

ONE NIGHT he had to leave the room for a while and get away from Poppy. And on the same night, on the other side of town, Rose left her hotel, wanting to escape the room McMahon rented for her. Pierrot's coat collar was pulled up so you could only see the top of his head. Rose had her fur hat down over her eyes so just the bottom half of her face was visible. Pierrot leaped back quickly as the trolley rang its bell at him and then surged by. Rose stopped at a streetlight as a car rumbled past the tips of her toes. Pierrot lit a cigarette. Rose inhaled from her cigarette. Pierrot exhaled smoke rings. Rose let white swirls escape from her nose. Pierrot tossed the cigarette onto the ground. Rose ground the cigarette with the sole of her shoe. Pierrot stopped to look at a mannequin wearing a pink dress in the window of a store on the west end of Saint Catherine Street. Rose stopped to look at a mannequin wearing a black suit in the window of a store at the east end of Saint Catherine Street.

"Are you there?" Rose said aloud.

"I'm here," Pierrot said to himself. "Where are you?"

"It's funny how often I think about you," Rose said. "I still miss having you in my life."

"Did you see the movie *All the Pretty Girls Live in Paris*? I thought it was so stupid. You would have laughed so much at it. I wish we could have laughed about it together."

"Remember those pink cupcakes with silver balls on them we ate at that mansion? Those were so delicious. I keep trying pink cupcakes to find ones that taste just like them. But I never can."

"Do you still read books? I wish you could tell me about all the things that depressed ladies in books are saying."

"Do you still play piano? I've never heard anyone play the way you do. There was a recording by a Hungarian pianist. There was something about the way she played that reminded me of you."

"I saw a kitten trying to catch the bottom of a curtain and it reminded me of you dancing."

"Did you fall in love with somebody?" Rose asked.

"Does your sweetheart look like me?" Pierrot asked.

"Do you like coffee? Or ice cream? Are you able to afford ice cream?"

"Are you having a hard time these days, like everybody else?"

"Do you remember when we used to pretend to be on a train next to each other?"

"Do you remember how you told me that unicorns were absolutely real?" Rose asked. "And that you thought you saw one out by the chicken coop?"

"Did you ever love me? You don't have to say. It's an embarrassing question. I'm just curious."

Rose sighed and turned around and walked back home. Pierrot sighed and decided to return to his room. Rose climbed up the stairs slowly. Pierrot stepped over someone sleeping in the hallway. Rose pulled her key out of her purse. Pierrot fumbled with the lock. Rose took off her hat. Pierrot shrugged off his jacket and left it behind him on the chair. Rose kicked off her shoes. Pierrot unlaced his boots and pulled them off. There were holes in the heels of Rose's tights. One of Pierrot's big toes was sticking out of its sock. Rose turned on the radio. Pierrot turned the dial to *Late Night Music for Restless Moonlight Listeners*. If she could, Rose never missed an episode of it. It was Pierrot's favorite show by far.

Rose clapped her hands when a song called "You're Not My Sweetheart" came on. Pierrot forgot about his problems when he heard this song. Rose felt the singer's voice sounded so familiar. Pierrot thought he himself could have written the words to the song. When the words came on, Rose began to sing along. Pierrot couldn't help but join in:

> *I don't like the way you wear your hat.*
> *I can't stand the way you hum to tunes.*
> *I don't like the way you laugh.*
> *I never liked the way you sing.*
> *So how come I get all crazy when you come around?*

All over the city, in living rooms and kitchens and bedrooms, and on factory floors, people burst out into the chorus:

> *Boom, boom, boom goes my heart, boom, boom, boom.*
> *Boom, boom, boom goes my heart, boom, boom, boom.*
> *Boom, boom, boom goes my heart, boom, boom, boom.*

⋅⊰ 25 ⊱⋅

THE CAT THIEF
IN THE NURSERY

Poppy always paid for the heroin. By the time he was twenty-one, Pierrot couldn't afford to get high every night with the pittance he was making being an usher and playing the piano on random nights. Poppy knew this too. The more he was dependent on heroin, the more he was dependent on her. Poppy's pet projects and prostitution alone certainly couldn't support Pierrot's growing addiction. She sometimes had trouble making any money at all. Men preferred the brothels. There was something about Poppy that made them all feel a little bit sad. They couldn't forget that they were paying for sex. She never seemed to have repeat customers. Whoever made love to her always seemed overcome by guilt that lasted, like a hangover, for three days.

Pierrot decided he would be a thief. He didn't have an elaborate inner debate over whether it was right or wrong. He had spent the last few years up in the mansions in Westmount, and he knew very well that they were loaded with fantastic items, most of which the owners didn't have a need for. There was such an enormous discrepancy between the rich and the poor that he felt he was in some ways providing society with a much-needed redistribution of wealth. He ought to be thanked for his actions. Of course, it was only he and Poppy who benefited from this redistribution, but that seemed like a rather minor hole in his economic theory. He had never been to university, so nobody could expect him to be Friedrich Engels.

Pierrot would leave his shoes outside the windows of the houses before he crawled inside. He preferred to creep into the houses while the occupants were at home, as they were less likely to have locked up. He would stand in his stocking feet, looking at the paintings in the long hallways as though he were a connoisseur in a museum appraising a traveling exhibition.

He was fond of taking paintings. They were quite light. All the French aristocrats with their big wigs looked like they had just stepped out of bubble baths. He chose what he believed to be the best painting and took it home. He would place the painting—and whatever trinkets had tickled his fancy—into his suitcase, put his shoes back on and saunter off down the street.

In his remarkable tailored suit he never attracted attention to himself, despite it being worn out and mended by Poppy. No one could imagine that his home was anywhere but this elite neighborhood. He was also a familiar face to the police officers. They didn't know his name, but they felt quite sure that they had seen him growing up around there.

The pawn dealer was always impressed by Pierrot's perspicuity when it came to selecting the paintings. He always plucked incredible works of art, the most valuable pieces in the collection. Yet he was unaware ahead of time of the priceless possessions in the houses he entered.

He crawled up a trellis one evening and climbed gently and quietly into an open window on the second floor. Pierrot put his black-stockinged toes on the carpeted floor, stood up against the wall and took a moment to ascertain where in the world he had found himself.

To his surprise, he was in a room whose walls were covered with a mural of mountains with sheep running across them. There were numerous astral bodies floating around his head. How peculiar to have Jupiter floating just inches away from him. He could reach out and touch it with his finger.

He looked down at the green carpet at his feet. He was surrounded by a flock of miniature sheep and cows and horses. How was it that he had found himself a giant?

Then he looked across the room and saw a very small bed in the middle. Ah, he was in a nursery. He was immediately calmed, then alarmed again when he noticed a small boy had sat up in the bed and was looking right at him. What could he do? His fate lay in the hands of an emotionally volatile and unpredictable child.

He smiled at the child. The child smiled back. He stood on his hands and walked across the room. The child rolled out of the bed as nimbly as Pierrot could do any trick.

Pierrot froze in one spot. Then he began to walk around the room with awkward, stilted steps. He looked like a mechanical doll. He moved as though each of his joints was stiff. There was no fluidity in his movements. But there was an awkward grace to it—as seen in giraffes that ambled about on the plains. The child laughed and laughed.

The boy brought him a tiny top that had on it yellow horses with flowing manes. When the top was spun, the horses became a shooting star whizzing through space at an extraordinary trajectory.

The child insisted that Pierrot take it. "It is for you, Peter Pan," the child whispered. Pierrot took the boy's hand and led him back to bed. And tucked him in. He juggled three colorful beanbags until the child squeezed his wee eyes together, his cheeks grew into round peaceful globes and he fell fast asleep.

IT TURNED OUT that the top was a treasure from the Byzantine Empire. The fence knew that although Pierrot had an extraordinary esthetic sense, he was clueless when it came to money or economic worth. And so for the Byzantine treasure, which had been twirled by the hand of empresses and would be cherished by any museum in the world, he gave Pierrot three dollars. Pierrot couldn't believe that he had been given so much money for a simple top. When he went home, he and Poppy rejoiced. It was enough money to remain high for two weeks. At one point one of Poppy's socks slipped off and they were unable to find it. That was the most eventful thing that happened during those weeks.

Pierrot fell asleep in the chair, his limbs hanging every which way, like a marionette that had just been abandoned.

26

THE GIRL WHO CRIED
"MARCO POLO"

On Christmas Day McMahon made an excuse to be away from the family for a couple of hours so that he could stop by and deliver a parcel to Rose. He said he had to go visit some charities, and nobody in the family questioned this.

When he arrived, he found Rose sitting on the end of her bed, weeping. She said it was the only time of year during which she got nostalgic. She told him about how she had liked performing at different people's houses with a young boy. They would dance across the carpets on tippytoe. Everyone around them would be so enchanted, they were overcome by rapture. The boy was a very talented pianist.

He had narrowly managed to keep his wife from going to the orphanage and reuniting these two. The very mention of the boy gave him a start and made him angry. He had taken her away from the governess job to get her away from him. He worked very hard not to roll his eyes when she claimed the boy was talented. He could only imagine what sort of ridiculous tunes he would be able to pick out. He felt sure that if Rose were to see this boy again, she would be utterly disillusioned. He was keeping Rose in the lap of luxury, and there wasn't another orphan in the world experiencing the same treatment. This delicate boy she spoke of was probably working at a factory. He had become hard. He was uneducated. Whatever bit of knowledge he had picked up in school with the nuns had no doubt been unlearned. Rose wouldn't even be able to have a conversation with him. McMahon was sure of that.

"When we went to the rich people's houses, they sometimes gave us warm clothes. Once the boy I traveled with was given a scarf that was much too long. It went around and around and around his neck. He looked as though his head were being engulfed by a huge boa constrictor."

Rose laughed. McMahon had an urge to slap her. He gave her his presents. He handed her red carnations. For some reason they looked to her like tissues that had been held up to a bloody nose. He presented her with a box of Turkish delight. The candies resembled slugs amassed on a dead thing. He gave her a black corset that looked like a cage. She thanked him and spread them out on the bed around her. She smiled. But her smile kept slipping down, like old stockings that wouldn't stay up. "I honestly can't tell you why I'm thinking about him all of a sudden. Silly, really."

ROSE ACCEPTED her role as a mistress. What else could she do? She was twenty-one years old. There was a Depression going on. Rose felt like a possession now. There was something that was capitalistic about her sense of self-worth. Things about her had definite currency: her jokes, her laughing at his jokes, her smiles, her hair, her sitting next to him in a booth in a tiny restaurant, her eating a grilled-cheese sandwich next to him—these things had a price. She ought to be keeping a receipt book to itemize her expenses.

McMahon sent her shopping at the giant department store. She went first to buy underwear in the lingerie department. She began her make-over right at the bottom. Like when you make a pencil sketch on the canvas before you put down the thick coat of oil paint.

She took off her woolen tights. They had been mended so many times. Her underwear was shabby and kind of loose. She had an undershirt that had been taken advantage of by a moth. There was a little hole that her

HEATHER O'NEILL

right nipple popped out of. She wasn't used to seeing herself in a full-length mirror, but there she was.

McMahon said seeing her in her old underwear was like taking the wrapper off a candy and finding a little stone underneath it instead of a sweet. She tried on some pink underwear the color of rose petals, made of silk. They were so cold they sent a chill through her. When you were wearing undergarments like that, it was important to hurl yourself into someone else's arms to warm up. She got a pile in her size.

She stopped to smell all the different perfumes. They were in round bottles. She wanted one that smelled just like her name. Everyone always said that she smelled just like roses. She thought that might be the power of suggestion. There was one bottle that smelled as if it had a hundred rotting roses crammed inside it. That was the one she chose.

She bought seven dresses, one for each day of the week. She had a dark blue one with a white belt that sat just below her waist. She got a pair of long white gloves that went up to her elbows, to accompany the dress. That was her favorite of the outfits, and she asked to wear it home. Everyone nodded at her as she walked up the stairs as though she were a lady, which she supposed that now she somehow was.

She fell asleep for a second while the saleswoman was slipping her feet into various shoes. She woke up as the saleswoman was crying out about how absolutely marvelous a pair of pink high heels were.

Rose quite loved the idea of being warm, and perhaps not having to wear two dozen layers of clothes. She remembered once, when she was little, stuffing a sock in her pocket to puff up her jacket in an attempt to insulate herself against the cold. She asked to be taken to the very warmest clothes. They led her to an elevator, which was a golden prison cell. There was a woman with a light blue pillbox hat inside, pulling the up and down levers. She brought Rose right up to the eighth floor, where the fur coats were. Rose chose herself a white mink coat to go with her old white hat, which was the only thing she had that looked fancy enough to keep.

She stopped at the bookstore on the way home. She bought herself a Russian novel. She stopped at the ice cream counter. She ordered herself a root beer float. She sipped at it as she read her Russian novel. She was content because she got to read. Maybe it wasn't so bad.

She stood in her underwear with all her different outfits lying on the bed. As though she were a paper doll.

MCMAHON CAME TO HER ROOM at the Darling Hotel. He held the two brandy glasses in his hand as if he were fondling breasts. She told him to take off all his clothes. Her favorite thing about him was just how fat he was. Whereas his wife would always say he was a pig and would beg him to lose weight, Rose loved how it felt to be squished underneath him. And she loved how it felt to be on top, riding him. Like he was a giant bear.

They still had very wonderful sex. It was sex unlike McMahon had ever had anywhere else and, for this reason, he would never leave her. He would probably have her shot if she tried to leave him.

He gave her a necklace with a single round pearl as a pendant. The pearl looked like the moon through a peephole.

ROSE WASN'T WORRIED ABOUT the children. She knew they were doing fine without her. In fact, they were probably doing much better. With her, it was as though they were at a birthday party every day of their lives. But she missed them.

Rose chose presents for McMahon to bring home to the children. The children believed they were seeing another secret and charming side of their father in these gifts. He knew them better than they thought. Perhaps he, not their mother, was the more loving parent. He brought the girl a globe of the moon, with all the names of its major craters written on it, which was phosphorescent and glowed in the dark. He brought the boy a golden toy poodle whose body was shaved, but it still had heaps of curls on its head so that it looked like a lion.

. . .

HE WOULD GO REGULARLY ON Thursday night for dinner at the Roxy. This was the event of the week, to which all the members of the underworld showed up with their mistresses.

McMahon was worried about Rose's performance at this dinner. They were not like events where you showed up with your wife. You had an excuse for your wife. You were contractually, legally bound to wives. They often changed their personality and physical appearance after having children. You never quite knew who you were marrying when you got married. Sometimes your wife turned out to be a dud, and there wasn't really anything you could do about it. She might have looked from the outside like somebody attractive and easygoing but then became ugly.

But a girlfriend was a different matter because she was someone you could update and change. She reflected the type of girl you could get on that day, at that hour. Everyone always knew that mistresses were only interested in your wealth and status, so they were your price tag, so to speak. They were like flashy cars, or incredibly expensive suits.

Rose was in the lobby of the hotel, waiting for him, on Thursday night. She wore a purple beret with a pom-pom on it. She had a matching purple jacket. She had on a black skirt. She had a pair of peach high heels with three buckles that went right up her ankles. She had her arms spread, and she was waltzing around the room with an imaginary partner. When he called her name, she stopped. She released her invisible beau. She made a tiny bow as though to dismiss her partner.

"Who were you dancing with?" he asked.

"Who do you think? You know. My friend the bear."

He didn't say anything but led her to the car. He warned her not to tell his friends about having been found under a tree. Most of the mistresses had completely invented their pasts. It was the polite thing to do. Nobody in the world wanted to know your sob story. What were they supposed to do once you told them? Go ahead and react to it? Nobody wanted to be reminded of poverty on a Thursday night. Thursday night was all about spending money.

They arrived at the restaurant, and the men and their women were already there. The women were supposed to say superficial things that did not cause you to reflect on what they had just said. They were just supposed to defer to being attractive. His accountant Desmond's new girl was a perfect mistress. She was some sort of showgirl, apparently from Louisiana. She had enormous breasts and laughed at everything that everyone said, and her hair was in perfect finger waves that ended just at her chin. She only asked questions that allowed people to warble on about themselves. She only talked about things that were easy to talk about.

Rose and McMahon were a strange-looking couple to begin with, just on a physical level. They were such an odd couple that they were almost charming. It seemed impossible that he could make love to her without crushing her and yet here she was, alive and well. You couldn't help but imagine mismatched couples having sex. Everybody at the table stopped talking to look at them.

"Hello, everybody!" Rose said, determined to fit in. "Pleased to meet you all in this splendid environment. We just saw some showgirls walking in, and they were fabulous."

She was introduced to everyone at the table. She gave each person a fantastic and gracious hello and managed to say something that delighted each person she spoke to.

"Oh, I love your nose! It's wonderful."

"I hear you own horses. I can see that somehow. You look like a man who owns a hundred horses."

"Are you the one who's trying to get into movies? I knew that right away just by looking at you."

"Oh no, don't worry, I'm coming over to you. You don't have to walk over to me. I heard that you gave a huge donation to the children's hospital. How do you even walk around? Your heart must be so enormous. It must weigh about a hundred pounds."

"The funny one!"

"I heard you like to read. You are like the intellectual of the group. You'll have to recommend some books to me."

"*On me dit que vous chantez merveilleusement.* Everyone says I have to hear you sing."

"What a fantastic dress. You have natural style. You have to be born with that, you know. I personally am just lucky if I don't put my clothes on inside out."

They weren't sure at first whether Rose was really pretty at all. But as soon as she was done going around the table, they all were sure she was beautiful.

ROSE TOLD EVERYONE that she would like to be excused to go to the bathroom. She hurried to the back of the club and into the washroom. She gave the attendant a nickel and sat down on the toilet lid. She put her knees together, her feet out to the sides. She put her elbows on her knees and her face in her hands and started to weep. What a horrific job it was to be a mistress. You didn't get to be yourself ever, and you had to perform unrelentingly. You had no security. You could be discarded like trash at any moment. She missed Pierrot violently. He had loved her for who she was. Hadn't he? She remembered a time when they were in the field working on the garden. He passed by her. He had a daisy tucked behind his ear. He winked at her. She was sure he was telling her that he loved her. Perhaps she was being naive. She had to admit that everyone sings for their supper.

WHEN ROSE WAS COMING BACK from the bathroom, she stopped on the dance floor, watching as the band set up. The drummer, seeing her, began to warm up by beating a tune on his drum. Rose started hopping to the rhythm. She looked down at her feet as though they were acting of their own accord. As though they wanted her to dance.

The drummer stopped playing and Rose stopped dancing. She smiled and started walking back to her seat. The drummer saw her and started back up. And in response, Rose's feet started getting all wild again. They started doing an out-of-control quickstep, kicking up in the air and dancing her about the dance floor. She was waving her hands all over the place. Her feet were making no sense at all, and her body was twisting in all sorts of directions. She kicked her legs up to the side, so high they seemed to almost hit her ears. She was so flexible and lithe. She had a body capable of expressing joy.

The band quickly caught on. They joined in. They all played wildly, whipping the girl into a frenzy, and then stopped abruptly, allowing her to walk to the edge of the dance floor before starting again.

The whole of the club wanted to join in. Patrons rushed to the dance floor. They danced like they were possessed by the devil, and then froze like funny statues once the music stopped.

McMahon watched her carefully. He had been cautious about getting involved with a girl who had such a lowly background and a loathsome pedigree. But she had the whole room transfixed. He was proud of her for being so wild and lovely. None of the other mistresses could compete. He was going to take her everywhere and show her off. She was the type of treat a man like him could afford. And at that moment, McMahon let himself fall deeply in love with her. Rose saw McMahon looking at her and returned his gaze. She felt a wave of affection for him. It was the serenity of being possessed.

When she sat down, one of the mistresses asked if she'd ever been onstage.

"I always wanted to be a clown when I grew up."

"Really? But why?"

"Well, some of the children must want to be clowns. Otherwise, how would clowns exist?"

"I guess I always thought people were just born clowns. Or maybe their parents were clowns and they had no other choice."

"So when they were very little, their mother put face paint on them? They went to school with their faces painted white, and with shoes that were too big for them?"

"Oh! That's so sad!"

"Rose, don't make everybody cry, please," McMahon said, and everyone laughed.

Later Rose asked the waiter to bring her six eggs.

"Please, please, please. Don't cook them or scramble them or anything! And I swear I'll give them right back."

"It's fine," McMahon said to the waiter. "Tell them they're for Mr. McMahon."

The waiter came back with a carton with six eggs in it. He placed the carton in front of her on the table as though he were sending the eggs off to a tragic death. Rose put her hand on the waiter's to reassure him.

She took three eggs and began to juggle, then took out a fourth and set it in motion, then a fifth and a sixth. She was as confident as Jupiter that those eggs would orbit around her. She did it so daintily that it was as if, each time she touched an egg, she was putting a magic spell on it. For a moment everyone around the table understood that magic absolutely existed. Every day the average person will witness six miracles. But it isn't that we don't believe in miracles—we just don't believe that miracles are miracles. There are so many miracles all around us.

ROSE LOVED THE ROXY. She loved to see all the people crowding into the nightclub. She loved the dancing and the smoking. She became friends with all the band members. And they would let her ding the triangle or smash the cymbals. Performers were always fond of her, which was one of the things McMahon liked the most about her.

There was something so generous about her personality. She spent her personality wildly. She spent her personality like a man on a winning streak in a casino. She tossed her personality out onto the table recklessly—like poker chips.

She was loud as a child, and she liked to be loud as an adult. She liked to say things that made other people burst out laughing and shouting. Not only did she like to be loud, but she liked everybody else to be loud too. She liked to be in places where the music was turned up, because it gave her an excuse to shout.

She liked to get up close to people when she was talking to them. Her breasts were often pressed up against the other person. She always acted as if they were squashed in a little elevator together. But after a night at the Roxy, Rose would always feel more and more alone.

ROSE PASSED A TREE in the park that was growing to the side so much that it was almost parallel to the ground. It was like a consumptive young lady reclining on a chair. The leaves were like poems that had fallen to the ground.

Since there was always an audience in Montreal, the venues could bring in any sort of act and it would sell out. The better cabarets had all the singers from the United States and Europe. The marquees were always bragging about what out-of-town *vedette* was going to be in their club. Rose went to see a touring American jazz band in a club downtown. A slender black woman in a white dress, wearing burgundy lipstick, and with wild curls piled up on her head, came out to center stage and stood behind the microphone. She opened her mouth and wailed a joyful, sorrowful tune. She sang louder and deeper with each refrain. And when she went low, she went so low. It was like she had eaten three men for breakfast to get her voice to sound that masculine. Her voice seemed too big for her body. It seemed too big for anyone's body. What she did with her voice seemed dangerous. Like when a surge of electricity passes through faulty wiring and burns the whole building to the ground. She wasn't afraid to see all the things that singing could do. What guts! Rose thought. She was proof that a woman could take as much from life as a man.

ROSE WAS IMPRESSED by the way McMahon did business. He got to be engaged in intellectual endeavors all the time. He and Desmond would sit and pore over all his books together. His desk was cluttered with plans. It seemed magical to her. You were able to make these plans at your desk, and the plans came to pass in the world. Just as with God at the very beginning, when the universe was nothing but a great desk and a blotter.

Everybody who gathered around McMahon's desk was always serious. They were always worried. What they did mattered. Without them, crime would become chaotic. They had the difficult, important task of overseeing drugs, gambling and sex. Those were what made a city a city. They made it human. Rose was very much attracted to the power and importance of the underworld.

When McMahon and Rose were at the hotel, she asked about the Roxy's books, about the gambling halls, about the liquor licenses; she asked about booking acts; she wanted to know about the dancers' true stories. She wanted to know about rents. She got to know the politicians and the police chiefs. And what made McMahon ever more frustrated: they seemed to be taking her seriously. They were forgetting that she was a girl!

He brought her along to a meeting with his business associates. They had brought their wives too. Whenever she asked a question, it was always to the men at the table, and it was always business related. She was curious about who did what.

"Do you move the gambling hall every time it's raided, or do you pay the fine and set up shop again?"

"How much is the lease for a theater? How much did you pay for the circus troupe you had from Moscow?"

He hated that she was asking questions like that. She was interested in their clubs. Everything was a little crooked, so these questions weren't supposed to be asked in the open. But it was more than that. She shouldn't be involving herself in his affairs. There was no possible reason for her to know these types of things.

"YOU MAKE THE MEN UNCOMFORTABLE when you talk about business shit."

"I've always been able to make people laugh. I want to be an organizer. Can I book some of the shows that come in? I mean, not right away, but I would like to work my way up if that is at all possible. I think the most amazing thing would be to travel. You know, I could travel through Italy, going to all the different circuses there and finding the really interesting performers. Like a strongman in Romania."

"Where do you even get these ideas?"

"I've read about them in books, of course."

"Of course you have. You shouldn't read so many ridiculous books. It isn't healthy."

"You were a poor kid and you went and built a fortune. You spent your whole life figuring out how to become something you were not."

McMahon squinted his eyes at her for a moment, then shrugged her off. It was beneath him to compare their life stories.

THE DEPRESSION WAS AFFECTING EVERYONE. Rose went to speak to Antoine, the booking agent of the club, one afternoon. He often went down to New York City to find the best acts. He was known for it. He was a middle-aged man with a jet-black toupee and enormous teeth that were always forcing him to grin, and he was known for having an agreeable disposition. Rose met him in the dining hall of the Crescent Dance

Hall. It was empty because it was the middle of the day. All the golden chairs were upside down on the tables. He took two chairs off a small table in the center of the room and sat down with Rose. "What can I do for you, darling?"

Rose thought they should try to save money by booking local, undiscovered acts. "I can help you find some. It would be my pleasure."

Antoine thought it was worth a laugh at least. They went down to Little Burgundy to see some acts in jazz clubs. Rose dressed in a white fur coat with dark swirls of brown, like a chocolate sundae.

They went to a small club that had a balcony that was being rented out as a storage space, and which was stacked with used furniture. There was a scared, skinny singer wearing an ugly dress, who didn't know what to do with her hair. She warbled so much when she sang that it sounded absurd. Her voice was shaky, like a fawn standing on brand-new legs. Rose thought they should give her a chance.

"When she gets a little bit of confidence, she'll be wonderful. When she stops singing as though she's standing in the rain, it will be something."

Antoine didn't see it, but he hired her and she turned out to be a favorite at the club. She even wrapped a silver turban around her crazy hair and it became her signature look. She joined a touring American jazz troupe and ended up making cameos in the biographies of several famous men.

Rose told Antoine about a magician who performed at children's parties. They met him while he was buying doves at the Atwater Market. His hands were all scarred from having been burned in an act gone wrong years before. He said he performed for young children because they couldn't write reviews. He was down on his luck. He used to make a silver dollar float in the air. The other night he had used a copper penny, which just somehow wasn't the same and depressed everyone in the room.

At the Roxy the magician had a dove fly out of a wallet. He couldn't afford an assistant, so he had Rose stand on a small chair as if she were a ferocious lion, and then she disappeared. Rose was really good at coaxing paranoid geniuses out of exile. She had her ear to the ground about new acts too.

There was a teenage boy who was able to do all sorts of tricks on his couch. They sat on the coffee table eating cucumber sandwiches with weak tea that his mother served them as they watched the boy. It was as though the couch were a trampoline—he bounded up off it and did a backflip on one of the armrests.

"He's been doing that since he was little. It's annoyed me for years, but I haven't been able to make him stop. Beating doesn't work on children anymore. If he's able to make some money from it, all those years of aggravation would be worth it."

He leaped off one armrest, did two flips and landed on the other armrest.

Since she seemed to have remarkable intuition, Antoine had Rose oversee the audition for showgirls for a club that was opening in Montreal North. She saw at least two hundred girls that weekend.

Antoine had trouble looking at the chorus line. All the showgirls looked the same. They were so perfectly in sync that, when they performed, it gave the impression that it was just one girl in a hall of mirrors. They came out onstage with their arms around one another like linked paper dolls. He couldn't believe it. A chorus was giving him a sense of the sublime. And it was made up of working-class girls from Pointe-Saint-Charles!

Antoine suffered a heart attack and died, not because of the chorus line but because of all the smoked meat he had eaten in his life. Rose decided to ask McMahon if she could replace him.

SHE KNOCKED at his office door, then said her name and opened it. She bowed her head and walked in. She stood there in her white fur hat, cheeks shiny from her excited march over. He stood up when he saw her, thinking she had a knack for appearing out of the blue when he wanted to see her the most. He could never get bored of her face.

"Wait," she said, putting her hand out in front of her to stop him in his tracks. "I wanted to ask you something important. Antoine passed away and you know I enjoyed his company a great deal, so it might seem a little inappropriate to bring this up so soon . . . but I was wondering if I could replace him."

McMahon didn't answer. He seemed to not quite understand her request.

"Take his place as the entertainment booker, I mean. I've been all over the city with him. A lot of the most popular acts were ones I discovered. I have a knack for it, and I know I can do it."

She looked at him sheepishly. She still didn't get an answer. He frowned. He looked as though he were about to say something in anger.

"Oh, and here—I have something for the children."

She reached into her bag and handed him a small light box she'd bought. It cast shadow puppets on the wall. McMahon took it from her, looking pleased that she remembered he was a family man. She had no actual place anywhere in his life. He put it on a shelf above the hook his coat was hanging from.

"I'll talk it over with everyone else and get back to you," he said.

She turned to leave the office, not quite sure who this "everyone else" was. Before she left, she felt his hand on her shoulder. He closed the door before she could leave. They made love against the door with their clothes on.

WHEN HE GOT BACK HOME to Westmount, the children loved the strange lantern. They lay happily in their living room, watching the horses run together joyfully all over the walls. They were bright orange and lit up, like warhorses on fire in battle. McMahon and his wife sat on the couch together, watching too. He was pleased with Rose because his children were pleased with him. His wife was happy too because she saw the gift as a reconciliation. He felt satiated. He had a family and a mistress, and everyone was perfectly happy.

If you ever experience such a feeling, you should probably realize that God will take notice. Something will be taken away.

Mrs. McMahon had a dream that she was sitting next to Rose on the couch. They were discussing love affairs. Mrs. McMahon was telling Rose about all the different suitors she had when she was young. Rose was so impressed in the dream. That was one of Rose's special qualities, her ability to be genuinely impressed by just about anything.

Mrs. McMahon buried her face in Rose's hair and inhaled deeply. She opened her eyes to find herself lying in her bed. She noticed that she could still smell Rose, if only slightly. Then she sat up abruptly. She climbed out of the bed. She flung open the closet door. She started yanking down jackets and inhaling deeply. She pulled off the jacket he had been wearing that night. And at that point she was absolutely convinced of what she had been smelling. It was Rose. She was on all of his clothes.

He was so surprised when she confronted him. His pupils always dilated for a split second when he was confronted with the truth. Once she saw his eyes turn black, he had already confessed to her.

"You took her away from the children and me. I liked her, that's why you went after her. She wasn't even pretty. She listened to what I said. She made me feel inspired again. I want a divorce. I want everything too. And then I'll burn it. You will never touch me again."

She called the police and told them about McMahon's crooked operations. The police were in McMahon's pockets. What could they do other than have her committed? She needed to have a rest. Most women became excitable.

When the truck came for Mrs. McMahon, there was a pile of her husband's clothes in the yard up in flames. The flames were fighting with each other. One flame grabbed another by the hair and shook it. The children were sitting around it like it was some sort of bonfire.

Her madness was a fact soon widely accepted as true. Although Rose never believed it.

"HOW ARE THE CHILDREN?" Rose asked a couple of weeks later. It was always a taboo subject between them.

"They are fine. They're both in boarding school, so they didn't have to witness the whole regrettable fiasco with their mother. I think you should move into a bigger apartment. We can't bloody well go back there together, can we? And I can use some fucking comfort. I've had it up to here with crazy women. All you have to do is be fucking pleasant and spread your legs, and you are taken care of. You don't know how easy you have it."

"So you would switch places with a woman, then?"

"Come on."

"Dogs are happy with that life, not me."

"There we go. I can't listen to this shit, really."

"Can I go see her?"

"Oh, fuck off, Rose. You're such a piece of shit. I feel bad enough about it. What do you care? You slept with her husband."

"I liked her. She was such a force. But she had been thwarted. She was meant to be on a horse riding into battle."

BUT ALTHOUGH he was paying for her whole life, McMahon still wasn't sure whether he truly possessed her. To make certain that he did, he tried to make Rose miserable. This was the only real proof that a woman belonged to you. Anybody could make a girl happy. It was only when a girl was in love with a man that he could ruin her self-esteem. He knew he would have to get around to that. He only had her for now.

. . .

ROSE WAS DRESSED to the nines that weekend. She was feeling optimistic waiting for McMahon's response. They shuffled into the Roxy together, sitting down around the enormous round center table with McMahon's associates and their girlfriends. In the middle of the dinner, McMahon got everyone's attention.

"Here's a question for you all. Rose wants to replace Antoine. What do you think of my girlfriend coming in as a business partner with me?"

Rodney Chesterwick, who owned the Toscadero Casino, looked up from his glass of whiskey, shook his head and stated, "Women ought to be at home. Otherwise, who prepares the food?"

"Can we just change the subject?" asked Harry Manuedo, who owned the Ravishing Hotel. "What movie are we going to see?"

They didn't want to get involved in a domestic dispute. If they did, they would go home to their wives. They thought Rose was crazy. Didn't she have any idea how good she had it, considering it was the Depression? She had a big plate of turkey in front of her. She had a little mountain of cranberries in front of her. They would turn her lips red and warm up her belly.

Rose realized that these men would never help her. She also knew that McMahon had made it clear to them that they were to treat her like an inferior. She was so humiliated, she couldn't speak. She didn't know how to talk back to a group of men like this. And she knew that if she tried to say even a single word, she would burst out crying, and that would somehow prove every point they had just made. So she sat there quietly through the evening. Everyone else went back to talking. All the molls went back to being delightful and screaming out loud in laughter.

McMahon wasn't satisfied that he had hurt Rose. Once he had gotten a sniff of her pain, he had to have more of it. He wanted to hurt her more. He was all of a sudden enraged that he had ever been under her spell;

now that the tables had suddenly turned, he was on her the minute they got back to the hotel.

"You think you're good in bed, but you really aren't. You're ridiculous. Other women are more passionate. They smell better. They buy themselves perfumes and bathe in them.

"Instead of asking people about what the seating capacity in their restaurants is, why don't you ask the women some of the things you need to know? Like how they all smell so good? Do you want to know how to identify a proper lady? You lift up her arm, you stick your face in her armpit and inhale and it still smells good. You know, most girls make an effort to please a man."

Rose sat on the bed. There was no point in defending herself against these accusations. She wouldn't dignify them. If you were stupid enough to listen to them, then you deserved them.

"It's bad enough that you flirt with other men, but it's the type of men you flirt with. It makes me really question myself. Like, if you're at all attracted to me, does that mean I'm a lowlife creep too? How stupid was I? I mean, it's one thing to fuck the help, but you don't go and set them up in their own apartment and parade them around town."

It made her feel like a rabbit caught in headlights. It made her feel as if a curse had been placed on her and now she was a little statue.

"Why don't you please tell me who you would be, if it weren't for me? I want you to explain it to me. You would be scrubbing floors, if you were lucky. You would be trying to seduce some other boss, who would have the good sense to ignore you."

"I don't know where I'd be?" she asked sarcastically.

"Why don't you gain some weight? You look like you're starving to death. I can see your rib cage poking out. No man wants to see something like that. Ask any man, he'll tell you that he likes a woman with flesh he can grab on to. He likes a big ass he can stuff his face into. That's it. That's the main value that a woman affords to a man. I should be a happy man. I'm rich. Everyone knows who I am. I'm a respectable member of the community."

"Are you?"

"What do you mean by that? Why would you question me like that? Who the fuck do you think you are? My equal? You think that sucking my dick gives you any sort of position or standing in this world? The minute I stop letting you suck my dick, you go back to being poor. Now take off your clothes and show me your ass, and I swear to God that better be in an enticing way."

She had no power at all. And she had to do it. Her fingertips trembled as she removed her clothes. She hated that he could see her crying. Her tears were ones of humiliation, impossible to stop. They were a different temperature than other tears—and they seemed hot as they streamed down her cheeks. After her outer garments were removed, she took off her slip. What falls to its knees faster than silk?

HE CAME BACK AND APOLOGIZED to her the next day. She didn't forgive him. She took out her old plan of the Snowflake Icicle Extravaganza from her pocket.

McMAHON HAD SPENT so much money on her clothes, there was no reason she ought to show up in anything other than spectacular outfits. But after that night she somehow managed to put her clothes together in ways that made them look odd.

She wore a headband so low on her forehead that a great black feather went down to her nose and almost obscured her eyes. When someone said something peculiarly interesting, she would blow on the feather in order to get a clear-eyed view of them. As though she were blowing bangs out of her face.

Another time she was wearing a black velvet cape he had bought for her. She was holding it up over her face as if she were a vampire. Count Dracula.

Also, he could never tell when she was actually drunk because she would often pretend to be inebriated. She pretended to be three sheets to the wind, and it made everybody laugh. And then she would say the types of things that she always wanted to say but that she knew she shouldn't, being a girl and all.

If he accused her of pretending to be drunk, she would claim that she had no idea what he was talking about. She would swear that she actually had been smashed, because she couldn't for the life of her remember a thing that had happened.

That was especially infuriating. He couldn't confront her about the things she had done. She would raise her hands to both sides and shrug.

Once she pretended to be drunk so she could act like a man. She started to flirt heavily with one of the girls. She held her finger under her nose, pretending it was a mustache.

"My darling, you are better than all the other girls. You are prettier than them all. It's true. You are gold and they are all bronze. Watch out for all the other girls. They will be so jealous of you that they will want to stab you to death."

All the men had laughed, but they were also a little alarmed. If Rose could see through them, perhaps every other woman could too. But then they decided that Rose was probably just a peculiar girl. And even though they suspected that she was very good in bed, and they had all fantasized about sleeping with her, they were rather relieved that it was McMahon and not them who had responsibility for this most unusual girl.

SHE WAS MAKING A CAKE in her hotel room. She had never made a cake before. She was doing it deliriously. She was whipping everything together violently. She dumped in a bag of flour and it blew up in her face. She crushed the eggs and tossed them in the bowl, shells and all. Then she poured in some milk and began to beat it all viciously.

"What in the world are you fucking doing?"

"I'm making a giant wedding cake."

"Oh, I see. I see. You want me to divorce my wife and marry you. Is that it? If that's it, I wish you would just have the courage to come out and say it."

"No, that's not it at all. It's actually the exact opposite. You see, I never agreed to marry you. I just woke up one day and I was married." She scooped up some imaginary icing with her finger. She held it out for him to come and suck it off. She gave a sickeningly sweet smile.

Her face was covered in white flour. There was no way in the world that McMahon would be able to hold on to this strange girl.

EVERYONE KEPT TRYING TO MAKE it clear to Rose that nobody really cared about what a girl had to say. She wasn't supposed to have radical and clever ideas. She was just supposed to try to vaguely follow what men were on about. They were supposed to bounce ideas off her as if they were playing racquetball. It was a more or less pleasant way of speaking to one's self.

It was important to be a little bit stupid as a woman. It was important not to feel proud of yourself. You were supposed to feel pride only when your husband did something. If you were talented, you ran the risk of making your husband feel bad about himself. So it was best to keep your talent in check. Or become talented at things that he didn't like to do himself. So you could be his very adept assistant. But Rose couldn't accept this.

OUTSIDE, THE SPARROWS HOPPED AROUND in the snow, looking for crumbs. They were the color of books whose pages had been ruined in a flood.

27

TWO MEN

ONE FAT, ONE THIN

McMahon was vaguely aware that one of his fences was making a fortune off the objects that a handsome junkie was selling to him. When Pierrot stole and then sold a tiny Modigliani sketch, McMahon became interested in this thief. Despite his aversion to drug addicts, McMahon had Pierrot come into his office.

McMahon stared at Pierrot, trying to figure him out. Although he was a handsome sort, he was clearly an addict. His arms curved around the back of the chair, and his head was slung forward as though he were stuck up on a crucifix. Not like Jesus but like one of the fellows next to him.

Pierrot did not behave like typical drug addicts off the street. He had these odd movements—he looked up into the air with his lips pursed while considering a thought. It made McMahon conjecture that he had come from a wealthy background. He seemed like a youngest son who had been disowned, possibly for being a sexual degenerate. It was hard to imagine his story.

There was something oddly familiar about him. Pierrot reminded him of someone, but he couldn't put his finger on whom.

"How old are you?"

"I'm twenty-one."

"Where were you educated?"

"You know, I don't know that I ever was. I did attend Selwyn House School briefly before they tossed me out on my ear. I've read a few of the classics, though. I stopped reading them because they gave me such a sense of ennui, you know? They made me deeper, and I didn't feel that I needed more depth. I feel like I'm at the bottom of a well as it is. Novels and ice cream—both are things whose depths of feeling I try to avoid."

How he had ended up with Poppy was a mystery too. McMahon told Pierrot, as a gesture of kindness, that he would erase Poppy's debt and obligations to him. Her criminal record was beginning to look embarrassing because there were so many arrests. It made the entire police system look ineffectual. In return, Pierrot would bring all his stolen goods only to McMahon.

McMahon looked forward to Pierrot's visits and finds. His art dealer came to the meetings. They would lock the office door after Pierrot entered, and he'd unveil his latest theft. No matter how much McMahon thought the painting or object of art was worth, it always turned out to be more valuable. Pierrot never argued about the money they offered him. Because of this, McMahon was a little more generous than he would have been with the average goon who tried to bilk them for tasteless items. But he needed Pierrot to run out of money so he would go steal more things, didn't he? So he had to keep Pierrot broke.

One afternoon Pierrot came in with a small pen drawing of a snowflake in a cheap frame. He was stoned—the irises of his eyes looked like garden flowers encased in ice. He held out the drawing as though it were going to bowl them over, exceeding any expectation they might have of his capabilities as an art thief. But this one turned out to be of no value at all.

"It was probably drawn by one of the children in the house and then framed by a parent in a fit of sentimentality," the art dealer said. "I can't imagine that this was made by any professional."

Pierrot looked disappointed. It was rare for someone as stoned as he was to experience genuine disappointment.

McMahon gave Pierrot five dollars for it nonetheless. He didn't disrupt the lucrative business they had. He put the painting on the hearth.

He told Pierrot not to worry, as he would keep that painting for himself. Pierrot walked out.

The moment the door slammed shut, the back door to his office opened and Rose walked in. She instantly gravitated toward the etching. "What's this drawing? Ooooh, it's so beautiful."

"Take it if you like it."

ROSE HUNG THE FRAMED SNOWFLAKE on a hook on her wall. Later, when McMahon walked out of the bathroom, Rose was staring at the drawing. He came at her from behind. He put his hands around her waist. After they had done making love, she got back up and stood looking at the snowflake, completely naked.

"This makes me feel so at peace, I can't even tell you."

Well, she was an orphan after all, wasn't she? McMahon thought. Sometimes he almost forgot. She put on so many airs, and she always did her best to impersonate what upper-class people with money acted like. Sometimes she actually had him fooled. But her admiration of this drawing reassured him on so many levels. She was a silly piece of trash that he kept for his own entertainment. She was so beneath him. He could treat her however he wanted.

AFTER MCMAHON LEFT, Rose had an urge to be out in the snow in her big coat and her fur hat and her four layers of stockings. She felt as though she had been swallowed whole by a hibernating bear. She lay in the snow just like she had when she was abandoned in the park at two days old. It had been the snow that had first comforted her. It had taken her in its big fat loving arms and it had whispered into her ears that she should just sleep, sleep, sleep and that everything would be okay. It was the only thing that had ever mothered her. There were piles of snow on the heads of the stone angels, making them look like they had on the same fur hat as Rose. Getting up from out of the snow, she made up her mind.

. . .

WHEN SHE STEPPED OUT of the Darling Hotel with her suitcase on Christmas night, she was surprised to see that the world had completely changed. She climbed onto the crowded trolley. There weren't any seats free, so she grabbed on to the pole. All the different mittens one on top of one another made it look like a totem pole. On the trolley, everyone's face seemed to have so much emotion. She could read everyone. She understood that everyone was living a great tragedy. Her tragedy had taught her the language of tragedy—and made her able to read that of other people. In that way, she supposed it was a sort of blessing.

·◦◄ 28 ►◦·

IN WHICH A GIRL IN CHEAP STOCKINGS SINGS THE BLUES

Poppy was standing in front of the window. She wore a yellow dress with golden stains in the armpits and a skinny white belt around the waist. The dress made her ass look so perfect. Pierrot was looking at her with something almost close to lust. She immediately went over to the bed. She knelt at the foot of the bed with both her breasts in her hands and her mouth puckered.

He would be a criminal not to have sex with her. If he could make this openhearted messed-up girl happy, shouldn't he take the opportunity? He propped his head up on the pillow and began to masturbate his penis with one hand until it was hard. He closed his eyes for a second and imagined all the pretty girls he had ever made love to. He imagined Rose lifting up her gray orphanage dress, showing him her underwear and smiling. He opened his eyes and gestured for Poppy to come to him.

She hurriedly climbed over and on top of him. She lowered herself on his enormous penis. It was larger than the penis of any man she had ever slept with, and she had slept with a lot of men.

The condom broke. Condoms almost always broke when Pierrot wore them. So he ejaculated inside her. She felt so warm and peaceful. Everything in the world was okay. Poppy's special gift was her ability to see the world in a grain of sand: to be happy with the small things. But is it a blessing to be satisfied with so little? Or is it a curse?

The condom lay on the floor, as if a snake had just shed its skin.

HE FELT GUILTY after sleeping with Poppy. The dissatisfaction reminded him that deep down, for some ridiculous reason, he only wanted to be sleeping with Rose. His longing for Rose became so overwhelming that it felt akin to paralysis. He lay on the bed, looking at the ceiling, picturing Rose. She was sitting on a bench in the hallway in the orphanage. She had her palms in front of her, pretending to read a book. She laughed heartily at the invisible words. She licked the tip of her fingers and turned the imaginary page. It was a stupendous performance. Even though she did not look up, Pierrot knew that the pantomime was for him.

Poppy, seeing Pierrot grinning stupidly, asked him what the hell he was thinking of.

Pierrot decided to tell Poppy about the girl he was infatuated with named Rose. It seemed ridiculous, but he thought that if he confessed his obsession, it might lose some of its power.

"Oh, I know Rose. She's really sweet, right? She's a lot of fun. Always dancing."

"You know her? Is it the same girl? She's our age? Black hair and very pale skin?"

"Yes, it's the same one. She grew up at the same orphanage as you. You both have a similar manner, come to think of it. I can see that you grew up together. But that was a lifetime ago, buddy. You should be happy with what's in front of you right now."

"I know, I know. Does she have a whole lot of children?"

"No. That girl is footloose."

"She doesn't have children? But she's married, though, right? Do you know her husband?"

"I'm beginning to think we might be talking about different Roses after all. She's not married. She was a rich fellow's mistress. Everybody knows her. She used to be at the Roxy every night."

"If I go there, will I find her?"

Poppy was momentarily disconcerted, realizing that Pierrot wasn't simply engaging in nostalgia, but was prepared to actually go look for this Rose.

"Who is this rich man she's seeing?" Pierrot continued probing.

"You've never met him," Poppy lied, determined not to give him any more clues. "And I said *was*. They split up. She left him. He completely lost his mind too."

"Well, I've got to go find her."

"What! Why?"

"Because I never explained anything to her. Because I never told her that I loved her."

"She goes with men for a short while, and then when she leaves them, they go completely mad. This rich fellow stopped being able to see prostitutes. He used to see two of them at a time. He just cries after having sex. And he paces back and forth. He can't sit through a movie. And he just wants to talk about how awful Rose is. The only way that you can get his attention is if you insult Rose. It's really boring."

Poppy saw Pierrot's expression and realized she had just made things worse.

PIERROT LEFT THE HOTEL, saying that he was going to wait in the work line. Twenty minutes later there was a knock at the door. Poppy flung it open, expecting to see Pierrot, but there she was. She was looking at the girl with the black bob. The girl with the pale skin. The girl who had grown up in the same orphanage as Pierrot. It was Rose. She wondered if she was dreaming. It was as though she had willed her into existence, like some sort of genie.

But Rose didn't act as if anything supernatural had occurred. She was looking for her fortune to be read again. Poppy led her into the kitchen, saying that her husband was out but would be back soon. Rose sat at a chair at the kitchen table, took off her gloves and said she wouldn't stay long. Poppy placed five cards on the table in front of Rose. They were all cards that had hearts on them.

"I think there is love on the horizon for you."

But Rose waved her hand as if waving away that useless fortune. "You can see the future, can't you? Do you think that it's possible in the future for a woman to start up her own company and for it to be successful?"

"Yes, it will be possible, but not for a long, long, long time."

"I mean, if it's possible in the future, then I might as well go ahead and get on with it now."

Poppy shrugged. "Nobody gives me anything and I'm a woman."

She looked at Rose. When Poppy had first met Rose, she looked like any of the other underweight girls who walked up and down the street. Now she noticed how pretty Rose was. She was the most beautiful girl. Poppy looked at her pale skin and the two pink spots in her cheeks that looked as if they had been painted with a thin brush.

Underneath the table, Rose put the tips of her toes on Poppy's toes. Rose had grown up in a room filled with sixty other girls. She was used to the intimacy of other female bodies. When a girl reached out a hand to her, Rose always instinctively grabbed it. Poppy was not used to touching other women. Poppy was that strange thing: an only child.

What could Poppy do but turn over another card? Every time she flipped over a card, it revealed itself to be one that foretold love. Each one was a heart card. Poppy almost felt as though the cards were hot to the touch. When she turned over a card, it was though she were opening the door of a stove. The hearts seemed to tremble on the cards like little butterflies.

Rose put her knees against Poppy's knees. Rose reached under the table and put her hands on Poppy's thighs. Poppy was burning with a strange desire.

When Poppy turned over the joker, she put her hands up in the air. There was Pierrot in his fantastic multicolored suit, with material of such fantastic color that it would never fade.

Rose sighed. "I'm making an ass of myself, I suppose."

Poppy said nothing, still aghast that Pierrot was in Rose's future. Rose put on her gloves, handed Poppy a dime, kissed her on the forehead, got up and walked out the door.

Poppy poured boiling water into her teacup. The tea leaves swirled around the bottom of the cup like a group of sharks in a feeding frenzy.

·⟨ 29 ⟩·

IN WHICH ICARUS LANDS
ON SAINT DENIS STREET

Poppy was in love with Pierrot and she would not let him go back to Rose. She always encouraged him to get high. If he cleaned up, he would be able to do all sorts of other things. He could be a great lawyer or a politician or a writer or an ambassador. He should rightfully be with educated and articulate people, but she loved him too much to let him become any of those things.

The girl next door came over with a black eye. Poppy took her hands and asked her what had happened. She sat the girl down at the kitchen table and spoon-fed her a watery egg. She gathered from the girl's hand movements and the few words she uttered through sobs that her beau had done this to her for dancing with another man at the dance hall.

Poppy's eyes filled with tears. She was jealous. Poppy wanted Pierrot to yell at her. She wanted him to be outraged. There is no love without fury. There is no beauty without ugliness. She needed a proof of love.

WHEN POPPY WAS YOUNG, she lived in a stinking, squalid apartment in Mile End with her parents and grandparents. Everybody in her family treated her with contempt. They criticized her every move. They were always disgusted with her because she was a growing girl.

When Poppy was ten, she and her mother were on their way home, carrying groceries from the market. As they were crossing through the park, a group of traveling puppeteers arrived. They didn't have a theater to host them, but they didn't need one. They had a small caravan attached to a white horse with black spots. The words *Puppet Master Puppetry Spectacular* was painted on the side of the caravan in glittery golden letters the same color as shooting stars. The back of the caravan folded down and transformed into a stage.

Poppy was surprised she was allowed to witness such a thing. Her mother never let her do anything pleasurable. She always had to do chores and chores and chores. But her mother used the opportunity to sit down on a bench and weep. The bag of potatoes next to her also bent forward in grief. Poppy left her mother and the potatoes' side and moved to the front of the crowd. The whole neighborhood hurried out to see it. Even the dogs gathered. They couldn't help it. It might as well have been the arrival of the Messiah. And who in the world could resist getting tickets to that?

When the puppets crept onto the stage, Poppy put her hands up to her mouth to stop herself from crying out. These odd dolls had come to life and were looking at her. Magic was possible. It was the first time that Poppy had been exposed to art. It changed everything she knew about physics.

It was a Punch and Judy show. The lady puppet was talking, talking, talking. She was nagging the male puppet. She was angry at him for drinking too much. She was very annoyed that he had gone out and had fun without her. There were so many words in her mouth. Words were free—that was why women used them all the time.

Poppy clapped her wee hands together in excitement. She knew what was coming next. So did everyone in the audience. She was going to get beaten! She wasn't allowed to say these things to a man. No woman was. And yet women did! They went ahead and complained to men, even though they didn't have a right to. Why did they do it? And it always ended up the same way. Everyone in the audience knew it. She was going to get beaten. She was going to get beaten!

When his bat came down on her head finally, they burst out laughing.

Poppy wanted to live in that strange box. She wanted to climb into the back of the truck and escape her life. Once she got that in her head, there was no way to get it out. She had run away from home because of that performance. And now she found herself longing for some of the perversion she'd witnessed in the puppet show. She wanted the ugly rage and depravity that came with love.

THERE WAS A MAN who often passed Poppy in the street and he was always aggressive with her. She knew that he was trouble, that he was vicious. His nose was long and tapered. His face was an acquired taste. A person might be prone to thinking of him as either incredibly handsome or downright ugly.

He had offered to be her pimp. He had told her he could take much better care of her than her faggot boyfriend could. They could make real money together, and she wouldn't have to live in a hellhole and dress like a piece of Swiss cheese. She had holes in all her clothes because she and Pierrot would fall asleep while smoking their cigarettes.

The pigeons were on the windowsill, making the noise of shuffling cards, as though they were playing poker. Poppy began to make a plan.

SHE SENT PIERROT OUT to deliver her jars of homemade maple butter. She looked out the window to watch him turn the corner. He walked down the street with three of the jars balanced on his head. All the children pointed and laughed. On the corner, a child let the air out of a balloon and it sounded like a Paganini tune.

Poppy was usually sparse with her makeup. Not because she was modest in the least but because she had so little of it. Sitting cross-legged on the toilet lid, she opened up a little compact of caked blush. She took out the cotton pad and dabbed her nose with powder, even though there was no powder left. She had just a small stub of lipstick, but she applied several layers of it so that her lips were of the brightest red.

She put on a white shirt that had a ruffle around the neck, and a black skirt. Poppy ran downstairs and down the street, heading to the building where she knew the pimp would be sitting on the stoop. She stood in front of him, took one of his hands in hers and invited the pimp over to the apartment.

"Where's your fellow?"

"He abandoned me."

"Why would he do that? I thought you were keeping the two of you high."

"Well, it's simple. He's a thief. He happened across a very expensive item that none of the fences in Montreal could afford. So he went off to Paris to sell it. I don't think he's coming back. He's always really wanted to be a European."

Poppy knew she had to tell a lie the pimp had never heard before. He wasn't particularly bright, so he was used to accepting that things might be going over his head. As they walked back to the building, the pimp put his arm around her.

"Will you please tie me up?" she asked once they were in the apartment.

"Is that what you like?"

"Well, I can't really say. But sometimes I like to try something new."

"All right. I mean, I don't care. I'm always up for anything."

She handed the pimp a box of old ties she had collected when she worked at the brothels. Men often forgot them when they were drunkenly getting dressed. They were like a group of slithering eels. The pimp tied her arms to the chair and then fastened a gag around her mouth. She kept hoping Pierrot would walk in at the right moment to rescue her.

They both heard Pierrot's whistle as he came down the hallway. Everybody in the hotel paused what they were doing to hear the bar of music Pierrot was whistling. It was a refrain from the tune for Rose. He was always working on that tune, even subconsciously.

When Pierrot opened the door, he saw Poppy tied to the chair at her wrists and ankles. She had a pair of yellow underwear stuck in her mouth. Poppy's eyes were wide, wide open. She watched the scene unfolding in her own little hotel room as though it were the most riveting movie ever made.

"Poppy!" Pierrot yelled. "What is happening?"

He twirled around to look at the pimp.

"You are a criminal, sir! How dare you! Get out of here!"

"You get out of here! You don't deserve your lady. You just make money off her. And you take off to Europe whenever you fucking please."

"I don't even know where Europe is!" Pierrot exclaimed.

"Anyway, I have more respect for her than you'll ever have."

"You've got her tied to a chair!" Pierrot attempted to push past the pimp, to untie Poppy.

The pimp reached into his back pocket and pulled out a knife. "I'm going to have to kill you now, buddy. I wasn't going to touch you, but you touched me first."

Poppy started to squirm about wildly in her chair, hoping to escape, trying to save Pierrot. It had all gone wrong. Pierrot didn't have a chance, and he was about to be cut into pieces. The underwear fell from her mouth.

"Run, Pierrot!" Poppy yelled.

There was nowhere exactly for Pierrot to run. The pimp was blocking the door, and the hotel room was too tiny for Pierrot to do anything other than run in circles. The pimp jutted his knife out and Pierrot had no choice but to go out the window.

HE CLIMBED UP the iron fire escape attached to the side of the building like a vine. Why he decided to go up instead of down might be regarded as either a metaphysical or theological question but is, in any case, unanswerable. Up he did go, with the pimp following close behind.

The pimp had the knife in his hand. He held it out in a stabbing gesture toward Pierrot. A little girl leaned out her window and handed Pierrot a butter knife to defend himself with. She had just been using it to spread strawberry jam on her toast. The red jam on the end of the knife made it look like it had just committed a bloody deed.

At the top of the fire escape, Pierrot twirled the butter knife around as if it were a baton. The children on the third-floor balcony began to applaud. Although this was rather esthetically impressive, it raised no fear in the heart of the pimp. The pimp seized the knife from Pierrot's hand. He held both of the blades toward Pierrot—like they were the horns of a bull that was about to charge him.

The sheets hung down from the laundry lines like they were the ceiling of a great, colorful, patchy circus tent.

Pierrot arrived on the roof and sprinted across, the pimp scrabbling up close on his heels. When Pierrot reached the opposite end of the roof, he momentarily considered himself trapped. He spotted a ladder and laid it down so that it extended from one building to the other, over the abyss. A girl looked up, let her skipping rope go slack and yelled, *"Regardez en haut!"*

Everyone came out of their houses to see. People crowded onto fire escapes as though the landings were theater boxes. They sat on the opposite roof with their legs hanging over the edge like they were in the very cheap seats in the balcony. Other people began shouting too. They yelled at Pierrot to not try to cross the ladder. They hollered that he would never make it.

The sun shone down on his head like a spotlight, but it was so bright that he wondered if he hadn't set his wings on fire.

This was a spectacle indeed. Pierrot cut such a peculiar figure in his fantastic threadbare suit. Everyone gasped and became silent as they watched Pierrot begin to tiptoe across the ladder. He hummed his composition under his breath, so he could focus. He stepped quietly from one rung to the next. He had always been able to balance so well. A rung cracked under his foot. He heard the sound so clearly, as though it were a bone inside him breaking, and then he slipped between the bars.

As he fell, he had a clear memory of himself and Rose when they were little. They had stopped at a park to play. They hung upside down on the jungle gym, facing one another. They had a conversation while they were upside down. Pierrot imagined that she was a mermaid, her hair floating so mysteriously and weightlessly below her head. Pierrot smiled in his memory.

And then he hit the ground.

A cat crawled up on him. It showed the claws on its paw like a switchblade.

POPPY FLUNG OPEN the glass front doors of the building. She had gotten free of the chair, and the ties were still dangling from her wrists. She ran down the front steps and over to Pierrot. He was lying on his back with his eyes closed. He looked so peaceful that it would be easy to assume he was dead. But his mouth kept opening and closing, as if he were a fish on the deck of a ship, breathing its last breath and thinking, I knew that worm was too good to be true. Poppy took his hand and lowered her face close to his.

"Please tell Rose that I'm sorry, will you?" Pierrot said. "And that no matter how poorly I've acted, for me, she was the one."

Poppy was taken aback and sat up. If you knew a little about Poppy's past, you might surmise that she could put up with just about anything. She had sucked men's dicks at the bottom of staircases. When she was done, she'd stood up, plucked out the pebbles embedded in her knees—like small diamonds—and then headed off down the street as though nothing had happened.

But this was where she drew the line. She had created this elaborate production just for him. And his last words were to Rose! Rose? She hadn't done anything for Pierrot in years and years, but now she was the one he would devote his last words to?

The pimp, who had run down from the roof, raised his gaze from the boy on the sidewalk and looked for Poppy. He put his hand out for her.

"Sweetheart," he whispered.

She took his hand in hers. The silver key to the hotel room fell out of her pocket like a scale falling off the Little Mermaid the moment she was transformed into a human.

30

STUDY FOR
BROKEN FINGERS

When he came to, Pierrot had both his hands in casts, as if he were wearing white mittens. He had trouble sitting up because his ribs were broken. Pierrot looked at the tips of his fingers peeping out from the cast. Each one was black.

The police officer at the side of the bed looked at Pierrot. He held up a piece of paper on which was drawn a sketch of his own likeness.

"Oh, how lovely," said Pierrot. "You've made a sketch of me."

"This is a drawing that a sketch artist made based on a description from a four-year-old boy. We believe this is the face of a thief who's been robbing houses all through Westmount."

Pierrot had a distinct flashback of the little boy with a top, smiling at him all those nights ago.

"On second thought, that face looks like nobody I've ever seen before."

"Mmmhmm. We tossed your place. And there's nothing. But you sell everything for the cheapest price so you can get high. We are onto you, Pierrot. You little schmuck. You keep your crime to your own neighborhood. If you so much as step into Westmount, I will come after you."

Although he couldn't tell the police officer, Pierrot had already determined he was done with that life. But what else could he do now that his hands were smashed? Could he still play the piano?

He asked the doctor who came in to see him next.

"I know it might be silly to tell you that you're lucky when you're lying there with all your bones broken. But it's really amazing that you are still alive. You might go down in the record books for this fall—if there were such record books."

"I wouldn't be surprised," Pierrot said. "There are books about all sorts of things."

"It's not the time to worry about playing the piano. Take it easy."

And Pierrot smiled as the drugs ran through his veins—they seemed to course with honey rather than blood. Poppy had left him. He felt rather relieved about this. Perhaps he didn't have a right to feel this way. He chose to believe that perhaps Poppy had found someone else to live with and love. This new gentleman would surely do better for her. He did have a rather alarming appearance, but who was Pierrot to judge a book by its cover?

By espousing this train of thought, Pierrot was willfully choosing to be ignorant. He found himself at a sort of psychic crossroads. He could choose the truthful path, with all its regrets and guilt and responsibilities. Or the other, which is what Pierrot did. Because deep down he knew that all the vicious-looking man could do was enable Poppy's descent into stranger and stranger realms of prostitution.

WHEN THE CASTS CAME OFF, Pierrot went back to work at the movie theater, anxious to test out his fingers. He wanted to see if a miracle had occurred. The owner was angry at Pierrot for missing work but told him to give it a try at the break in the film. After the cowboys had been making threats for an hour, the screen lit up with the word *Intermission*. Pierrot made himself comfortable at the piano, flexing his shoulders, stretching his arms, rolling his head from side to side and wiggling his fingers in the air above the keys.

He had become quite fond of this piano. It had a lot of character. The keys were so light, he felt he really didn't even have to touch them. He would just put his fingers on the keys and imagine the tune and it would begin to play as if by itself. There was a love affair between the piano and Pierrot's imagination.

It kept him company. Some pianos had nothing to say. But this piano wanted to converse. This piano wanted to complain to Pierrot as much as Pierrot wanted to complain to the piano. The piano was his support group. It was his advocate. It was the only one that had tried to talk him out of being a drug addict over the past years.

His fingers ached when he placed them on the keys. He pushed the keys tentatively, so that his fingers were like the legs of a girl playing hopscotch. His whole body was in pain, racked with guilt and sorrow and loneliness. And then he let himself begin to play quickly, wildly, expertly. He played for having lost Rose. He played the tune he thought of as hers, but in a more grievous and sorrowful way. The tune now wove the frivolity of youth with the gravitas of maturity.

When he was finished, there was absolute quiet and Pierrot was confused. Where had everyone in the audience disappeared to, and shouldn't they be done with the washroom by now? He looked toward the seats. The cinema was completely full. No one had left their seats during intermission. They were weeping silently.

And so it was that Pierrot played better now that his fingers had been broken. It made the notes sadder. There were people who came to the theater to hear Pierrot rather than to see the movie. The owner gave him a two-penny raise. He stayed at a men's hotel and slept in a room with twenty-five other men. He spent his pay on getting high enough to prevent his body from going through withdrawal in the evenings.

31

PORTRAIT OF LADY
AS ALLEY CAT

Rose had filled her pockets with the jewelry McMahon had bought for her. The necklace had a pearl that looked like a seed you were supposed to plant, which would grow into a real moon. The diamond earrings were like tiny stars far, far, far away in other galaxies. There was a ring with a giant red stone that was like Mars, all poisonous and angry in the black sky.

She took the trolley from the Darling Hotel down Saint Catherine Street to the red-light district. The narrow streets perpendicular to Saint Catherine were lined with lazy buildings that had let themselves go. They needed new windows and new steps and new paint jobs. They were cantankerous and moody. They refused to open or shut their windows. They let the cold in through the cracks in the doors, and mice into those in the walls. They acted as though they had been awoken from deep sleep when you turned on the faucet or tried to use the stove.

On the front arch of an old abandoned bank there was a gargoyle of an angel lying on its back, looking up at the clouds in the sky, having completely lost interest in the world.

Rose was moving to the area where girls like Poppy plied their trades. But she didn't mind. She was tired of pretending she was anything other than an unfortunate young woman without a penny to her name—who fucked for a living.

One of the governesses had told her about a pawnshop in the neighborhood that would take your riches without asking questions. There it was, just like she had said. The pawnshop was dark inside and had a small cabinet filled with all the stolen jewels in the city. There was an expensive suit hanging from a coat hanger and a pair of fancy shoes. It was as if a man had sold his clothes and then walked out of the pawnshop naked.

On top of her jewelry, Rose sold all her fancy dresses. The pawnbroker told her that he would give her an extra dollar for the exquisite fur hat she had on as well. But Rose shook her head. She wasn't going to give up that hat. It seemed like the only old friend she had. It had come all the way from the orphanage with her. She knew that it made no sense for her to wear it. It was as though she were walking around with a crown on. But that was why she liked it. She wasn't about to give up a magical talisman at this point. Not when she was a girl alone in a land where everybody was a cross between the Big Bad Wolf and Puss in Boots.

Even though the pawnbroker had wildly underappreciated the worth of the objects she had pawned to him, she was still in possession of what was, to her, a small fortune. She intended to buy herself a holiday, time off from her life. She felt like spending some time in the city, the way a seven-year-old might.

SHE MOVED INTO A LITTLE ROOM at the Valentine Hotel on the corner of Saint Catherine and De Bullion. She told the woman that she could only afford the cheapest room they had. Her room was pretty, though. It was tidy. The tenant before her had lived in the room for twenty years and she had kept really good care of it. The wallpaper wasn't torn off at all. The floor wasn't scuffed. The washbasin looked like it had never toppled off due to some sort of drunken escapade. And the wallpaper was covered in yellow roses. There were white doorknobs with flowers painted on them.

The widow's cat peeked its head in the window, asking Rose whether it would be okay if it continued to reside in that room. Rose held its head in her palms and said, yes, of course, of course, of course. The cat had gray and white stripes, as if it had just escaped from prison.

She ended up loving her little room, which she paid for all by herself. The floors were so thin you could hear somebody making love three floors up. A woman singing a lullaby to her baby could put a lonely junkie on the fifth floor to sleep. There wasn't much secrecy in that building. If you saw one of your neighbors walking into the confessional, you already knew everything he was going to tell the priest. If you saw a man sleeping on the bench outside the building, you knew why his wife had kicked him out. His children kissed his cheeks on their way to school as they passed. The proximity of all these people made Rose feel less alone. She fell asleep listening to the voices of other people through the walls: it was what the world sounded like to an unborn child.

The windows were covered in frost in the morning when she woke up. She pulled on three pairs of stockings and two sweaters, then her overcoat on top. And she walked through the snow. She ran around with her hands out, catching snowflakes with the children.

She had time to see the neighborhood without worrying about getting home to the orphanage or McMahon. It was the first time in her life that she could do something like that. When she returned to the hotel, the concierge reached behind the wall and plucked off Rose's key for her. All the keys hung in a row, like a very simple musical score for a child to play.

32

PORTRAIT OF LADY
WITH WHIP AND DONKEY

Despite residing in the world's cheapest hotel room, after a time, Rose began to run out of money. Rose wasn't sure how she would survive in the city on a day-to-day basis, however. McMahon had put out the word that she wasn't to be hired at any of the city's nightclubs. Since they were under his protection, the owners told Rose that they couldn't let her in. It was as though all those years of learning the business and meeting people hadn't even existed. They had all been a waste of time. She understood exactly how all those Americans had felt when they jumped out the windows of tall buildings in 1929. She was twenty-one years old. She amounted to nothing.

There weren't any other sorts of jobs either. She went to the factories. She went to all the restaurants and knocked on the back doors. She went to the five-and-dime. She went to a spruce-beer manufacturer. She knew that they didn't have any signs in the windows asking for help, but she went in just in case.

She was walking down Saint Alexandre Street, where there were prostitutes in cloches milling about on the sidewalk. You could only make out their pouty lips. They walked like hens with their chests stuck out. As Rose passed she saw a sign on the door of a narrow building. It said: *Help Wanted: Seeking the Most Beautiful Woman in the World.* There was a descending row of white doorbells, like the buttons on a dress. She went up the marble stairs to the third floor of the building, even though she knew it had to be a trap. She knew that telling a woman she was beautiful was almost always setting a trap.

A man greeted her when she arrived at the door on the top floor. He brought her down a carpeted hallway. They passed a door through which she heard the sounds of people making love. There was a great bright light coming out from underneath it. Also, there were wires all over the floor leading into the room, so she assumed some sort of pornography was going on. One of the mistresses at the Roxy had gossiped to her about such a place.

Rose was directed into an office at the end of the hall. Another man was sitting behind a desk. He held a cigarette between his fingers and pointed it at her. "Will you pretend to look frightened, like the zookeeper accidentally left the cage door open and the lion got out?"

Rose made a funny look of horror with her mouth open and her eyebrows arched way up and her hands in front with all her fingers spread. Then he asked her to act as though a man had come up to her, unzipped his pants and let his erect penis out of it. She made the exact same expression and they gave her the job.

ROSE WAS ASKED TO POSE for photos in the nude. The photographer was making postcards that would be circulated discreetly around the country. Maybe they would go to Europe. But Rose knew, no matter where they went, the photos were for men to look at and fantasize about. They were against the law. In her first photo, Rose was wearing a little black masquerade mask and riding a hobbyhorse, and holding a whip in her hand. There was another girl named Mimi who was dressed the same. Rose didn't care. She got paid that evening.

She ate steak for dinner with a tumbler of whiskey. She'd had a taste of the type of life crime could bring you. After she was reminded of it, there was no going back.

THEY TOOK HER PHOTOGRAPH sitting on a wooden moon that had a little seat on it and was attached by cables to the ceiling. Silver cardboard stars were glued onto a black backdrop behind her. In another photo, she was in a dress, sitting on a chair with her legs spread. You could see her underwear. She was reading a book. This was for a popular series of postcards. They all displayed the literate whore.

She and Mimi dressed up as maids. They took turns feather dusting each other's fanny.

In another she was wearing lace underwear and a veil. There was a dog that wore a little tuxedo. She didn't know what it was supposed to mean. Perhaps the dog was her master and not the other way around.

SHE STARRED IN some movies too. She was usually naked in them, running away from priests and schoolteachers or men in black masks. In one movie a police officer made her sleep with him to get out of prison.

She pretended to be a girl working in an office. In the film she became so overheated that she could barely stand it. She tried to open the window but it was jammed shut. In frustration, she took off all her clothes. And the boss came out and started yelling at her as she happily typed away.

There was a dirty movie called *Florence Nightingale*. In it a patient was brought in, suffering from hypothermia. She took off all her clothes and climbed under the blankets with him. And they rolled around together until he was revived. Then she tried to get away, but he rolled on top of her and started having sex with her. The movie ended up with them wiping the sweat off their foreheads. In another film where she played the same character, in order to revive a man who was having a heart attack, she gave him a blow job.

. . .

SHE DIDN'T THINK it was any different from the other make-believe games she had played. How different was it really from when she pretended that the great big bear was pawing her at the dinner table?

She liked performing. When she was young, she hadn't realized how much she liked it. She didn't realize that the feeling she had while performing was unique to performing. She thought it was just a regular feeling one went about having. But looking back on her life, she realized that she had not had that feeling since. It was a feeling of completion. It made her feel safe. It made her feel intelligent. It made her feel like herself.

She washed up in the bathroom at the end of the day and reapplied her makeup. She took the trolley home to the Valentine Hotel.

THE DIRECTORS WERE AMAZED by how quickly Rose would catch on to instructions. She made them laugh out loud. They were wrapped up in the tale and the personas that she embodied. They almost wanted it not to end with her having sex or doing something dirty. They wondered about her character later in the day. They wondered about what would happen to her afterward. They wondered if she ended up happy.

They thought about the dear little perverted nurse and wondered if she would ever settle down. They wondered if she would be so enthusiastic about every patient. They hoped she would never become jaded. They hoped the hospital knew how lucky it was to have her. They wondered if they could meet their own little nurse someday and live happily ever after. And so they fell asleep without masturbating.

Sometimes her performance was too good and it took away from the sex.

SHE HAD ON a black Napoleon hat. It was like the black part of a crescent moon. She was riding around on a hobbyhorse. There was a backdrop of the frozen Russian landscape stuck up behind her. How cold it was meant to be in this make-believe Russia! The white makeup on her face made her as pale as the snowflakes. She was wearing a long black coat, and she had on a pair of bloomers but no shirt. She made love to Mimi, who was also dressed up as a soldier.

"Did you know that Napoleon was afraid of cats? But that he liked women's pussies?" Mimi asked Rose. "Did you know that he used to dress in the clothes of a poor person so he could walk through the streets of Paris to find out what people really thought of him?"

"How do you know all that about Napoleon?"

"I have a book about him that you can borrow."

Mimi was the only person Rose had ever met who liked to read as much as she did. Rose kept the things she read stuffed messily in her head like a walk-in closet. Mimi kept them all organized in her head like a scientist. She filed them away like a stack of cue cards. The facts were always there when Mimi needed them. She was a genius. She should have been a lecturer at the university. She should have been touring around in a black suit and tie, talking about French history. She was here without her clothes on, though.

MIMI WAS GETTING DRESSED in a maid's outfit. She turned her back to Rose so that her friend could do up the little buttons at the back.

"What in the world do our clothes say about us when we put them on?" Rose said. "There's no real dignity in any of these costumes. If I'm a maid, I do what the owner of the house tells me to do. If I'm a nurse, I do whatever the doctor tells me to do. What are we as women, other than barnacles that attach themselves to higher life forms in some pathetic attempt to clean up messes? Tidy up what men have left behind—make the world a lovelier, better place for men. I would like to play a part in which I don't have a superior."

The director told Rose that she should save her philosophical specula-tions until after work because they were causing the male actors to lose their erections.

Rose looked over at the male actor. He was wearing a long white wig and a black judge's robe that went down to his feet. He was casually stroking his cock to get an erection so they could start the film again.

A man walked by with a mask of a donkey head and a tail attached to a belt around his waist. Rose looked down at his penis to see if she could recognize who it was by the organ. It seemed to be a rather ordinary penis.

"Have you watched any of the movies we've been making?" Rose asked. "In every one of them, the woman is hunted. She's subdued, isn't she?"

"Oh, you're not supposed to look into them so hard, you know. They're just there to let some lonely people get their jollies," said Mimi.

"A girl's desire is like a pretty butterfly. And a man's desire is like a butterfly net. His desire captures and kills her. He turns her into an ob-ject to be pinned on a corkboard. I don't think I'm interested in the tyr-anny of the couple. I'm more interested in what a person does when they're forced to be by themselves."

"You just want to sit on a chair naked and masturbate?"

They both laughed.

"Are you going to get into your costume soon?" Mimi asked.

Rose had said all that while being stark naked, not a stitch on her other than a string of fake pearls, a pair of black high heels and a little tuft of pubic hair.

33

STILL LIFE OF MURDERS

McMahon had thought about Rose compulsively during the past year. He had stopped sleeping around. It was too emotionally risky. Before Rose, he had always felt completely in command when sleeping with a woman. Now he felt vulnerable, like the woman could take something from him. He felt as if he were begging them for something they could never give him. The emptiness and longing he felt after sex made him sick inside. He blamed Rose for this.

And he sometimes even felt strange when he masturbated. He always felt like weeping after he came and his fantasy dissipated. It wasn't worth the orgasm. He sometimes wondered whether the sex had affected Rose similarly. After all, he had been her first. So he had to have registered in her consciousness in some fashion. He had to be emotionally important. If he knew she felt the same, he thought that perhaps he could go back to being a man.

McMahon kept expecting Rose to return for money, but she never did. He thought maybe Rose had died. He had everyone in the police station paid off. The crime-scene photographer put together a portfolio of Jane Does in the city who had died suspicious deaths since Rose had run off on him.

Every time he looked at one of the photographs, for a split second he was sure it was Rose.

There was a woman with a tie around her mouth, put there no doubt so that she couldn't voice her own disappointment at being murdered. There was a woman fastened to a kitchen chair. Her head hung forward, almost like she had fallen asleep that way. There was a girl with a pillowcase over her head. He thought for a moment that if he were just able to pull off the pillowcase, he would see Rose. But the body of the girl was quite plump. Too plump to be Rose. There was a girl lying on a bed with a bullet hole in her forehead. She seemed to be looking up at the hole. There was a girl in the park. Dark-colored autumn leaves had fallen on her. She had on boots and a hat but nothing else.

There was a girl who was found beside the fairground. She'd had a good time there, as she had a stick of cotton candy lying next to her, and a stuffed black panther with a red bow tie around its neck. It was something she had won, tossing balls into baskets and rings around the necks of bottles. She was wearing black tights. Those black tights reminded him so much of Rose. He liked when she would sit in her tights on the side of the bed with her legs dangling over the side. They reminded him of a little girl, but a little girl he could fuck.

He loved Rose so much, he needed her dead. It was a man's right to kill the woman he loved. McMahon closed the portfolio and went to find Rose. The smoke ring from his cigar hung in the dark like an eclipsed moon.

34

TINKER BELL'S REAL NAME

Pierrot was feeling lonely. He looked up at a building whose windows were all lit up at night. They each looked like a luminous oil painting hanging on a wall. There was a girl with a big fat ass trying to get a knot out of her hair with a brush. It looked like a Rubens painting. There was a skinny girl with her hair pulled back reading a recipe book. It was a Giacometti! The girl with the strawberry-blond hair—with her arms folded over her large breasts and sticking her toe in the bath—was a masterpiece by Botticelli.

He didn't have the will or drive or courage to make love to anyone ever again.

Pierrot made friends with an usher who worked at the Savoy with him. They were walking home in the same direction along Saint Catherine Street one night after closing up. Pierrot was staying at a men's hotel on Saint Dominique called the Conquistador. The usher lived with his mother on Saint Christophe.

They passed a noisy proscenium that had the word *Arcade* written in tiny red lightbulbs across the top. There were blue and green tiles leading into the arched glass doorway. The usher grabbed Pierrot's wrist and dragged him down to the front of the establishment. "Let me show you the greatest footage ever recorded by mankind. I'm going to show you a wonderful film. I mean, this is going to change the way you think about everything. This is real moviemaking."

"You didn't like the film tonight?"

"Not my cup of tea. I hate singing and dancing. And I despise sailors. If I didn't live in Montreal, I might feel differently about American sailors. But I do happen to live here, and I hate their guts. Come on! I'm going to give you culture!"

He led Pierrot into the arcade. They passed rows of colorful new devices called pinball machines. They were dinging and whistling and making a racket. The noises reminded him of the nursery at the orphanage, the babies shaking their rattles and the bars of their cribs. The noisy babies were the ones who lived. The silent ones slipped away into the great eternal quiet they so clearly preferred.

He passed by a miniature racing track with wooden horses making their way across. They were black and white and dappled. The jockeys riding them had their backs hunched and their heads down, imploring the horses to advance. It made him think of the horse-drawn carts at the orphanage at Christmastime. He didn't know why everything was reminding him of the orphanage and his childhood.

The usher gestured toward the back of the arcade. There, up against the wall, was a row of three light blue machines screwed to a heavy wooden table. A sign on the wall above them had the words *Peep Show* written in red letters. Written on the machines themselves in red glittering letters were the words *Beautiful Ladies*. Underneath, the fine print swore that for a penny you could have all your earthly desires met.

Pierrot had so little money. Naturally, he didn't like to waste it. He didn't even want to part with a penny. But he was enticed and frightened by the machine. He instinctively knew that it was more than it seemed. You could look through a keyhole and have everything you knew about people transformed by what you saw on the other side. It reminded him of Sister Eloïse having him peek under her habit.

And he wasn't quite sure what he felt: terror or desire. He was unused to desire because he was a junkie. And when he felt it, he got it confused with all kinds of other things. Nonetheless, he dropped his penny in. He had the feeling that he had dropped it down a well. It was irretrievable now. He lowered his head. He pressed his eyes against the telescope that looked down and not up.

There was a girl with a black mask flittering on the screen. She had on a black corset and black panties. She had leather high-heeled boots that went up to her thighs. She was carrying a long riding whip in her hand. She tiptoed quietly and cautiously around the room. She seemed to dance about on her toes as she looked about, searching for a victim who was apparently eluding her.

He didn't have any trouble recognizing her with a blindfold. They had often played hide-and-seek when they were at the orphanage. In so many of his memories of Rose, she happened to have a blindfold on. Because children who couldn't hold in their laughter were usually discovered, Rose was often it.

In the film, she was tiptoeing back from the closet when she noticed a pair of men's shoes sticking out from beneath the bed.

You might think he was upset by what he saw. But Pierrot felt the opposite. He didn't judge Rose for this. He had also had sex with people he hadn't loved. Rose was silent up on the screen. He thought she was like a fairy trapped inside a bottle. He had never wanted to make love to someone so badly in his life.

This meant that she wasn't married. It was a lie. Eloïse had lied. She was by no means leading a conventional life. By no means! And Poppy had been incorrect. She was no protected gangster's moll. She was free to do as she pleased. She belonged to no man. He could find her. Rose lifted up the bedspread and bent down to peek under the bed.

"Oh, come catch me! Catch me!" Pierrot found himself saying. The screen went black, as if a guillotine blade had dropped.

. . .

Pierrot decided to go through withdrawal. For the first time since he had become an addict, he had a reason to get clean. He wanted to have an enormous hard-on when he found his Rose again.

He was sweaty all night. He reached for a teacup. The teacup shivered and shook as though it were a tiny boat on a terribly tempestuous sea. Everything he touched he seemed to electrocute. It was as if his finger were a lightning bolt. He picked up his jacket and it shook like a man being hanged and jerking around trying to stay alive.

He was too cold and too hot all at once. He didn't know whether or not he was suffering. His body was restless no matter what he was doing. When he was sitting down, he wanted to be standing, and when he got up, he wanted to be lying down. He sat on a chair as he crossed and un-crossed his legs. There were bugs all over him. There were ants in his pockets. He had ants going up his sleeves. They were all around his neck. They were stuck to the sweat.

He puked into a bucket. There was nothing but a little bit of bile. But he knew he had exorcised the demon inside him. How mundane demons were, he thought as he flushed it down the toilet and then washed out the bucket. Our trials always seemed so tiny and insignificant in retrospect, once they faded away into the distance.

He thought of the enormous erection he would have when it was all over. He thought of the look that would be on Rose's face when he penetrated her the way no man had ever penetrated her before. But most of all, he wanted to do something he had never done before.

He wanted to have sex with someone he was in love with.

ROSE IS A ROSE IS
A ROSE IS A ROSE

One night Rose went out drinking with the other girls after a long day of shooting. They sat on the row of stools at the bar together.

"Isn't it an obvious fact that the pursuit of happiness always makes a person miserable?" Rose said ponderously after two beers. "So do you think that if we went out of our way to look for things that made us miserable, we would find ourselves perfectly content in the end?"

"*Oh, ne commence pas avec tes idées folles, Rose,*" said a girl named Georgette. "Anytime you start thinking and drinking at the same time, you end up going a little bit cuckoo."

"Don't worry, my pretty darling. All of you are worried about me steering the night into melancholic waters, but don't be! I'm in a fantastic mood tonight."

A man asked her to dance, but she waved him off. She didn't like following the same steps that everybody else was following. She took a flower from the vase on the bar, stuck it behind her ear and stood.

"Ladies, have you met my beau? Don't judge him because he's a bear."

She put her arms around her imaginary bear and they waltzed around the dance floor. People stopped to look. At first they thought they were looking because it was so incredibly odd. But then they started looking because they wanted to watch the expression on Rose's face as she waltzed. It was a look of rapture, as if she were having the most wonderful dream. They wondered whether they would be able to find love like that in their own lives. They all wanted to hurry home and jump in their beds and have the same dreams she was having.

OF ALL THE GIRLS, Mimi was her favorite, because they could carry on such interesting conversations. On a Friday, Rose and Mimi tried to figure out what they would do with their Saturday.

"There's a movie theater where a really great piano player works," said Mimi. "Let's go there."

"I'm not a fan of movies," said Rose. "I prefer live performances. But anyway, let's go somewhere where we can talk."

ROSE AND MIMI MET UP outside the Valentine Hotel the next day so they could go see the Picasso exhibit together. It was fall. The curled-up brown leaves fell from the trees like sea horses.

"It's going to be wonderful," Rose exclaimed. "All these paintings where he sticks a nose on a cheek and an eyeball on a forehead. He captures the modern condition. All our thoughts are fractured. Everything is a dead end. You have to look at something from all angles at once to see it from the inside out. Not just be obsessed with the obvious, stereotypical way of looking at something, you know? To make things appear as they really are."

THE MUSEUM WAS a distinguished-looking building with columns, in the middle of downtown. They had to climb up a flight of rather large marble stairs. Rose quite liked the feeling because it made her feel as though she were a little child again. The building had a huge echo inside it. All the noises were amplified. It was like you were on a stage, speaking into a microphone.

. . .

ON THE WAY TO THE EXHIBIT, they passed through a display of the wildlife that lived around Montreal in the woods, that never dared to venture into the city limits. If you were a creature afraid of fire, you could only imagine the sight of marquee electric lights. A taxidermied wolf stared at them, its giant teeth bared and one of its paws raised, though it really wasn't frightening in the least. It just seemed odd out of context.

"All fear is dependent on context," Rose said.

THEY STOOD LOOKING AT the portrait of Gertrude Stein together. The subject was so serious and intelligent-looking. Rose had read her poetry and had admired it. It had made her feel better about herself and her sex. Everything written by any woman was written by all women, because they all benefited from it. If one woman was a genius, it was proof that it was possible for the rest of them. They were not frivolous. They were all Gertrude Stein. Rose looked at the portrait of herself as a poet.

"Isn't she the most beautiful woman you've ever seen?" Rose asked. "If someone made a portrait of me, I would want to look exactly like her."

"Oh look, Rose!" Mimi exclaimed. "Let's go into this room. It's called the Rose Period. It's been named after you."

Rose looked around the room at the paintings. They were all of circus performers. They were colored the pink of a sunset. She stopped in front of a painting of a slender clown in a leotard and a two-cornered hat seated on a red couch. Mimi came and stood next to Rose, looking at the painting.

"This painting! It looks so much like Pierrot. He was my first love. He abandoned me because I wouldn't put out, I think. Or actually, I don't even know why he left me or what he thinks of me or why he fell out of love with me.

"It's so wonderful looking at him now. It makes me remember how I used to feel about him, or that you could feel like that with a man. Just like companions and not like competitors. I stopped worrying about things. It was like I was in a boat and the boat stopped rocking. He made me feel safe so I could have all these dangerous thoughts. I think that might be what love is."

"I don't know if I necessarily agree with you. I think you're just describing one of the eight thousand ways to feel horny. But I do think you should go find him. Just to see what he's all about, so you can stop mooning over him."

"I've always wanted to. But I never knew what had become of him or where I could find him. But now I see it perfectly. Of course, Pierrot is a clown!"

Then there was a *swoosh* as water came out from between Rose's legs and splattered on the floor.

"Oh my God, I'm going to have another baby."

ROSE AND MIMI HURRIED BACK to the Valentine Hotel. Rose was trembling as she went into the cupboard and pulled out an old blanket. It had been on the shelf when she moved in. It was old, and the colors were unattractive, and the padding inside was not cushy at all. That was probably why it had been left behind. There were strange purple mushrooms on it. She spread it on the bed. She felt as if the blanket had been put there especially for that purpose. She lay down on the strange field.

"Did you know you were pregnant?"

"No!"

"I thought you had a paunch. How far along do you think you are?"

"No idea."

Mimi knelt next to the bed and took her hand. Rose felt like she had done forty shots of whiskey in a row and now couldn't throw up. Then she felt as though a great fist were punching her in the stomach, over and over again. It was just like at the orphanage all over again. The girls were always punished worse than the boys.

The pain was terrible. Why didn't you hear women wailing in pain all the time? She tried to stop herself from screaming out loud. But she couldn't help it. She yelled and yelled.

"Push, push, push," Mimi begged.

"Why?" she cried.

"Push, push, push, and it will soon be over."

She didn't know if she was pushing. She kept wanting to pass out but then not being able to. Her clothes were wet with sweat. Her knees were bent and her legs were spread. Mimi was looking between her legs. She had never felt so naked. How many people in this world had seen her cunt? How many people had looked at her cunt for answers? As if it were the sort of place where miracles happened.

Mimi swore she could see the baby. She knew more about the baby than Rose did. Mimi had proof that it was a mortal, that it wasn't just an imaginary pain in her stomach. Mimi promised her that the baby was practically out of her body. So she kept pushing until Mimi, all at once, stopped saying anything at all. She went all quiet, as though she had decided to say a prayer. Rose waited for the baby to make some sort of noise.

Rose wished that she had the energy to sit up and look at the baby. But she didn't. She couldn't do anything at all. She couldn't will her head to tilt forward, and her eyes wouldn't stay open, and she couldn't even move her lips so that she could ask whether the baby was a boy or a girl. These were all things that could be figured out in good time.

Mimi would take care of her, she thought. She imagined Mimi standing next to her with a little black mask over her eyes and a whip in her hand—protecting her like the angel that protects the Garden of Eden.

ITS SKIN WAS THIN and delicate as the petals of a flower. It was shocking to look at. Its skin was the color of a galaxy, of a tiny cluster of stars.

It kept changing different shades of pink and purple and blue, like an aurora borealis.

You could see that it was animated. It had been touched by the magic wand that was life. You could see its heart beating in its chest. You could see goose pimples on its skin. You could see the little eyeballs moving behind the little eyelids. You could see the tiny fingers move, almost opening, as if reacting to a thought. It was a girl.

There was nothing anyone could do to keep a baby that small alive, and soon its heart stopped beating. Rose washed it off in a bowl of warm water. When it was underwater, it almost seemed to move its arms and legs of its own accord, as though it were a sea creature.

She had never wanted to be pregnant. She had never wanted the baby. But now she was devastated that it was gone. She stared at it like she was a little girl looking at a doll and expecting some sort of reaction from it. She wondered why it had insisted on growing and living inside her. But now that it was out of her body, it would no longer admit that it had been alive.

She, of course, knew the origin of the baby. It was either the child of the man with the donkey mask or of the bear she had danced with at the nightclub.

SHE HEARD MCMAHON'S VOICE in her head: "So you prostitute yourself with a third-rate actor just to be able to afford soup and to live in a fleabag hotel. Wonderful. So that's why you left me."

Later that night she informed Mimi that she was no longer going to work at the movie studio. "I'm starting my own touring company. Watch this, please."

She picked up the eggs and began to juggle them. They spun around like the lights on a Ferris wheel. She withdrew her hands and suddenly all the eggs fell to the table and broke.

"Oh dear," said Mimi. "You've completely lost your mind. But don't worry. I'll just scramble up all of these into a nice omelet."

. . .

LATER, AFTER MIMI LEFT, Rose wrapped the baby up in a stained napkin with orange orchids on it that she had never liked. She put the wee parcel in the inside pocket of her coat. Feeling famished, she stopped at a restaurant to have something to eat. The waiter asked if she would like him to take her coat. She shook her head. She sat at a table in her coat by herself, sighing, with a bowl of soup.

When she was in possession of the baby, she felt people would find out about it. They would judge her entirely unnatural. They would say she was some sort of witch, and they would burn her at the stake.

When Rose got back home, she took the little girl wrapped in the colorful napkin and put the package in the garbage chute and then sat on the bed staring at its closed door. As though she were expecting to hear a knock from behind it.

Outside on a branch, a crow cawed suddenly, as if it had something very hot in its throat.

·≈[36]≈·

THE ANATOMY OF MELANCHOLY

ater that night Rose yanked on her dresser's top drawer, the one that got stuck, until it jerked open. She reached in and pulled out the tin cigar box she liked to keep her condoms and money in. There was a barrette with a tin rose on it that McMahon had given her, which was the only one of his gifts the pawnbroker had declared absolutely worthless. And there was the plan she had made with Pierrot.

Every time she looked at the piece of paper, it distracted her because it was so whimsical and absurd. It amused her that she had come up with something so outlandish and impossible. She liked to think that who she was as a child was entirely different from who she was now. This is a common phenomenon. It's because people don't like themselves, but they believe they are inherently good and that it's life that has made them wicked. So they look back at themselves as children in an idealized, unspoiled lovely state.

The crazier she found the plan as an adult, the more special she felt she had been then. However, this time when she looked at the plan, it seemed to make absolute sense. Why couldn't she put together this plan now? If it was created by a thirteen-year-old, it should feel easier to accomplish, not harder.

THERE WAS A CIRCUS PERFORMING "Leda and the Swan." She watched a girl in the circus leap off the strong man's shoulders, do two flips in the air and then land back on his shoulders. There was no way any scientist could explain such a feat taking place on earth. The atmosphere was different onstage. It was that of another planet altogether. The atmosphere was not composed of oxygen, but rather it was composed of sadness. Sadness was dense—as if it were liquid. You could leap higher up into the air when you were onstage, and sometimes you were suspended there.

Most of us hide away when we are sad, Rose thought. But performers were sad in public. She liked how honest they all were. They opened up their hearts. They took out every emotion—no matter how small or pathetic or odd—and celebrated it. It was as though each trick they performed was an attempted suicide, proving that you could indeed survive the human experience.

They were much more naked than Rose had ever been in the pornographic films. That was for sure. It was much harder to look at. Rose knew she could create an even more provocative show of her own, as sad

things can also have other sides, miraculous ones. If you don't feel sadness, there are types of happiness and compassion and torture and insight
you will never know. Sadness has all sorts of truths that allow you to
experience joy. She remembered reading with Pierrot the flyers of visiting
circuses. They came from faraway places—like Poland and New Orleans
and Moscow and London and Bombay and Hong Kong. They brought
stories of different lifestyles.

She wanted to create a group from Montreal. To make people wonder
what it was like to live on the snowy island. Where there was nothing but
crying pregnant girls. Where you could have sex with a girl wearing nothing but a fur hat and socks. Where there were churches and horses and too
many babies and too much snow. Where everyone fell in love only once.

SHE WAS GOING TO FIND her partner. He must be performing somewhere because he couldn't help it. He must be a sad clown in some smaller
revue. Once she got that idea in her head, she couldn't let go of it. She
stepped out of the theater. It was hailing outside, as if a bottle of lozenges
had fallen over on the shelf.

·❦[37]❦·

ON THE FIRST DAY

n one week she saw seven different clowns. On Monday she went to a
theater that had paintings of blue skies with white cumulus clouds floating on all the walls.

There was a clown whose act revolved around the use of a spotlight.

The spotlight would turn off, and when it came back on, he would be doing something completely different with other props. He changed his clothes in the darkness. He sat on top of a ladder. He lay under a blanket, sleeping. He sat on a chair, reading a novel. He wore a chef's hat and stirred a pot of soup. Rose found his routine almost miraculous. It seemed as if he were part of the light, like he completely disappeared and reappeared when it went on and off.

Rose watched the artists leave backstage but didn't spot the clown. Rose knocked on the door to the artist's dressing room backstage. The clown opened it. He looked tipsy and was wearing pants but no shirt. His face paint had mostly been wiped off, but a ghostly pallor remained.

"I found your act truly transcendent."

"This was nothing. I used to have a wife who worked the lights. Because we'd been together for so many years, we were so amazingly coordinated. I really seemed like I was supernatural. I wish that you could have seen the act then."

He poured them each a tumbler of gin.

"But then I cheated on her. At first I thought she was turning the spotlights on and off at the wrong times and in the wrong places on purpose. But then, you know, I realized it was because I'd broken our trust."

The gin inside Rose's glass looked like a tiny calm lake. She held the glass to her lips and took a sip. She immediately began to feel relaxed and loquacious.

"I think clowns feel the consequences of things more than other people do," said Rose. "We clowns are larger than life. We hold a microscope up to things. I think if you want to be a better artist, you have to be a better person. How else would you be able to express innocence—which is what every clown is after?"

The clown nodded. "Thank you for sharing that philosophy. It's quite useful to me. I'd very much like to see your act."

"I'm looking for my partner. He's an absurdist. He's always doing something wonderfully peculiar, like balancing plates on his head."

"There's an interesting act over at the Neptune. A clown who spends all his time in a bathtub."

"Thanks. I'll go looking for him."

"Come back and see me sometimes."

He winked.

Pierrot went by the pornography studio looking for Rose. He asked about the girl with the black hair who stared right into the camera. They said that her name was Marie but that she only answered to the name Rose. They said that she no longer worked for them. She had arrived at their door out of the blue one day, and then she had left with just as much resolution and as little explanation.

As he turned to leave, Pierrot saw a man with a huge mustache in socks and his boxer shorts eating a sandwich, sitting on a stool. He often played a landlord who extorts his tenants.

"Keep looking," the man said to Pierrot. "She's around."

-⸬[38]⸬-

ON THE SECOND DAY

On Tuesday Rose went down to a theater whose name, the Neptune, was painted in blue and white on the light box out front. There were murals in the lobby with paintings of different calm seas with magnificent ships sailing on them. There was only one mural that showed a turbulent sea. On this particular sea, there was a huge ship with broken masts being pulled under the waves. And tiny terrified people in those waves, trying to cling to the flotsam and jetsam while sharks approached them from the rear.

Rose sat in the audience, and when the stage lights came on, a clown was revealed, sitting in a bathtub. He wore a bathing suit and pirate hat and looked out of a periscope, as if his tub were actually a little boat. He was peering through it in what could only be a desperate search for land. It was unclear, metaphysically, whether the water was inside the bathtub or outside it.

He took out a pair of large oars and stuck them into the imaginary ocean and began to row. He put the oars back into the infinite bottom of the tub. Then he pulled out a fishing rod. Casting an imaginary line, he caught himself an imaginary fish. He then took out a gigantic pot to cook the fish in. It surprised the audience that such huge things were coming out of the small tub. The bathtub actually didn't have a bottom to it, and he would position it above a trapdoor on the stage.

"I'm never sure whether people understand my act. I don't know whether they think I'm just clowning around. What did you think I was trying to say?" the clown asked Rose later.

"We all struggle with contradictions. Contradictions are marvelous. If you don't believe that everything contains contradictions, then there is very little you can understand. We know ourselves by embracing what we are not. We become good by taking evil head-on."

"Exactly!" exclaimed the clown. "You can't have land without water. You can't have water without land."

"In my own clown work, I'm interested in the wonder in tragedy and the tragedy in wonder, that type of thing."

"It's not so often you see women going into clowning these days."

"Why do you think that all the clowns who I've met are men?"

"Because clowns are supposed to be funny. Clowns are supposed to be allowed to fart all the time. They are supposed to be honest. They get to expose their flaws. They get to confess to all sorts of funny emotions. Men are happy doing this but women are not. It wouldn't be funny if women did this, just ugly."

"What you are describing is freedom. And, trust me, women want it too."

"There's an effeminate clown at the Parisian. Perhaps he's the clown you're looking for."

Pierrot called the operator, looking for Rose, but her number wasn't listed. So Pierrot went to the police station. There was a cop who knew absolutely who he was describing. He remembered Rose from when she was dating McMahon. There was, however, no way he would give up any information about that girl to this young bozo.

"She always wanted more than she deserved out of life. McMahon did everything for her, all she had to do was spread her legs. But no, she went off. Left him destroyed. I have no interest in women who don't know their place."

"So you can't help me?"

"It's in the home."

"What is?"

"A woman's fucking place."

Anyway, McMahon had taken it very hard when Rose left. There was an unwritten agreement among all McMahon's friends that they were not going to have anything to do with her. The cop had never really liked Rose because he was so attracted to her too.

39

ON THE THIRD DAY

T he Parisian Theater had ornate boxes on the side for rich people to sit in. The wood around the stage had depictions of flowers and teacups and unicorns and lilies carved into it. Onstage, a fat clown walked around in an imaginary garden, bending over and plucking different flowers, which he would inhale from deeply.

It was as though the scent of the flower made him stoned. He danced about the stage. He had on a pair of ballet shoes under his spats. He danced on pointe, gracefully and wonderfully. He took off his jacket to reveal that he wasn't fat at all, and that it was just the parameter of a stiff tutu creating his girth. He danced to Stravinsky's *Rite of Spring*.

When he picked up one of the flowers, he made a terribly loud and rather shocking buzzing noise, as if there were a bee inside the flower. As his nose approached the flower the buzzing became louder and louder, until he yelped out loud, obviously bitten. He held up his hands to his face. When he put them down, he had on a big red clown nose.

Backstage, sitting on the fire escape, the clown and Rose looked down at his toes. There were bandages on every one of them.

"I bet your act was so beautiful," the clown said to Rose. "You're allowed to be affectionate and loving. You're allowed to go around telling people and things that you love them. You don't know how lucky you are sometimes, being a woman."

Rose smiled. "There are some strange advantages, it's true."

"Was your partner handsome?" the clown asked. "I saw the most devilishly fetching clown at the Razzle Dazzle Circus. Go check him out, even if he isn't the guy."

Pierrot stopped by the main library. It was made of orange bricks and had gargoyles of squirrels on the walls. He remembered that Rose always read anything she could get her hands on. He described Rose to the librarian and asked if a girl fitting that description ever came in.

There was a tunnel on the side of the library that led to a magnificent greenhouse. Pierrot headed down the tunnel into the glass structure, which had white tiles on the floor and pots of flowers everywhere. He went to have a conversation with the roses. There was a load of huge roses. He was always surprised at how voluptuous they were. Rather like a white handkerchief tucked into the breasts of a woman at the opera. Where shall I find my lovely Rose? Have you seen her?

The roses were desperate to have their portraits painted. They complained to one another that they hadn't been born in the Netherlands, where all the great still-life artists had lived. It was a waste to be a rose in Canada. There were still some drops of water on their petals from having been watered. They were like tears.

40

ON THE FOURTH DAY

here was a theater in the East End called the Velvet that was surrounded by factories. Nobody noticed the theater during the day. Women with little kerchiefs on their heads would stand outside on their breaks to smoke a cigarette. But when the sun went down, and the factory workers had gone home, and all the trucks were in garages, the theater lights would come on and that glowing palace was all that seemed to exist on the block.

Rose stepped into the theater. The carpets were a deep burgundy, and the seats were all made out of vermilion velvet. The curtains were such a heavy red that they looked as though they had soaked up the blood from a hundred murders. When the curtains rose, the stage was lit up and seemed like a tiny womb, with the performer tucked inside. The clown on exhibit had an enormous trunk that seemed as long as one that might belong to an immigrant family going across the ocean to the New World.

The trunk held all manner of unusual and extraordinary objects to juggle with. There were bottles that the clown pulled out and spun around quickly. He had colorful balls and pins and a group of butcher knives. Rose wondered if he used these same knives in the kitchen to cut up salami.

But those feats were nothing, as the clown was just warming up. He had some sticks with rags on the ends of them that he dipped into kerosene and proceeded to set on fire. He dipped his white skullcap into some water and then put it on his head. That way his head wouldn't catch fire if one of the balls of flame chanced to land on it.

He juggled so many at a time that Rose felt like she was hurtling through outer space, passing different constellations. If you were in the audience, you couldn't help but reflect on all the winking stars immeasurable distances away, which blazed so we'd have something to wish on, and lit up the sky so that we could walk our dogs in the evening without bumping into trees.

His pièce de résistance, which he had worked on for several years before mastering it, was to keep one burning giant ball in the center, with colorful balls spinning around it, creating in essence a map of the universe.

After his performance, the release of anxiety was so intense that he went outside behind the theater to throw up three or four times. Rose met him there. He led her back to his dressing room. He was still so exhausted by his performance that before he could talk he had to weep and weep and weep.

"*C'était magnifique. Je comprends que ça puisse vous vider.* That was magnificent. I can see how it could drain you," Rose said.

"*C'est ce que fait Dieu, chaque nuit.* That's what God has to do every night on an infinite scale. He invented the whole universe, and now he has to pay attention to it. Otherwise all the stars will go out one by one. We complain that he sometimes doesn't get around to the things we want him to, but look up at the sky! Always more spectacular, the people say. Always more spectacular. *Les gens en veulent toujours plus.*"

"*Oui,*" said Rose.

She wanted to be a full participant in that extravaganza too.

"*Connaissez-vous un clown du nom de Pierrot?* He's so very light on his feet, it sometimes seems as though he is floating above the ground."

"*Il y a quelqu'un qui correspond à cette description au Théâtre Magnifique.* Go try there."

Pierrot looked up at the night sky. The North Star was twinkling so bright that it was surely a sign. He wished to find Rose. He never really put much stock in the stars. He rather fancied himself a lucky person. He didn't feel as though he could impose on the universe and ask for any more favors. And should he find himself needing to make a demand or recommendation to the universe, he would have to be in dire straits before doing so. Although he could not call his situation distressful by any stretch of the imagination, he nonetheless looked up at the big night sky and he asked it for Rose.

41

ON THE FIFTH DAY

The clown performing at the Ocean Theater was wearing a wig with hair that twirled upward in roped braids as if he were submerged underwater. He had a deep-sea-diver outfit on. He looked incredibly clunky and ungraceful as he lumbered across the stage in his flippers.

He climbed up the scaffolding to above the stage. He stood on the tiny ledge, and after attaching two ropes to the hooks that were on the back of his outfit, he dove! Right down he went, and then before he smacked the stage, the complicated system of pulleys attached to the ropes yanked him so that he was able to land on the ground with a certain delicacy. He leaped up again and he floated magically through the air with the slow-motion grace of somebody who is underwater. He flipped around. He did a breaststroke. It was beautiful and ludicrous.

He and Rose sat across from each other at the theater's café, off the lobby.

"All life began underneath the ocean. So I'm giving people a taste of what existence might have been like before civilization."

"But we were amoebas and tiny shrimplike creatures. We didn't start off in deep-sea-diving outfits."

"We all come into this world with an oxygen tube in our belly button."

"True."

She put her hands up to her own belly. There had so recently been a sea creature evolving in there, trying its best to get its act together. It had perished under the deep, deep, deep sea.

McMahon had put the word out that he wanted Rose found. Someone tapped McMahon's shoulder at a restaurant. It was a burlesque woman with a white fur coat and thick black liner surrounding her eyes. Her face was so overdone that he assumed it must be stage makeup.

"What?" he asked.

"I just saw Rose. I swear it's her. She's backstage across the street, talking to the clown."

McMahon stood up from the table, grabbed his coat, hurried out of the restaurant, knocking over a chair on his way, and stomped across the street. He went through the lobby into the main hall and up onto the stage, then tossed aside the curtains and walked backstage. He pushed open the door that had *Snoop the Magnificent* written on it.

"Was a black-haired girl just in here?"

"Yup. You should be able to catch her."

Her wet footprints hadn't dried yet and they headed down the back hallway to the back exit that led to the street. McMahon ran, even though it made his lungs burn. He pushed open both doors. There was nothing in the alley but the wind. And a trembling fourteen-year-old girl with heart-shaped cookies she had made for a performer. She held one out for McMahon. He sneered like an enraged horse.

PIERROT WENT TO THE PUBLIC BATHS. There were dark brown and white square tiles, as if the floor of the pool were a chessboard. A tall, old, skinny man walked slowly, step by step, across the pool, as though he were a king piece. Pierrot took off his towel and walked to the edge of the pool, sat down on the ledge and lowered his feet in. The water was warm and melted his toes. He slipped into the water, closed his eyes and sank to the bottom, where he landed painlessly on his behind. He imagined

Rose underneath the water with him. Why she would be there, he could not fathom. But it seemed as likely that she would be there as anywhere else.

He lay on his back, floating in the large bath, his penis like a lily pad.

·⊰[42]⊱·

ON THE SIXTH DAY

There was a theater all the way on top of the hill in the park, known as the Beaver Theater. Inside the theater, paintings of forests with deer galloping through them hung from the walls. The curtain was striped green and brown.

This clown was known for his animal acts. He would take off his top hat to reveal a duckling on his head. He had a legendary dog that had been with him for years. He was quite miserable, as it was hard to rent an apartment when he had such a ridiculous menagerie. He was kicked out of the Saint Martin's Children's Circus because one of his geese snapped at a child.

Rose watched his hectic show. He was an enormous clown. He wore a white skullcap. He had on a white one-piece suit with three large red pom-poms as buttons and a red ruffle around his belly, like icing surrounding a cake. He had on white silky pants. He had on large red shoes that must have been about size twenty-six.

He pulled a dove from out of his top hat, followed by a white rabbit and then a white kitten. A tiny goose maniacally drove a little mechanical car around the stage. A small white pony came out from behind the curtain, confused, as though it had just woken up, and the clown proceeded to climb on top of it. The small horse didn't seem to mind, even though the clown was approximately three times its size.

His famous dog looked like it had seen better days. It looked as if a cigar had exploded in its face. That was the trouble with white poodles: they always looked older than they were. The little dog had on a tuxedo. It was able to walk on its hind legs with fantastic ease. It seemed to be as at ease on its hind legs as it was on all fours, quite possibly because it had been doing this for so many years. It walked across a low tightrope the clown had set up.

He was backstage with the dog in the dressing room. All the other animals were presumably in their cages. But he seemed to treat the dog like it was his equal and so it was allowed everywhere with him.

"I've worked with all kinds of animals. I had a great little lamb for a few years. The kids went crazy for him. They wanted to run their fingers through his wool.

"I usually can only afford to keep one exotic creature at a time. It stresses a person out. I'm never sure about them. I don't know when one of them will turn on me. It was okay to put myself through that kind of excitement when I was a younger man. But now it'll give me a heart attack.

"I had a lion for a few years. He had a nasty temperament. I sold him to a zoo when I was drinking and needed to pay the rent. You name the animal, I've worked with it. I'm a lot like Noah, you know."

"Have you ever worked with a bear?"

"Ha-ha-ha! You have me there! I never have. Are you in the entertainment trade yourself?"

"When I was young, I had an act with an imaginary dancing bear. We would waltz around the room together."

"Hmmm. Well, it's easier to rent a hotel room without a menagerie. Sometimes an imaginary animal can be just as effective as a real one."

"The Mother Superior said that I was dancing with the devil. But it was kindness and love and warmth and compassion that I was spinning about with. I was welcoming those things with big open arms into the orphanage. I wanted that kind of warmth."

"Of course. We clowns must tame some of the great metaphors of the world."

"I'm looking for a partner who I used to work with when I was very young."

"Describe him to me."

"He's a daydreamer, always has his head in the clouds."

"There's a clown at the Velvet who's always half asleep."

Pierrot went to the zoo. He passed by the different glass exhibition cases. He never could spend too much time with reptiles. They seemed so lacking in compassion, hardly part of an animal kingdom character-ized foremost by its penchant for feeling sorry for itself and fretting about what tomorrow would bring.

He stood in front of the swans. Rose had always liked swans. This was the type of exhibit she would come and look at. He remembered the big angel wings that they wore when they were in the Christmas pageant that had changed his life. He threw a small chunk of stale bread into the water. The swans, unaccustomed to being fed in those bleak times, spread their wings and rose up toward him in one movement like a wave.

43

ON THE SEVENTH DAY

T he tiny theaters were hard to find, the ones that seated only a hundred spectators at a time. One such establishment was on top of a spaghetti restaurant. Patrons would sometimes smell the sauce cooked in huge vats and get hungry during the show. The owner of the restaurant took the lids off the pots at opportune moments so he would be sure to get the post-theater crowd.

Rose arrived last minute at this theater on a miserable day with freezing rain falling from the sky and hurried to her seat. The spotlight revealed a clown and a bed in the middle of the stage. The clown was dressed in polka-dotted pajamas and a nightcap. He kept opening his mouth and making incredible yawning noises that sounded like an elephant had suddenly been alarmed. Then he picked up a teddy bear and clung to it amorously and dropped into bed and underneath the covers. He put a night mask over his eyes.

He then got out of the bed, not removing the mask, as if he were sleepwalking. He got on the bicycle with his night mask. He began riding his bicycle backward. He was riding it right alongside the edge of the stage, coming dangerously close to falling off. The audience gasped.

He climbed up a ladder at the side of the stage. A child in the audience yelled at him to wake up. He proceeded to walk the tightrope with his night mask on. He ended up in the middle of the rope and began making his outrageous yawns once again. Then he lay down on the tightrope and fell right back to sleep, as unself-conscious of his height as a cloud.

The audience should not have been alarmed. Nothing can really happen when you are dreaming.

Rose went to see him in his dressing room. He was sitting on a long green couch that was against the wall of the room. He was too exhausted to wipe off his white face paint. He had a rag in one hand and a pot of cream in the other, but he kept them separated.

"I get paid practically nothing these days. I guess I'll have to reconcile myself with the fact that I'm a failure. Why is that always so hard? I wish I could just pack in being a clown."

"What else could you do now?"

"Did God create us so we can spend our time speculating how much better He is at absolutely everything? He made us in His image, so naturally we want to create from nothing. It's a maddening task, isn't it? The reason He doesn't do anything or take interviews these days is because He's completely lost His marbles. We'll go up to heaven and discover that He's in a straitjacket, no doubt."

"So you are a religious man? Do you go to church?"

"Obviously not."

He looked at Rose quizzically.

"I'm not at all who you came here looking for, am I?"

"No."

"Figures."

He stretched out on the couch and pulled his jacket over his head to take another nap.

"Nothing really matters on a Sunday," his muffled voice said from under the jacket. "Everybody gets to have a day off from who they actually are. Don't you think? Your crimes don't count, your achievements don't matter. You just have to curl up in your bed and take a lovely siesta. You are both nothing and everything in your dreams."

What in the world was Rose doing when she interviewed these clowns other than trying to rediscover a certain innocence that she had once felt? Maybe if she could hear it explained back to her, she could have it once again. A hallucination is no longer a hallucination if somebody else sees it. Then it becomes an apparition.

"Do you want to have sex with me, darling? If not, for the love of God, let me sleep."

Every time she knocked on a door, Rose was made aware of the fact that she was a girl. Everything she did along the way was something a girl wasn't supposed to do. She was not allowed to have dignity.

She went home and dreamed that she and Pierrot were underneath the sheet, doing things they had never got a chance to do together.

It was miserable and wet and cold that day, and Pierrot didn't know where to look anymore. He went to see a private investigator. The man had just come in from the rain himself, as he was still wearing his checkered rain hat. The water from it dripped off the brim and onto the papers and photographs on his desk. The drops of water caused the ink to bloom into small black irises. He smelled like cigarettes.

The investigator said he could help, but he charged. He wrote his fee on a piece of paper and handed it to Pierrot. Pierrot was taken aback by the amount. He could not save up the money to pay him to find Rose. Why was a pauper like him looking for Rose? What would he have to offer her if they did meet? It wasn't meant to be.

PIERROT LAY BACK DOWN on the mattress in his room. He had spent the little money he had on the one luxury he could afford. He rolled up a bit of tobacco and decided he would never find her. When he lit up the thin cigarette, it made a slight sizzling noise, like the sound of a writer's manuscript being tossed into the fire.

44

THE MOON IN C MINOR

ose heard Pierrot's piano tune playing in her head every time she walked down the street. It haunted her. She worried it would play in her head until she found Pierrot. She began to frequent all the circuses. She had become an aficionado when it came to clowns. She would wait for them backstage. She brought a notebook along with her, jotting down names of clowns and clues she was able to gather. Rose had dinner one night with Mimi at a bistro. Mimi kept talking about a pianist she had heard playing at the Savoy.

"It's a laugh. Some of the girls and I like to go. They play old silent films, from when we were little. But the best thing is the piano player. He plays these wonderful tunes. They seem simple, but they put you in a good mood for three days. He's gorgeous too. Some of the girls try to seduce him, but he's got his head in the clouds."

"Oh, right, you've mentioned him before."

After dinner, they kissed each other on the cheek and headed their separate ways home. But Rose didn't want to go home to her lonely room. It had started to snow, and the flakes were blowing in eddies, like jacks hurled in the air by a young girl. Instead she wandered farther west down Saint Catherine Street, toward the Savoy. Perhaps there was a slight chance the piano player was Pierrot. When she arrived at the cinema, only half the lightbulbs of its marquee were lit, and they were blinking on and off.

Rose looked at the schedule. An old silent film was playing: a sailor falls in love with a party girl who is married to a brute. In the end, he puts her in a trunk and takes her off to the open sea, to freedom. Rose thought that sounded all right, and she paid for a ticket to the late showing. The only decor in the cinema seemed to be little golden stars painted all over the proscenium. To her surprise, the theater was full.

When the lights went down, a girl's face appeared on the screen. She was blowing kisses. Her face was so white and round, there wasn't a person alive who wouldn't compare it to the moon. Her husband didn't respond to her kisses, but wagged his finger angrily at her. As she was heading to the grocery store with her shopping bag in hand, a friendly sailor on a bicycle began cycling figure eights around her. The sailor put her on the handlebars of his bicycle and they headed down the street, swerving in and out of traffic. How marvelous, Rose thought. She clapped her hands in delight.

The piano player was as good as Mimi had said. She realized that most of the audience members were there to listen to him and not to see the film.

It seemed that the strange black-and-white people on the screen were really dancing to his playing. And that if he played a different tune, they would act in an entirely different manner. If he didn't play fast enough, they wouldn't be able to escape their captors. His hands would fly up at the end, and she could see them up above the heads in the front row. She hadn't heard anybody play the piano in a way that pleased her in a very long time.

Toward the end of the film, the pianist began to play a slow, light-hearted tune when the heroine and the sailor finally fall in love. Rose knew that tune. She recognized it. How could she not? She wanted to get up and dance.

It was the tune Pierrot used to play when they went to the rich people's houses. All the old people used to dance to that song. Their breasts would jiggle, their jewelry would make clinking noises and they would put the palms of their hands together and make silent claps—like two pieces of bread put together.

Could she actually be in the same building as Pierrot? Were they occupying the same time and place once again? She stood up. She ran down the aisle of the theater. She hurried through the lobby and pushed her way out through the big glass doors framed with gold. She felt the rush of cold air outside. She could escape. What could there be other than disappointment? She had snubbed him years ago. He had made it clear he didn't want anything to do with her. He had never written to her. But here he was, playing the piano in a small theater on Saint Catherine Street. Shouldn't she at least find out if he still had a bit of affection for her? Rose was terrified. She had spent so much time looking for him. What if he didn't care at all about her? Of course, he wouldn't have thought about her through the years, the way she had thought of him.

WHEN PIERROT WALKED OUT of the cinema, there was a woman standing under the marquee, dressed in a simple black coat. She was the most beautiful woman he had ever seen and he recognized her immediately. He wanted to run up and throw his arms around her. He tried to light a cigarette, but his hands were trembling. He finally succeeded. He inhaled. He was freezing all of a sudden. Trembling violently. What if he blew this again? She might spurn him. Of course she would. Why had he been looking for her? She was too good for him. He closed his eyes and began to pray. He was afraid to approach. Pierrot waited for her to notice him.

Rose looked at her reflection in the glass of the theater front, wondering how she would appear to him. She was thinking she would go and come back another night when she was more prepared. When she knew what to say. But she couldn't move.

Pierrot thought, She's waiting for a lover, anyone can see that. She's worried he won't find her lovely. What type of fool wouldn't find her lovely? She didn't see him staring. Even if her lover came out of the blue and killed him, he wouldn't care. He wanted to say hello to her again.

"Rose!"

And she turned.

"Pierrot! How did you know it was me?"

"No one in the world is so beautiful. I would know you anywhere."

She smiled. She put her face in her hands. She had not expected a statement like that so quickly. He had always professed his love so easily.

"Thank you," she said.

"What are you doing here?"

"Waiting for you."

"Waiting for me!"

"I came into the movie. I recognized that tune."

"It's your tune. I've changed it so much over the years."

"Have you? It sounded exactly the same."

"I . . . I've been wanting to see you lately."

"Really? I've been thinking about you too."

"You have?"

They stood there with the snow coming down, making their shoes wet. Neither of them felt the cold. Neither of them wanted to move, in case the other disappeared. They hadn't seen each other in six years.

"I'm sorry. Can I just hug you?"

They threw their arms around each other and stood like that, terrified of letting go, weeping into each other's shoulders. For so many years neither of them had had a shoulder to cry on. They just wept now. They stopped for a moment and pulled away to marvel at each other's face again. Then they hugged again and wept some more. They finally let go just to laugh. Although they didn't know why they were laughing. Nothing was funny; it was all just so pleasurable.

. . .

THEY WENT TO the Little Burgundy neighborhood to go to the city's most popular jazz club. It was run by a black man who had been a railway porter and a bootlegger. Pierrot loved the place and decided to bring Rose to it.

He hadn't gone in a while because the music put him in such a state—it was so close to being high—that it would push him over the edge, causing him to use drugs. There was a trombone player who made him feel the rush that comes right after shooting. Once there was a touring singer who, with her eyes closed, sang about being left by her lover, and it made Pierrot feel so melancholic, he couldn't bear it, he had to get high. Beautiful things made him sad. But now that Rose was back, wonderful things would make him happy—there could be no such thing as sadness. Sadness was nothing more than a variation on happiness.

They sat at a table in the corner and ordered a pitcher of beer. They sloshed it all over themselves as they poured it happily. The two of them were piss drunk by the time they pulled each other over to the dance floor.

It was very wonderful. A perfect, splendid night. By the time Rose requested "Lovebird Nestle," the orchestra was either drunk or stoned themselves. There were a couple of players who passed out. The drummer had untied his bow tie and was lying on the stage near the drum. The flute player, who was an insomniac, played a tune like a little breeze getting through a crack in the window. The piccolo sounded like a young child pinching his nose and singing like a cartoon character.

Rose and Pierrot clung to each other as they made little steps and kissed each other's faces. They couldn't bear to be apart, even for one moment more. They danced around, and she swooped under his arms. They put their foreheads together. They shimmied away from each other. They clung together. The few customers drinking at the ballroom that night put their elbows on the table, settled their chins in the palms of their hands and watched. This was so much like performances they had done when they were children. Except they didn't have to go back to an orphanage afterward and sleep in separate beds.

They were adults. They could make love.

WHEN THE BALLROOM CLOSED, they walked down the street together.

"When I went back to the orphanage looking for you," Pierrot said, then paused. "I saw Sister Eloïse."

"That crazy bitch. What did she have to say?"

"She said she told you about me and her."

"I don't know what you mean."

"We had sex in the bathrooms."

The spots on Rose's cheeks began to glow bright red.

"Starting when?"

"I think when I was eleven. Yes, when I was eleven."

"Oh, it's not your fault, my darling. She was a lunatic. Surely you can see that?"

"You don't think less of me?"

"If I knew it would make you feel better, I'd go there now and put a bullet right in her brain."

"No, I don't think I'm angry with her. It's in the past. I just worry that it's done something to me. That it's rendered me in some way unlovable."

"Don't be silly. I will kill her for you one day."

"Ha-ha-ha. What? Thank you, but you don't have to."

And then Pierrot began to weep.

"Look, since you've given me your secret, let me give you mine. I was a man's mistress, as you heard, but when I left him, for money I would dress up in high heels and garter belts and make love to men dressed as zebras. And those little films are being shown in small rooms all over the world, and men are masturbating to them right now."

"Oh, I saw you in one of those movies! You were splendid!"

. . .

SHE OPENED THE DOOR to the Valentine Hotel and Pierrot caught it behind her before it closed. He came right up the stairs after her. She felt like he was her shadow. She felt as if he was stitched to her. The stairs were doing marvelous things. They were so much like the stairs in dreams. They were like accordions. Some of them took an unnecessarily long time to get up. Rose could fly up some of the stairs, gravity seeming not to exist.

That was desire messing with physics: putting its finger on the record and then slowing it down, making sure you heard every word spoken, and memorized it.

When they walked into the room, Pierrot pushed Rose up against the blue wallpaper. One of her legs was around his back. As soon as he was pressed up against her, she could feel his penis. She looked down in disbelief. She unbuttoned his pants and reached down and felt it.

His jacket came off to the ground. She'd never been so excited to see someone take their clothes off. As she took off her clothes she was delighted with her own body, as though she were seeing it for the first time, and she was very pleased with what she was witnessing. She pulled her stocking off her leg and she was thrilled by how skinny it was. And then she wiggled the toes at the end of her feet, very satisfied with those too.

When Pierrot saw Rose's tits, he grabbed them with both hands and stuffed his face between them. He pulled off his suspenders. And he was inside her before his pants had even hit the floor. The belt buckle hit the ground like an anchor.

They moved over to the bed. Pierrot held her shoulders as he pushed harder and deeper. She cried out so loudly that Pierrot was afraid the neighbors would hear. Not that he imagined they were the type to mind. They would probably quite enjoy hearing Rose's lovemaking. But he wanted to keep it all to himself. It turned him on so much that other people hearing it would be like others seeing her naked.

He pulled out and came all over her. And when he was done, he felt like his whole body was ruined in a wonderful way. Because she had squeezed every bit of life out of him. After they were done gasping for air, they looked at each other and laughed and laughed and laughed.

He didn't feel like a criminal for having made love to someone. How wonderful! He couldn't quite believe that Rose was next to him. How wonderful! And she didn't have any clothes on. How wonderful! He wanted to find her clothes and throw them out the window so that she would always be naked next to him, so that she could never go anyplace again.

"What's your favorite color?" Pierrot asked.

"Dark blue. Almost black," Rose answered.

"What was your favorite age?" He pressed further.

"Eleven."

"Do you have a favorite bird?"

"A robin."

"You seem like the type of girl who would like a robin. You appreciate what a devastatingly handsome bird it is."

"Thanks?"

"What is your favorite book?"

"I saw a puppet show of Molière's *Tartuffe* that made me laugh so hard."

"How are you so cultured?"

"I used to read books to the children when I was their governess. They could understand anything. And even if they didn't, they would just lie quietly through the adult parts."

"You probably ruined them for life! I don't care what anybody says, all those strange novels about complicated problems only have the effect of making children melancholic."

"They're rich. They're going to end up melancholic no matter what."

"True, if you can afford to be melancholic, why the hell not?" Pierrot agreed. "Enjoy it. So what's your favorite food of them all?"

"Lobster."

"Lobster! I've had it with these highfalutin answers. I don't know what type of men you were dating before me. I can't give you those marvelous dishes."

"I like toast and jam the most lately."

"Me too. I love eating toast and jam in the morning. You were always so good with all the younger children at the orphanage. You would make such a wonderful mother."

Rose blushed. Pierrot loved when her cheeks turned red like that. It always drove him wild with desire.

"We should have a baby," he said.

"No, don't say that. We can't. You know that. We're broke."

"I will make a fortune so that you can have our baby," Pierrot insisted.

"How will you do that?"

"I do not know. But the baby will smell like pastry sugar."

"And it will have big, big blue eyes," Rose added.

"And dark hair."

"No, light hair like yours."

"And we will read it complicated novels so that it will be confused all day long!" Pierrot exclaimed.

"And you should play it sad tunes on the piano so that it will weep for no reason at all. And we will say, 'Baby, oh, our dear little baby, what in the world is wrong with you?'"

"And the baby will have no idea what it is crying about."

"Let's make it afraid of the world so that it will want more hugs from us," Rose said, sitting up. "When it tells us that it thinks there is a monster in the closet, instead of telling it that it is a fool we will board up the closet with planks and nails."

SOMETIMES WHEN PIERROT WAS NERVOUS about feeling good, to his dismay he would find himself thinking about Eloïse. He saw Eloïse anywhere out of the corner of his eye. He saw a woman in a habit step onto the trolley when he was riding back home from work. Anxiety spread through his veins like a hive that had been upset and all the hornets were buzzing out. He leaped off the back of the trolley. He dove into a roll and landed on the ground. Everyone on the trolley stuck their head out the window to look at him. The nun also looked out. It was obvious upon second glance that she was at least seventy. Sketches of all her old expressions were visible on her face like rough drafts.

He suddenly wanted to get high. When he shot up, the heroin flowed through his body, turning on light switches in every part, like someone showing a child there were no ghosts in the house. And then he thought about Rose. She would never be with him if she saw him stoned. The feeling passed.

AFTER THEY HAD MADE OUT that night, Pierrot told Rose about his addiction. She instinctively looked down at his arms. They were covered in scars like black smudges. She knew they were track marks.

"I'm not going to lie to you. During the years before I found you again, I was completely addicted to heroin. In part I felt that I had nobody in my life. I was a man without a family, and so I was in many ways a man without an identity. I didn't care whether I died. The addiction gave me a purpose, even though that sounds pathetic. It is so pathetic. But I woke up in the morning knowing what I wanted. Otherwise the sense of loss I felt waking up was treacherous. Then I got it into my head that I could find you. And I wanted to be free of my addiction. I couldn't bear for you to see me like that."

"And I didn't."

"And you never will."

PIERROT HAD A SUITCASE in one hand and a painting in the other. He went to stay at Rose's apartment. When he came in, the powdery snow, like dust from a child banging two blackboard erasers together, was all around him. Rose left the room messy, like a girl who was used to having a maid. There were irises carved on the wooden back of the chair, though its cushion was totally ruined. The teacup was broken and it had been glued back together. The yellow blanket lay on the floor all jumbled up like scrambled eggs.

SHE LIKED THE WAY he got her undressed. But she also liked the way he got her dressed. He helped her with her buttons. Or he picked up her hat and put it on his head. It was like he forgot what was his own self and what was hers. She liked the way he rode her around on the handlebars of his bicycle. She liked the way when they had a conversation while walking, he'd jump in front of her and walk backward so he could look right at her when they spoke. She liked the way he laughed uproariously at any joke on the radio.

He liked the way she would laugh uproariously at any joke on the radio. He liked that she would write words in the air with her fingertip. He liked the way she put her hand out to check whether or not it was raining, when it clearly was. He liked the way she helped out the older people in the hotel. He liked how all the children in the neighborhood seemed to know her name.

She liked how all the children in the neighborhood seemed to know his name. She liked how he could fry up an egg while smoking a cigarette clenched between his lips. She liked the way he called up to her from the sidewalk. She liked the way he put his arm around her. She liked the way he talked about paintings when they went to the museum. She liked the things he noticed about the world.

He liked the things she noticed about the world. He liked the way she looked when she was wearing underwear and sitting cross-legged on the bed and describing bad things that had happened to her. He liked when she read passages that she had underlined in novels. He liked how she got involved in other people's arguments on the street. He liked how she always read the newspaper first thing in the morning. He liked how she made him feel about himself.

She liked the way he made her feel about herself.

A YEAR PASSED, during which Rose and Pierrot lived in a happy state of penury. Because times were so difficult all around, Pierrot's paycheck was often short. Rose sporadically found and lost jobs. She worked for a period in a dress factory, and then as a soda girl, and then as a maid at the fancy Ritz-Carlton Hotel. Every place she worked had to let her go in the end. Yet she and Pierrot still scrimped together enough to pay the rent and have a meal at the end of the evening, under a dim lightbulb in their hotel room. Despite the Depression, they were a happy unit, and it seemed as if the world, which had once been so cruel to them, had mercifully lost interest.

Rose was scribbling in her black journal one afternoon.

"May I look at your journal?"

"Yes! It's not private at all. In fact, I hope to one day share it with the whole world."

Pierrot picked up the book and flipped through the thick pages. The journal was filled with crude illustrations in black pen.

What marvels were there?

There was a sketch of a girl wearing a Napoleon hat. There was a drawing of a clown on a bicycle whose wheels looked as big as a house. There was an illustration of footsteps with arrows—a pattern to an extraordinary drunken waltz, no doubt. There was a drawing of a top hat with a lever so the crown could open and close like a chimney flap and smoke would come out of it. There was a tuxedo with a carnation tucked into its pocket, with holes in the elbows. The drawings on the paper became animated in his head, a Disney cartoon. It was Rose's circus dream.

Pierrot sometimes came across Rose doing something incredibly odd.

But it wasn't because his darling had lost her mind. It was because she was working on different things for the show, which she never quite gave up on.

Once, she was balanced on the edge of the roof. A passerby might have assumed she was about to plunge to her death. Suicide wasn't uncommon for women in the Depression. Having your husband home all day long drove women to great despair. But Rose happily waved to Pierrot.

The next day Pierrot came up to the room and found Rose sitting with a wooden spoon with a rag wrapped around the top. The rag was on fire. She had a little teacup that she filled with kerosene.

"Remember when we used to perform in those rich houses?" Rose said. "We seduced them. When we showed up in their living rooms, they didn't know what had hit them. They were under a spell. We could have asked them to hand over the keys to their houses and they would have."

She took a sip from the teacup and breathed a huge bolt of fire that shot halfway across the kitchen. She hiccuped afterward and a small flame shot out. They were both a little bit startled and frightened.

"I can't believe I'm still here," Rose said, looking up and down at her body.

"Never try that again."

Rose shrugged. She wasn't exactly sure how the plan would come together. But sometimes you just have to work at something for the end to appear in sight.

ONE AFTERNOON, Pierrot was taking a piss in an alley when a man came up behind him and tapped him on the shoulder.

"You owe me money," the stranger said.

Pierrot buttoned up his fly and turned around. There was a man with a peaked cap down over one eye and a missing front tooth.

"Have I had the pleasure of making your acquaintance?"

"That redhead you used to go around with ripped me off. And now you're going to pay for what she took."

"Poppy? How is she? I think about her often."

"She took all my money. I woke up and it was gone."

"Well, I hesitate to say this, but Poppy was a generous person—so if she stole from you, there might have been a reason."

"You're going to pay for what she owes. So hand over a hundred dollars."

"I don't have a cent."

"She said that I should come see you. She said that you would do right by her."

"If I had money, I would give it to her. Or to you for her. But I have a new girlfriend. Doesn't she still have that new fellow? He seemed to have his wits about him, an aggressive gent, a real go-getter."

"He threw her out. She robbed me. Now you're going to pay me."

"I am no longer a thief. I can't be, they have my fingerprints."

"Buy a pair of gloves and act like a man."

"I've never had any idea what that means."

The man took out a knife. Pierrot closed his eyes, accepting his doom or fate or whatever. He didn't know how to fight back. All he knew was how to sacrifice himself. But nothing happened. There was a crashing sound and Pierrot opened his eyes.

The man looked stunned. His jaw dropped as though he were about to say something. He fell to his knees. At first Pierrot wasn't sure what had happened. The man seemed to have been struck down by God. He was in the presence of a miracle. But standing behind the man was Rose, holding a broken chair in her hands. They both looked at the body as it slumped to the ground. Rose quickly squatted—her coat tucked underneath her buttocks—and she checked the pulse of the man lying there.

"Oh, he's okay. Let's move along, though. He won't be in a good mood when he wakes up."

They headed off toward the street. The alley was filled with furniture that had been thrown out after evictions. There was a mattress covered in blue violets—the color of the blue lips of corpses. An overturned crib looked like the carcass of a dead buffalo.

"I'm not ever going to let anybody hurt us again. I'm going to fight back."

"You are so brave!"

"I'm not brave. I just can't take it anymore. You have to smash people over the head with chairs and bottles in order to be taken seriously."

Her hat flew off and her hair blew up in the air. Pierrot had never seen her look so dazzling, but he also found her quite mad. He wondered why she was even dating him. He was not ferocious. He wasn't good enough for her. Rose would realize this any second and leave him. Pierrot was concerned about Poppy. Had he abandoned her? Did he have to help her if she was in trouble? He didn't want to think of himself as the type of man who treated women badly. But was there any way to have sex with a woman without being unkind to her? Wasn't sex always a vicious act of cruelty? He couldn't go back to Poppy. He wanted to be with Rose. It was the only thing he had ever wanted. Would he end up hurting Rose next? Was his relationship to her unholy and unkind as well? He wanted to be true to Rose. He couldn't be true to any woman but Rose.

She was walking down the street, ranting about how she wanted to bop everyone in the face. Pierrot had stopped in his tracks, and she was walking alone. She started walking toward him with both her palms up and out to the side, like an Egyptian who didn't know which way to go. Asking, "What the hell?"

"Will you marry me, Rose?"

ON THE DAY of their wedding, they took a bath together in little pots of warm water they had to waste hard-earned coal to heat. They asked Mimi to be their witness when they got married at City Hall. They were twenty-two years old.

Rose had a tiny white veil pinned to her black hat. She wore a navy blue dress with discreet polka dots and a white collar. She held a bouquet of cloth flowers that Mimi had picked up from the costume room at the film studio. Pierrot was wearing his famous suit.

The lace of her wedding veil made it look like they were peering at each other through a window covered in frost.

"I don't deserve you. If anyone wants to come up here and stop this, they most definitely should. I will do anything for you. I have never put anyone ahead of myself. And I have always wanted to. I want to devote my life to making you happy. After spending this past year with you, were you to leave me, I wouldn't be able to survive."

"You are my Napoleon. You have stuck a stake in my heart. You are my Alexander the Great."

Pierrot shrugged, because he wasn't anything like those guys.

"I don't care if you are making the worst decision of your life," Pierrot said. "Because I want you to belong to me so badly."

It was very short. She liked that. They went into a door single and unmarried, and came out a couple. Just like a transformation that occurred in a magician's box.

They had a dollar that Mimi had given to them as a wedding present. They had to decide what to do with it. They decided on getting their photo taken. When they each saw how nice and cleaned up the other one looked in the photo, they were delighted they had chosen to have their photos taken that day. It was a black-and-white photograph. For reasons he could not even be sure of himself, the photographer decided to add a touch-up to the photograph. He took a little paintbrush and added a dab of pink paint to both of Rose's cheeks.

"LADIES AND GENTLEMEN, I am giving a toast to a girl I have known my whole life. We were left as babies at the same orphanage. We were put in cribs that were adjacent to one another. And the moment I turned my head and saw her on the other side of the bars, I said, I'm going to propose to that baby."

At one point in the evening Pierrot sat beside the pianist. They engaged in a four-hand tune that sounded like a hundred pianists playing all at once. As the girls in the bar began to feel tired their heads sank forward, as though they were lost in reading novels on the train.

Pierrot had tied soup cans to the back of his bicycle. They made a rattling, clattering, wonderful sound, like a drunk party girl falling down the stairs with bottles in her hand. There was a nip in the air. Later that night they sat on the rooftop, wrapped together in a blanket, and looked up at the constellations in the sky. Rose knew what they were from looking through the telescope at McMahon's house. But she decided to rename them all for Pierrot.

"There's the Unicorn. See its long magical horn?"

"Oh yes!"

"There's the Pony with the Broken Leg."

"Don't look at that constellation. It'll make us too sad."

"Look at the Cartwheeling Girl."

"That one's my favorite."

"I like the Girl Who's Puking over the Toilet after the Orgy."

"She needs to slow down!"

"The Boy Blowing Out His Birthday Candles."

"Oh! How old is he?"

"Eleven," they say at the same time.

"All I want, Pierrot, is for you to be happy. I can't make myself happy. Nobody can really make themselves happy. But they can make other people happy."

"Don't say that! Don't ever worry about me. If ever I'm standing in the way of your happiness, I swear I will throw myself right off a roof. All I want is for you to be happy. I'm broken, and you're perfect. You come first."

"No."

"Yes, I insist. Please. It will make me so happy if we just agree on that."

"Okay. I love you, Pierrot. You're the only thing and person I've ever loved."

"What did I do to deserve someone as wonderful as you? If I knew I was going to die tomorrow, I wouldn't mind, because this is the perfect feeling. It doesn't get any better than this in the entire universe."

Rose's white undergarments were all over the floor—like eggshells on the ground. They felt silly because they both began to cry.

·◖ 45 ◗·

NOCTURNE IN PINK AND GOLD

On Saturday night, sometime after closing, there was a fire on Saint Catherine Street. The Savoy Theater went up in flames, like a page in a book. Its fuse box had exploded. It was as if the building had had a heart attack. Perhaps it was just the building's time to go. The fire trucks came, but there was nothing anyone could do. Pierrot was now out of work, like most of the pianists and just about everybody else in the city, it seemed. On top of that, Rose was also unemployed.

The landlady came right into their room on Sunday. She begged them for rent. She took Pierrot's trousers and shook them upside down to see if any money came out. They wouldn't get out of bed to stop her. They were too hungry and tired.

People were being evicted everywhere. Pierrot and Rose stopped on the street to allow movers to pass in front of them. The possessions of an apartment were being loaded onto a cart pulled by a white horse. There were black spots on the thighs of the white horse that looked like the footprints of children in the snow.

The movers were carrying a dusty red couch. There was a green piano among the possessions. The sound the piano made when jostled by the couch was curious and soft and lovely. Pierrot hadn't played a piano in weeks, so there was no way he was going to pass by this one without playing it. He had resisted heroin, but there was no way he could resist this piano. He leaped onto the back of the truck and scrambled over the furniture before anyone could stop him. He sat on a kitchen table and began to play the green piano. It played so gentle and sweet.

One of the movers hurried out to tell Pierrot to knock it off, but the playing stopped him in his tracks. He had an instant change of heart and wished that Pierrot would never stop playing, that he would play for the rest of their lives.

Rose also felt like letting go of her problems. She began to dance to the piano tune, and her breath made puffs of clouds come out of her mouth. Some children peeped at her. The tone of the piano was so coquettish that it made Rose bat her eyelashes and hop lightheartedly from toe to toe. Then Rose pretended she was being blown violently by a gust of wind. She held on to the pole of the street lamp and lifted her body until she was hanging horizontally, as though she were trying to resist the pull of a hurricane. She had been working at that trick for a week. Some children ran across the street to see. It was truly wondrous.

When Pierrot stopped and Rose took a bow, the small crowd began to applaud. A child threw a handful of bottle caps into the jacket that Pierrot had laid on the ground. A man tossed in a rolled cigarette.

Rose and Pierrot stood in front of the window of the butcher shop. There were links of sausages, and the head of a pig was suspended from a hook like a mask. The meat was making Rose ravenous.

"I've been all over the city. No one performs the way we do. We're just as good as any of the acts coming in from European cities. I know we can be stars. Those people are starving to death, and yet they would've parted with their pennies if they had any."

"We got a cigarette out of it," said Pierrot, lighting it up.

"We need to get the rich people to pay for expensive tickets to see us," Rose said. "They don't like anything unless they have to pay huge amounts of money for it. They want what other people can't afford. It reminds them that they are rich. We need to get their money. They want to see experience and pain up on display—we have heaps of that."

Rose reached over to take the cigarette Pierrot extended toward her. She exhaled a row of smoke rings that looked like a row of ballerinas in tutus spinning by.

"We've got to get ourselves into a *big* theater," she continued. "We have to advertise ourselves as a rarity. Expectations are all part of a performance. We have to get everyone worked up. Telling people who will like it is half the work of any show."

"I love when you talk about taking over the world. How are you going to put this together?"

"I don't know. I can see it now clear as anything. We're going to have an army of tap dancers. If only we had some money to invest. What are our options? Rob a bank? Ransom a millionaire? Find a patron?"

They both laughed.

PIERROT KNEW, like every young man in every bedroom in every apartment in every building on the block, that it would be an idiotic move to get your wife pregnant. They would never be able to afford anything that married couples in the past were able to afford—like a house or food for the baby.

He always made certain to withdraw after they had sex. It felt so good. Each time, he was certain that he would mess up and that he would never be able to pull out on time. He pulled out his dick like it was a frying pan taken off a fire. It always put into stark relief just how ludicrous the actual act of sex was. If you weren't having sex to have a baby, then it was a really ridiculous and absurd endeavor, wasn't it?

Rose logically had no desire to have a baby, but she wanted one just the same. Every time they made love, there was nothing on earth she wanted as much as to be impregnated. Everything in her body wanted it. She never said so, though.

Pierrot was afraid to even think of the possibility. And because he was afraid to think of having a baby, he ended up thinking about having a baby. And it was with the thought of the baby looming in his mind that he came inside her that night. He couldn't tell for the life of him whether he did it on purpose. And he was wondering whether she would think he had done it deliberately and be furious with him. To his surprise, she leaned over and planted dozens of kisses on his face.

Their baby began to slowly exist, like a tiny little footnote kicking at the bottom of a great physics text. A cashew at the bottom of a glass dish.

ON A MONDAY MORNING, Pierrot went to wait in the unemployment line. This was an acceptable way to spend your day. There weren't any jobs available. So, instead, life had evolved into these sad rituals. If you didn't engage in these rituals, you were less of a man. It revealed what a sham dignity was.

THIS TIME, ROSE WAS PREGNANT longer than before. She had more time to think about it, wonder about it, reflect upon it. For a time, she hadn't dared to think about the thing inside her as an actual baby that might one day leave her body and inhabit the world. But he began to grow in her imagination. She didn't have any say in it. The little boy in her mind had a life of his own. She gave up fighting and joined the child in her imagination.

She pictured them sailing together on a boat on the Saint Lawrence River. He was dressed in a little sailor's suit and hat. They leaned out the side of the boat and they saw that the water was absolutely swarming with belugas. The belugas were like slabs of marble that had not yet been carved into angels.

She imagined the two of them in safari hats in a jungle in Africa, with binoculars around their necks, waiting to spot wildlife. She imagined them at the Eiffel Tower, wearing berets and eating baguettes. She imagined them in London with pigeons on their heads, sipping tea.

As Rose walked home she noticed a little girl putting a mirror up to her doll's mouth to see if it was alive. She smiled.

Pierrot began to imagine the baby also. He imagined a tiny little girl with black hair. She would always be asking him questions about the natural world and the universe. He quite liked that. Little Rose asked him whether it was possible to travel into outer space and shake hands with aliens. Little Rose asked him whether it was possible to travel back in time to see dinosaurs. Little Rose asked him if it was possible to have a zebra as a pet. Little Rose asked him whether it was possible to find a genie in a bottle. Little Rose asked him whether it was possible to find a flying carpet in Chinatown.

And to all these questions, he answered yes.

There was a statue of an Iroquois warrior that he always passed on the way home. Today there was a crow on its right shoulder, its beak a piece of charcoal. He hoped it was a good omen.

46

THE HEARTBEAT OF A RABBIT

Rose couldn't really be a performer now that she was pregnant. To be a performer, you had to be reckless. You risked your life and security and the safety of your body to make the audience laugh or feel sublime. Therein lay so much of the beauty. The sacrifice was beautiful. But now she didn't feel that way. Now the baby came first. She didn't care to do a cartwheel or anything like that. Even the idea was horrific to her.

Rose was so sick in the morning it was difficult for her to get out of bed. She was exhausted all the time. She felt as though she would die if she weren't able to take an emergency nap. And her lower back felt like someone had come up behind and stabbed her.

She had trouble looking for work. She lined up at a factory but fainted on the street.

THERE WAS A KNOCK ON the door one afternoon during that time. When Rose opened it, she found a girl who looked no more than thirteen standing there and holding up a dead rabbit by its ear, as though it were Exhibit A.

She informed Rose that the rabbit was for sale. The little girl had a rabbit-skin jacket that she had probably sewn all by herself out of the furs of rabbits she had eaten. Rose asked her for a live rabbit. The girl said she'd have to follow her back to her apartment.

They only had to go around the corner, to the skinny triplex that the

Rabbit Girl lived in, on the top floor. There was another bedroom at the very back of the apartment, where the big rabbit cage was. There were patterns of poppies in the molding along the top of the walls. And the wallpaper was a very pretty blue. She had made a cage out of an old armoire. She had replaced the glass on the doors with chicken wire. A rabbit lived on each shelf as if the cage were an apartment building. It was really rather ingenious.

Rose wondered what would happen to this extraordinary child after the Great Depression. She hoped she wouldn't just become someone's wife.

"Would you like me to wring the rabbit's neck? It's messy to cut off its head. I hit it on the head with a mallet. It's pretty quick. I cried about the first fifty times, but I don't anymore."

Rose was carrying a suitcase—she put the live rabbit inside. She walked down the street with the suitcase, with the live rabbit inside it. Perhaps she wanted to save the life of just one living thing. It thumped around in there as though it were someone's heart she had stolen.

"WHAT IN THE WORLD have you done, Rose, my darling?" Pierrot asked when he got home.

Rose was sitting next to the rabbit on the couch.

"I thought we could use the rabbit in our show. But I need a bit of meat. I'm feeling dizzy all the time. It's only a matter of time before I say something and all the teeth fall out of my head."

"This just won't do. Next you'll be bringing me home peacocks from the zoo to put in the stew pot to eat."

"Very funny."

ROSE FELT BAD for the rabbit. But she needed to eat some meat, otherwise she would faint dead away. And the baby was inside her, demanding sustenance. Her appetite was ferocious. In her heart she felt like a wolf.

As if she would do absolutely anything to get what her heart desired. There was nothing she could do for the creature sitting pert and attentive and eager to please on the couch next to her. It was an object of prey.

THAT NIGHT ROSE AND PIERROT ate the rabbit. The power had been turned off and so they ate by candlelight. It was like they were out in the wilderness, in the light of a campfire, eating their wild game. There was nothing but darkness all around them. They would return to civilization tomorrow. And they would have new wisdom and knowledge for the others.

TWO DAYS LATER, Rose stayed home, feeling sick to her stomach. She lay down all by herself on the bed and let out a groan as she delivered a tiny baby on the mattress. She put the baby in the little suitcase that had once held the rabbit. She was terrified of the actual body. It was something you shouldn't be looking at. It was unholy. The dead baby was not her baby but the opposite of it. It was only after she had disposed of it that she could begin to grieve.

As she stepped outside the Valentine Hotel the sun was going down. The sky became darker and darker shades of blue, as if it were applying more shades of eye shadow, until it was finally sufficiently mysterious to go out on a date.

Rose walked to the edge of the water. She opened the lid of the suitcase. She piled some rocks inside it and then she closed it and tossed it into the river. She was too ashamed to tell anyone that she threw her babies away. But she couldn't bring herself to ask what she should do with them. She felt terrible and bleak, as if under all her clothes she were naked, which essentially she was.

At dusk Pierrot found Rose sitting on a bench, facing the river. She was having morbid thoughts. She was descended from people who had come to this great land, killed off its inhabitants and settled in with their treacherous ways. Did you have a right to expect anything from God if you were white and North American?

"What's the point to any of this?" Rose asked. "Do you think that our mothers went on to have amazing lives after giving us up? I hope it was worth it."

"Don't start asking yourself those types of questions, Rose, sweetheart. You are pursuing a dark train of thought."

"I bet they did and repeated their mistakes. I bet they got pregnant again the week after they left. It was just their fate to keep raising up their dresses in alleys. They were going to get pregnant their whole lives. And they wouldn't know what to do with all those babies."

"What's wrong?" Pierrot asked.

"I lost the baby. I threw it in the river."

Pierrot hadn't expected it to hurt so much. Rose had already been through this. Pierrot ran down to the river to look for it. Rose put her hands over her face so she wouldn't have to watch him. Fireflies danced around her like embers after someone has thrown a log into the stove.

ROSE WOKE UP in the middle of the night and saw that Pierrot was putting on his coat and heading toward the door. "Where are you going?" she asked.

"I'm sleepwalking."

The drugs cried out to him like a siren's song. He so wanted to walk down the corridor and jump off the plank. She jumped up out of bed and ran after him.

"I can't do it, Rose."

"You're going to ruin everything if you get high. We tried so hard to find each other."

He put his hand on the doorknob, which was shaped like a rose.

"If you get high, don't come back. I don't want to spend my whole life trying to stop you from doing drugs."

All over the city, women were begging their partners not to go out and get drunk or high. Rose was used to seeing them. It was one of the most common sights during the Depression. They pleaded with their husbands as though the men were angry gods. Rose had always felt sorry for them. But she knew that any good relationship involved a constant willingness to go to war.

She leaped in front of the door. She spread her arms out to both sides as if she were being crucified, as if she were some sort of natural barrier, like she was a dead bolt. He took both her arms and pulled her out of the way. She grabbed him from behind, jumping onto his back like a banshee.

He bent forward and she toppled right over him and onto the floor. As he stepped over her to get to the door, she grabbed his leg, causing him to fall down and bang his head on the counter. All the dishes that were stacked on it to dry fell to the floor. He started struggling to get free from her. But she hung on to his leg with her whole body. He tried to shake her off.

They started wildly slapping each other. Their hands were like two birds fighting in the sky. He grabbed her by the waist and shoved her aside. She whipped sideways across the room and tripped over a chair. He was shocked by his own strength and ran to see whether she was okay. As he crouched beside her, she kneed him in the groin. He clutched his crotch and collapsed on his side as though he had been shot.

They lay there weeping in each other's arms. They had fought the addiction together. On the floor, the broken plates looked like the surface of a frozen pond a child had fallen through.

47

A CHURCH BELL RINGING

The landlady banged on the door so loudly one morning that they both scurried underneath the table. The landlady warned them that if they didn't have the money by the end of the day, they'd be thrown out.

Rose began to pace around the little hotel room, back and forth, like a frustrated lion inside a circus cage: despising being entrapped and dreading being released to perform humiliating acts.

She looked so skinny and pale that she wondered whether she could even get a role in a pornographic film now. She took off her clothes and looked at herself naked in the mirror. Her black pubic hair against her pale skin looked like a splotch of ink on a piece of paper. At twenty-three she had the look of a harried wife. Rose gathered together all her underwear to sell it. She wrapped it in a bundle. "I've found a couple of things to sell," she told Pierrot.

Pierrot told her he would rather starve to death than not be able to see her in her pretty pink silk underwear. Pierrot knew that Rose had had a boyfriend who bought her anything she wanted. He couldn't expect to sleep all day and keep a girl like that. All over the city, men out of work felt they no longer had a place in the world. They felt useless. Pierrot had to do extraordinary things. She would get bored with this tiny world. He had to keep her. He had to make some money.

It was truly amazing to him that he had not thought about the apple in all this time, especially when he was on heroin and desperate to get high. If you have trouble believing that Pierrot hadn't thought about the apple, trust me when I tell you that no one was as surprised as him.

PIERROT TOOK HIS BICYCLE to Westmount, pushing it all the way up the hill to where the massive houses were. He went out of his way to avoid the giant mansion he had lived in with Mr. Irving, which had become the old man's tomb. He couldn't bear the sadness of thinking of his dearly departed friend. There was the tree. He prayed that God would make him invisible, then up he went. He hopped from one branch to another and then reached into the hiding place. He felt all sorts of odd soft objects, and beneath them, a hard, circular form.

HE HADN'T LOOKED AT IT in a great while, and Rose had never seen it at all. It was so sparkly and spectacular on their kitchen table. Pierrot had taken it when he was living in rather splendid circumstances, so it hadn't seemed quite as amazing as it did now. It was so unlike anything else in their grubby little Depression-era world that it seemed surreal and ethereal. It was absolutely out of context.

"How have you kept this until now? We've been down on our luck for so long and you've had this strange priceless apple all along."

"When I stole it, I was surrounded by splendor. It was nothing to me. So I forgot it!"

"How much do you think we'll get for this apple?" Rose asked.

"Surely we'll get enough money to get by until Sunday."

"I'll go with you, then," Rose said. "I'm quite worried you'll get ripped off."

"Mr. McMahon always gives me particularly good deals, so long as I promise to sell only to him. But it would be nice to have you along."

Rose was shocked when she heard Pierrot say the name. She felt a numbness, as though she were standing too close to ringing church bells.

She had never realized that Pierrot and McMahon could exist in the same reality. She had managed to avoid him for so long that she believed she was done with him. Of course he would come back. Pierrot was going to see him right this second. This was dangerous, but she had to take a risk. She wouldn't go—she knew full well that she would get her head blown off.

He attached the suitcase to the front of the bicycle with belts. Rose had changed her mind about coming along.

"Are you sure?"

"Isn't he a violent gangster?"

"Well, yes. But I thought you had no problem with murderers and whatnot."

"Just don't mention that you have a wife."

"And why not?"

"He might use it as leverage."

"Hmmm. I have no idea what that means, but since you are smarter than me, I will defer to your judgment."

McMahon was surprised to see Pierrot, having assumed that the idiot was long dead. There was something about Pierrot's smell that took McMahon aback. McMahon had a strange impulse to seize Pierrot in his arms and inhale him.

The sparkling, jewel-encrusted apple was priceless. The art dealer said he wasn't giving them nearly what it was worth, but they had to understand he would have to sell it on the black market, maybe to someone with European connections. McMahon gave Pierrot twenty thousand dollars for the apple. He kept the same amount for himself and watched Pierrot leave, confused.

Pierrot walked into the room at the Valentine Hotel with a suitcase now filled with cash, completely in shock. He plopped the suitcase on the bed. It rocked like a ship on a stormy sea. Rose came up to him as he unfastened its clasps and threw open the lid.

"What in the world will we do with this?" said Pierrot.

"Let's start a business."

"The Snowflake Icicle Extravaganza!"

THAT WAS WHAT THE DOVE first brought back in its mouth. It wasn't a little bough with a pretty leaf on it. It was a dollar bill.

SELF-PORTRAIT ON TRAIN

Rose woke up one morning and Pierrot was still fast asleep. He would be for several more hours. She was restless and wanted to get out into the world. She had spent the past two weeks visiting different venues. Each had turned her down because they were afraid of repercussions from McMahon. He had ordered that she not be allowed to work in any club, and the indictment was still nonnegotiable. They would end up out of business or have their legs broken for booking Rose's show.

She wanted to have something to read, it didn't matter what. She walked toward the café. She picked up the newspaper at a stand next to it. She settled into a table, ordered herself a cup of coffee and unfolded the paper. On the cover was a story about the arrest of Montreal heroin dealers on their way to New York City. A group of gangsters had gone in a boat that had been stopped by customs officers at the border. Half of them had been gunned down, and the entire shipment had been seized. The border guards were on the lookout for the heroin dealers coming in from Montreal. They declared that it would be almost impossible to move anything across now. Those routes would be too carefully monitored. All the customs officers and the state patrolmen would be on the lookout for more men from Montreal.

Rose laughed. This was McMahon's organization. How would he be able to get his drugs into New York City? McMahon would have to recalibrate his entire operation. This would piss off all sorts of gangsters in all sorts of places—he'd be stepping on their toes and territory.

She worried for a moment about his wild children, who would be by now fourteen and fifteen. She wondered if they would get fewer gifts. But, as always, she was a little impressed by McMahon too. There was something oddly amusing about the idea of hometown criminals making a splash in New York City.

Then Rose had an idea. McMahon didn't run New York City, did he? There was a massive audience just a few hours across the border. She would make her mark in New York City. She would stage her grand revue there. Why not? It was there that all the world's greatest acts got their beginnings. There were dreams that you could realize in New York City that were impossible in Montreal. She sat back as the possibilities grew exponentially in her head. She was aiming high. New York City! She felt almost dizzy by the new heights of her own ambition.

The ink from the newspaper had come off on her fingertips, as if she had just had her prints taken.

SHE HAD TO LOOK THE PART of a professional producer. The first investment she made with the money Pierrot had acquired was in clothes. She went to a seamstress and had an outfit made for herself out of a long roll of black velvet. The light shone off it and the velvet appeared to be a strange shade of blue—the way the fur of black cats sometimes did. The dress fell straight to the floor, with a black jacket to go over it. And a hat she wore at an angle.

After two days of phone calls made from the lobby of the Valentine Hotel, she was able to secure an interview with a theater manager in New York City. The rotary dial of the phone was like the barrel of a shotgun. She told him she would be in New York City, as was her custom, on Wednesday and agreed to a time to come by his theater and present him with an exquisite idea that would knock his socks off.

At first she considered taking Pierrot with her. He had the gift of the gab and could certainly impress the people in New York City. But he was unpredictable and might make them come off as lunatics. She knew how to deal with high-powered men.

The very next morning, Rose went to the train station and bought herself a ticket to New York City. Just like that! She showed the conductor the ticket and he ushered her into a compartment. She sat next to the window. There were two men beside her and three men across from her. She put her little valise, which held a change of underwear, a cucumber sandwich and the original plan she had written in pencil when she was just a child, in the shelf above her head.

The train pulled out of the Montreal station. The movement sounded like someone typing, becoming more and more inspired, hitting the keys faster and faster to keep up with the ideas. The train traveled over a bridge, away from the place she had spent every day of her waking life. The cliffs of sedimentary rock along the train track looked like different bits of ripped wallpaper. She was impressed with herself. She smiled at herself in the small mirror in the train's bathroom. Even if nothing worked out in New York City, she was about to achieve the extraordinary accomplishment of just laying eyes on it.

When she stepped off the train and into New York City's Grand Central Terminal, she saw the ceiling arched up above her. It was as if she were in an air balloon.

There was no way you could capture New York City in a photograph. Each building was beautiful. There were iron staircases running up the sides. There was all sorts of fancy masonry in the shape of leaves and vines and waves. There were more gargoyles hanging out on the top of one building than there were in an entire Montreal neighborhood. She peeked into building lobbies with golden tiles and doormen with small hats. There were rows of people in business suits. There were department-store windows filled with gloves for women of every temperament. There were so many grand church spires, which stuck up straight into the heavens, daring lightning bolts to strike them.

She hit Broadway, and the different marquees distracted her from looking way, way up into the sky. There were neon lights and paintings of showgirls, and lightbulbs that spelled out words. And it was noisy. Nothing had prepared her for all that noise. It sounded like children. If all the children stood on their balconies and banged pots and pans at once. Or if all the babies in the world took their rattles out and shook them. It always sounded as if there were a parade just around the corner. There was something so joyous about all the noise in New York City.

The ground shook because there was so much activity, and you could feel a pulsation. She realized that it was all the hearts beating. Everybody was so excited that their hearts beat louder and stronger than anywhere else. Her own heart was practically smashing against her rib cage. It was a good feeling. Surely the blood racing through your body made you braver.

Because Rose was out of her context, she was able to think clearly. How marvelous this world was. She was amazed by it. Humans were always more capable of evil than you could imagine. And they were also capable of more wonderment than you could ever fathom. People had come up with this city. And what was different between them and her? They had hands and eyes. They had imaginations. They went to bed at night, and they had funny adventures in their heads. Anything was possible.

But the effects of the Depression were everywhere here too. This was the heart of the Great Depression. So much of Montreal's economy hinged on its exports to the United States—its economy mirrored theirs. If the Americans were unhappy and miserable, Montreal was too. She passed a breadline, and she had never seen anything quite like it. It went all the way around the block. She couldn't see the beginning or the end.

It was made up of men whose furtive eyes peeked out from the collars of the coats they huddled in. Their hostile eyes were vicious with shame, because anyone could look down on them. Trying not to make eye contact, Rose hurried by. Men were taught to have so much pride, to go out into the world and make something of themselves. This Depression was deeply humiliating. Since women were taught that they were worthless, they took poverty and hardship less personally.

Rose passed a thirteen-year-old girl with grubby cheeks, wearing a light blue dress. She was leaning against a wall with her foot under her ass and her knee up, smoking a cigarette. She had scabs on her knees that looked like strawberries. Her beige hat looked like a cake that hadn't risen. She exhaled smoke rings, unconcerned.

ROSE HAD AN APPOINTMENT at the New Amsterdam Theatre. It was stately on the outside, but breathtaking once you stepped across the threshold. She took a peek into the theater itself. The rounded ceiling was covered in star-shaped pockmarks, and inside each one was a tiny painting. There were small arches around the proscenium that made it look like the edges of a tea biscuit. The curtain was green velvet with enormous golden tassels at the bottom that looked like manes shaved off lions on the African plains.

It was the type of theater that gave you the excuse to wear your most fancy clothes, and all your best jewelry too. You could even wear a tiara to a place like this. In fact, it would be impossible to be considered overdressed at such an establishment. At night the coat check would be filled with every type of fur coat, like a line of bears waiting to get into a soup kitchen.

She went down a narrow white hall and up a flight of wooden stairs to get to the manager's office. The manager was an enormous fat man, crammed into a wooden chair behind his desk. He didn't bother to put his jacket on. He just leaned over, sticking his pudgy hand out for Rose to shake. He was wearing a white blouse with a purple silk vest that was very tight. It was as though his great belly were an Easter egg and his clothes had been painted on. Rose found his appearance delightful. It was comforting to see a fat man during the Depression. He leaned back in the chair behind his desk, listening to the pretty girl's pitch.

"Well, good-looking," he said, "make it quick."

"I intend to bring to your city the greatest sad clowns that the world has ever seen."

"What do you call yourselves, did you say?"

"The Snowflake Icicle Extravaganza."

"I generally only book world-renowned acts, my darling. And I've never heard of this."

"These performers have no shallow inclination to travel around exposing their talents so that they can receive accolades. Whether they are at Carnegie Hall or performing in front of four children at a park, they do not see the distinction. They are not interested in glory. They are not interested in immortality. They've a duty to create beauty. And it is my duty to allow the whole world to see it. They understand that every gesture is a work of art. A girl cracking an egg on the side of a bowl is exquisite to them. For a clown, there is no difference between a singer onstage at the Paris Opera and a woman singing in the bathtub."

"I like the way you put it. So I'm going to give you a chance. But only because I just had a cancelation from some Russian ballet dancers. Now there's a country that never lets you down when they send performers on tour. They were supposed to use the theater in six weeks' time. Does that work? It's the only spot I can give you."

"Six weeks is perfect. Plenty of time."

"Although a bunch of Canadian clowns might not bring in the crowds on its own. You'll have some chorus girls too, I hope?"

"Only the best."

He put seven stars on his calendar: days that the Snowflake Icicle Extravaganza would be staged at the New Amsterdam Theatre in New York City.

ROSE WENT TO SLEEP that night in a dingy hotel called the Truelove Hotel. She lay in the tiny room that was not much bigger than the bed. She was happy. It was the first time she had felt fulfilled in this way. It was silly, as she had only accomplished the very first part of her enterprise. She hadn't engaged in anything strenuous yet. She hadn't worked day and night assembling the strangest, most unusual clown show anyone had ever seen. She hadn't yet found the people who would put Montreal on the vaudevillian map. But she had taken one step. The red lights on the marquee across the street were like the cigar tips of men smoking in the dark.

As she walked down the street to the train station the next morning, she noticed that everyone was smiling at her. The reason was simple: *she* was smiling at *them*. They were all simply smiling back. She had an egg sandwich from the dinner cart on the train. There was a skinny vase on the table that looked just like an icicle, a single flower sticking out of it.

49

THE COMPLETE MAN

ose began planning her extravaganza the minute she got home. She ordered:

40 tubes of white face paint
20 spools of black ribbon
40 sticks of brightest red lipstick
25 skullcaps
18 yards of white silk with red polka dots on it
40 Elizabethan ruffs of all sizes
20 Napoleon hats (two-cornered, black)
14 pairs of XXXX-large black shoes
1 pair of XXX-large black shoes (with the sole unstuck)
25 sticks of black greasepaint
7 attachable red wax noses
10 bright orange buttons
1 box of detachable polka dots made from fabric of various colors
3 poodles, white
3 packets of pink hair dye for poodles
17 white rabbits
3 geese
27 doves

40 pairs of white gloves
35 cardboard clouds
5 spools of yarn
1 tiny violin
1 tiny piano
1 tiny trumpet
8 gallons of shredded newspaper for papier-mâché
Paste for papier-mâché
Chicken wire

She rented out a vacant hangar at the port in Old Montreal for her company to practice and rehearse in. She had to walk through Old Montreal to get there. Then she went in search of clowns. She put an advertisement for clowns in the newspaper. She went by all the theaters she used to frequent, rounding up her favorite clowns and talking them into joining her revue.

Clowns from all over the city joined Rose's troupe. She wanted a clown whose performance was as rich as a Tolstoy novel. She wanted a clown as sophisticated as a Chekhov character. They understood that the clowns were not going to be in the background. They would not be running around the perimeters of spectacular acts, like lion tamers and elephant trainers and ringleaders. They were not to be considered children's entertainers. No! They were artists. They were the most intrepid performers in any circus. They delved into the dark heart, plucked out the secret flowers and offered them to members of the audience.

Clowns of all shapes and sizes came to the hangar leading out to the river, which led out to the sea. They auditioned. It was a strange sight to see all the clowns sitting together and having lunch. People didn't know whether what they were seeing was a marvel or whether it was unholy.

Rose and Pierrot had a wonderful time looking for the clowns that Rose had been impressed by and luring them into their new company. Pierrot went to bail the clown she had seen at the Ocean Theater out of jail and get him a lawyer. Having accomplished this task, he was walking down the street, completely absorbed in his thoughts. He was humming the last bar of his musical composition when a large black car pulled up beside him. The car door opened and two arms reached out and snatched him up as easily as if he were a child.

Pierrot found himself sitting in the backseat between two rather severe and ugly men. He thought these might be McMahon's men, but there was no talking to either of them. The looks on their faces implied they would respond to any query by belting him in the mouth. Pierrot thought it was probably a defense for not knowing how to make conversation.

He assumed there might be some sort of fee McMahon would charge him for doing any kind of theatrical enterprise in the city. He relaxed and thought this was simply a matter of course. McMahon just wanted to have a business tête-à-tête.

Despite the absurdity of his profession, Pierrot now liked to think of himself as a working stiff.

The car bounced as if someone was jumping up and down at the foot of a mattress.

The men brought him up to McMahon's office, where he had, of course, been many times before.

"It turns out that your apple was a lot harder to move than anybody could imagine. No dealer would touch it. So what do you think about that? It belonged to a Russian princess, if you can believe it. It was stolen from the home of the Russian ambassador. It was going to be temporarily put on display at the museum here in Montreal. And what should happen but it got swiped five years ago and disappeared without a trace. There was never any ransom for it. It never turned up on the black market. The

Russian government put the pressure on the police to get that apple. And guess what?"

"Yes, I understand."

"Do you? You have the worst head for business that I've ever encountered. So allow me to deliver to you the long and short of it. You owe me twenty thousand dollars."

"Hmmm. That's difficult. You see, I of course had no idea about this unfortunate circumstance involving the Russian princess, one of the unlucky Romanovs I've read about in the paper, no doubt. And I don't have any of the money left."

"What the fuck did you do with it? What did you buy? A house? A car? I don't believe it. You're not that type. You're too lazy to spend the money that fast."

"I invested it in a theatrical revue. The money mostly went to clowns. Some of them had previous commitments, so they needed further monetary incentives."

"You invested your money in clowns? Did you come up with this on your own? Or did someone encourage you to do this?"

"My wife. She has a wonderful flair for organization. It's going to make a lot of money. Let's consider it an initial investment. We'll give you our returns!"

"Who's your wife? Who would marry a fuckup like you?"

"You wouldn't know her. Though it's possible. She has worked her marvels in different clubs around the city. Her name's Rose."

"Rose?"

"Yes. That's what she likes to be called. Her real name is actually . . ."

"Marie."

"Good guess!"

A strange hunch came over McMahon—it couldn't possibly be true. He had always assumed that Pierrot had come from an upper-class family. He was sure he had seen him in Westmount a couple of times when he was driving to work. He had thought Pierrot might be one of Irving's children but assumed he had been disowned from his family for drug addiction. He also assumed that was why he had any sort of intelligence. Pierrot had once said he'd gone to Selwyn House, the same school as his own son. But it occurred to him in a sudden flash that Pierrot was the little boy from the orphanage, the little boy with a big scarf around his neck, the only boy Rose had ever thought enough about to mention.

He remembered Rose saying that a person couldn't possibly imagine just how delightful and absurd Pierrot was unless you actually met him. He remembered Rose telling him how sweet and refined and fair the boy was. What an air of sophistication the boy had, despite being an orphan.

"Where did you grow up, anyway?"

"I was Al Irving's ward for many years. But before that, I spent my formative years in an orphanage."

"Where did you meet your wife?"

"I've known her my whole life. We were raised in the same orphanage."

McMahon had to sit down. All his stories and narratives about Rose suddenly needed revising. The psychic energy devastated by this revision exhausted him. He had not taken her affection for the blond boy seriously. But clearly she had been thinking about him the entire time they were together. He was her first love. McMahon had only ever been her second choice.

He immediately wanted to murder Pierrot.

50

THE TOWER OF BABEL

cMahon sat in the car at the port, watching Pierrot being strung upside down from a mast of a ship on the docks. When that task was completed, he got out of the car and headed toward the hangar. McMahon could hardly be prepared for the group of men he would encounter as he walked toward the end of the hangar, where Pierrot had said he would find Rose.

He passed a clown standing with his skullcap on and his large pants unbuckled, smoking a broken cigar and juggling plates.

There was a clown with his poodle. It was white and middle-aged. You could tell that it had worked long and hard for a living. The clown had a tiny rag that he dipped into warm water to remove the gunk around his dog's eyes—as if he were removing its clown makeup.

A clown was dressed as a black chimney sweep. He had covered his face with black soot and carried a little broom over his head. Tears made pathways down his dark cheeks.

There was a clown spreading muscle relaxant all over his arms and legs while smoking a cigarette. There was a lot of chain-smoking. The rooms were filled with little clouds of cigarette smoke, as if it might suddenly start to rain.

Another was balancing a stack of ten hats on his head. He had his jacket off, and he wore a fake belly under his suit to appear corpulent and well fed. He was actually very skinny—he could barely afford to feed himself.

Another clown, dressed in a black suit he had bought for a deal from the undertaker, was playing a tiny trumpet. Another was playing the violin, trying to pick up the trumpet player's tune. Another clown appeared to levitate an inch off the ground.

One clown, who had his hair pulled into triangles on the top and sides of his head, began singing inscrutable words in a low and magnificent voice.

They were all babbling in gibberish. There was no universal clown language. Every clown spoke his own particular tongue and had his own odd dialect. One sounded like he had a piece of electrical tape over his mouth. Another spoke as though he had something hot in his mouth. Their speech varied from sounding like a record played backward to a bicycle horn being honked. McMahon felt annoyed and frustrated. He wished to God they would all just speak English. He tried to ignore them as he walked past.

The huge desk was covered in stacks of paper. And there she was in front of him, sitting on the chair behind it. She looked like a million bucks, wearing a black velvet dress, with a white silk scarf tied in a knot at her neck. It was as though their breakup had not affected her at all.

"How did you finally find me?" she asked.

She was so calm. It was strange how different she now looked. She was older. She had become much more beautiful. He was appalled that she would sit across from him acting as if she were his equal.

"Your *husband* told me where you were."

"Where is he?" Rose asked, showing some alarm finally.

"What a ridiculous fool you've aligned yourself with." McMahon's anger surprised even himself. "I couldn't believe it when he told me that he had a wife named Rose, and I put two and two together. I mean, in what universe does a lowlife junkie and a man like me share a lover? It's so fucking ridiculous. It's a tragedy that makes me laugh. What would you call such a thing?"

"A comedy."

"No, my darling. This is no comedy. If you actually think that you're going to have a happy ending with that piece of shit, you are out of your mind."

"Where is he?"

"You must have had a laugh when he sold me that apple. Your husband owes me. He fucking owes me!"

She was afraid to move her hands or to pick up anything. She was worried that her hands would shake. Her heart was beating too quickly. He was in control now. He had Pierrot. She wasn't allowed to say what she wanted. She might as well have a nylon stocking tied around her head, gagging her, and her hands fastened behind the chair.

"Pierrot didn't know about our relationship. He never set out to dupe you."

"What didn't I give you? You ruined my life. You ruined my wife's life. Weren't you supposed to be friends? Don't act like a victim. I swear to God, I'll kill you if you do. I couldn't walk down the hallway of my house without running into you half-dressed and acting like a dog in heat."

Rose just looked at him.

"I'm embarrassed for you. I'm embarrassed for myself. It's disgusting."

They stared at each other. Full of hatred but with a visceral awareness that they had been naked and carnal with each other.

"Just tell me. Come on. Does he lick your pretty little cunt? Do you make all those same noises? Remember how you used to beg me to make sure you felt good? You were so tight that first time. Remember how I opened you up. You were ruined after me. I destroyed your cunt and that's how you'll always like it. I know you think about me sometimes. When he's on top of you."

She hadn't, though. She sometimes thought of the man with the donkey's head right before she came. She wouldn't dare give McMahon the satisfaction of seeing her change her expression.

"I need to know what you've done with him or I won't sit here another second."

"Relax. He's alive and fucking well, hanging upside down at the dock. He's happy there. But he's not safe. You are going to do something for me and I'm not going to murder your husband. I need to move dope across the border, a magnificent trainload of the shit."

She paused, considering his offer, knowing she could not say no.

"I need more money, of course."

He flopped a suitcase onto the desk.

"Take it. It's fucking nothing to me. I have more money than you can ever imagine, Rose. So here's some money, because it's what you love. It's what you'll never get enough of."

He stood up, buttoning his jacket. He leaned over the desk toward her. The white ostrich feather on the back of her hat made it appear as if her thoughts were on fire.

"Admit it, you hate me more than you love him."

As soon as he drove away she was released from his power. She opened her mouth and let out a loud wail. She overturned her desk; it made a large booming sound. The suitcase thudded to the ground, the latch clicked open and stacks of bills rolled out.

When she saw the money, it shocked her. She stopped worrying about Pierrot for a moment. She got down on her knees and began putting the money away. The money dazzled her, changed her mood. She loved the feeling of being in possession of it. She put it in the safe. For a moment she didn't even think about where the money had come from. She didn't care at all. She felt only excitement. She loved the money's proximity to her and the possibilities it opened up for her.

She didn't believe a thing they said in church about material possessions being of no value. Money gave her confidence. It made her feel powerful. Oh, certainly the money hadn't come to her in the most straightforward fashion. But it never does. And a person has to be willing to meet money on its own terms.

Pierrot!

THE WHITE SHIPS docked in the port were like wedding cakes on display in a baker's window. Pierrot was hanging upside down, tied by his ankle to a hook from the deck of a steamer. The clowns came running with a long ladder, which they had used for a traditional house-on-fire scene. Rose stuck her hands up in the air. Pierrot put his hands out to her.

"How are you?" she asked.

"I don't know. You can get used to anything."

"I'll find a way to get you down."

"I should hope so. What were you talking about that took so long? Were you engaging in small talk? Were you exchanging recipes?"

Pierrot was actually laughing when they took him down from the hook. Pierrot's pride wasn't injured easily, the way McMahon's was. He didn't have any pride—and, surprisingly, that made him noble.

"Is there something you'd like to tell me about your relationship with McMahon?"

"Oh God, I told you about the married man."

"Yes! He informed me that the two of you were quite the pair back in the day."

"I thought you might not sell him the apple if you knew."

"With good reason."

"Sorry!"

"I always had these intuitions, even when we were kids, that you liked tough guys."

"Don't be ridiculous. I abhor brutes."

Pierrot smiled kindly at Rose. He had suspected she had a penchant for ruthless, ambitious men, and while he did not in the least doubt her affection for him, he sometimes felt that even though he was the love of her life, he was not necessarily her type.

"What are we going to do with all this money?" Pierrot asked her when she showed him the suitcase.

"What is the thing that money always buys you?"

"I don't know."

"Girls, of course."

"Ha-ha-ha! I almost forgot about the dancing girls you promised."

⊷⊰ 51 ⊱⊷

THE WORKING-GIRL
REVOLUTION

With McMahon's investment, Rose was now able to afford her chorus line.

"I have to do some serious recruiting today," she told Pierrot. "I promised top-of-the-line chorus girls too."

"You're crazy. Where will you find showgirls in Montreal as good as the ones in New York City?"

"No, no, no, no, no. I have to find showgirls who are better than the ones in New York City."

"Where are you going to find these girls?"

THERE WAS A LINE OF GIRLS outside the fabric factory near the port, waiting to see the owner. Little white clouds came out of their mouths as they spoke. There had been an announcement in the paper that there would be a job opening that week. They had hats pulled down almost to their noses. They had long knitted scarves that wound around and around their necks. Their black tights had been mended and darned over and over again. They were tiptoeing up to the door as if the sidewalk were thin ice and they were about to break through and be swallowed up by the water. They had such a tenuous grasp on their own existence, they could disappear from this earth and there wouldn't be a trace left. They stomped their feet up and down to stay alive. Everywhere Rose looked, there were strange chorus lines of girls.

Rose almost didn't want to change anything about them. She wanted them to line up on the stage in their hats and their wet boots, with a little bit of lipstick they had borrowed from their mothers, coughing and cold, the roses in their cheeks blooming, holding their letters of reference. How could art ever capture that?

THEY ALL WILLINGLY WENT ALONG with Rose. They liked the sound of the Snowflake Icicle Extravaganza. They immediately believed they were taking part in something special. And also Rose had promised them soup.

They were a little bit defiant. They knew somehow that all the men in their lives would be opposed to them joining Rose. Because she was independent, wasn't she? But no matter what they did, they were probably going to end up beaten by their fathers when they got home. So what did it matter in the end?

When they lined up in the hangar with their coats and woolen tights off, their bare skinny limbs were covered in welts. Their dads beat them for standing on the corner and laughing. Their dads beat them for being pretty. Their dads beat them for putting lipstick on. Their dads beat them for taking too long to come home from the school, for forgetting to take their baby brothers out of the bathtub, for having a snarky expression while putting jam on the table, for leaving kiss marks all over the bathroom mirror.

A skinny girl in a black sweater, who looked as if she'd had a blocked nose her whole life, could sing really quickly, as if she were hyperventilating, as if she had been running and now she was trying to tell you a story. Everyone applauded.

A few could dance, and they tapped to the right and to the left. They looked like they were running on a log knowing that if they stopped some sort of horrible fate awaited them.

But she almost preferred chorus girls who didn't have any talent. Women were still strange and inscrutable creatures. Men didn't understand them. And women didn't understand themselves either. It was always a performance of some sort. Everywhere you went, it was like there was a spotlight shining down on your head. You were on a stage when you were on the trolley. You were being judged and judged and judged. Every minute of your performance was supposed to be incredible and outstanding and sexy.

You were often only an ethical question away from being a prostitute.

SHE HAD TO BUY THEM new clothes. They all looked so damn homely. None of them could afford proper stockings. They didn't look like a troupe of exciting, spoiled chorus girls. And so they were all fitted for new, sparkly dresses. One girl, covered in beauty marks, stood in her underwear, as though she had just come out of an enchanted forest and was now covered in ticks.

When the tailor was done, there was a pile of measuring tape on the ground as if a mummy had just performed a striptease.

When they arrived, the dresses were the color of the rain. The girls had sashes around their waists, looking like presents that could be opened.

There were also little see-through beads on the dresses that made them look like flowers covered in dew.

The girls all leaned together in their gray dresses, eating their bowls of soup. They were squished up together like a storm cloud. And all their slurping sounded like rain rolling through gutters. Everybody in the company was kind of horny because they had been well fed. They chatted about eligible nineteen-year-old bachelors in the neighborhood. There is no sex without a sandwich.

WITH ONLY FOUR WEEKS LEFT to get the show together, there were still a hundred little things Rose had to attend to. She looked at the costumes pinned onto the mannequin torsos. She counted the order of twenty Napoleon hats, trying one on herself. She described the set to the carpenters. She raised her arms above her head, clenching and unclenching her hands, illustrating how she wanted scintillating stars hanging from the sky. Part of the show was to take place under a huge blizzard, so the whole troupe furiously cut snowflakes out of the newspapers that described scandals and mob killings and trouble in Europe.

They had also collectively made a giant moon out of papier-mâché. Every now and then the moon would get loose and roll across the hangar. There was a joke in the company that the moon was possessed. They said that it wanted to be up in the sky and resented being pulled down to earth. They were afraid it would roll down the boulevard, women and children and dogs jumping out of its way, until it plopped happily into the river. And then what would happen? It would lie under the water every night, glowing. The moon up in the sky would be the reflection, and not the other way around.

Some of McMahon's men came late at night and filled the moon with heroin. The drugs were in tiny little bottles, themselves inside a huge trunk. Rose helped the gangsters hide the trunk deep inside a crater she had kept open in the moon, then sealed the crack with buckets of plaster.

THE PRESSURE OF getting the show done on time was getting to Rose. She threw temper tantrums in front of the performers. Everyone knew these were just passing moods, but they were still alarming. Rose could listen to a children's choir for ten seconds and then point out the future opera singer with her finger. But she wasn't especially good at managing and encouraging the talent. She threatened to bury a clown and his dog alive if they showed up tardily for rehearsal again.

Later that day, Rose passed a couple of girls sitting half-dressed and cross-legged in front of each other. She was shocked to see them doing nothing. She stopped for a second to overhear their conversation.

"It's violent in New York. I'm a little bit worried about walking around on the streets alone. Can we make sure that we don't lose sight of one another when we're there?"

"*Voyons!* How can it be worse than here?"

"Because Jimmy Bonaventura runs the streets down there, as a matter of fact. He's a psychopath. If you look at him the wrong way, you might get shot in the back of the head."

"*Oui, mais . . .* I wouldn't mind if he asked me out for filet mignon. Have you seen photographs of him?"

"Yes, I saw his arrest photograph."

"He is so handsome. He has a reputation as a ladies' man, you know."

"And then what would happen if you got on his nerves?"

She pointed her index finger, as though it were a gun, at the other girl's head. She pulled the trigger with her index finger. She said, "Pow." The other girl toppled over to the ground.

"Knock it off, will you?" Rose said. "Get back to work. Are you two out of your minds? Playing cops and robbers at a time like this? I'm paying you! Never mind Jimmy Bonaventura, I'll murder the two of you myself!"

AFTER THAT EXPLOSION she went to find Pierrot. He was sitting in the middle of a circle of crushed top hats.

"I've just finished with these hats," Pierrot said.

"How did you get them to look like that?"

"Frankly, I jumped on them. It was a dirty business, but someone had to do it."

"Pierrot, you're going to have to be in charge of all the performers. Or else they'll drive me nuts."

"What if I lead them all astray?"

"Everything I know about performance you know too. I trust you implicitly."

"Oh, thank you. And what are you up to today?"

"Gangsters. Drug dealers. Thugs."

"The commonsensical ones!"

She smiled, not disagreeing, and hurried off, leaving Pierrot to take care of the rehearsals. Pierrot was terrified for a second. He couldn't believe he was in charge. It seemed like a funny dream—like realizing you are naked in a very public place. But Pierrot answered fifty questions over the course of that one afternoon.

"Which of the noises sounds closest to a rooster: *Cockalooalooaloo* or *Cowarooraoooaroo*?"

"The second."

"Do you think that when I make a farting noise, I should have a look of pleasure on my face, or should I just completely ignore it and not acknowledge it?"

"Be surprised by it."

"What do you think of me reciting a famous poem at the moment I am about to blow my head off?"

"I'm for it."

"Do you think that I need to look at the heavens—the ceiling—when I sing, or out at the audience?"

"The audience."

"Spongy nose or painted one?"

"Painted."

"What color of carnation goes with this suit?"

"White."

"What do you think about this?"

"No."

"Do you like this?"

"Magnificent."

"Can I have your opinion on this?"

"Oh no. That's all wrong."

"Pierrot, look at this for a second."

"Hmmm."

LATER, ONE OF the less talented clowns, Fabio, walked past Rose while she was crunching numbers. Although he was fifty-seven, rather obese and had drooping gray cheeks, he performed an act wherein he pretended to be a toddler.

"Oh, I've always loved numbers," Fabio said. "They behave so prettily, don't you find?"

Rose immediately made him wipe off his face paint and work as her accountant.

THAT EVENING Rose hurriedly undressed and climbed into bed. She rarely had an hour to herself in the evenings, but this night she needed it. She switched on the lamp next to her bed. The lampshade was yellow with pink blossoms painted on it, and the lightbulb was the wattage of an early day in May. She pulled a book out from a paper bag and began reading it eagerly. It was a pulp novel with a character based on Jimmy Bonaventura and his exploits. Rose was curious and had bought herself a copy at the drugstore. It was horrendously written, but it was a page-turner.

Jimmy Bonaventura had no idea who his father was. His mother was a maid who had been seduced. When she got pregnant, she thought that the baby was her ticket to the high life. Instead, Jimmy's mother became a prostitute. Jimmy had grown up in a tiny brothel. He used to sleep in bed with her after the clients went home. He used to sometimes hide under the bed while she was making love. He was so used to seeing her sitting on the laps of different men that he didn't think anything of it.

When his mother jumped out the window of the brothel, Jimmy was sent to the boys' home, where he met his right-hand man, Caspar. All the other boys were repelled by Caspar because his forehead was too big and jutted out. There was no haircut known to any barber that could hide that forehead. They thought he was mentally deficient. Jimmy thought this was a rather ridiculous assumption, because he could see right off the bat that Caspar was a genius. He could count cards. He could memorize phone books. He calculated odds for Jimmy.

When Caspar and Jimmy were fifteen, they turned a little ice cream parlor into a bookies' den. And that was their first official headquarters. They wiped off all the names of ice cream flavors in chalk on the blackboard above the cash register. In their place they wrote the names of the racehorses. Which actually could have been the names of ice cream flavors and specialty sundaes: Rocky Road, Chunky Monkey, Slippery Banana, Marshmallow Darling, Cotton-Candy Heart.

They met a girl who was taking bets on skipping-rope tournaments. These were popular because boys liked to watch the girls' skirts bop up into the air. She offered to turn tricks in the back room of the shop. The mafia came after them soon after that. Jimmy felt that if he could defend his ice cream shop, he could take over the entire city. He killed twenty-six men before the mafia backed off, and then it was all over.

A young, overly imaginative journalist had coined the name the Ice Cream Mafia. The author of the book suggested the name was inappropriate, as it seemed childish and sweet, when this was a group of most violent thugs. Rose closed the paperback, put it on the night table and felt happy thoughts.

She rather liked that she would be dealing with such a character. It occurred to her that she liked the mechanisms underground. Other than the fact that she had to communicate with McMahon again, she was pleased to be dipping her toes into those dark waters.

Her reflections were interrupted when she saw Pierrot standing at the foot of the bed, watching her. "What?" she asked.

"You read that whole book in two hours. You were enraptured. Just enraptured."

"You know I like books."

"I rather think it has something to do with the subject matter."

"We are meeting him in a week."

"I think it's incredibly risky to have any dealings with Jimmy Bonaventura. He's a psychopath, a murderer, a drug dealer and a pimp, with a flair for torture and a notoriously short fuse."

"And he's handsome."

She started to laugh. Pierrot crawled onto the bed, moving toward her slowly on all fours. Rose squealed with laughter, and Pierrot pounced on her. The combination of danger and money was making her giddy.

JIMMY BONAVENTURA WAS SITTING in his kitchen, reading the newspaper, when he saw an advertisement for the show from Montreal, which would be arriving in several weeks. There was a picture of a clown standing under an umbrella in a snowstorm. Jimmy cut it out and put it on his fridge. But upon second thought he crumpled it up and tossed it into the garbage. He hadn't been pleased when McMahon told him about the plan.

A few days later he heard an advertisement for the show on the radio. The radio was on in the kitchen, and Jimmy was sitting in the bathtub, with the bathroom door open. He was anxious for the show to arrive. He was worried about the streets going dry. He needed to get those drugs out to the junkies—before they began to find other ways, or got new addictions, or some other dealer moved into town.

"Hurry up and get your goddamn choo-choo train here," he yelled like an impatient child. Then he held up his foot to scrub between his toes with a bar of soap. His attractive head leaned against the edge of the bathtub for balance.

IN THEIR HOTEL ROOM, Rose and Pierrot sat on either side of the kitchen table. There was a mouse on the counter, looking at different crumbs like a woman selecting fruit at a market, but they couldn't be bothered to pay it any mind. Rose took out the piece of paper and stub of a pencil that she kept in her pocket. And in a simple diagram no more or less complicated than a spider's web, they constructed the order of the acts in the Snowflake Icicle Extravaganza.

"What is reserved for this last act?" Pierrot asked. "Why don't you have anyone's name written down here?"

"That's always the most important slot, isn't it?"

"Indeed. I was wondering what you intended to put there."

They smiled at each other.

DETAIL OF WALLPAPER

His whole life, McMahon had been consumed with pride. He never let his guard down. He had always considered his actions carefully. Even when he was a little boy, he acted in a way that nobody could mock. McMahon sat leaning against the leather seat of his car. He couldn't believe what he was doing. McMahon hated himself for following her around. But the minute Rose appeared, he forgot himself entirely and stared. Rose and Pierrot held hands and walked down the street.

Pierrot was an altogether different person when he was with Rose. He was wide awake and so alive. He swung his hands all over the place as he spoke. And he made her laugh uproariously. She looked at him with an unmistakable admiration. They whisked happily into the doorway of the Valentine Hotel and disappeared from sight.

McMahon sometimes felt that alcohol and drugs actually revealed the true personality of people. Rose hadn't seen Pierrot stoned. That was a whole different man. That was who he truly was. Drugs scratched off people's veneer. It made them abandon manners. Then you could see what was left of them, which was not much.

He couldn't believe that she liked sex with Pierrot as much as she had with him. In fact, he couldn't really bring himself to believe they were having sex at all. He didn't want to get out of the car, but that's what he found himself doing. He walked into the lobby of the Valentine Hotel and rented a room from the decrepit concierge. He gave her a two-dollar bill and she gave him the key to the room right next to Rose's.

When he walked into the room, he felt like a giant. The room was exceptionally tiny. He felt as if he were trapped in the dollhouse in his daughter's room. The wallpaper was green, with tiny brown birds. The bed frame was carved out of burgundy wood and had tiny roses on the back of it. The mattress was thin, and the bedspread had brown and pink flowers. He couldn't imagine fucking on that bed. The weight of his body would break it.

He didn't want to sit on a bed that so many people had had sex on. Instead he sat in the armchair, whose back was shaped like a shell. The legs of which were so thin, they were like those of very tall birds. He wondered how it held him up. Things that he had previously judged weak were now proving strong—to have no trouble supporting themselves and others. He was in an alternate universe, where skinny was fat, weak was strong, small was large.

There was a glass tumbler on the side of the sink. McMahon picked it up and put its mouth against the wall. He put his ear to its bottom, listening carefully to the movements in the other room. He wondered what colors the wallpaper was in Rose's room. He wondered whether it was the same as that on his side. It was actually green and pink, but he could not know this.

Suddenly there were voices in the glass, swimming around like two fancy goldfish.

What he heard was the longest-running one-act play of all time, mounted in cities all over the world, interpreted by different directors, starring different actors but always sold out.

McMahon dropped the glass to the ground in horror. The words scurried around the floor like spiders. He threw on his coat. He opened the door and headed down the narrow, carpeted corridor of the Valentine Hotel, and didn't breathe again until he was across the street.

He would have his revenge. He would end this love affair. He didn't want to just kill Pierrot. That would be too easy. Then Pierrot would certainly be the love of Rose's life. In his experience, dead men were the ones who fared the best in the opinions of women. Instead he wanted to break them up. He wanted Rose to be disgusted by love the way he was disgusted by love. He wanted her to look back on everything Pierrot had said and judge it to be a lie.

·⊰[53]⊱·

STUDY OF GIRL IN A SAILOR HAT

McMahon sent a girl named Lily to seduce Pierrot. He would have been sleeping with her himself if his rage for Rose hadn't rendered him impotent.

Lily was the opposite of Rose. She was pale. She had blond hair that she wore in a great bun heaped on her head. The bun always looked so messy, just on the verge of collapsing. It never did. Her green eyes were the color of marbles that any boy would go crazy trying to win. But she squinted. She'd had trouble with her eyesight when she was little but didn't get glasses. Now her face was sort of permanently squinted up. She had the look of a Persian cat sitting in the sun.

Her legs were so long she made any dress she had on seem indecent. She always seemed naked. Businessmen paid ludicrous sums to have sex with her. They only slept with her because the price was so high. They could be sure that no poor man was able to afford her. They would be sticking their penises only where the best penises had gone.

Pierrot was on his way home from the hardware store. His pocket was filled with screws for a pulley mechanism being built to hoist up a two-hundred-pound clown into the air. Lily took Pierrot's arm as he passed by. "Please, come upstairs with me. I need some help. Quick, it's an emergency." She scrunched up her face a little—like a rabbit sensing danger—and tried to convey her distress.

Pierrot followed her. It made him nervous. He was generally very nervous when women called on him to help them. They usually asked him for something he couldn't provide. He hoped she didn't want him to lift anything heavy, or to fight off some terrible brute she had become involved with. Pierrot wasn't good at that sort of thing.

To his surprise, she sat down on the edge of the bed in her room and spread her legs. On the mattress next to her was a tea tray with cups and a vase with wilty-looking mauve flowers in it. Poised on the corner of the tray were a spoon and a syringe atop a tiny bit of newspaper with last week's headlines.

"Will you shoot this dope into my thigh? I can't have anyone see marks on my arms."

He was so surprised. He was in the room with heroin itself. It was as though heroin had taken on the form of a girl. He found the heroin was much more seductive than the beautiful woman. He hadn't expected to confront it like this. Imagine answering the door and finding your ex-lover standing there, saying she had changed her mind and wanted to come back. How could you resist? What would it hurt to spend a moment more in the room and help this girl out? He liked the ritual of cooking dope. It made him feel important, like someone with an actual profession—a doctor, say. He took a stocking of hers from off the bedpost and tied it around her thigh. The instant he injected her, Pierrot felt high by proxy. They were curiously upside down. The bed was on the ceiling. The rug too was on the ceiling. The table, with its teacups and lamp, wasn't crashing to the ground. Clever girl! What a way to decorate a home. She looked at him with her eyes closed and laughed.

Then abruptly Pierrot came to his senses and the room righted itself. He had to get out at once or he would succumb to the drug and live on ceilings, floating over life like a ghost, for the rest of his life.

When he flung open the door, a man stood there with a camera. It was the detective with the checkered hat, the one he couldn't afford. Pierrot nodded to him, but the detective pretended not to notice and moved on.

HE ENCOUNTERED another odd woman a few weeks later when he stopped to look in a bakery window. Montrealers gathered around bakery windows as if the cupcakes on display made a sort of comic opera. You would look at them like you were looking at a Hollywood musical but it was even more marvelous, as it was right there at your fingertips. How could any Hollywood starlet compare to a vanilla cupcake topped with red candies in the shape of tiny stars?

In the window, he saw the reflection of a woman coming up behind him. It was as if she were a submerged body rising up in the water. She wore a man's black wool coat and had on a sailor's cap. She came up next to Pierrot and whispered into his ear.

"*Tu me reconnais?*"

"What's your name?"

"I like to change my name every week. Once my name was Marguerite, but all I did when my name was Marguerite was get into trouble. I was such a bad girl when my name was Marguerite that I changed it to Natalie."

Pierrot looked at the girl, his mouth hanging open, not sure what to say.

"We can call ourselves Lucille and Ludovic. We can do whatever we want. And then change our names to something else."

"My name is Pierrot. I'm quite happy being called that."

"*T'aimes fumer?* Do you like to smoke?"

"I like it more than anything."

She opened her coat to reveal her completely naked body underneath. He wasn't expecting that. The stretched lining of the coat made her look so skinny, a streak of lightning in a big black sky. She let her coat close and reached into her pocket for a long pipe with a glass bowl.

She lit up her pipe. Pierrot looked around. It was odd to light a glass pipe like that out in the open. The smoke swirled around, not like a dragon, as the drug was fancifully called on the street, but more like a tiny newt.

A light flashed at the corner of Pierrot's eye. A man across the street with a camera was taking photos of them. He recognized the checkered rain hat. It was the same private investigator he had tried to pay to find Rose. Here he was again: he was following Pierrot! He popped up right after these lovely ladies tried to have sex with him. It was a setup! Brilliant! He realized that, of course, McMahon had hired him. He was the only person they knew who had money to afford this type of absurd luxury.

"Who do you work for?" Pierrot asked, wanting to make sure.

"Why do you think I work for anybody? I have no idea what you're talking about. I'm flabbergasted. *Est-ce que c'est le bon mot?*"

"Can I ask one question?"

"*Oui, mais* . . . just one."

"Is he, like, a really powerful black-haired mafia guy who runs the Roxy downtown?"

"Yes. But I won't say anything else."

As Pierrot walked home, reviewing what had just happened, he decided not to tell Rose. She lost her temper so easily these days, especially with the pressure of putting the show together. And since McMahon had visited, she seemed ready to kill someone at the drop of a hat.

As Pierrot was walking up the stairs he heard Rose yelling, "I'll wring your neck, you lousy bastard! I'll teach you to come up against a woman!"

He flung open the door to find her in the kitchen, struggling with a jar of jam. No, he would not upset Rose further.

MCMAHON HIRED a girl named Colombe to seduce Pierrot. She was the girl who worked in the brothels and most resembled Rose. She had the same build and the same short, dark hair. But the thing that most distinguished Colombe from Rose was the expression on her face. She always looked disgusted. She pouted and complained about everything. Her main topic of conversation was how she couldn't stand other women. She thought she was better at making love than any of the other whores.

McMahon had the madam smack Colombe across the face so that she looked like a victim and Rose would take her in. She showed up at the door of the theater wearing a raggedy old blue dress, holding a suitcase.

When Pierrot went to the bathroom, Colombe was standing there, wearing black-and-white-striped stockings and black high heels. She had on black lingerie that ended above her crotch. He could see her tuft of pubic hair and the bottom of her ass cheeks underneath it.

"Take me like a beast, mister. Degrade me. You teach me how I want it, daddy."

Pierrot sighed and walked out of the bathroom. Pierrot had by now became accustomed to women showing up out of the blue and propositioning him. He knew McMahon was sending them. They didn't want to be taken for a hamburger or a movie, or to meet any of his friends. They just wanted to go straight to bed. When he was a boy, he had often fantasized about such a scenario, where he lived in a city filled with nymphomaniacs who ran around on the street wearing coats with nothing underneath and offering him money or whole chickens if he would just have sex with them and end their misery. But he realized now that the fantasy was a depressing reality.

As he was walking away Pierrot turned around and called back to Colombe, "Hey, you wouldn't be able to carry a tune, per chance?"

He was desperate to find singers. Colombe ended up having a pretty singing voice, and Pierrot offered her a solo.

"What do you want from me?" Colombe asked McMahon. "Those two are in love. He's in love with Rose. He thinks she's perfect. She sort of is too. I'm going to New York City with them. I'm done here."

··=》 54 《=··

THE ARRIVAL OF A TRAIN

McMahon came to see Rose before she left for New York City. He inspected the papier-mâché moon in the corner of the warehouse. "Well, you pulled the moon right out of the sky. You didn't think the rest of us wanted to look at it?" McMahon smiled, seemingly trying to make peace. She didn't laugh, however. She stared at him. McMahon abruptly took the friendly look off his face.

"Jimmy is going to come closing night," McMahon continued. "They are going to take the moon in a truck down to the riverbank, where they can open it. Go with them to oversee. I've never liked the guy. He's always had this arrogant way about him. Like, the minute you walk out the door, he starts laughing at you. He doesn't like Quebecers. He thinks we're beneath him."

Rose shrugged. She had been given so many reasons to look down on herself that she couldn't be bothered considering any more. Being a Quebecer was the least of her worries.

"When do I get the money?" she asked.

"They won't be giving you the money. I'm making a trade. Jimmy Bonaventura has a bunch of buildings he bought to launder money in the red-light district. He never wanted to sell. But when the price is right, anything's for sale. When you come back, even your hotel will be owned by me. It's the biggest real estate grab I've ever made. Too bad, it could have been yours. All those cabarets. But you prefer to fall in love with junkies."

McMahon watched Rose's face carefully to see if she would flinch or reveal even a tiny flicker of remorse for having left him. He saw nothing.

"Even if they don't understand this show you're putting on, don't feel badly. This is the first thing you've put together. You're young. You're an amateur."

He thought he saw the color in her cheeks darken. He decided to immediately continue the condescension.

"Are you excited to meet someone like Jimmy Bonaventura? What an adventure that will be for a nothing girl like you. You can tell me all about it when you get back."

"I don't think so. I think I would prefer never to see your face again."

"It's because I broke your heart."

"I never loved you. I was with you because I didn't have a choice. I threw myself at you because I was terrified of poverty."

She looked into McMahon's eyes. She was watching his reaction carefully. People gave away secrets when they were angry. You could read their emotions when they were enraged. She knew that McMahon had arranged to have her killed. He turned without saying anything and walked away.

IN THE HANGAR NEXT TO THEIRS, they were manufacturing bathtubs. They were carried out on the back of a truck that day, like a school of beluga whales.

. . .

THE CLOWNS ROLLED the papier-mâché moon down the street, from the hangar to the train tracks, which wasn't that far, only a few hundred feet. They were laughing. They were amazed at how strong the gravitational pull of the moon was. It was heavier than usual, and given its propensity toward escapism, they were afraid the moon would for sure make a break for it this time. The moon took up half a baggage car by itself. The sides had been scuffed when it was squeezed into two large doors.

Rose looked at all the trunks piled high in the baggage car. They had everything they needed to build a brand-new universe. One trunk contained small planets and shooting stars. Another had clouds and lightning bolts and snowflakes. There was a fake ocean and a pirate ship in one. Several contained costumes for aristocrats, generals and paupers. One was filled with flaming hoops and tiny tuxedos for dogs. Each was as full of wonders as Pandora's box.

Rose was the last to board the train. She wore a red velvet jacket and matching trousers. Once she had slid the door closed behind her, everyone in the troupe popped their heads back in from the windows, because the action was now inside. When the train began to move, everyone let out a huge whoop. They were impressed by the sheer realness of all of it. This was the train she and Pierrot had been sitting on when they were very little, though then it was an imaginary train, heading to an imaginary place. Now it weighed thousands of pounds and could run over anything in its path.

THEY ARRIVED AT THE BORDER in under an hour. The longer part of the trip would happen after they crossed. But getting past customs was the real challenge.

The customs officers took a peek into each baggage car. They all looked the same as the baggage cars of American troupes and circuses that came up north across the border. The custom officers laughed at the moon. It was scratched and dented from rolling down the sidewalk. But this seemed to make it look more like the real moon: nothing more than a dented hand mirror up in the sky. One of the officers shook hands with a Chihuahua. The officers smiled to themselves. In their minds, the boxes contained only the components of a wonderful show. They wished the troupe luck.

When Rose showed their papers and the train was then waved across the border, she knew the whole world was hers.

SHE WALKED DOWN the shaky corridor of the train. The landscape was flashing by through the square windows. There was so much land, open and empty. All the trees stood there, naked without leaves, their arms supplicating the sky. They were so chaotic and full of longing.

They went through a series of old, crotchety mountains. They were so old they didn't look dangerous anymore. Occasionally a big boulder rolled off them into the middle of a road or landed on top of a deer, but on the whole they had found their place in the world. The rain had worn their peaks down, one argument at a time.

Rose understood why hobos would ride the train. It made you feel like you had escaped from time. That you had gotten ahead of it. It was as though you were the hare and time was the tortoise. And now you could just dally until the future caught up with you. Rose plopped down in one of the seats among a group of girls and decided to enjoy the journey with them.

They had packed sandwiches for their daylong train ride south, so nobody was hungry. There was a peacefulness that settled over everyone in the train now that their bellies were full. It allowed them to luxuriate in the moment as if it were a warm bath.

The girls were having thoughts they hadn't been allowed to have before. Rose liked listening to conversations. Every conversation was like a scientific experiment that sought to find a cure for the human condition.

"I'd like to have a stage name. Something with a little razzmatazz."

"Once you start with the razzmatazz, you'll never be able to knock it off."

"I read *Frankenstein*. Do you know that a woman wrote it? She ran away with this poet named Percy Shelley. They had an orgy in a castle and she made up the story to amuse their friends."

"Where did you find out all this?"

"At the library. If you keep reading past *Winnie-the-Pooh*, most books are actually really dirty."

"I hated school so much. I was so happy to leave it."

"I couldn't make out the blackboard. I have bad eyesight. When my grandfather died, I took his glasses. All the other girls laughed at me but I was able to read the blackboard."

"There's going to be another war, and there will be all sorts of jobs opening up. You can do what you want."

"*Penses-tu qu'ils ont les même tablettes de chocolat aux États-Unis?*"

"My mom wanted to get a job to make more money, but my father said he would die of shame if she did that. I like having money in my pocket."

"Nothing feels as good as having money in your pocket. *Rien du tout.*"

"I never minded giving my parents my whole paycheck, because they pay the rent and buy the food and they have all my brothers. But I have to beg and beg and beg just to keep enough money to go to the movies on Saturdays."

"I love the movies."

"Did you see *King Kong*? It was the first movie I ever saw, and I couldn't stop screaming. I couldn't sleep at night. I kept looking out the window. I was sure that a big gorilla's hand was going to reach in the window and snatch me out of my bed."

"I know what you mean. After I saw *Frankenstein*, I was cycling down the street. I was sure the monster was just behind me. I started hurrying to get home."

"Joannie read that book."

Rose adored the brilliant repartee of the girls. It was like the train it-self, traversing all domains—trivial and profound subjects, both at once.

IN THE DINING CAR, Rose sat across from a ventriloquist clown. He had a rat in a jar. He opened the lid of the jar and once he took the lid off, the rat began to sing in a melodic, high-pitched voice. He had been work-ing with the clown since he was a pup. He liked to be rocked to sleep in the clown's pocket.

The rat was nervous. The rat had come from Montreal. It had heard of the New York rats. They could intimidate dogs. And if cats saw them coming, they would cross to the other side of the street.

The clown told him not to worry, they wouldn't be meeting any New York rats. This was a very reputable theater, and there wouldn't be any rats in the audience.

But the rat knew that all he needed was for some New York rat to say he was a loser and he would never, ever recover. They would say that no respectable rat would be traveling with a clown. He sat behind the glass, wringing his hands, worrying about being judged. He had never felt so small in his whole entire life.

SHE STOPPED IN A COMPARTMENT to talk to Fabio, who had a huge accounts book spread open. The two of them looked at the book as though they were children searching for a foreign city in an atlas. Fabio had turned out to be unexpectedly good with numbers, and Rose was the first person in his life who had found use for that skill. She had been consulting more and more with Fabio about numbers and business affairs. Fabio was the only person in the company other than Pierrot who knew about the drugs. There was no point telling the others. They believed they were on this trip because of their artistic abilities. They looked so innocent, they would never be suspected. They were just enjoying the ride. They were all crowded up against the window, gaping at the Adirondacks. Even the sad clowns were laughing. The sad clowns weren't worried about their arthritis, or their ex-wives, or their failures. They were all smiling.

ROSE WALKED INTO the small cabin where Pierrot sat, a compartment they had reserved for themselves. The seats had been reupholstered with brown and green and gold material. There was a pastoral mural painted on the walls. There was a small bed that folded out from the wall. Rose closed the door behind her. She began to unbutton his jacket and he swayed back and forth. Pierrot pulled down the bed, and the pillows hopped up in surprise.

·◦[55]◦·

THE BIG APPLE

t was unseasonably cold in New York City that morning. The quality of the air was different from that of Montreal. But it was so subtle. It was crisper. It smelled like someone who was about to kiss you. It smelled a little bit like Coca-Cola.

They could suddenly see better. Many people who needed glasses found their eyesight rectified for just that moment.

The minute the first member of the Snowflake Icicle Extravaganza stepped off the train, tiny snowflakes began to fall from the sky. They were so minuscule that at first nobody was able to see them.

As soon as the sun went down, the snow began to fall in huge flakes.

They were like girls in Communion dresses doing cartwheels. People in mourning discovered that they were actually quite lucky. They could see momentary proof of the snowflakes on their black clothes before they melted and disappeared.

JIMMY SAT IN HIS OFFICE in the Romeo Hotel with Caspar. There was a fishbowl by the window with two fancy goldfish that swam in circles, like tassels on a burlesque dancer's nipples. The mobsters were staying in for the night because of the snowstorm. They were both aware that Rose and her troupe had arrived in the city. The radio was on; a singer who sounded like she had a clothes-peg on her nose whined about not getting what she wanted for Christmas.

"Did I ever tell you just how much I hate Montreal?" Jimmy asked. "And every asshole I meet from that place?"

"Yes, many times," Caspar answered.

"Is this dope worth it? Can't we buy from anyone else?"

"It's been tested. It's incredible, supposedly. Like nothing those morons have ever had before."

"Tell me again why the fuck we have to wait until the show is over to pick up the dope?"

"Because the dope is inside a moon."

"Because the dope is inside a fucking moon! That's the most ridiculous thing I've ever heard in my life. Why did I agree to this shit? What are we doing tonight?"

"Playing cards."

"Never mind that. Let's go. I need to see this. Come on. You like the theater."

"I don't know. We have to blow the girl's head off. It's inappropriate."

"Come on. Let's not start worrying about what's appropriate and what isn't at this point in our lives."

"It's starting in less than an hour."

"Then we have no time to lose."

"What if all the tickets are sold out?"

"Ha-ha-ha!"

Jimmy grabbed his coat and flung open the door to his office and leaned out into the corridor. "Girls, come on!"

Jimmy came down the stairs with his arms around two girls. When the other gangsters saw Jimmy heading toward the front door, they immediately wanted to join him. They grabbed their coats and hats, took their girlfriends' hands and left their meals behind and followed. There was no point hanging around the hotel on a Friday night if Jimmy wasn't going to be there.

The girls found the sidewalks icy and slippery, especially as they hurried along in their pretty high heels. When they arrived at the theater, there was no lineup outside. A sandwich board said that last-minute tickets would be sold for half price.

Five minutes before the curtain rose, they were able to pay half price for excellent seats. Jimmy wasn't happy because he had hoped to sit at the back of the theater. He wondered whether tomorrow's show would be canceled and if he would have to kill the girl in the morning.

WHEN ALL THE PEOPLE had been seated and had settled down and when the curtains rose in small, soft jerks, snow began to fall heavily outside. It came down over the whole of the city. It filled the palms of all the statues of angels. It covered all the roofs of the buildings with a giant down quilt. The audience inside the theater completely forgot that the outside world existed. Because, really, it wasn't there at all.

THE SNOWFLAKE ICICLE
EXTRAVAGANZA

ACT ONE

The chorus girls came out. They were dressed like little girls in short white dresses, with ribbons in their hair. Because of the identical make of their dresses and their woebegone faces, the audience was able to ascertain that they were orphans. They carried mops, and they swept in perfect unison. Except for one girl, who wore a black wig. She stood completely still in the middle of the stage, while all the chorus girls did wild movements with their mops around her.

ACT TWO

A clown dressed as an aristocrat in a checkered suit with a top hat came out on his bicycle. The lid of his top hat hung off the side, like an opened tin can. It was as though his head were a pot and his ideas had overcooked and blown the lid right off the top of his head, to let off steam, so to speak. He had his chin so far up in the air that he couldn't see where he was going. He drank from a delicate porcelain teacup as he cycled around. He leaned the bicycle all the way to the ground so that he was almost doing a handstand—and then when his nose was almost at the ground, he plucked an imaginary flower and inhaled it.

ACT THREE

A group of clowns came out. They wore shorts and striped T-shirts and beanie caps. They leaped about and kicked their legs. They were acting like children. It was so ridiculous and absurd to see grown adults acting in such unself-conscious ways. The audience was holding their sides because they were laughing so hard. Women pulled out their handkerchiefs and dabbed the tears of laughter from their eyes before it ruined their makeup.

ACT FOUR

There was a clown sitting inside a bathtub, all alone on the stage. He started to weep. He squeezed a rag under his eyes and water just poured out. He wept and wept, until it became apparent that the bathtub was filling with water. He stopped crying. He noticed the audience and looked immediately shocked and ashamed. He clearly wanted to get out of the tub, but looking around, he could not find clothes or a towel. Finally, he decided to climb out nonetheless, to escape. He was naked, but he wore a huge prosthetic erect penis wrapped around his waist. The audience laughed hysterically at his member as he hurried off.

ACT FIVE

Then came the act that had required the Napoleon hats. The clowns came out riding on hobbyhorses, which encircled their bodies. They brandished swords and fought one another. Then, all of a sudden, a bell rang gently. They put their horses on the ground and gathered around for a picnic together. The orchestra went from playing loud, thunderous music to playing soft, tinkly music. There was an abrupt change of mood. How fickle and superficial are our attempts at grandeur.

ACT SIX

A group of alcoholic clowns came out. They wobbled about with their eyes half-closed. It was as if the drug had taken away all their physical substance. They moved around, gravity seeming to have no pull on them.

They practically floated like feathers and tufts of milkweed on a breeze. Three of them climbed the ladder up to the tightrope. They tiptoed across wires, despite weighing hundreds of pounds. They walked across with the same assurance they would have walking down a chalk line on the sidewalk.

The last clown suddenly turned at a ninety-degree angle and strode off into the air. Everyone gasped, thinking he would plummet to his death. But he had wires attached and so he just appeared to walk on the air. The reprobate clown walked on the air the way Jesus walked on water. Right out over the audience's heads.

And didn't the whole audience find it in their hearts to forgive him for wasting his afternoons getting intoxicated, and throwing his whole life away.

ACT SEVEN

In the next act, a girl was getting ready for an important date. She had gas, however, and she kept farting every time she sat down. She bit into a cake and had icing all over her mouth. She lit up a cigar. She exhaled a series of smoke rings, which floated above her head. The audience all said, "Ooooh." They had never seen a lady do such things.

She was looking at a large magazine so she could see the latest fashions. She was having so much trouble behind the partition getting her clothes on. At one point she knocked the whole thing over, revealing that she had her dress on backward.

A group of girls ran onstage and rearranged all the furniture so that the girl was no longer in her bedroom but at a table in a restaurant. A clown sat at the opposite side of the table. He wore a tuxedo and a giant red bow tie. He was wearing spats over his bare feet and had an enormous prosthetic belly.

She was decidedly the most unladylike of ladies, but that made her wonderful and sweet and honest and trustworthy. She climbed across the table, knocking off everything that was in her way, and onto the lap of the man she was dining with.

She had trouble getting her arms around his enormous belly. But when she did, she gave him an enormous messy kiss. They fell underneath the table. When they crawled back out from under it, they both had large red grimaces on their faces, like clowns. It was rather delightful. Everyone in the audience was on her side.

ACT EIGHT

After the pair exited to the right, the chorus girls came out on roller skates. They were dressed in the shabbiest and oddest ways. They had tried to doll themselves up, they had tried to look pretty for the audience, but they had done so out of rags. Their bright little young sweet faces smiled from underneath crushed mushroom hats with crooked flowers, and black handkerchiefs tied in bows at their foreheads.

They began to take off the scruffy layers. They unbuttoned their threadbare coats and stuffed them into garbage cans that sat in the middle of the stage. They roller-skated with giant smiles on their faces. They were freer with every layer they took off. Some of the girls had become so talented and free with eight small wheels underneath them.

One girl skated backward, her hands up in the air, with such assurance. There was one girl who could barely stand up on her skates, and she kept toppling over. Everyone laughed at her struggle, but not at her.

They took off their gloves that had holes in the fingertips, their moth-eaten scarves, their patched-up sweaters, their faded dresses. They took off their roller skates and their stockings. They stood in their skimpy peach-colored chorus girl costumes, which covered them like undergarments. They pranced to the front of the stage in bare feet, until they were underneath the footlights. They each found a pair of sparkly silver high heels, which they put on.

They were all so naked and they were all so perfect. They all exited the stage, leaving just one girl all alone. She was wearing a ridiculous red wig. The audience thought she was supposed to Little Orphan Annie, but Pierrot and Rose knew that she was supposed to be Poppy. She kept kicking her legs up in the air, not noticing that all the other girls had left and that the music had stopped. She was just too busy experiencing abandon to bother. She opened her eyes, noticed her predicament and stopped in her tracks. She looked out at the audience and laughed and laughed and laughed.

FINAL ACT

There was a clown who was dressed as a shooting star, who rode his toy gangster car across the stage. He spotted a lasso on the ground. He got off his bicycle and picked it up. He kept throwing the lasso up into the air, up toward the ceiling, over and over again. The lasso kept falling right back down. And then, finally, it got stuck up in the air. It was affixed to something above in the rafters that could not be seen. He pulled on it as hard as he could, but no matter how hard he tried, whatever it had caught would not budge.

He began to climb the rope and found himself upside down and tangled in it. Another clown came in with his dog. That clown took the rope in his hands and both men began to pull together. The dog took the rope in his mouth and he began to pull too. Then the other clowns came out. They all began to pull the rope. Three of the chorus girls climbed up on the rope in order to pull harder. Finally, with everyone pulling, it slowly began to budge.

And from above the curtains, the most enormous and lovely papier-mâché moon began to slowly descend as the clowns fulfilled what they promised to do in the advertisements for the performance: to bring the audience the moon.

Rose's greatest theatrical gift was her stage presence. It was evident when she tiptoed out onto the stage in sparkly slippers. She had on her head a triangular hat with a little pom-pom glued on top. She had on a silk jacket with big polka dots. She had on a skirt that jutted outward, little white pom-poms attached to the edge of it like snowballs that were attached to a dog's chin. She had wires attached to a great big bear puppet that was behind her.

A piano and a bench were suddenly rolled onto the stage with none other than Pierrot seated at it. He was wearing a loose white clown outfit. He had a ruffled white collar, large black pom-poms for buttons, and pants that drooped down at his feet like melting candles. His face was completely covered in white face paint, except for a tiny little black tear on his cheek.

Rose's face was similarly covered in white face paint, except for a red dot on either cheek—just like the ones on her face when she was found in the snow as a baby.

Pierrot began to play the tune he always played. Rose began to dance her funny dance. When she danced elegantly, so did the bear. Every time she leaned forward, it seemed as though the bear was certainly going to swallow her. But then Pierrot played higher on the scale of the piano and the bear changed his mind and began to dance elegantly behind her.

Pierrot had been working on this peculiar score for years now. It was his magnum opus. He had been working on it since he was a little boy—perhaps he had been playing the same tune since he first put his long fingers on the piano keys. And that night onstage, he finished it.

For the last bar, Pierrot paused for a moment and tapped the keys delicately, as if he were trying to wake someone from a deep sleep. Paper snowflakes came down one by one from the ceiling. It was quite lovely.

When the stage was covered in paper snowflakes, and Pierrot stopped playing the piano, Rose and her bear took a bow. The heavy, heavy curtains tumbled down like lava on the side of a volcano. And the show was over.

THE AUDIENCE WAS QUIET. There was a hush. They were not sure what they had just seen. They did not want to breathe. They did not want to clap, because their applause would mean the show was over and they did not want it to end. Then it came. A wonderful sound. They applauded joyfully.

The audience was filled with a hundred nine-year-olds dressed in furs and fancy pearls.

·≈[57]≈·

JIMMY'S ONE-POINT PERSPECTIVE

Jimmy wasn't sure what to think about the clowns. He felt a little bit weirded out by men who had chosen clowning as a profession. He only regarded being a murderer or a politician as sufficiently masculine. He was so cautious of betraying any emotion or sign of weakness that he felt alarmed by these men who just paraded about in front of an audience, weeping and farting and dropping things.

He did, however, like the chorus girls. There was something so odd about them. Some of them weren't even pretty. A few of them had no chest at all. They weren't the sorts of girls who he would have working at the Romeo Hotel. He liked the show, though. It started reminding him of his past, when he was a little boy in the whorehouse.

He looked at the faces of different chorus girls to see which one he was supposed to kill. But none of the girls seemed to have the face of someone who had managed to get such a large sum on her head.

He looked at Caspar and raised his hands as if to say he didn't know who their mark was.

"You'll know her when you see her," Caspar said.

They believed in all sorts of omens—anyone who had been around a lot of deaths always did. You came to think of superstition as common sense. They both believed that you could spot right away when someone had a price on their heads. They had a weird aura, like saints in medieval paintings.

Jimmy leaned back into his seat and the last act commenced, wherein right before his eyes, a moon began to be lowered down on cables. This was going too far. He turned to Caspar, whose mouth was open and who seemed stunned by the enormity and reality of this moon. McMahon was out of his mind. Montreal had gone too far this time, Jimmy thought. It must be the cold. Everyone who traveled there said they couldn't put into words how cold it got and how miserable they had been trudging through the snow. They would often hold up their feet for him to get a look at how their shoes and boots had been destroyed. They seemed a little bit mad when they returned from Montreal. But it was as if they had caught just a touch of madness—like the flu—that passed after three or four days. He could only imagine what living through an entire winter would do to you.

And then someone tiptoed out onto the stage. There was a smattering of little moans in the audience, with people oohing and aahing. It sounded as though they were making love. When the woman stepped out onto the stage, everyone in the audience stiffened their spines and stared. Jimmy felt a small surge of desperation when he looked at her. There she was. That was her. She was the one.

She was different from the other girls. She moved wonderfully. She landed so lightly on her toes. She landed as quietly as a snowflake on a mitten. Her face seemed so interesting. He wanted to look at her forever.

Of course this was the girl he was supposed to kill. Indisputably she was the type of girl who could drive a man so crazy that his only option would be to stick a bullet in her head. He hadn't even met her yet and she had already driven him quite mad.

JIMMY WOKE UP in the morning feeling hungover: melancholic and lazy and afraid of death. But it was the show, and not drinking, that had caused him to feel this way. He was distracted all day. That evening he kept staring at the outfits in his closet, trying to decide what he should wear. He put on the black suit he only wore on special occasions. Although he had been told a hundred times in his life that he was good-looking, he found himself standing in front of the bathroom mirror wondering.

He hurried out of the building, not wanting to tell Caspar that he was going to see the show again. He had always looked down on guys who fell in love with chorus girls. Those women only got into that racket to get married. But she wasn't a chorus girl anyhow. He didn't know what she was.

There was a larger crowd than on opening night. He rented out the box to the right of the stage and sat there by himself. He felt lonely. He felt completely lost. But then she came onstage. She reminded Jimmy of something that was buried deep in his childhood.

Jimmy went to see her every night. At each performance more and more of the seats were filled up.

58

THE HONEYMOON HOTEL

Pierrot and Rose stayed at the Honeymoon Hotel on Forty-Fourth Street, only a few blocks from the theater. There was a framed ink drawing of a bluebird on the wall in their room. Their room's windows were arched like those in a church. The tiles were a lovely shade of light blue, blue like the type of cloak the Virgin Mary liked to wear. Rose looked out at all the different lightbulbs on the theater signs across the way and felt like anything was possible. She felt that the world was gigantic. She was suddenly taken by just how beautiful the world was, and how lucky it was that she had been born, especially since her parents hadn't wanted her.

Pierrot was lying on the bed, his arms spread out on either side of him. Rose had a bare foot on either side of his hips. She slowly descended. She seemed to be descending for five years. It was so lovely. He put his hands on her knees. He put his mouth on her cunt and gave it a kiss. Rose could put on some very pretty little private shows.

THE CLOWN SHOW was a huge success. They all crammed around a table in a diner to listen as Pierrot read the papers out loud to them.

"The clowns seemed to imply that we are really nothing more than our foibles and that, were we to eradicate our flaws, there would be nothing left of us at all."

They laughed and held up their big glasses of beer and clanked them against one another. And they all felt really good. And they drank until their foreheads were sweaty and flushed, as though they'd just made love. And the words in their sentences crashed into one another like clown cars, because they really had nothing important that they needed to say.

AN HOUR BEFORE SHOWTIME, there were always people lining up outside the theater to get in the door. They blocked the sidewalk. And when it was over, they all rushed out the door like carbonated bubbles heading to the top of a bottle, to go off and tell their friends. What in the world did Pierrot and Rose's absurd and sad story have to do with them? How had it become entertainment? Pierrot knew that he shouldn't be surprised. When he and Rose were little and performed before rich people, they always enchanted their audiences. But it was still quite something to see it on a larger scale like this. It was that sweet and happy feeling he had when he was with Rose. They had somehow managed to convey that feeling of innocence and play in the face of oppression and calamity, and this had proven an addictive elixir. There were more and more dates booked, and the show's run was extended for a month. Much to Jimmy's consternation.

PIERROT WAS IN A GOOD MOOD as he strolled down the street. He reflected on how he adored New York. The buildings were so tall and skinny, they seemed like ladders up to the heavens. Because he was new to the city, he noticed all the details that someone who had grown up there wouldn't. It was as though he were on a first date with the city. Every building made him curious. In Montreal, every building reminded him of something really shitty that had gone on in it. With Montreal, it was as if he were spending time with a spouse who just criticized him all the time. And who kept bringing up mistakes that he had made years and years before. And almost seemed to be mounting an argument at the breakfast table about why he was, in fact, an abominable person.

He felt he had escaped his past. His past was back in Montreal. It was checking out all the clubs where he used to hang out. It was knocking on the door of friends he used to know, asking if they'd spotted him, or if he'd mentioned anything about where he might be headed. It would not find him.

Rose had been offered touring dates from a big-time producer. When their run was finished in New York City, they would be going on the road. He would never have to set foot in Montreal again, and he was surprised at just how good that made him feel.

THIS WAS A TIME for them to enjoy their lives. They weren't going to have any worries at all for the next while. But Rose was wary the whole time. She knew that McMahon was going to have her killed. She expected the gun to be stuck behind her head at any moment. Everywhere she went. Just because the show was extended didn't mean that the gangsters were going to honor this arrangement. She kept a handgun under the counter in her dressing room.

After the show, she called Colombe into her dressing room. She needed to send a message over to the Romeo Hotel, where Jimmy Bonaventura and his men lived. The girl was out of her mind, but she had worked for McMahon and didn't get giddy about gangsters.

"I want you to go see Jimmy Bonaventura. Let him know that the show has been extended and I need to speak to him. I'll give you his address. It's not far."

"I know where to find him," Colombe said matter-of-factly, and turned and walked off.

Minutes later there was a knock at the door. Rose flung open her dressing-room door, expecting to see Colombe. But there stood none other than Jimmy Bonaventura. They looked at each other, unable to speak.

"How did—"

"I was sitting in the box. A sort of moody-looking girl said you wanted to see me backstage."

She was wearing her black coat as a robe. He could see her bare legs underneath it. So he assumed that, other than the coat, she was naked. She let him in. There was a photograph of Pierrot from a newspaper that she had Scotch-taped to the wall. There were vases on the table that were filled with roses. Because there was nowhere else to put it, a vase with roses was on the floor. They seemed lackluster somehow, compared to her.

"You want the moon," Rose said. "But I can't give it to you tomorrow because the show has been extended. By popular demand. They've sold out another month."

"I know, I got the message from McMahon."

"Perhaps there is some information that gets lost this way. It might be efficient if we communicated one-on-one in the future."

"Yes."

"Yes?"

"Yes, I think that's a good idea."

"Can I come to your office tomorrow to review the situation with you?"

"Yeah, we'll discuss it properly . . . when you're dressed."

He stepped back and she closed the door. She was so nervous that she leaned her forehead against the door, the tip of her nose touching it. On the other side, Jimmy, overcome by the urge to be closer to Rose, stepped up against the door and pressed his face against it. Only a few inches of wood prevented them from kissing.

59

THE HERO OF
ANOTHER NOVEL

The next morning Rose neurotically did her hair and sat at the end of the bed, cleaning the toes of her button-up boots with a brush. She had on a white veil—as though a spiderweb had formed below her hat. She had arranged to meet with Jimmy that afternoon. Pierrot was dressed in his checkered suit, which was just back from the cleaners.

"We have to look professional," Rose stated as Pierrot put out their breakfast.

"But why?"

"You know why. This isn't Montreal."

The New York City mobsters were murderers. They carried around machine guns, and they would actually kill each other. That's why they were each so famous. She had been reading about the New York City mobsters in the newspapers since she had arrived. They assassinated each other on a regular basis. They were merciless. You couldn't be an actual mobster unless you killed somebody.

In Montreal, the mobsters would come up behind you with a stale loaf of bread and bang you on the head. They would kidnap your dog if you weren't careful. They would pick on women. They were cowards. They weren't real mobsters. This meeting with Jimmy was just as much of a performance as the clown act they had put on the previous night.

"Don't be so erudite today," Rose pleaded. "Don't say anything at all. Can you do that? Don't say anything about your ideas about life and the universe. Don't say anything about just how happy we've been during the last few days."

"I get it. We have to look like maniacs. Damn you, croissant. Oh, I thought you were a smile, but all along you were nothing but a frown!"

And with that Pierrot launched his croissant across the room. Rose put her hands up to her mouth and started to laugh. She knew that Pierrot could play any role except that of a tough guy. But she wasn't entirely certain that Jimmy wasn't going to shoot her the minute she walked in, before listening to her proposition. And if she was to die, she wanted to go out the way she had come into this business—holding Pierrot's hand.

She tapped the shell of her egg with a spoon. A little earthquake spread across its surface.

THEY PASSED ONE of their chorus girls in the lobby. She was squashed in a love seat with an extravagantly dressed bald man. She was teaching him how to speak French, and judging by his flushed face, he was finding it adorable. She pointed coyly to each of her body parts as she recited its French *nom*.

"*Voici mes petits doigts. Et voici mes genoux. Et ah, ça, c'est mon oreille! Qu'est-ce que j'ai sous ma chemise! Je ne connais pas le bon mot!*"

Rose and Pierrot laughed.

THEY SAW THE NEON SIGN as soon as they turned onto the street where Jimmy Bonaventura and his men had their headquarters:

It was a gray stone building that looked very much like the other buildings on the block. All the buildings were so old and stately compared to the ramshackle houses and skinny churches in Montreal.

There was a guard standing at the door. He looked the couple over as they walked up the steps of the establishment. They had not expected it to be so beautiful inside. They were used to the Montreal whorehouses, which were just duplexes converted into brothels. This was a regular hotel, and a rather splendid one too. The large lobby featured a pianist playing a grand piano. Wooden staircases rose on either side of the lobby, polished and shiny. Everything was so clean. Well-dressed men sat around tables, playing cards. A mural of baby angels cavorting hung on a wall. The chandelier was magnificent, with hundreds of little pieces of crystal hanging down from it and tinkling.

Pierrot and Rose sank a little bit into the carpet, which was covered in a pattern of pink and blue flowers. They stood there looking at their feet, wondering if the ground would continue to swallow them up. It did not.

The whores were all magnificent. Rose had, of course, heard tell that Jimmy had the most beautiful whores in the city. But she had had no idea what that meant. She had had no idea how one type of woman could be considered more beautiful than another. She saw that they were all buxom. Their asses were huge and lovely, and when they sat down it was like giant parachutes descending. She saw that they weren't only better-looking but also so well groomed. They smelled so good when they walked past her that she wanted to inhale deeply. One girl, wearing white stockings over her muscular legs, looked like she had the limbs of a unicorn.

A man appeared with a bullet hole in each cheek: one scar from where the bullet went in, and one scar from where the bullet went out. He led Rose and Pierrot upstairs and down the hallway to meet Jimmy.

MCMAHON AND JIMMY were each the head of a crime syndicate. Professionally, they were equally powerful men. But they presented themselves very differently to the world. McMahon kept a small, makeshift office in downtown Montreal so he didn't draw attention to himself and his criminal activities. He was very safe. He isolated his home life from his criminal life. He wanted to eventually wrap up the criminal world and become an upright citizen.

Jimmy didn't have a double life away from the Romeo Hotel. He loved an ostentatious display. He loved to rub his ill-gotten wealth in everybody's nose. Even in the police officers' noses. Even if it ended up getting him arrested. Even if it was his downfall. He didn't really think that life was worth living unless people were watching him live it and were impressed with how he was living it. His life itself was an ornate Broadway production.

Jimmy had made a fortune when booze was illegal. A crime that wasn't really a crime—only temporarily a crime. Now that Prohibition was over, he continued to engage in all sorts of other crimes, amassing more and more wealth.

But he didn't have a pretty wife at home who he cheated on and whose self-esteem he ruined. He had never had a serious girlfriend. He slept with different prostitutes. Sometimes he slept with one girl for a few weeks, but never for much longer, and he never deluded her that he was sticking around. All in all, it has been suggested by some that, murders aside, Jimmy was a more moral man than McMahon.

He wasn't pretending to be anything other than who he was and who he was raised to be.

He was elevating crime. He was making the underworld a part of everyday life. He was making sure that the criminals ran the city. He wanted everyone to look up to criminals and wish that they could grow up to be one.

Jimmy had thick, dark brown hair that always flopped messily about. His nose was too big. Even when he was a little baby, people worried that his nose was going to end up being too big. He had heavy, arching eyebrows that made him look skeptical, and fantastic blue eyes. When he smiled, all his perfect and big teeth lined up, and his eyes grew wide and their blueness took away from the overall darkness of his face.

His face matched his unpredictable moods. You couldn't be bothered to think of killing him or overthrowing him. He doused his words in alcohol and set them on fire. They were inflammatory. The reason he was so successful wasn't that he was a calculating workhorse, the way McMahon was. The reason he was so successful was that he took wild risks, his moves were inscrutable, his intuitions almost uncanny.

And here was Rose sitting on the chair across from his desk with her partner. McMahon had told Jimmy that after she had delivered the heroin and the show's run was up, he was welcome to shoot Rose between the eyes and put her out of her misery. He was also supposed to kill the love of her life, Pierrot, who was certain to show up with her.

McMahon warned him not to be fooled, that the girl was far, far more violent than the man. He said that even if Pierrot was dressed the part of a gangster, he was incapable of violence. He moved in slow-motion. If he tried to punch you, his fist would probably feel like a pillow.

Pierrot reached for a flower from the vase on the table. He shook the water from its stem and tucked it behind his ear. A black cat jumped from the window to the desk and onto Pierrot's lap.

"Drown that thing in the bathtub," said a gangster. "Jesus."

Pierrot ignored him and stroked the cat's head. The cat was all black, except for the lower half of its face, which was white, as if it were covered in shaving cream. "Hello, my darling. Well, we're here no doubt to discuss pleasure in the most unpleasurable of manners. You'd best do something wicked in this life so that you don't get reincarnated as a man. There's nothing to walking on two legs. Highly overrated."

The gangsters looked at Pierrot, who they were sure would have been murdered if he'd been a New Yorker. Why had this good-looking moll chosen this effeminate buffoon, they all wanted to know. But Jimmy understood why immediately. Because he allowed her to be free.

Rose and Jimmy just sat there looking into each other's eyes. Then it clicked why McMahon hated her. And he suddenly knew something about McMahon that he hadn't known before. He knew that McMahon was a certain type of man. McMahon was the type of man who had hated Jimmy's mother. McMahon was the type of man who had looked down on Jimmy's mother. He was the type of man whose lousy opinions had pushed Jimmy's mother out the window.

Jimmy's mother was all these amazing things. She was able to make him stop crying. She had drawn a tiny black cat on a piece of paper and she held it up to her face and made a meowing noise and it was just as if the drawing had come to life. She had put both of his socks on her hands and they told him about how much they enjoyed going for walks.

"Once a whore, always a whore," she had said to Jimmy the day before she leaped out a window.

Jimmy surprised everybody in the room by saying: "When that clown walked off the tightrope, what was that supposed to mean? Like, that he might be a bum but he had highfalutin thoughts?"

"Exactly," Rose answered. "He thinks that he's confined by a social order, but he's not confined."

"How come you guys have so many clowns in your show?"

Rose turned to Pierrot, offering him the opportunity to answer. He was just sitting there, looking rather uncomfortable and upset by the men around him, as though he were still on the side of the cat. He found it difficult to even look at Jimmy Bonaventura. He couldn't get the image of all the things that the mob boss had done out of his head. He knew that a lot of people saw Jimmy Bonaventura as a romantic figure. Look at all he had. He had started off with nothing at all, and now he ran the greatest city on earth. Was this the American dream, then? At what expense did it come? Could a person only become wealthy if they had no regard for anyone but themselves?

"Je vais t'attendre dehors," he said to Rose in French, because he wanted to speak to her and no one else in the room.

"Why do we have so many clowns? You weren't careful in the 1920s," Rose went on, letting Pierrot leave. "You never thought that everything would get terrible again, and so you had no need to invest in sad clowns. In Montreal we understand that everything in life is seasonal. Winter is always going to come, and then summer is always going to come. You have to prepare yourself for the eventuality of every emotion. We've always had clowns."

"They make a living off that?"

"Have you seen the reviews? This troupe is successful. We'll be able to go back and forth across the border any number of times in the next year. It's the perfect cover. The police are on to McMahon. It isn't just this. They are always looking to catch him. They'll never look at me. They'll never think that a woman would be in charge. I'm a woman, so I'm invisible. I'll never be a suspect."

"Are you saying that you'll never get caught?"

"No, we'll all get caught eventually. And it's only by accepting this that we can make any sort of bold decisions. Do you believe that?"

"I do. I never thought about it like that, though. You put things in a very intelligent way."

"Once he's dead, they'll leave this all alone. Everything exists only within a temporal framework. Every clown knows that."

Jimmy paused for a second, staring at the girl, needing a moment to take in what she had just proposed to him. Then he said, "Are there other people who speak like you in Montreal? In Montreal are you considered unique?"

"For a woman, yes."

She gently leaned across his desk and took a piece of paper off a stack and a pencil from the jar. She felt confident. There was something magical about a piece of paper and a pencil. It was with them that all the new things of the world happened. She began to map out on the paper a diagram of downtown Montreal and its crime organization and holdings. She began to draw all the different nightclubs; all the little theaters; all the narrow backstreets; all the *boulangeries*, with their tiny pastries in the window; and the hospital, with all the newborns in the cribs. She made everything into a little grid, as seen from up above. The whole city was like a seamstress's box, with everything divided up into its proper compartments.

It was as though she were laying out her entire city and childhood for Jimmy. When she drew the hotels, he could see her standing in her stockings over a little blue sink, brushing her teeth. When she drew the café, he saw her eating chocolate pudding and reading an Honoré de Balzac novel in it. When she drew the church, he heard all the different confessions she had whispered into the ears of priests over the years. She was not at all afraid of this Montreal that she could fold up and fit into her pocket.

And then, with several swipes of the pencil and various arrows and lines, she explained how he could easily take over the heroin trade that was coming into New York through Montreal. The tip of the pencil moved across the page like a bullet in slow-motion. She drew *X*s along the docks where the heroin came in.

"You know which of his guys will turn, no problem?"

Rose nodded. She had watched their expressions at the Roxy for years and knew without a doubt which ones despised McMahon. She also knew they were all upset about the last major bust. She put a circle around the hotels that she wanted: the ones that he had purchased for McMahon in exchange for the heroin.

Jimmy liked the idea of any sort of power grab or a coup d'état. And he especially liked the sound of this one. He had never had a woman make a plan for him. He had always worked with men. They had designs that sometimes worked and that sometimes didn't work at all. The strategies he chose were the ones he was curious about. And the ones he was curious about were the ones that had a spark of newness about them. These were always the most powerful plans. Nobody knew quite what to do when faced with the very electric power of new things.

ROSE WAS IN A GOOD MOOD when she rejoined Pierrot, who was smoking a cigarette on the street outside the Romeo Hotel.

"And so?" Pierrot said. "You worked out your business?"

"Yes!" Rose exclaimed.

Although Rose was light-footed and smiling, Pierrot felt concerned as he walked back to the hotel. At the beginning of the venture, he and Rose had collaborated on all aspects of the show. Then, as things became more hectic, they had divided up tasks, but now they seemed to have completely separated their jobs, to the point that they were no longer working together at all. She wanted to focus entirely on the drug trade.

He could tell that she didn't really care about the reviews as much as the other performers did. She had immediately set her sights higher than the show and was interested in negotiating with gangsters, not tour managers.

He had never been jealous about Rose having been with other men. He thought what they had together was so much better than what she had had with other men that he wouldn't even deign to compare the unions. But she had been in the room planning a future with another man. He had known since even before he had met him that Jimmy Bonaventura was a threat.

On the window ledge was a robin that looked like a fat man who had been shot in the chest by his business partner.

·◄[60]►·

CONEY ISLAND BABY

Jimmy had to take Rose to meet the rest of the commission. On a Saturday afternoon they drove together to a restaurant that was built under the tracks in Brighton Beach. The elevated train roared over them and suddenly they were all characters in a silent film, mouthing their words. Although the ground under their feet shook, nobody walking by seemed to mind. They weren't worried about everything crumbling down around them.

The restaurant was a small, unassuming place. You wouldn't imagine that it was the type of place where a contingency of gangsters would meet. It was built out of red bricks and had red-and-white-striped curtains over its windows. The name *Luigi* was painted on the glass with sparkly gold paint, and there was a blackboard on the sidewalk out front with the names of all the types of pasta written in cursive.

A man came and took their coats. And while doing this, he very quickly and subtly patted them down for weapons. Rose found herself rather liking the way the strange man's hands felt on her body. They made her feel dangerous.

The walls inside were covered in white tiles. There were large, circular wooden tables. The waiter threw the red tablecloth up into the air as if he were a matador gracefully challenging a bull. Jimmy and Rose sat at the big table by themselves.

The other heads shuffled in shortly afterward. One man was enormous. He ate beautifully. He twirled the spaghetti around his fork perfectly. He puckered up his mouth as though he were about to give a kiss and then dabbed it with a napkin. There was a squat man. His face was round and his features all seemed to be squashed up together within a very small area. Another man kept making jokes that weren't funny. Another had a receding hairline that made him look intelligent and like some sort of scholar, but when he spoke, he had a thick Bronx accent and used the word *fuck* at least twice in every sentence.

A man in a pin-striped suit arrived, apologizing that he was late because he had just come from a funeral. The way he said it, Rose wondered whether that meant he had been at a funeral parlor seeing off a beloved aunt, or out on the side of the highway burying someone in a shallow grave.

They were all rather frightening and intimidating. But Rose liked that this was the sort of company she was now keeping. She knew that she could not even for an instant reveal any form of self-doubt, or any hesitation, or be in any way threatened by the men who were sitting around the table. In other words, she was not to show any signs that she was a girl. They made small talk among themselves, and Rose joined in as if it were perfectly normal for her to be there. The gangsters didn't really understand Canadians—everything they did seemed to be ass-backward. Perhaps the women ran the show up there. There was no way the gangsters were going to turn down Rose's plan. They nodded that McMahon would go. It had to be soon too because he was pestering Jimmy about bumping off Rose.

The noodles on her plate looked like a ball of yarn thoroughly messed up by a cat. She couldn't eat a bite because she was so nervous. She smiled.

AFTER EVERYONE LEFT, Jimmy and Rose walked down the street to the boardwalk. The ocean was right there in front of her. She'd never seen the ocean before. It was so vast compared to the rivers she'd seen. The sand resembled brown sugar. The seagulls leaped up and down as if they were at the ends of yo-yos. The waves made the sound of someone biting into an apple. When they crashed, they were a hundred thousand chorus girls raising up their dresses at once. And then the water receded again like the train of a jilted bride walking off into the distance.

Jimmy couldn't stop glancing at her. Her hair immediately seemed to curl. Her cheeks, which always seemed to turn bright pink when she was out in the cold for too long, were suddenly all rosy. While he was looking, his eyes turned a brighter blue. It was something the ocean did to blue eyes. It turned them on as though they were lightbulbs.

They were both dressed more formally than everybody else on the beach. Their careful outfits looked absurd. The sand kept trying to get into her shoes. And the wind kept trying to knock her hat off.

A woman walked by in a long green wool coat, a striped headband tied around her forehead with a big bow at the back. She looked as though she were off to fight a dragon, Rose thought. She resembled a warrior. Her four children followed her at an increasing distance. She turned and called back to them by their absurd nicknames: Cricket and Frog and Booboo and Bird. They all laughed and hopped and skipped, but didn't really hurry up at all. When we were free and easy, that was when we felt like ourselves. That's what children with mothers feel like, Rose thought: free and easy.

JIMMY AND ROSE SAT AT the counter of a hot dog shack on the boardwalk and ordered pints of beer. After taking a sip of her beer, Rose had a white mustache on her lip. She felt a hundred pounds lighter. She wondered how that could be, and then she realized that it was because she had very temporarily lifted her business concerns and efforts off her shoulders. The beer was making them happy, like children at a birthday party. The beer made their words come out of their mouths like carbonated bubbles.

Jimmy kept looking to Rose for some sort of encouragement. She hadn't come out here with him to discuss love. He knew that. He had just been trying to convince himself that the situation was otherwise. Jimmy handed Rose the petite briefcase. It wasn't the ordinary kind of briefcase that a man might be in possession of. It was a dainty, thin black briefcase with a black handle in the shape of a swan biting its tail. Two clasps on either side of it made the swan's golden wings.

It was a briefcase that only a girl would feel comfortable toting down the street. Jimmy had bought it especially as a gift for Rose. As a subtle indication to Rose that he wanted their relationship to be more than a business one.

Rose opened the briefcase. She looked at the deeds to the hotels. She read the names on the papers. She imagined what she was going to do with each one. How she would make it wonderful.

She closed her eyes and imagined the Valentine Hotel. Chandeliers sprouted down from the ceiling. The floors grew fantastic carpets. Magnolias and tulips and violets sprouted on the wall. Statues of nude girls climbed onto the empty plinths in the lobby. She opened her eyes again and smiled. She was in a good mood.

Jimmy had always been incapable of making a connection between sex and love. Sex was something that you purchased, like an Italian ice. He noticed how Rose stuck her thumb in her mouth to suck off a drop of beer. He noticed the way she shooed away a pigeon that was walking toward the shack, using just the tip of her toe. He noticed she smiled at a fat baby passing in a stroller. He was surprised at just how much her smiling at a baby got to him. She twitched her nose when she drank the beer. She crossed her ankles under the stool.

He just had to look at women and tilt his head at a certain angle and they would always blush—and it would make them have a dirty thought in their heads. And after that, getting them into bed was downhill. Many other gangsters had tried to figure out the exact degree of this angle, but they never could.

He tilted his head at Rose just to see what would happen. The sun reflected off her wedding ring and stabbed him in the eye, and for the moment he had to turn away from looking at her.

THERE WAS A LITTLE GIRL with black hair standing out at the edge of the water. The ocean kept casting a wave like a net at her feet to try to pull her in—but failed each time. She wore a white coat and a scarf with red polka dots. She was waving at someone. It seemed to Rose that she was waving at her, though she knew that this couldn't possibly be the case.

The driver of Jimmy's limousine was reading a newspaper that described the Night of Broken Glass. He had spent the entire time that they were at the beach reading about how in Germany a few nights before, Jewish shops and synagogues had been raided, and tens of thousands of Jews had been rounded up. Jimmy ran the shipyards—the advent of the war was going to make him even richer than he was before. The war was frankly about to make a lot of people very rich. But nobody knew that right then, except perhaps the limo driver.

JIMMY LOOKED FOR AN EXCUSE to meet her backstage the next night. He came with a bottle of wine that he had been given as a gift by a politician. He said there were some details about their plan he needed to clarify. They drank the wine together. She said that she couldn't concentrate on the numbers now that she was tipsy. Her thoughts were like corks that couldn't stay below the surface of the water. He said he couldn't remember the name of the street he lived on. She smiled and her teeth were purple. He was keenly aware of the fact that he was making another man's wife laugh.

Caspar looked at Jimmy when he walked into the Romeo Hotel. "What the hell are you doing?" Caspar asked.

"I have no fucking idea," Jimmy answered.

He went to his room to be alone. He couldn't stop thinking of things that he wanted to do to her. He wanted to take her to the ice cream parlor that had twenty types of strawberry ice cream. He wanted to take her to visit his mother's grave. He wanted to ride on a roller coaster with her. He wanted to go for pie with her after a movie. He imagined them listening to a record in a booth at a record store.

He imagined her in a nightgown sitting across the kitchen table, sipping coffee. Having that picture in his head made him feel almost delirious. He imagined her reaching over the table and picking up his piece of toast and eating it. He could almost hear the way it would sound.

He closed his eyes. He unbuttoned his shirt. He imagined it was Rose's fingers undoing the buttons. He imagined it was her hand slipping down his pants. And he whispered, "I don't have time for that now, sweetheart. I have to go to work. Cut that out!"

THE CHILDREN'S WAR

Pierrot woke up with a start, feeling sad for their tiny baby, somewhere in a suitcase in the Saint Lawrence River. Perhaps it had floated off to sea. Would things have been any different if their child had survived? He couldn't imagine it now. They would be in Montreal, performing for an audience of one in a high chair. A baby makes the ordinary miraculous.

Rose was asleep beside him. She was so pale and serene when she slept, as though she were frozen in ice.

When he began thinking about the baby, it was an indication that his mood was about to go to hell. It was like feeling a sore throat and knowing that it meant that the flu was coming on. He didn't want to stew in those thoughts all day long.

Whenever he was depressed, it made him want to get high. He was surprised by this craving. He always assumed that the craving had disappeared—that its hold on him had weakened. And when it came back, he was surprised to feel it so strongly.

Imagine, if you will, the taxidermied corpse of a wolf. Dead for years, its insides gutted, its organs removed, its hide stuffed with wood chips, and sewed back up. With glass eyes, it's been mounted in a position and put on display at the museum. Imagine then that, despite all that, there was the wolf strutting around, acting as if nothing had even happened, drooling and famished, its joints all elastic, pacing at the foot of your bed, as absolutely real as anything real could ever be. Imagine the shock you would feel.

Pierrot jumped up out of bed—as though the desire were in the bed, as though he could get away from it. He put on his clothes and quietly headed out for a walk.

As Pierrot was passing through the lobby, the concierge called out his name and said he had a letter for him. Pierrot walked over to the desk and took the letter from the man's hand. It wasn't exactly for him personally per se. The words on the envelope were written in a studied print that had curlicues at the end of the strokes of each letter, making them look like the tendrils of flowers. On the envelope was written: *To the members of the fine circus with many clowns in it, to be read by someone in charge.*

Pierrot ripped open the envelope, pulled out the letter and perused its contents:

> *Would you find the time to send one of your clowns to visit the children at the Downtown City Hospital for Sick and Unfortunate Children? We cannot afford to pay for your services. But if you found it within your charity, the unfortunate children would see it undoubtedly as a great blessing.*

He was surprised and touched by the letter. He liked the very honest manner in which it was composed. He also quite liked that something good was being expected of him. And, frankly, he was in the mood to see some children.

On his way to the hospital, Pierrot stopped by at the theater and went into the prop room backstage to find himself a clown costume.

He stuck a round, red nose on his face. He took out a top hat that was crushed at the top and had a red cloth carnation affixed to the side. He picked up an old battered suitcase. He looked at himself in the mirror. He found it almost alarming just how quickly he had transformed into a clown.

WHEN HE ARRIVED, Pierrot was escorted to the common room on the second floor of the hospital. A nurse lifted up a hand bell over her head and rang it, and children immediately began to be assembled.

A little girl had an intravenous drip that she was walking along like a pet ostrich she was taking for a walk. There was a girl covered in stitches where she had been mauled by a dog. She looked like a doll that had been mended with black thread. There was a boy with a cast on his arm. It was covered in ink drawings—no doubt he would one day be a sailor covered in tattoos. There was a boy in leg braces who seemed to nonetheless have a joyous sort of walk. There was a little boy with a bandage around his head. There was a little boy whose skin had been burned. There were some children who were pushed into the room in wheelchairs.

They were like tiny battlefield veterans, injured by the trials of being young, in the Great Children's War. Perhaps he himself had never escaped his childhood wounds. The only difference was that these children wore their injuries on the outside.

There was a piano on a small raised stage in the room. He sat at it and began to play for the children. It was a cheap piano. It had a tinny sound. There was something childish about its sound, akin to striking a xylophone with a metal stick. It reminded him of the piano that he had learned to play on at the orphanage.

It was a little bit stubborn. It didn't want to play. It just wanted to be left to its own devices in the corner of the room. Pierrot made it feel as though it too was capable of great things. It was as if he were getting a shy girl to dance. And then Pierrot and the piano understood each other and a delightful cascade of notes poured out of it.

The children couldn't believe their luck. They began to jiggle their bodies around in their seats, which made them look like sauce pots rattling on the stove. Some got up and danced in place.

It had been so long since he had performed for children. He had forgotten how wonderful they were to entertain. Who forgot about their problems the way children did?

You couldn't really achieve happiness as an adult. It was something that belonged to children. It was a fool's errand to try to experience it as a grown-up. Once you were old, all you could do was make others happy, and that gave you a deep sense of fulfillment. He had always liked delighting others, and it had been his job since he was a boy. It was how he and Rose had first started out doing their tricks.

He felt as though he had remembered his purpose in life. Ever since the meeting they had had with Jimmy Bonaventura, he had been feeling sort of empty.

PIERROT FINISHED HIS TUNE and stood up to take a deep bow. The children applauded. As he straightened back up, he put his palm out as if he had felt a raindrop and was looking to confirm his conjecture.

"Did you feel that?" he asked a boy with an eye patch sitting in the front row.

"We're inside," the boy answered. "The rain can't get us here."

Pierrot went to the back of the stage and retrieved his suitcase. He put it on the ground, unlatched it and raised the lid. He reached into the suitcase with both arms, burying his head and neck inside it. A girl with an oxygen mask over her face inhaled great lungfuls of air, anticipating what Pierrot would find. He then withdrew from the suitcase, holding in his hands, for all to see, an umbrella. It was an umbrella that Rose, in her infinite wisdom, had had constructed. She had come up with the design for it in her notebook when they were first together and broke in the Valentine Hotel. They hadn't ended up using it in the production, not because of any faults exhibited by the umbrella—it was splendid—but because of the cost. Rose had said the umbrellas cost too much to fabricate. But Pierrot had wondered if it wasn't because the black umbrella had made her too nostalgic and sad. As it did himself.

Pierrot opened the umbrella and it immediately turned inside out as if it had been caught by the wind. He whipped to one side as though a strong gust had seized it. It spun him around on his toes, almost as though he were performing a ballet. The umbrella kept twirling him around the room like a mad top. He was fighting against the wind beautifully. And then the wind let up, Pierrot settled down and the umbrella popped back to its true shape. He put out his hand to feel whether it was still raining. And then he closed the umbrella.

A little girl applauded by clapping her prosthetic hands together.

The nurse told Pierrot he had to leave, as it was time for the younger children to take their naps. The children begged him not to stop. Not to leave them. They started to come after him in the hall. And as he was leaving he noticed that the corridor behind was filled with children. It was as though they were coming for him.

"Don't go. Don't go!" the children yelled.

They would murder him by loving him so much. A nurse opened a door to the fire exit, and Pierrot zipped down it and stumbled out onto the street.

PIERROT REMEMBERED all the children in the orphanage. The ones he had left behind. He had been so in love with Rose that he had rarely thought about the other children they had grown up with. He had thought about them so little in the intervening years that he still pictured them as being little, as if they were in a state of limbo, unable to grow up. They would be tucked into the same beds in their early-century pajamas until the end of time. They were still waiting for him to perform his tiny feats for them. It broke his heart.

He and Rose had used their gifts to rescue themselves and no one else.

As he headed back to the Honeymoon Hotel, Pierrot began to feel conflicted once again. How had this happened? He had been so caught up in the frenzy of the planning during the past few months that he hadn't had time to really reflect on what they were actually creating. This was not a clown show—it was no Snowflake Icicle Extravaganza—it was a criminal operation from start to finish. And he had been the most complicit of them all in it. If he hadn't stolen the apple, none of this would have been possible.

The only people who had any actual grasp on morality were the under-eight demographic. They hadn't created all sorts of loopholes in their understanding of it. Children are born with eyes as large as those of adults. Children keep theirs wide open. And children know, without a doubt, that there is a difference between right and wrong.

He had been a thief. He had been unkind and irresponsible to Poppy, tossing her aside. He was now a large-scale drug importer. He wanted to be good. He made a resolution as he walked. They would stay in the United States as performers with no criminal ties. It had been the original plan. He hurried back to the hotel to tell Rose his decision.

It had been so long since he had made an important one without her.

·⊰| 62 |⊱·

NAPOLEON, *MON AMOUR*

W hen Pierrot got to the Honeymoon Hotel, he didn't find Rose in their room. He looked in the dining room, but she wasn't seated at any of the tables. He searched in the lobby, as there were always members from the Extravaganza there. He saw Fabio taking up a gold love seat. He was looking at his untied shoelace, clearly making plans with himself to tie it sometime that afternoon.

"Do you know where Rose is?" Pierrot asked Fabio.

"I do. She's gambling across the alley."

Pierrot knew the place Fabio was talking about. He went around to the back of the hotel. Across the alley was another doorway that led to the back of an old community center that had been turned into a gambling den. There was a man guarding the door who let Pierrot in without asking any questions. As soon as the doors opened he heard the sound of boisterous men talking over one another. They were congregated around a ring made out of wooden boards painted red and blue and hinged together in a circle. And there squeezed among them was Rose. It was easy to pick her out in the crowd because she was the only woman. Rose had started gambling again since they arrived in New York City. She worked so hard that she liked to throw herself into the randomness of the universe. She wore a hat with a veil on it and a new black coat. Her cheeks were flushed. He found her more beautiful than any other woman. He had been looking at that face his whole life. It had gone through so many different stages of beauty.

Pierrot pushed his way to the side of the ring, opposite to where Rose was standing. There were two dogs, one on either side of the enclosure. One was a boxer, which looked as if it were squeezing its face out of a turtleneck sweater. The other was, to Pierrot's surprise, a poodle. The poodle had a mass of gray curls in its face, like a girl who had just been woken from her sleep.

He waved at Rose. She opened her mouth happily when she saw him. "Pierrot!"

She disappeared into the jungle of men. And then reappeared at his side. He was about to kiss her, but she turned to hand a pile of bills to the bookie.

"What sort of matchup is this?"

"I've put all my money on the poodle. The odds are entirely against her. You have no idea how much of a pot I'll get if she wins. It's about having faith, I think."

"What does she go by?"

"Treacherous Storm Cloud."

"You're making that up."

"No, it's true."

They both laughed. The poodle stood up on its hind legs and began swatting its paws in the air as though it were looking for a fight. It looked absurd.

"The poor thing looks as though she doesn't even know what's about to happen," Pierrot protested.

"Don't you believe it!" Rose said. "She knows what's going to happen. Isn't that wonderful? I'm going to give the sweetheart her own act! She ought to be onstage! I've never seen anything like it!"

The toy poodle ran around barking, almost as if it were laughing.

"Oh, Rose. Look at that lunatic! Your poodle doesn't stand a chance."

"Darling! You can do it!"

"Even if she survives it, she'll be completely mad from this experience."

"Pierrot! Why don't we pray! We never pray anymore. And we spent so many years living with nuns. Let's ask for a miracle! We'll pack her up and bring her with us next week to Montreal."

Pierrot stopped laughing and looked pale when he heard the word *Montreal*.

"What is it?" Rose asked.

"Well, it's just that, see, I went to the children's hospital. You should have come, Rose. It wasn't sad, it was full of so much hope and life. It reminded me of the orphanage in a funny way. We could perform at some for free when we're on tour. I thought about it, and I do not think that we should return to Montreal. Nothing but a life of debauchery and violence and iniquity awaits us there."

"We can't go back on tour," Rose said. "We're returning to Montreal at the end of the run."

"I'm not trying to be cruel. I just need to know what is going through your head. Why would you want to go back to a place where we were treated horribly our whole lives?"

"I'm homesick."

"Do you miss the cold? You're forgetting the way it is there, the way it feels like your clothes are made out of paper. Do you miss waking up and seeing your breath in little clouds above your head?"

She put her arms around herself and hugged tightly. She was feeling the cold as he was describing it. She pulled Pierrot away from the ring so that she could speak to him.

"Do you miss the horny sailors harassing you as you go about your business?" Pierrot continued. "Do you miss all the cockroaches and the mice? They have those here too. Do you miss all the dirty looks from priests as you walk down the streets?"

A bell suddenly rang. The dogs were let loose. All the men began to scream and yell at once, encouraging the dogs to rip each other apart. Rose and Pierrot hardly noticed. They had to finish this conversation.

"Things will be so different," Rose said. "I'm going to fix up the buildings that I got the deeds for. Do you remember the Ingenue Hotel? That place is falling apart and is so decrepit. But every time I walk by it, I always think it could be turned into something wonderful. There's the empty ballroom near Saint Dominique that could be turned into a cabaret. The checkered floors in there, under all the trash, are so great. I would hire a band too, a wonderful quirky band, a new sound. You could play with them! I was thinking that we could name the club after you, and you could headline there whenever you like. There's going to be a lot of money to be made in the city in the next decade. We'll never get this sort of opportunity again."

"You can make anything sound splendid, Rose. But we have an opportunity also to go on tour. That could also be successful."

"It won't be, not if you look at the details of the contract, which I did with Fabio. We'll be living an existence that is just short of starvation. We'll be getting such a small percentage of the door. We'll never be able to put anything away. We'll be staying in fleabag hotels. It's a trap if we sign it. We'll be exploited by the producers. We won't run our own show."

"But the tour is an opportunity that we earned legitimately. We got it because of our own talent and not because of wheeling and dealing. I don't think we should be involved in anything corrupt."

"Pierrot! Don't be a fool. Don't be naive!"

"Stop talking to me like I'm an idiot, Rose. I can't stand it. Whatever happened to us making decisions together?"

"I'm bringing it up to you now."

"But McMahon will never let you run those clubs. He'll fight back. So I don't even know how you're considering it. I mean, just tell me, what do you intend to do about McMahon?"

Rose didn't say anything. He looked at Rose's face. The black lace veil over her eyes gave him the impression that he was speaking to her through a screen in a confessional. The answer to that question wasn't the sort of thing one could speak out loud. It was something that was insinuated. Something that just became known.

A sickening feeling came over Pierrot. It was that strange feeling you get when you realize you've missed out on something that's been under your nose all along. He almost felt high; the realization sent a flood of adrenaline through his body. She meant to have McMahon executed.

Rose was terrified as she watched Pierrot figure this out. Her heart beat desperately in her chest, a frog newly trapped in a jar. She didn't know how he would take it. She was afraid he would leave her. She knew that she had risked their marriage for this enterprise.

"Of course," Pierrot said. "It's the only way that your plan will work. It's so obvious. But I didn't realize it because I couldn't imagine that such a thing was possible. It's monstrous. Diabolical."

The dogs began viciously barking at each other. Rose was angered by Pierrot's accusations. She raised her voice to talk over the ferocious barking and snarling.

"I was an orphan, Pierrot. My body never belonged to me. You must have felt that too. If someone wanted to beat me, they could beat me. If someone wanted to lock me in the closet, they could. They didn't even have to have a reason. Childhood is such a perverse injustice, I don't know how anyone survives it without going crazy. But I have a chance to turn the tables. I have a chance to run the streets and be a very wealthy woman. No one is ever, ever, ever going to treat me with disrespect again."

Rose's eyes had grown large and dark as she spoke. Pierrot looked at all the men around him. They were yelling and waving their hats up in the air over their heads. She was right. Maybe there was a certain amount of aggression that a person needed in order to get by. He had felt much more at ease in the children's hospital with all the broken children.

"I can't go with you, Rose."

"I can't go back without you, Pierrot."

At that moment he was seized by such a terrible sense of loss that he thought he might begin to weep. He was alone and bereft. Because he knew what Rose said wasn't true. Whether or not she was aware of it, she had begun to imagine her future, and he was not in it. She had already left him behind.

And if he did manage to make her stay, it would only be out of guilt and an old promise they had made when they were younger. He was standing in her way. She was meant for great things; he was not. Perhaps he was just a fool who couldn't grow up and understand the world.

Pierrot straightened up and held Rose's chilly cheeks in his hands.

"My darling cynic. You were always the one for me. You were the only one I ever loved. You've been breaking my heart since I was fifteen years old," Pierrot said. "I only wish that I had known."

"Known what?"

"That you hate McMahon more than you love me."

Just then the sound of a dog weeping and whining, as though fatally injured, emerged from the ring. Pierrot began to retreat, backing away from Rose. Men who had been standing behind Rose now rushed toward the ring to see the dogs. The fight was reaching its final throes: its apotheosis, its climax, its denouement. They got in between Rose and Pierrot. She reached her hands out between their bodies to get Pierrot's attention. There was a wall of men separating the two of them.

"Oh, where are you going? Pierrot! Pierrot! Pierrot! Come back! Come back."

When Rose finally got through the men, Pierrot was nowhere to be seen.

The sounds in the ring abruptly abated. There was a terrible *crunch*, almost certainly that of a neck being snapped. And it was followed by a terrible silence. The dogs stopped making noises. A quiet came over the hall. The crowd quieted down too, as if they were ashamed of their own violent natures. They couldn't believe that moments before they had been desperate for something terminal and tragic: for a dog to die. In fact, now they were struck by the brevity and sweetness of life, which only death can make sense of.

Rose turned to the ring. She was terrified to approach. She couldn't bring herself to view what she knew everybody else was looking at: the tiny gray poodle, its beautiful limbs still, its neck snapped and its head backward, its big dreams having got the creature nowhere. She began her walk over to see it for herself.

·¾{ 63 }¾·

LADY OF THE POND

Pierrot ran far away from the hotel and Rose. When he was out of breath, he slowed down and wandered for an hour, ending up on Forty-Second Street, with all its brothels and whorehouses. The street was filled with girls leaning against poles. They were tying their shoes in strategically provocative ways. They were opening and closing their coats. One girl opened up her cheap brown fur coat as he was passing by, revealing pale breasts, like two cognac glasses filled with milk. One woman wore lipstick that had been mostly kissed off, and eye shadow that had been smudged, making her resemble a watercolor. When she spotted Pierrot, she blew him a hazy kiss.

He had rather surprised himself by showing up here. He didn't think he wanted to be with anybody but Rose, but here he was. He wanted to hear some compliments. Even though he knew they weren't real. They were just a sample of what the women were selling, hors d'oeuvres before the meal.

"Hello, handsome. What a face!"

"Look at you. Nobody as good-looking as you should have to be lonely."

"You want to call me names? Come upstairs and call me names."

"I'm dying for your cock. I'm desperate."

"I painted my toenails pink this morning. Want to come back to my apartment and take a look?"

It was probably a mistake to walk down the street in his very handsome suit. Because it was like holding out a rose to a bunch of starving bees.

"Poppy, Poppy, Poppy," he thought, letting it sink in what she had done for a living while they were together.

"Oh, fine. Who cares, anyway? You're just a skinny broke-ass loser. You can't afford to pay for me. Go find yourself some form of employment, and then you can come back and afford to make love to me."

PIERROT WANDERED INTO A PARK. There was a rock next to a pond, and Pierrot climbed on it and sat on its rounded edge, looking into the water. He had the sudden urge to walk into the pond with his shoes on. It was an impulse he hadn't had since he was a little boy. A swan approached him from the middle of the pond. When it got to the pile of rocks, it walked out of the pond, looking like a bride holding up her dress as she stepped out of a car. He wondered for a second if it would approach him and declare its love.

"How you doing, huh?"

He was startled for a moment, thinking the swan had spoken to him. But then he spun his head around to see a woman standing next to him wearing a white dress under a navy overcoat. There was a row of buttons along the sleeve of her jacket like an octopus's tentacle. She had light brown skin and short black hair that she seemed to have brushed all the kink out of. Her eyebrows had been drawn on her face expertly with makeup. She sat down next to him. There was something so relaxed about her face; she gave the illusion of having just been made love to. The swan turned and returned to the water.

"I'm all right, I suppose," Pierrot answered.

"So what brings you to the edge of the pond?" she asked.

"I don't know. I've wandered farther than you would think. I'm from Montreal."

"I've heard of Montreal. I heard that the girls all have diseases and stuff like that. I've heard that it's cold. Like, colder than here in the winter—and I can, like, barely stand that season here. My daddy went up there once. He told me *allllll* about it."

She looked straight at him. She had this wonderful way of looking at people, Pierrot thought. So unafraid.

"What did your father do?"

"My daddy played the trumpet. He was always walking out on us. But then he would come back. And it was the most wonderful thing. Just when we thought that we would never ever see him again, the door would kick open and there he would be, in all his glory. He would have these presents from faraway places. Like, once he got me this hairbrush from Kansas. I was so in love with that brush. I took it with me everywhere that I went. I sang into it for hours."

"How marvelous."

"It was! It didn't matter that we had to live in this tiny apartment with bugs creeping around under the wallpaper, or that we were hungry all the time, or that my mother made us scrub floors. That's all you get in life—a childhood. And you get a mommy, and if you're real lucky, you get to have a daddy. And that time is filled with all these feelings of love, even if you get the worst parents in the world. And then as an adult you always have to go around trying to find fake ways to get that feeling. You have to do the dirtiest, most lowlife things to find that feeling. That feeling is always in the strangest of places."

Who was this philosopher? Pierrot wondered.

"You hungry? Want to come back to my apartment? I'm going to make stew."

"Really?"

"Yeah, it's a recipe my grandma taught me."

"All right. I'm actually hungry."

"My name's Coco, by the way. You can trust me."

THEY STOPPED AT A STORE so that Coco could get the ingredients for stew. She came out with a paper bag with some onions and a turnip it in.

"Is that all you need?" Pierrot asked.

Pierrot had never had anyone make him their grandma's special home-made stew, but he knew it had to have more ingredients than what Coco had haphazardly stuffed into the bag.

"I don't know. The owner gets on my nerves. He's so in love with me. Everyone's in love with me around here. But you can trust me. Right?"

"Right?" Pierrot answered hesitantly.

Pierrot felt very wary of anyone who insisted that they were trustworthy. People who really were trustworthy believed the attribute to be implicit and the assumed, normal way to be. Why was she feeling guilty?

"Would you like to maybe go to a movie with me?"

"Not right now. Let's get up to my place and start on this stew. It's really the most important thing."

Yes, thought Pierrot. She possesses all the traits of a lovely spy sent by McMahon. But so what if she had been sent to ruin his life? So be it, he thought. He wanted his life to be ruined.

They stopped at the window in the lobby. An old lady with blue hair and dressed in a man's coat handed Coco a key with a pink ribbon on it.

There were a lot of stairs up to Coco's room in the skinny Desire Hotel. It surprised Pierrot. The building hadn't seemed so tall to him from the outside. Every time they got to a landing, he was sure they must have reached the top floor, but then there was yet another level.

An artist must live in one of the apartments, he concluded, because the walls of the stairwell were covered in oil paintings. They were all of different sunsets and were quite arresting. There was one that was just of a group of cumulus clouds. The others were of the sky being shocked by pink and yellow and orange streaks.

"There are a lot of stairs in this building," Pierrot commented.

"If you're an old person, you just stop going out. You just stay up on the higher floor for eternity."

THEY FINALLY ARRIVED at the top floor. Coco opened the door to her room and Pierrot followed her in. There was nothing on the walls and, in the center of the room, a large bed whose mattress caved in the middle. Coco put the paper bag down on the counter in the small kitchenette, then rolled over the bed as a shortcut to the window. She swung open the blinds.

THE DETECTIVE SAT in an apartment in the building across the alley. He pulled a yellow armchair with a pattern of pink roses up to the window. He took his camera out of a medical bag with a broken clasp that had belonged to his father. He put a book, a copy of *David Copperfield*, on the radiator, placed the camera on it and parted the green curtains.

PIERROT WAS STANDING at the end of the bed, and Coco came up to him. They were practically nose to nose. She turned around and leaned her forehead over in a slight bow, as an indication that she wanted him to help remove her clothes. As Pierrot unzipped Coco's dress at the back, the zipper got stuck on her lace undershirt. This took a lot of time to untangle, and Coco kept yelling at him to watch out because he was going to tear the best dress she had.

"Man oh man, would you watch it, buster," she yelled.

However, in the photo the private investigator took, she appeared to be moaning in ecstasy.

COCO GOT ON ALL FOURS on the mattress and immediately let out a yelp. The mattress was so cheap and thin that her weight caused one of the springs to clang up against the bones in her knee. She had stretch marks on her breasts and her thighs, having gone from being a girl to a woman too quickly at some point. She was wearing plain white underwear, but they had slipped into the crack of her ass and her butt cheeks were sticking out. They were enormous and round and wonderful. And when he stuck his face into them, he was filled with desire that he couldn't contain. On all the big screens, in all the tiny cinemas, there were gangsters pulling their machine guns out of their holsters. They were holding their handguns stretched in the darkness in front of them. They were crossing fields with shotguns straight out, heading toward their victims. Everyone had to face the fact that fate was coming. It was going to outsmart you. It was unforgiving. Pierrot stood up. He unbuckled his belt. He pulled down his pants.

She turned her head around. "Yes! Do it! Do it! Do it!" she cried.

He went deep into Coco. A mortar seemed to erupt inside him. And when he rolled off, it was as though he had tumbled into a mass grave.

Afterward he sat on the edge of the bed, inhaling a cigarette, no longer a married man. She turned off the light next to the bed and closed the curtain. She was sure that the detective had gotten enough of a show and she would get paid properly. She lit a candle next to the bed.

"Let's get high," she said.

"Sure thing, baby," Pierrot answered.

"We could do it after the stew. But we should probably do it before the stew. Right? Because stew takes a while. And a lot of the time you are just standing around, waiting for things to boil."

She sat on the edge of the bed next to Pierrot. She opened up the drawer on the tiny spindly-legged night table. Inside was a small pewter baby spoon. On the handle was a round image of a baby. Its eyes were squeezed shut, and its mouth was open wide in a scream. She didn't even bother putting any clothes on before she started preparing to cook up the dope.

There was a teapot on top of a bureau. She grabbed it and poured some water into the spoon. She shook a tiny bit of dope into the liquid, stirred it up with the tip of the needle and then heated it over a candle. She took a tie out of her pocket and wrapped it around Pierrot's arm. She injected the heroin, and he waited for the old sensations to come.

As he and Coco lay next to each other on the bed, the onions rolled out of the bag and off the counter. They landed on the floor like asteroids falling to the earth.

·⊰[64]⊱·

THE HEART IS
A TRUMPET SOLO

Rose couldn't bring herself to leave her room. The chorus girl Colombe said she could replace the star. Even though she wasn't as charismatic as Rose, they figured she would do. They tried to hire another pianist. A line of them arrived in the morning at the New Amsterdam Theatre. Pierrot had never written down his score. The girls hummed and whistled their interpretations of Pierrot's tune. It was always lacking when someone else played it. When ticket holders heard that the stars of the show would not be appearing in that night's performance, they began to demand that their tickets be refunded. The remaining Snowflake Icicle Extravaganza dates were canceled. And the dates were given to a troupe of twelve-year-old ballerinas who had just emigrated from Poland and were called the Flying Mice.

FABIO HAD THE MOON DELIVERED to Jimmy and his men. It was tied to the back of a delivery truck as all the neighborhood children stood on the sidewalk watching and laughing. It was driven out to a rendezvous point down a rural road half an hour outside the city. It was a spot where they usually whacked people. A deer stepped out onto the road, making wide, slow steps, as if it were sneaking up behind a friend.

After the moon was unloaded from the truck, the driver climbed back in the vehicle and drove off down the bumpy road. The gangsters walked around the moon, assessing the best way to open it.

"Is there a trick to this?" Jimmy asked Caspar.

"I don't think they thought that far ahead."

"Let's shoot the fucking thing," a gangster suggested.

Another gangster brought an ax out and started to strike it. The moon began to crack, as though it were an enormous egg. They waited to see. There was the feeling that just about anything could happen. A dinosaur might suddenly appear and unfurl its claws. White dust and plaster spilled everywhere when the shell cracked, but there it was: a trunk of heroin, freshly imported from the East into Montreal, meant for immediate distribution in the streets of New York City. The gangsters laughed at the absurdity of it all.

They carried the shell of the moon to the nearby lake and pushed it in. It bobbled about in the water before sinking. It looked like a reflection of the real moon.

Jimmy went back to the hotel feeling miserable. Rose hadn't come with the moon. He hadn't seen her in days. In the evenings there were usually gangsters in Jimmy's room. There was a huge ballroom downstairs, but people always liked to be wherever Jimmy was. They would crowd into his tiny room. There would be six or seven gangsters sitting on the side of the bed. There would be one sitting in the cushion of the armchair and one on the arm of the chair. There would be a gangster leaning up against the bureau and one checking himself out in the bathroom mirror. But in this case, he wanted to be all alone. His white carnation boutonniere looked like a crumpled-up love poem.

OVER AT THE HONEYMOON HOTEL, Fabio was sitting in his room, shirtless and hunched, like bread dough that had yet to be beaten into shape. The show had closed and the moon had been delivered. McMahon would be waiting for word of Rose's execution. If McMahon didn't hear that Rose was dead, and soon, he would be sending his men down to start a war. Or Jimmy might change his mind and kill her himself.

So for days Fabio had been trying to get Rose to pack up the troupe and head back on the train to Montreal.

But Rose never looked as though she had any intention of leaving. Every time he went to her room, he could see that her clothes were sprawled everywhere—over couches and chairs. She had a half-eaten cupcake on her boudoir table, as she hadn't even bothered to let one of the maids come in to clean up the mess.

She didn't appear to have bathed either. She sat in a dirty slip, her hair greasy and sticking up. She had been afflicted by guilt. She was going to give up the entire project just so that she could devote her life to sitting in a hotel room, feeling guilty about having chased Pierrot away.

That morning, just to be dutiful, Fabio had checked in on Rose. He had opened the door and saw that she was sitting on the edge of the bed with her back to him, looking toward the window.

"Any word from Pierrot?" he had asked.

Rose hadn't had to turn to know it was Fabio who had poked his head into her room. She knew his cigar-scarred voice.

"Maybe he doesn't know we're leaving," Rose had answered faintly. "He might not have heard that the show was canceled. I'm sure he went to the zoo."

"Are you out of your mind? Nobody goes to the zoo for five days. I've had people go there looking for him. He isn't there."

"So?"

"Well, what do you believe happened to him? Do you imagine that he got eaten alive by a polar bear?"

"Get out of here!" Rose had screamed.

She'd stood up, spinning around, and picked up an ashtray and flung it at his head. He'd slammed the door just in time.

FABIO PUT ON A SHIRT when he heard a knock at the door. He hoped it was Rose, coming to apologize for her behavior. He opened it to instead discover a timid-looking maid with extraordinarily plump pink lips, dressed in a black uniform.

"I have an envelope that I'm supposed to deliver to Rose's room."

"Well, this isn't Rose's room, is it?"

"It's because, sir, well, last time I went to Mrs. Rose's room, she threw a cupcake right at my head, you see."

Fabio held out his hand. The maid handed him the brown kraft envelope and then darted off, clearly relieved to be free of it.

Fabio was nervous about the mysterious envelope. He didn't know who it was from. He felt ill at ease as he shuffled down the corridor to Rose's room to deliver the letter. He stood bent over, catching his breath at the elevator.

Fabio knocked on Rose's door and opened it. He slipped in like a cat and discovered Rose lying on the bed, reading a paperback book. She looked up from it. "You're back," Rose said. "What can you want now?"

"I've this for you. Should I open it myself?"

"No, let me see what it is."

Using a five-dollar bill as a bookmark, Rose gently put the book aside. She got up off the bed and took the envelope. The flap was tied with a piece of string, so she only had to pull at it to open the envelope. She walked over to the window as she pulled out the contents, a stack of large, glossy photographs. She whipped through them maniacally, then shoved them back in the envelope, holding it up against her chest. She went into the bathroom and slammed the door behind her, only to step out a few seconds later looking deranged.

"He's been with another woman. He cheated on me. He wants to break me so that I won't be able to work. He wants me to go and find him and beg him to come back. It's not going to happen. Because I don't care about him. I don't give a shit about Pierrot. I wish that skinny fucker was dead. I really do!"

She walked to her dressing table, picked up her powder compact and hurled it at the wall. It exploded upon impact and powder flew everywhere, creating a white mist in the room. Rose disappeared for a moment. But then she stepped out of the cloud, her finger pointed right at Fabio.

"You know, it's because he's onstage that this type of girl is attracted to him. That's what happens when you're an entertainer. Stupid, fucking shit. This isn't real life. It's not my cup of tea. I was forced to dance in front of rich people when I was a little girl. But let me tell you, I'm not going to do it anymore."

"Well, you've already expressed your desire to no longer be a performer."

"You don't roam around sleeping with random women, do you?"

Rose just looked at him, desperate for some sort of answer that he could give her to stop the emotions that were coming.

"I haven't had a hard-on in two years."

Rose stopped short for a second, having no idea how to respond to that statement. Then she flung her arms toward him violently, as though she were trying to throw her hands away.

"Well, we're leaving New York without Pierrot."

"Of course. I'm ready to go. We've all been ready to go. If we had left as soon as we handed over the moon, we might have avoided this scenario altogether."

Rose just grabbed her hair in two fists and screamed, "Ahhhh!"

She threw the envelope at Fabio and then collapsed on the bed.

Fabio reached down to the ground to retrieve the fallen envelope. He couldn't help himself, and he opened it to peek at the amorous photos inside. His sigh was so loud it was almost a cry. Pierrot looked so lost in the photographs. He knew Pierrot didn't have the stomach for where the plan was going. He knew this was Pierrot's way of cutting them all loose. He had always known that Pierrot was altruistic. Pierrot had had so much patience with everybody. There were tears in Fabio's eyes because of Pierrot's sacrifice. Because Fabio believed in love again.

THE MAID FROM the Honeymoon Hotel was standing in front of Jimmy's desk. The state she was in—out of breath and with the buttons of her coat in the wrong holes—indicated that she had rushed over. Jimmy listened to the maid telling him that Pierrot had betrayed Rose. She had opened the envelope and had seen the photos herself. Pierrot had also disappeared, not bothering to take anything with him. According to the girl, Rose was presently in a state of hysteria.

Jimmy had a sudden urge to have the maid killed. It wasn't her knowing what she knew that bothered him. It was that she knew how much he wanted to hear this news. She had hurried over to tell him before anyone else had the chance, because it was exciting to her to be part of this big moment in his life.

But Jimmy was inscrutable when he wanted to be inscrutable, which was most of the time. He stared at the maid blankly, not letting on how the news affected him. He reached into his drawer and pulled out a ten-dollar bill and handed it to her.

"Good. Continue to bring me interesting information."

She walked out, tucking the money into her pocket and looking mildly disappointed. When she was gone, Jimmy looked over at Caspar, who was sitting in an armchair by the door.

"How do you think this affects things?"

"Not at all. She's the brains behind the operation."

"I meant . . . never mind."

What in the world was he supposed to do now? Go over to her hotel room with a white rose and ask her out to dinner? He hadn't a clue how long it took someone to get over heartache, as he himself had never really been heartbroken. He was frightened, for the first time ever, that he might be rejected by a girl.

⋅≺∣ 65 ∣≻⋅

THE *TITANIC* SAILS AT NOON

Rose hadn't left her hotel room since learning about Pierrot. She had had trouble sleeping. She dozed off in the late afternoon. She dreamed that she was in a pair of black boots and her underwear. She was up in front of an audience. A strange man came up onto the stage. He made her get down on her hands and knees. He unbuckled his pants—the audience broke into applause. She woke up and walked to the bathroom. It was only nine o'clock.

She couldn't be alone in her room anymore. She threw on her coat and wandered out of the room and down to the small bar next to the lobby. Everybody else was already down at the bar, drinking to the end of a successful run and the abrupt ending of their show. The bartender lined up a row of shot glasses. He poured the brandy in right up to the lip of a glass. She swallowed it. And it burned. It lit up her heart as if it were a candlewick. She just needed to let the candle burn down through the night.

She threw off her coat. She was only wearing a black satin slip, as she hadn't bothered to get dressed. She drank longer than anybody else. For a couple of seconds, the booze lifted her up. It made her feel as though everything was as it should be in the world—that everything was fine.

She stood up. She held her glass up in the air. It wavered back and forth. Little drops of alcohol dripped onto her, like splashes of holy water.

"This is to Pierrot! My husband!"

"Hear, hear!" everyone yelled.

Someone put some music on the jukebox. She wandered into the middle of the floor to dance. A gangster, taking pity on her, or overcome by desire, or just being plain stupid, moved to the middle of the floor to put his arms around her and dance too. She clung to him. They moved wonderfully together. Every man danced so well when he danced with Rose.

Then her expression changed. Her face seized up as if she were going to be sick. She shoved the man so hard that he fell to the ground. Then she just danced by herself, her arms out around no one. It was so upsetting that a lot of the men left. They went to their own rooms and sat on the ends of their beds and stared at the walls, not understanding what the point of anything was. She was hoping the imaginary bear would comfort her, but tonight she just felt as though she had her arms wrapped around emptiness.

Rose hunched over as if she had been kicked in the stomach and let out a yell. She didn't think she could stand it. She slipped for a second as though her shoe heel had broken. There were about seven or eight men around her to catch her.

Her arms were up in the air. She looked at the cheap wedding ring on her finger. She would always wear it. It was like a small snowflake that had landed on a mitten—and it was so beautiful. It was always just about to melt. If anyone were to try to touch it, or to breathe on it, or speak too close to it, it would turn into a bead of water and would deny that it had ever been the most beautiful thing on earth. She had loved Pierrot.

She propped herself on a stool like a rag doll. She straightened her back. She felt a desire to go down the street to the Romeo Hotel. She found herself thinking about Jimmy. His hair was dark, dark brown, like chocolate. It was the color of chocolate syrup on sundaes. She knew that Jimmy was picturing himself down on his knees, kissing her pussy, right at that second.

She wanted to feel desired. She wanted to feel sexy. She wanted to break the spell that Pierrot had over her. Oh, however fucking irrational it was, she wanted to feel that he didn't matter and that any man could replace him. She went back up to her room and, with meticulous care, got dressed for the first time in a week, and she headed off down the street to the Romeo Hotel.

She entered through the large doors, she strutted across the lobby and she went up the stairs. The man with the scars in his cheeks let her go. She opened the door to Jimmy's room. He was sitting on the window frame smoking a cigarette when she walked in. She closed the door behind her and Jimmy chucked his cigarette out the window.

She took off her white fur hat. She took off her gloves and her scarf, and she tucked them into her hat. She placed the hat on the little night-stand by the door. She unbuttoned her black coat and let it drop off her shoulders. She pulled her dress off over her head. She stood there in her thin lace lingerie. It looked like frost had formed on her body.

He didn't know what to say for a moment. Because he was doubting what he was seeing, it took a short moment for his reason to catch up with the situation.

When he came toward her quickly and violently, she put her skinny arms out with desperation and they hugged each other so hard that their hearts beat against each other. He tossed her onto the bed. And she felt as if she weighed as much as a bagful of feathers. As if she weighed no more than her slip. As if she weighed no more than a single snowflake coming down from the great, great blackness.

They curled up in each other's arms afterward. She felt so unlike herself that she didn't even really feel like a person anymore. She felt like a skinny white cat stretching out its graceful limbs.

One of Jimmy's men went up later to see what was going on and what was holding Jimmy up. He looked in and was surprised to see him in his room with a girl. And under all the nakedness was Rose herself.

He had never seen either of them look so peaceful. It was the first time they had ever slept so deeply. That's the way you got to sleep before you were born.

WHY HAD SHE DONE IT? She wasn't sure. It was to end her body's pining for Pierrot, perhaps. It was to remind her that it was only sex but that, as a woman, she could give herself away to love so easily.

The sex had been good. There was nothing like having sex for the first time with a man who has been pining for you. He tore you open like a present and found wonderful things inside. Something wonderful inside that he had to stand back and admire.

Meaningless sex meant you could make love, put your clothes back on, get up and walk down the street and leave it behind you on the bed. Like discarded nightclothes. There was something freeing about it, the feeling of having power over sex. Of having it and then not being a slave to its drives. Or having it and not feeling ashamed of it. Or having it because you find yourself between a rock and a hard place.

WALKING BACK TO the Honeymoon Hotel the next morning, Rose passed a hotel that had a paddy wagon parked out front. Police officers came down the stairs single file, each with a girl in handcuffs. They were being loaded into the police van like a group of stray dogs that had been rounded up by the dogcatcher. The last girl to go in had on an orange-flowered cotton dress and dark blue high heels with the felt scratched off the toes. Rose could see the bump under her dress from her round pot-belly. She was probably four months pregnant.

Rose thought about the time she had spent with McMahon. What had she been other than a prostitute? She had worn her white fur hat around to all sorts of fancy places and ordered great meals in restaurants, acting as if she were a member of an empowered class. While the only females in society who had any real bargaining power were the dopey little virgins with rags safety-pinned to their underwear, filling up with blood the color of fallen dead rose petals. The minute they gave them-selves up, they really had no agency whatsoever.

ROSE COULDN'T put her finger on what had happened to her. But she had fallen from grace. That was the most surprising thing. Because she had not realized that she had been in a state of grace. She had at least figured that as an orphan she had been born with nothing to lose. When you fall from grace, time passes quicker. Time begins to make sense. It moves in a linear fashion. It begins to trickle through the hourglass. It no longer belongs to you.

Her cheekbones seemed higher when she looked at herself in the bathroom mirror. Her teeth were yellowish. They were the color of a wilting white rose. She was wilting. She realized for the first time that she had a face that could age. Was actually aging. Now that Pierrot had left, she was no longer young.

SHE LEANED UP to the reflection in the mirror. Her lips were almost touching her reflection's lips. Her reflection was seduced despite herself—despite the fact that if she were to enter into this relationship, she would be dominated and told what to do all the time. The reflection closed its eyes and puckered its lips, waiting for the kiss.

Rose whispered, "Whore."

The reflection's eyes shot open and she bolted back.

ON HER WAY HOME, she had noticed an abandoned skipping rope lying on the sidewalk like a chalk line around a dead body.

·⊰[66]⊱·

PRIMER FOR A REVOLUTION

Fabio knew what had happened the night before. Everyone knew what had happened the night before. News of such a coupling spread in the underworld quickly. Fabio assumed that Rose would want to postpone leaving again. On some level, she had bought herself some time.

He went down to the lobby to talk to the clowns, who were standing around there, to tell them that they might not be going anywhere that day. They had given up their hotel rooms and packed their bags. Their trunks were piled in the lobby all in a row. A clown sat on top of one of the stacks of suitcases, smoking a cigarette.

As Fabio explained the situation to said clown, the clown squinted and pointed behind Fabio. Fabio turned his head to see.

There was Rose. She was coming down the stairs in a black dress and a coat, perfectly composed.

She had done something with her rage and her anger. She knew that exhibiting it was a sign of weakness. She knew that she didn't have to show it anymore. She didn't have to engage in ridiculous, over-the-top displays of rage. It was already obvious how angry she was. Her rage permeated her entire body. There was a feeling that she was dangerous. You felt it intuitively. Even people who had just walked into the hotel that moment averted their eyes and moved out of her way. The way that every creature in the jungle gets quiet when a jaguar is passing.

People would no longer address her in a familiar way. She had closed the door on her private life. Whereas before it was something she had paraded onstage for everyone to mine, now she would have people enact her rage for her.

A bellhop followed behind her. He was carrying all her extra baggage, as she had purchased so many clothes while she was in New York.

THE GANGSTERS CLIMBED onto the train with all the dancers. They mussed up their hair and fidgeted with their ties and dabbed a little bit of alcohol behind their ears so they could more properly pass themselves off as traveling clowns.

Rose oversaw each member of her entourage as they stepped onto the train. She saw a black car pull up, the back door open and Jimmy Bonaventura step out. He approached with another man beside him. He looked up and down at the train with the mixture of incredulity and amusement that he maintained for all things Snowflake Icicle Extravaganza related. He walked over to Rose and stood on the steps opposite her compartment.

"This is Tiny," Jimmy said. "He's going with you."

Rose looked at Tiny. He looked like a gangster, not a bohemian, like the rest of the men traveling with her. She took hold of the front pocket on his jacket and in a swift motion tore it off. Then she mussed up his hair.

"Here," she said.

She handed him a book of poems by Baudelaire for him to peruse on the train. He needed some practice in introspection in order to pass as a tormented clown.

Tiny opened the book at random and read out a line. "An artist is an artist only because of his exquisite sense of beauty, a sense which shows him intoxicating pleasures, but which at the same time implies and contains an equally exquisite sense of all deformities and all disproportion."

His delivery was awkward and the words came out sounding stilted and rough, like those of a tough guy.

"Very nice," Jimmy said.

After Tiny stepped onto the train, Jimmy and Rose both laughed. And in that moment Jimmy was glad that Rose was leaving town. His feelings for her frightened him. If she stayed in New York any longer, he would end up wanting to see her every day. She would end up owning him. Jimmy saw what Rose had done to Tiny. She had turned him into a clown.

They stared at each other and then blinked. For a second each imagined the other completely naked. And then they blinked again and they were both fully dressed. And it was all over.

A gray poodle that had a bandage on its head where it had lost its ear walked up to the train.

"Hello there, Treacherous Storm Cloud," Rose said.

When Rose had mustered up the courage to look into the dog-fighting ring, to her absolute shock, she saw that it was the boxer that lay on the ground. Sitting woeful in the corner was the poodle, very much alive. The poodle now looked up at Rose hopefully, as though making sure she hadn't changed her mind about it coming.

"We'll have to change your name to Trix."

Rose nodded to the dog and it jumped on board, wagging its tail joyfully.

⋅❧ 67 ❧⋅

POSTCARDS OF THE HANGING

McMahon had been drinking since five o'clock that afternoon. The last shot of whiskey seemed to swim around his belly like an eel. The air was heavy, and time slowed down. He couldn't hear what anyone was saying to him. For a moment he thought he might faint. He was waiting to receive word that Rose had been shot, and it was making him nervous. He decided that he'd better go home and wait for the news. Who knew how he would react, and he didn't like other men seeing his emotions.

He stepped out onto the street and waved to his driver.

As the car headed toward Westmount, the downtown lights receded behind him. It was as though he were departing from the Milky Way. He stepped out of the car and told the driver he could go home for the night. He stood outside his house for a moment, watching the few snowflakes come down, like bits of confetti falling to a ballroom floor.

He knew the big house would be empty. His children had gone to live with his wife's parents. The servants would have gone to their own homes. He no longer liked having people living full-time in the house.

. . .

ROSE'S TRAIN came to a rest in Old Montreal. The trip back had been so much longer than the way there. She had stayed alone in her compartment, looking out the window. She felt lost and terrified leaving Pierrot behind in New York City. Every mile seemed so long.

When the troupe stepped off the train, the clowns and chorus girls fastened the top buttons of their coats and tightened their scarves. The air was so much colder here. You always forgot how cold Montreal was until the minute you arrived. Everyone kept yelling how tiny the city looked to them after coming back from New York. It looked like a row of dollhouses!

She walked home to the Valentine Hotel, with the gray dog hopping behind her. The street was more beautiful than she remembered it. She noticed all the details on the outside of the hotel with such affection. It was hers.

WHEN MCMAHON OPENED THE DOOR to his house, he was taken aback by its eeriness. The house was so dark and quiet that he felt as if he were in his coffin. The darkness in the houses in Westmount was lush, like velvet. It never got this dark in houses downtown. Lights from the streets always got in. There was always the noise from the cars and the people passing by. The streetlights made it so that you could always see the naked body of the person whom you were sleeping with. Nobody could sneak up to you in the dark.

WHEN SHE STEPPED INTO the lobby of the Valentine Hotel, the old woman who worked behind the desk greeted her but had no idea that Rose now owned the place. She put her suitcase down next to her. The carpet didn't sink underfoot the way it did at the Romeo Hotel. It had been worn down and was as hard as the floor, the patterns hidden under dirt. She stood taking in the room.

Everything in it belonged to her. It felt like she was home in a new kind of way. She felt proud of it. The wallpaper was telling her an old children's story. There was an iron faun in the grate of the fireplace.

She noticed that the golden velour couch had springs coming out of it. She used to be able to ignore the broken things before. But now they were her problem. She liked that. She felt responsible for them. She knew exactly what this hotel could look like. There was a mural on the ceiling at the entrance. It was all grimy and dark. But if someone got up on a ladder with a bucket of soapy water and a sponge, the stars and planets would begin appearing and shining once again.

McMahon opened the closet in the hallway to hang up his coat. He was startled and leaped back. There at the bottom of the closet was Rose, her hands over her eyes as she counted to ten, playing hide-and-seek with the children. But then he realized, of course, that it was just a folded blanket that had fallen from the shelf.

He walked to the staircase that led to the bedrooms. There was Rose again. She was wearing a three-cornered hat and a tuxedo jacket, a thin mustache drawn on her face. She was on her way to the masquerade with the children, no doubt. He hurried up the stairs, knowing it was too good to be true, then realized it was a coatrack.

He looked up the flight of stairs to the third floor. There was a tiny plume of cigarette smoke escaping from the keyhole of the nursery.

As Rose turned up the stairwell she stopped abruptly. There was McMahon at the top of the stairs, just around the bend. He'd come to kill her. He'd come to put her in her place. She almost dropped her suitcase, but then she realized it wasn't McMahon at all. It was the curtain on the hallway window that had been puffed open by a breeze. She walked to the second floor. The lightbulb had burned out at the end of the corridor that led to her room. There was a black shadow lingering by the door.

It occurred to her that Jimmy might have betrayed her. How did she know that this was hers? Perhaps he had told McMahon her plan. Perhaps he had allowed McMahon to kill her. McMahon was still alive. Maybe Tiny had been put on the train to kill her. She hadn't seen where he went after they arrived in Montreal.

As she approached the door her eyes adjusted to the darkness and she could see that there was nothing at all in the darkness. She stood outside the door of her room. She heard something inside fall to the floor.

McMahon opened the door of the nursery very slowly and carefully. He thought he would have a vision of her in there. He was sure he would see her. She would be eighteen again. She would have no one else but him. She would be a virgin. With an apple balanced on her head. Waiting for him. Wanting him again.

"Rose," he whispered.

The pug, looking like a butted-out cigar, tiptoed uneasily around the house.

She opened the door to her room. She thought he would be there, sitting on a chair, waiting for her.

"Mac?" she whispered.

The poodle carefully looked into the room, as though it had come home late and was trying not to disturb anyone.

There was the sound of a gunshot.

On opposite ends of the city, McMahon and Rose clutched at their hearts. Each had arranged to have the other killed. Who had actually shot whom? Neither of them seemed to know. An act like that takes down both the victim and the aggressor. They both closed their eyes.

. . .

ROSE OPENED HER EYES. She felt sick to her stomach. She could have sworn at just that moment that a bullet had entered her. She looked down, searching her body for the bullet wound.

She felt nothing. She wanted to feel the bullet hole. She needed to feel the bullet hole. She wanted to ascertain the gravity and reality of what she had just done. She wanted the bullet to kill her too. But she knew that it hadn't. It would take a very long time for her to understand how she had done something evil like that.

MCMAHON OPENED HIS EYES for the last time. As he lay on the floor, the last thought he had was, Thank God. Thank God I meant something to that lovely girl. And he looked up at the heavens and hoped, probably without any reason, that he would be going up there. And then he saw nothing ever again.

THE POODLE BARKED at the rat on the shelf that had knocked over the vase. The rodent hurried out through the crack it had come out of.

Rose closed the door behind her. How had she abandoned all the men in her life? She felt the grandeur of being responsible for oneself. She was independent, and her actions had enormous consequences. What she did mattered. She had to get on with her path in life.

The pattern of red flowers on the carpet spread out around her like a pool of blood.

68

BALLAD FOR THE MOON
IN C MINOR

Rose had a pink suitcase filled with money delivered to Pierrot at the Forget-Me-Not Hotel a few months later. She felt that he had earned it, after all. Rose treated everything in life as if it were a business now. She knew that Pierrot had helped her inestimably in her theatrical revue, so he was due his share of the profits.

Pierrot put the suitcase on the bed. The bedspread had a pattern of orange and brown autumn leaves and tiny red berries. He was reminded of a storybook for children, *Babes in the Wood*, in which two children were abandoned in the middle of a forest. He unlatched the suitcase and stared at the money. He had never been around this sort of money. He had hardly been around money at all, since it was Rose, and before that Poppy and before that Irving, who handled all the finances. He had preferred it that way. He sat on the edge of the mattress, the money next to him, and imagined the two of them abandoned together in the middle of the forest. It seemed to be the fate for orphans in fairy tales. He wanted to lie back on the quilt and imagine the sound of crickets and birds chirping.

But the money said, "Spend me, spend me, spend me." That's what money wanted. It wanted to be spent. And it really wanted to be spent on luxury items. Its greatest thrill was just to be gambled away. It wanted to change hands. It wanted to find itself at the racetrack, it wanted to be thrown into the center of the table at a casino. Money is a masochist.

He wondered whether Rose wanted to kill him by sending him all that money. But that would be assuming that she cared. Underneath all the money was their wedding photo.

PIERROT HOLED UP in his tiny hotel room. The walls were a dingy off-white. He hung the wedding photo of himself and Rose from a nail in the wall to have something to look at while he lay in bed. He had no intention of even trying to fight the addiction now. He would wake up in the morning and shoot up. Occasionally he wandered outside, looking for some sort of human intimacy. Women wouldn't come close to him. Sometimes when a woman walked by him, he would reach out his arms to her. She would shrink from him and hurry away. It wasn't that he actually wanted to touch them. It was that he missed the feeling of reaching his arms out toward someone. He missed that tenderness.

He lived in the hotel for almost a year. When he got to the end of the money, he was not at all surprised. In fact, he was surprised that it had lasted that long and that he was still alive.

He sat in a diner, trying to eat a plate of eggs. He didn't understand quite how he had come to find himself sitting at this table with a plate of eggs in front of him. He didn't know how anyone could eat. He really didn't have the ambition to eat anything else at all.

He had lost weight. He had always been slim, but he had never been quite this skinny. His tailor-made suit that had always made him look like a dandy, no matter what sort of financial situation he was in, now seemed loose and baggy on him. It had lost its magic charm. Or anyway, perhaps that was what he wanted to tell himself to justify trading in his suit at the pawnshop on Eighth Avenue.

The owner, a white-haired, older woman with a pair of glasses on a fake pearl chain, gave him enough money to get high for a couple of days. She also gave him an outfit to change into. It was a black suit. Because of its slim fit, it had been hard to sell. But Pierrot wore it well. Although when he looked in his oval mirror, he couldn't help but notice that he looked as though he were preparing ahead of time for his funeral.

HE WOKE UP in the morning three days later. But was the suit really his last possession? What else could he say belonged to him and nobody else? What else did he have the right to sell?

He wandered across the street to the library. There was a girl sleeping in one of the phone booths, Snow White waiting to be kissed. He pulled open the door of the phone booth next to her and sat down on the wooden bench. He asked the operator for the number to any recording studio. The phone swallowed the coin quickly, like a dog that doesn't chew its treat. He could hear the nickel being digested by the telephone. The man on the other end of the line knew of the Snowflake Icicle Extravaganza. He had remembered the tune at the end of the show. He said that he was indeed interested in recording it.

"It was really the best thing about the show. I mean, it's the part of the show that's going to last. How come you never recorded it before?"

"I used to be worried about recording my music. Because I thought that other people would hear my melodies and steal them and get credit for them. I figured that they would be able to study my playing and get how to perform like me. And I wouldn't be unique anymore. But that's just fear giving me crazy reasons. I have no right to keep a good tune for myself. I have to let it go out into the world, man. It wants to have its own life in other people's hearts."

Pierrot was quiet for a moment.

"I also have to get high."

"I'll pay you up front so you don't have to wait around for royalties or nothing like that."

He said he'd love to make it into a record. He asked Pierrot to bring a photo of himself.

All that Pierrot had was the portrait of him and Rose, which hung from a nail on the wall. He did feel rather sad about unhooking it. But at the same time, he felt full of pride that morning, for the first time in months. Because he had been reminded of two things. That he had once been married to a very beautiful woman, and that he had written this tune that everybody in the world seemed to like.

THE STUDIO WAS IN A narrow building. It was squeezed in between a church and a department store, like some skinny man on a bus at rush hour. The man who had spoken to Pierrot on the phone met him in the lobby and they took the elevator to the ninth floor. In the studio there was a great big microphone hanging down on a pole over the top of the piano. The floors were wooden. He looked at technicians on the other side of the glass. There were so many levers and knobs, like a city seen from up above.

He began to play the tune. It had been a while since he'd played it. To his surprise, the tune was slightly different from before. While he had sunk into oblivion, the tune had continued to work on itself. It had to get up in the morning and get itself dressed and take care of business. And so Pierrot listened to the tune that he was playing, instead of performing it. A work of art when it is good and completed exists independently of its creator. It is indignant, even—it doesn't want to have an author.

All children are really orphans. At heart, a child has nothing to do with its parents, its background, its last name, its gender, its family trade. It is a brand-new person, and it is born with the only legacy that all individuals inherit when they open their eyes in this world: the inalienable right to be free.

The tune was a thing of great wonder.

ONCE PIERROT HAD FINISHED RECORDING, he knew that he had captured it. He had finished the elusive tune. The simple little number was his life's work. He didn't have it in him to spend the next twelve years of his life working on another fifteen minutes. There were great musicians who were capable of producing great and fantastic bodies of work, but he didn't have that sort of tenacity or intelligence. Unlike him, those musicians had been raised to have the constitution to do great things. Artists from poor backgrounds couldn't bear their own genius for very long.

He signed the first contract they put before him, not bothering to negotiate. He knew that he had to do it quickly and impulsively or he wouldn't be able to do it at all.

A squirrel holding an acorn as though it were a tiny bongo drum stood up on a branch outside the recording studio and worriedly looked around.

When he stepped out into the shining street, he was a completely different person. He was walking around, but he knew that his story was over. His life story was written, and he was living in the extra blank pages at the back of a book. There was a beginning, middle, end to his life.

On the corner of the street, Pierrot spotted a curious-looking boy. The child had folded a newspaper into a Napoleon hat and was wearing it on his head. He looked up at Pierrot with a deep frown. Pierrot knew what the newspaper said. It was becoming more and more likely that the world was going to war. The world didn't need Pierrot's type of sadness now. No, the world was a violent place, and it was gripped by a madness that Pierrot had no way of expressing. He didn't want to read the newspaper or listen to the radio anymore. He didn't want to be a grown-up. There are some people who are just no good at it.

69

UNKNOWN HEROIN ADDICT, NEW YORK CITY

A nd the score that Pierrot had sold in New York City went on to be recorded, and it became a huge hit. It was made into a record entitled *The Ballad for the Moon* and was played by children all over North America. They often asked for the tune for their birthdays and would receive the record wrapped in green or pink or blue paper. They would unwrap it and find the photo of young newlyweds on the record cover. The children were so surprised that they had gotten the present they wanted. They were used to not getting any treats at all. They didn't know why the hard times were over. But they did notice that, little by little, things began to change in their lives. When they put on their socks, their toes did not peek out of holes at the ends of them. When they went to bed at night, they noticed their bellies weren't rumbling. They opened their lunch bags and noticed a cookie inside. They noticed that they couldn't feel the ribs of their cat when they lifted it up. When they woke up in the morning, little puffs of smoke didn't appear out of their mouths.

Their mothers had roses in their cheeks. They sewed themselves smarter dresses. They came home with groceries and cooked decent meals and sang while they fried up the tomatoes. The coffee was creamier. There was dessert several nights a week. Tiny cupcakes and slices of pie on small dishes appeared like fairy tales on the kitchen tables.

The Great Depression was over. The children associated Pierrot's tune with the end of hardship.

For all they knew, the tune itself was the cause of the new, more fortunate times. They had begun to hear the tune on the radio and then all sorts of interesting things began to happen. The more Pierrot's tune was played on the radio, the better things became.

PIERROT HIMSELF paid very little attention to the success of his tune. He had no way to track it, as he wasn't receiving royalties. One day he had only two dollars left to his name. He owed five dollars to his regular dealer, so he couldn't go see him. He went to the back of a building that another junkie had told him about. He rang the doorbell, and a man came out into the alley to meet him.

"You're in luck. I just got some new shit in from Montreal. It is the best I've ever tasted. You'll never want to touch anything else, trust me."

"Montreal," Pierrot said in a sad way, as though it were only a mythical place for him now.

He took a room at the Lonely Hearts Hotel. The floorboards in his room had been painted green. There were swans on the wallpaper. He thought that was a good sign. He shot up some of the Montreal heroin. He felt that feeling that you get when it's quiet right before the snow comes. It reminds you of being under the covers as a child, and learning that school is going to be canceled because it is snowing so heavily. The streets are empty, but you can hear laughter somewhere in the distance. You can hear the church bells ringing with a clarity that is so pure and sweet and perfect.

He injected the rest of the heroin into his arm all at once. He stared at the swans on the wallpaper, waiting for them to start moving, but they did not. This was it. This was his last hotel room. How strange. He would never get old.

When they say that your life flashes before your eyes, what they mean is that you can choose to go to any moment from your past—and almost everybody wants to go back to when they were little. Pierrot selected a memory of Rose. There was Rose with a blindfold on her eyes while they were all playing hide-and-seek. Pierrot hadn't hidden. Instead he had made his footsteps and breathing deliberately heavy, and tried to get in her way, just so that she would reach out and touch him. In the memory her hands came closer and closer to him.

Rose didn't reach him. A great loneliness came over him. He thought that he had lived a most wonderful life.

BY THE TIME HE PASSED AWAY, Pierrot was world famous. When the maid who found his body realized who he was, she let out a yelp. The maids, in their black uniforms, their hats like white daisies, crammed into the room and stood around his body.

∙⪤[70]⪥∙

THE FUNERAL PARADE

Rose looked at the little boy who was standing at the door of her hotel room with his lower lip jutting out. It was early in the morning and she was in her dressing gown, the birds embroidered on the silk unfurling their wings as she moved. She had no idea why there was a newspaper boy standing with his pile of papers at her door. Rose was often known to be quite generous to single mothers when they asked her for help—perhaps he was here to beg.

"What do you want?"

"You're the last building on my route, but I decided to come to you right away."

"And why is that?"

"There's news that is of interest to you, ma'am."

Rose reached into her pocket and took out a coin. The boy stuck his hand out. Rose dropped the coin into the boy's palm. He looked at the coin; pocketed it; handed her a newspaper; said, "I'm very sorry, ma'am"; turned; and ran with his stack of papers out of the building.

Rose's cry woke up the whole of the building.

A child on Saint Dominique Street, in a building in the alley opposite, sat up in his bed, certain that she had heard someone yell in terrible pain. But when she went in to see her parents and wiggled her sleeping mother's toe, they told her to go back to sleep.

PIERROT'S BODY WAS RETURNED to Montreal to be buried in the cemetery on top of the mountain that was in the middle of the city. The funeral was held in the tiny church where Pierrot and Rose used to go to get free soup during the Depression and where they were married. The clouds seemed heavy that day, like a pregnant lady rolling in a pool. Pierrot didn't have any family at the funeral. He was obviously related to people all over the city. He had cousins and aunts and grandparents. He had not just dropped from the sky. But there was no way anybody could find his family. The Hôpital de la Miséricorde had made sure of that twenty-five years before. All anyone knew was that there had once upon a time been a girl named Ignorance who didn't follow rules and was so many millions of miles away from being a saint, and who had played a foolish game with her cousin.

So the church was instead filled with the clowns to whom Pierrot was closest. And, of course, Rose, who sat in the front pew with a veil over her face, unable to say a word. She had wept for three days.

Hundreds of red roses lay across Pierrot's coffin as it was carried down the steps by six strapping clowns. Rose followed the coffin and walked down the narrow stone steps of the church. To the people outside staring at the door of the church, waiting for the funeral party to exit, Rose looked like she had aged ten years. She always said later that her hair started to turn white that day—afterward, people found it difficult to tell exactly how old she was because her skin and eyes had an impish, youthful glow but her hair was white.

Fabio was at her side. You would never know that he had been a clown, however. He looked like a fat, serious businessman. You would never know that he had been any sort of artist, as he betrayed no emotions. He was the type of person you would have trouble imagining as a child, even. Occasionally, in a very stressful circumstance, he might take off his hat and wipe his bald head with a handkerchief and then put his hat back on. That was just what he did on this occasion after stepping out of the church and witnessing what was going on outside.

The streets were filled with all sorts of people who had come to show their respect. The sounds of car horns could be heard in the distance. People were crowding the streets for blocks, preventing traffic from moving. People stood on stoops to get a glimpse of the casket. People perched on the roofs of buildings—it looked as if all the gargoyles had come to life.

There were adults from all walks of life. Some had come from the wealthy neighborhoods in their fur coats, and some had come from the poorest neighborhoods in their threadbare ones. People from all backgrounds had been touched by Pierrot.

There were loads of little children, who had gotten permission from their parents to put on their Sunday clothes and go to the funeral. There were some that had single flowers they had plucked from their yards or had begged the florist to spare. They followed the clowns. Many of them wept openly at the death of their hero.

And scattered everywhere in the crowd were young men in military uniforms. Canada had declared war on Germany that week. Before going overseas, they wanted to pay respect to Pierrot. It was as though they were kissing their wonderful and broke-ass and big-hearted and unpredictable Montreal childhoods good-bye. They were burying them with Pierrot. Many of them, like him, would never grow old enough to understand that you only go from one hardship to another. And that the best we can hope from life is that it is a wonderful depression.

The coffin was loaded into the hearse. The clowns climbed into the limousines parked behind it. None of the men were in costume. They were dressed in black suits. But there seemed to be a little detail on each one of them that betrayed that they were clowns. One had a cloth carnation in his lapel that would squirt water in your face. Another had a small trembling Chihuahua in his inside pocket. One had black shoes that, although recently shined, were at least six sizes too big for him and turned up at the toes.

A black, squat bulldog waddled after a clown and jumped into the limousine. But before hopping in, the dog turned to look at the crowd. There was a round white circle around his right eye, like an eight ball.

THE FUNERAL PROCESSION moved slowly down the street. The clowns didn't care that they were blocking traffic. When the limousines began to move hesitantly through the crowd and down Saint Catherine Street, a woman sitting on the sidewalk pulled on her accordion and started to play Pierrot's tune, and it made everyone feel wonderful. It brought out their feelings and made them more intense, the way spices do to the flavors of meat. And Pierrot, who had been terrified of the feelings that accordions gave him, seemed to no longer mind. And the people in the crowd felt terrible and full of woe that Pierrot had died, but they also felt grateful that he had been in their lives. He was from Montreal, and he had proved that they all had beauty and art inside them as much as any other person anywhere in the world. They felt happy about exactly where they were in the universe.

All the children in the city put candles in their windows that night. The Milky Way became for one night a tiny island in the Saint Lawrence River.

···⟨ 71 ⟩···

FINAL CHAPTER

t was late in the afternoon and Rose was walking down the street. She wore a long, straight navy blue dress. It had different layers, different rows of lace that had been sewn together—it looked like a multistoried apartment building. She had a giant white pouf attached to the side of her head.

SHE WAS ON HER WAY from the audition of a new brother-and-sister act for the Rose Theater. The eighteen-year-old boy played the ukulele with such an odd solemnity. The sister sang a letter to a sweetheart who was overseas. She had a squeaky voice, slightly off-key, but confident for no reason. Only an act as awkward as this could dare to convey the tragic events that had occurred overseas, so Rose booked them on the spot.

The pair threw themselves into each other's arms and wept when Rose offered them a job. In the three years since Rose had returned to Montreal, she had turned her clubs and hotels into vibrant, lucrative businesses. Her most magnificent accomplishment was the cabaret on the corner, the

Rose Theater, which she had constructed out of an abandoned ballroom. The building itself was beautiful, but it was the acts that were extraordinary, universally regarded as the best in town. No one ever quite understood where she was able to find them. There were always lineups around the block to get in.

There was also something romantic about the atmosphere. It was the place to go on a first date. People often found themselves proposing to their partners there.

Rose stopped to chat to four young girls sitting on a bench. They weren't any better-looking than other girls. The prettiest thing about them was that they were nineteen. But there's always something eternally lovely about being a girl. They had fixed their hair in various waves on top of their head with bobby pins. Two of the girls were looking at a magazine together. Another girl, dressed in a beige coat with beige socks, was eating french fries out of a paper bag, looking straight ahead. You might not think that the girls were prostitutes if it wasn't for the fact that the girl at the end, who was wearing a light blue cotton dress with puffy sleeves, couldn't seem to keep her eyes open and her head kept jerking up and down.

The city's nightlife exploded in the 1940s, with all the sailors and army ships docking in Montreal before heading out to Europe. Montreal became world famous for having pretty girls you could fuck for cheap. But Rose refused to ever make a cent off an unfortunate girl. She never operated any brothels or allowed any in her buildings. She never had a back exit at her clubs that led to a brothel across the alley. She never allowed pimps to prey on young girls at her clubs.

Of course, it all happened regardless of whatever Rose did, but she wouldn't be a part of it. There wasn't anything she could do about the heroin either. People used heroin when reality was starkly different from their dreams. Thus there would always be heroin addicts, like the lovely girl on the nod at the end of the bench. And the drug connection between New York and Montreal was growing stronger and bigger every day. Rose paid the gangsters the tax they demanded of all the businesses in the red-light district, because she wanted to make herself psychologically free of them. Or pay some sort of penance. In any case, she had as little to do with that lot as she could.

Rose offered the girl eating french fries her business card and told her that if she needed help, she ought to come by the Valentine Hotel. Because although she couldn't stop the economics of poverty, she did encourage women who were in predicaments or who were down on their luck to come by her office and ask for her advice or mentorship. She often got them jobs in her clubs or hotels, or spoke to other proprietors on their behalf. She paid their doctor bills without asking questions, and paid their tuition when they took courses. She thought all girls should be independent and should have money in their purses. She wasn't afraid to speak up to an abusive husband or a pimp.

She was that rare person who gave without expecting anything in return. Many girls rented rooms in her Sweetheart Hotel, which was exclusively for single women. The laughter that came out of the windows during the summer was one of the most beautiful sounds in the world. It was like the percussion section of a children's orchestra, in which a musician was hitting the triangle with a steel rod in the most charming way.

AFTER SPEAKING TO THE GIRLS, Rose walked into the lobby of the Valentine Hotel. Completely renovated and transformed, it was now a place where artistic and bohemian types converged. Poets sat at the tables, trying to put into words things that they themselves didn't understand. The walls were covered from top to bottom with wonderful abstract paintings that artists brought in. Over the fireplace was a large oil painting composed of white and black chunky squares. It reminded Rose of the huge yard in front of the orphanage, and the ocean of snow that had separated it from the city.

Everyone knew to find her at the Valentine Hotel. She had a schedule that she kept to. She had her own office on the second floor. She had a desk. It was piled with account books and receipts. She was often booking out-of-town acts, as well as local ones. She was known to enjoy talking on the telephone.

BUT ALTHOUGH SHE INTERACTED with so many people during the day, no one could actually say that they were close to her. There is an aloofness to the permanently heartbroken, a secrecy. There was something impenetrable about her. There was a door that she had closed, which no one could get in.

There were rumors that Rose had been the one who had had McMahon killed. Instead of making her unlikable, it made her seem deeply romantic, wonderfully other and untouchable. It gave her an aura of respect. She was a woman who had done what she needed to get free. Men discovered that they had no trouble relating to her as an equal. The men who had ridiculed her when she was dating McMahon found that they had changed their minds about her.

People also talked about how she had been a performer herself once. The clowns from the Snowflake Icicle Extravaganza would talk about the fabulous show she had directed and starred in, which had won over the American crowds. But nobody in Montreal ever got to see a Rose production. Despite the success of her first, Rose never staged another of her own shows. And she never graced the stage again, in any capacity. In fact, she never even went out dancing. She never balanced an egg on the tip of her nose. She was too old and dignified to do a cartwheel. If there was a puppet lying on a chair, she never picked it up to bring it to life.

SHE WENT BACK TO HER OFFICE. It was the end of the business day. She spent a few moments completely lost in thought. That was her favorite time, right at the end of the day, when she would reflect on the control she now had over her time. Framed behind her was a creased and stained piece of paper that had the original blueprint of her whole life, drawn in the handwriting of a child. Her most prized possession. It was the beginning of her enterprise.

She lit up a cigarette and listened to the conversation between Fabio and Tiny outside her door. Tiny had never gone back to New York City. He had taken a fancy to the Valentine Hotel and the Montreal winters. She needed him for when sailors got out of hand, or a pimp showed up looking for a girl. He had become more and more bohemian. He had recently fallen in love with a chorus girl, who was giving him a hard time.

"Last Tuesday she told me that she had been waiting for a man just like me since she was five years old," Tiny was saying. "She said that it would be a tragedy if we didn't end up together. And then I went to see her Wednesday and she says, 'Go away, even looking at your face suffocates me.'"

"Would you ever consider dating a girl who was less erratic?" Fabio asked.

"Never."

The two men were interrupted by the sound of a very soft voice asking for Rose. It was followed by the sound of a small sneeze, one a child might emit.

"Come in," she called out abruptly. She had no idea why she did that. Except that she had the irrational feeling that she recognized that strange sneeze. It seemed to have come from a long, long time ago. She felt as if she were hearing the voice of someone she had known a long, long time before, when she was a child.

When the door cracked open, she was surprised to see not a child but Sister Eloïse. Rose hadn't seen her face since Rose was fifteen years old. Pierrot had sometimes imagined that he'd seen her and would jump, but he had always been mistaken. Sister Eloïse had come to seem, in Rose's mind, like some villain who belonged strictly to childhood, like the Big

Bad Wolf. Something incorporeal, like a monster in a closet, but which in adulthood turned out not to exist. But here she was in the flesh, looking exactly the way Rose remembered her. She seemed to have gotten even younger. When Rose was a little girl, a woman of twenty-seven seemed to be ancient. But now that Rose was that age herself, a woman of thirty-eight somehow didn't seem old at all.

Rose was shocked that Eloïse would even come near her. It was like a mouse striking up a conversation with a cat. Didn't Sister Eloïse realize the extraordinary reversal of fortune that had befallen Rose? She could not be ignorant of just how dangerous and powerful her old foe had become.

"Hello, Rose. Do you remember me?"

Rose didn't answer. She would not allow Eloïse to know the enormous influence she had had on her and Pierrot's sad youths.

"I had a child brought into the orphanage," Eloïse continued. "His mother was a prostitute. She had every manner of disease that you can imagine. She died, you see. From what, it doesn't matter. The child himself came to us with tuberculosis, though he's got over the worst of it. We thought it had affected his mind. It's hard to say because he has a very peculiar disposition, which we don't know what to make of. But perhaps he'll turn out all right. I mean, we did always think that his father was a complete idiot, but he turned out to be a clever, affectionate fellow, didn't he?"

Rose looked at her. She was confused. She realized that she had missed a very important part of this story. "I'm sorry, but who in the world is his father?"

"Joseph. Or as we all used to call him, Pierrot."

Rose looked at her, now completely shocked. She felt her cheeks burning. She crushed her cigarette in the ashtray on her desk. The smoke furling out of it seemed to be revealing too much.

"His mother was a strange redheaded girl, rather likable. She told the priest she had had an affair with Pierrot years before. She didn't want to tell Pierrot because she knew he was so happy with you. But I just thought that you would want to know that this little guy was out there in the world without a soul to look after him. I don't even rightly know whose responsibility this child is, seeing that his mother was Jewish and his father was Catholic. We didn't immediately know which orphanage we'd send the boy to, and then I thought of you."

She handed Rose a small photo of the child. Rose stood up from her chair. She didn't doubt the veracity of the story, as the child looked so much like Pierrot had at the same age. She moved around the desk toward the nun. Here was a child that fortune would spare from Sister Eloïse and her kind.

"I know I was harder on you than I should have been," Eloïse said. "Maybe it was because of a certain amount of envy, as I could tell that you had an extraordinary future ahead of you. We all could."

Rose touched the woman's hand. Then there was another tiny and wonderful sneeze from the hallway.

"Is he here with you?"

"Yes."

"Let me see him. Bring him in to me."

Sister Eloïse hurried into the hallway. She reached out and grabbed a hand and brought the little boy into the room. And there he was, standing in front of Rose only feet away. The tip of his nose was bright red—he probably had a cold—and his blond hair stuck up on top of his head. Rose smiled. She got down on her knees in front of the little boy. She turned her head upward and looked into Sister Eloïse's eyes.

"You have done me a great kindness," Rose said.

Eloïse looked down at Rose with a look of surprise and relief. She had the urge to let out a cry of laughter.

"It would give me such peace if I knew that you forgave me," Eloïse said hoarsely.

HEATHER O'NEILL

"Yes. None of that matters now. Thank you. You can leave him with me. Is that all right?"

"Yes, of course!" Eloïse said.

Sister Eloïse didn't lose time getting out of the room, proud of herself for taking such a risk and having it pay off. She had been waking up every night for the past few years, terrified of Rose, certain that she was next to the bed, still a tiny girl but with a look of judgment on her face. She imagined the grown-up Rose coming to the orphanage and denouncing her. Everyone would believe Rose now, she was so powerful, she had pull. Eloïse didn't want to stay a second longer and risk her fortunes changing. Rose didn't even seem to notice her leaving. She was transfixed by the miraculous six-year-old boy with bright blue eyes who was staring right back at her.

"What is your name, darling?" Rose asked the child.

The boy looked at her with a guileless self-assurance she recognized, and offered her a beautiful smile by way of introduction.

"Isaac," he said. "Am I to live with you?"

"If you would like. I would love nothing but. You're a generous little soul, aren't you? Shall we get to know each other a little?"

"Perhaps we can go to the zoo?"

"There's a lovely polar bear there, darling. It wants to meet you."

"It will eat me!"

"I would never let anything touch a hair on your sweet head. The polar bear is behind a cage, and I swear he'll act like a gentleman or we'll walk off and have *chocolat chaud* without him."

"Chocolat chaud!"

Rose began to laugh. It had been so long since she had allowed herself to feel joy, as it made her feel unfaithful to her dead husband. There were tears in her eyes, as though her eyes were ice cubes that were melting. She looked at Isaac. The thought of pleasing the boy made her mind fill with all sorts of ideas. For this little boy she would create a new puppet theater.

388

For this little boy she would have clowns from Europe arriving by sea in no time. For this little boy she would create a wondrous animal show, with geese that sang traveling songs, and an elephant that played the trumpet. It all came so clearly to her mind. She would have the world's greatest juggler to teach him the rules of science and of the natural universe, and the world's most amazing escape artist would teach him to tie his shoes, and a white cat that walked on a tightrope would be his best friend. Their life was to be a marvelous circus, on and off the stage.

She went to get her coat. She swung open the door to tell Fabio and Tiny that she was going out for the afternoon. The small framed drawing of a snowflake that hung from a nail on the door swung back and forth as she spoke into Tiny's ear. She went and took Isaac's hand in hers, determined never to be apart from him again, not even for a moment.

As Eloïse turned down the street and headed along Saint Catherine, a man fell in behind her. He pulled out a gun and put a small bullet in the back of her brain. Her body was cleaned up quickly, so that Isaac would not see it or be disturbed by it.

Rose and Isaac would have a wonderful childhood together.

ACKNOWLEDGMENTS

This book would not be what it is without the wonderful imaginations of my editors: Jennifer Lambert, Sarah McGrath and Rose Tomaszewska.

Also, thank you to my agent, Claudia Ballard.

Additional help and feedback came from my trusted associate Arizona O'Neill.

And thanks for financial support from the Conseil des arts et des lettres du Québec.